NO RETURN
HOME

DISCARD

NO RETURN HOME

▶ SEQUEL TO BEWARE THE WOLVES: A SOVIET WWII LOVE STORY ◀

VICTOR MOSS

TATE PUBLISHING
AND ENTERPRISES, LLC

Published by Tate Publishing & Enterprises, LLC
127 E. Trade Center Terrace | Mustang, Oklahoma 73064 USA
1.888.361.9473 | www.tatepublishing.com

Tate Publishing is committed to excellence in the publishing industry. The company reflects the philosophy established by the founders, based on Psalm 68:11,
"The Lord gave the word and great was the company of those who published it."

Book design copyright © 2015 by Tate Publishing, LLC. All rights reserved.
Cover design by Norlan Balazo
Interior design by Angelo Moralde

Published in the United States of America

ISBN: 978-1-68118-608-5
Biography & Autobiography / Personal Memoirs
15.03.31

Acknowledgment

I EXPRESS my sincere gratitude to my children, Paul Moss and Katherine Stafford, and my sister, Mary Moss Janssen, for their discussions regarding the direction of the text.

Enormous thanks are given to my friends Gayle Branger, Marsha Butkovich, and Melanie Tappen, for their encouragement and useful comments and suggestions, and to Charles Bedard, MD, for his help with the medical aspects of this novel.

But above all, I thank my wife, Rita Moss, for her support and the many hours we spent discussing each segment of the story. Her suggestions and editing were truly invaluable.

The names of the characters, except for Vladimir, Slava, Victor, and their families, are fictitious.

World War II created the largest migration of humanity in history. Fifty-five million individuals fled their home, their homeland, and the lives they once knew. Demographics throughout the world were forever changed. Eleven million, alone, flooded into Germany, escaping the Red Army as it moved westerly.

Chapter 1

ENVELOPED IN steam, the train appeared a mirage. The chain of drab olive-green wooden coaches, topped with shadowy cylindrical roofs, ominously waited. Faint glimmers of light, defused by the thick fog, emanated from windows. The future remained uncertain for the young couple standing on the platform, their hands clasped together. They shivered, either from the cold October morning or from apprehension, or from both.

The motionless train at the bullet-riddled depot in Baranovichi, Belarus (formerly Poland) stood as a symbol of a new and somewhat mysterious beginning for Vladimir and Slava Moskalkov. Each struggled with the thought that they might never return home. At least they'll leave this accursed city—a place that held Vladimir captive for a year in the dreadful Nazi prisoner-of-war compound. Their fate lay in that train heading westward. Hearts thundered as one, ready to explode. Was it the anxiety of the unknown? Was it that they must leave their homeland, possibly forever? Or was it the overwhelming joy of reuniting with each other after seventeen gut-wrenching months? They knew only that to avoid further punishment, or possibly death, by the Nazis, they had to obey the orders to set up a medical clinic in Slonim. These orders were tucked in Vladimir's breast pocket.

War-torn Eastern Europe in October of 1942 held little hope for the young couple. Their hometown of Vitebsk, Belarus remained occupied by the Germans since July 1941. Since then the German lightning campaign to conquer the Soviet Union pressed onward. Vladimir became a victim of the onslaught when his medical unit was ensnarled by enemy encirclement in October 1941. Enduring inhumane conditions as a captive in Baranovichi, Vladimir's only goal was to survive to see his wife again. Meanwhile, Slava, fluent in German, avoided a labor camp for herself and her parents by doing forced work as a document translator.

Little more than a week before, neither knew of each other's whereabouts or whether the other was alive. Now they waited in the cold air on the well-worn brick-lined platform to board a third-class coach. Most of the other passengers were helmeted German soldiers wearing their long brown military coats. Several had guns draped over their chests or rifles slung over their shoulders. Cigarette smoke comingled with the heavy, humid air. Little attention was paid to the anxious couple dressed in civilian clothing. Vladimir embraced the anonymity. Twelve hours before, he was a captive. Today he was free. How wondrous freedom felt. Yet, how long would freedom last? He distrusted the Germans. The mere sight of the armed uniformed soldiers left a lump in the pit of his stomach. He struggled to suppress flashbacks of his months in cruel confinement. He wanted to hurry and board the train and go anywhere to escape the sight of the soldiers and their rifles. The more he thought about it, the tighter he gripped his wife's hand and tried to focus his thoughts on her, who, miraculously, at long last stood by his side.

He marveled how Slava knew how to find him upon his release. He understood that she had no food to eat, yet took up a daily continuous vigil at a window in a rented room in Baranovichi overlooking the street that he would have to take. He replayed in his mind the sight of her racing out of the house into his arms as he walked down the street, not knowing if she would find him.

No matter how hard Vladimir tried to avoid eye contact with the soldiers milling about, his eyes, nevertheless, strayed. Vladimir's surreptitious gaze once again noted the man dressed in a black trench coat and hat. He spied him the moment they left for the station. Vladimir felt his heart beat faster. *Is he here to take me back? Surely he would have taken me back before now? I can't dwell on this,* he thought. *I can't do anything about it except run, but where could we run to? The enemy is everywhere.*

They traveled light. Slava packed her small suitcase with a few items. Vladimir possessed only what he wore. The overcoat, now wrinkled and terribly stained, was the same one that Slava had insisted he take with him when he went off to war in June 1941.

Finally the doors of the train opened and the passengers shoved their way on board. The train car reeked of urine and cigarette smoke. Vladimir glanced around to see if that man in black boarded the car. He saw only soldiers taking their seats on the hard, splintered, wooden benches. *Look at them laugh and joke around,* Vladimir thought. *They are going home on leave, those bastards. None of our men have that luxury. There are no breaks from the war for Soviet soldiers.*

The couple grabbed two seats toward the right center of the coach. "It feels good to finally sit down," Slava said as she squirmed to find a more comfortable position. "Did you know that on the train from Vitebsk to Minsk, they took all the seats out so that more soldiers could be transported?" Noticing Vladimir fidgeting about, Slava did not wait for an answer. "You have lost so much weight. These seats must be really tough on your boney rear."

"Slavochka (diminutive for Slava), I'll be all right. The Germans gave me two hundred marks. Surely in Slonim we'll stumble on some food. It's only about fifty kilometers from here. We should be there soon."

"Good, I'm absolutely famished," Slava said. "I haven't eaten anything for two days. But I can wait. How are you doing? When was the last time you ate?"

"Actually right before they came to release me, I had a morsel of bread with some hot water last night—my portion for the day. I'm all right though."

"That's all! Oh my God, no wonder you're a walking skeleton." Slava shook her head in disgust. Thinking about the food they'll need to buy, she asked, "How long do you think the marks will last us?"

"I have no idea, but we'll get by until we start earning money at our clinic. Oh, Slavochka, I'm so enthusiastic at the prospect." Slava saw, at least for a fleeting moment, the excitement light up his face at the thought of working again as a physician. She knew that Vladimir yearned to work, had to keep busy. His opportunity would come in Slonim.

Vladimir assessed everyone in front of him then glanced over his left shoulder. He could not understand if his empty stomach was creating a sense of paranoia or if there was a reason for his anxiety. No one looked suspicious on board, just soldiers going home. All the while he held Slava's delicate hand, stroking it, perhaps too strenuously in anticipation of the train's departure.

Slava sat silently for several minutes, then said, "I just can't imagine how we are going to do it."

"Do what?"

"I mean, for us to come to a strange town, under enemy occupation, not knowing anyone, and find a place, equipment, and instruments to open a medical practice of our own. It's hard to imagine how we can possibly accomplish it."

An optimist by nature, Vladimir did not show any despair. "Don't fret. We'll do it. We must."

"What if we can't? Do you think we'll be sent to a labor camp somewhere in Germany? Oh dear Blessed Virgin Mary! What if they send you back to that inhumane camp?"

Letting go of her hand, Vladimir gently caressed Slava's cheek with the back of his hand. Bringing her closer to him, he kissed Slava's cheek. "Of course we'll do it. Don't worry."

"Well, I know you're just saying it to make me feel better. But you don't know." As soon as she said that, she realized that she was being too hard on him. She needed to ease off and temper her fears so not to distress her husband. She realized that he also must be stressed with the daunting task ahead. "Oh, Volodya, (diminutive for Vladimir) as you know, I worry about everything. If anyone can do it, you can. My main concern now should be how to fatten you up."

"That's a deal. I look forward to lots of food." Vladimir smiled broadly, and she returned his smile with a mischievous grin.

As they sat, waiting for the train to move, Vladimir, once again, turned towards the back. *So far, so good. Hopefully he won't board this train. I may be worried about nothing,* he thought. He faced forward again. As Slava looked out of the window, he studied the car. Cardboard and wooden planks covered glassless windows. Bullet holes pocked the ceiling and walls, some large enough to allow light from the depot to filter through. *This train had been under attack. Dear God, protect us to Slonim.* The floor was wet and slick from melting snow trampled in by boots. A smelly toilet stood at the front of the car. They were the only civilians in the car—Slava, the only female.

The train whistle startled them. Relieved that they would be on their way, Vladimir glanced back and blew out a breath when he did not see the man in black. The whistle blew again, and the train jolted. Vladimir looked back once again and suddenly spied the man in black as he hurriedly entered the car and take a seat in the back. Their eyes locked. He felt the man's cold glare penetrate him. Vladimir's heart raced. His muscles tightened. His breathing slowed. *Oh God! Who is he? What does he want? I know he is here because of us. I can feel it.*

Chapter 2

THE TRAIN chugged along toward Slonim. Vladimir, still tense and breathing heavily, joined Slava in gazing out the window, willing himself not to dwell on the last passenger. Through the lifting fog, gray stucco buildings, unpainted wooden houses, barns, outhouses, and electric poles with sagging wires passed by as the train picked up speed. He was glad to leave Baranovichi and what it meant to him.

Slava's thoughts turned to her parents. They were elderly, neither one in good health. They assured her that they would be fine, encouraged her to go to Vladimir, and not to worry about them. Slava continued to worry. *Will they really be all right? They're resourceful, they probably will survive. Would they be able to obtain travel permits to Latvia? Maybe because of their age, they would. Maybe there is no turning back—ever.*

Slava's contemplations then focused on how the war had changed her own life. The cost was high. Her dreams of finishing medical school and practicing medicine were extinguished, like a candle that was abruptly snuffed out. *That's all inconsequential now because I'm with Vladimir. He is the most important thing in my life. I'm so blessed to be reunited with him.*

Turning toward her husband, Slava gave him a beautiful smile. "I'm really thankful and excited. We're alive, together again. You're right. This will be the beginning of a whole new life for us. We'll make a new home for ourselves in Slonim. And, who knows, maybe we'll be able to return to Vitebsk. You'll see. We'll have that clinic set up in no time. Oh, Volodya, I missed you so. Promise me we'll never be apart again—not for even one day." As the sun began to stream into the car, Slava noted that a familiar sparkle was missing from Vladimir's eyes. "What's wrong? Your color changed from ashen to white?"

"Oh, it's nothing, I'm just wondering about a man that appears to have followed us."

"You mean the thug in the black coat and hat? He looks like death or the grim reaper."

"You noticed him, then?"

"Of course. How could I not have? Such a nasty looking man, who do you think he was? At least he's gone now."

"We're not rid of him. He's sitting behind us, a few rows back."

"Oh God! What do you think he wants?"

"I don't know. It's probably just a coincidence. We've learned to live in fear. We can't trust anyone. If he had wanted something, he would have approached us by now. I didn't mean to worry you, darling." She slowly looked back and did, indeed, notice the man. He met her glance. His fish-like grey eyes seemed as cold as the weather outside. "You're right, he's there and staring at us."

Vladimir and Slava sat silently, Vladimir gently tapping her left thigh with his right fingers. Slava laid her head onto his shoulder. Her red knit cap slipped slightly and he kissed her exposed brown hair. "I've decided that we needn't worry about it. We're on our way, following their instructions. We've done nothing wrong."

"All right. I'll drop it from my mind."

Soon Vladimir's eyelids drooped over his previously vigilant eyes. Exhaustion overcame him, and he was lulled to sleep by the sway and the rhythmic clacking of the cold metal wheels on cold metal rails. Slava dozed off as well. It had been a sleepless but joyous night for both.

Suddenly a deep growling voice awakened the young couple. "Travel papers!" Slava's body tensed up. Vladimir jerked awake. The sight of two men, one in a pale blue uniform and one in a military uniform, standing over him sent electric shocks throughout his body. Stunned, he was unable to utter a word.

"Documents now!"

With a trembling hand, Vladimir reached in his coat pocket and pulled out a carefully folded half sheet of paper. Slava reached into her purse. With her shaky hand, she removed the passport issued by the German occupiers in Vitebsk. A folded piece of paper was tucked inside. The helmeted soldier with a ruddy complexion and a square jutting jaw told the conductor to go on, that he will handle these people. His protruding, washed-out blue eyes peered down at them with contempt. He snatched the items from their hands.

"You are without authorization on this train," the soldier barked. "This is not a passport," addressing Vladimir. "I want to see a passport and official documentation that you can travel. Otherwise I must arrest you. And as for you, lady, I see your passport but no authorization for you to travel."

"It's in the passport. It's a slip of paper from the chief medical officer in Minsk."

Vladimir thought his heart would burst. He could hear Slava's heart pounding. "That paper I gave you is from the Commandant from the Baranovichi prisoner of war camp. It authorizes my wife and me to travel to Slonim," Vladimir tried to explain in his broken German. "It is an official document. I was told that this paper was all I needed until identification papers are issued to me in Slonim."

"Who told you that?"

"Colonel Klaisle, the commandant of the camp at Baranovichi. It was also cosigned by Colonel Neusbaum, chief medical officer in Minsk for the Group Center Command."

The soldier rolled his eyes. "I don't give a damn. I don't know those officers. How do I know you didn't forge this piece of paper in your attempt to escape? Do you take me for a fool?"

"I assure you that our papers are genuine," Vladimir's face turning crimson in color. Slava noticed veins popping out of his temples. She grabbed his hand, squeezed it tightly.

"Calm down," Slava whispered in Russian.

"What was that you said?" The soldier barked, turning his attention to Slava.

"I'm sorry, I just told my husband to calm down. Can't you see how nervous he is? He has been through so much. He's lucky to be alive." Slava answered in perfect German.

"What is the purpose of your travel?"

"We are on our way to Slonim. My husband has orders to start a medical clinic there."

"Yes, please look at the documents again," Vladimir said.

"Yes, please," Slava pleaded. "Everything we told you is the absolute truth. These are all that we were given. The officers told us that these papers will suffice."

The soldier studied Slava for a moment. "I should arrest you, you know." The man considered the documents again, holding them up to the window. He twisted the papers forward and backward, obviously pondering what he should do. "All right. Your story seems more like a fairy tale, but then, what the hell." With obvious disappointment he threw the documents in Vladimir's lap and walked away.

If Vladimir had anything in his stomach, he would have lost it. "That was close," he told Slava. He looked back to make sure the soldier had not returned, but his eyes caught the glaring stare of the man in black. Vladimir shuddered and quickly turned around. He sat quietly, worrying about that individual. *Who is he? What does he want? Is he government? Military?*

Suddenly, the mysterious man appeared right there, looming over Vladimir. He squeezed hard on Vladimir's left shoulder, causing immediate pain.

"Why don't you jump off the train and run for the forest so that I can shoot you down like a dog. You Slavs are all savages, and that is the fate you deserve," he hissed maliciously.

Vladimir chose not to respond. *I can't argue with a fanatical Nazi.* Instead, Vladimir sat still and looked away from the man, his insides about to burst. He could hear Slava gasp.

"Ah, so you have nothing to say. Well, let me assure you I have plenty to say. I do not agree with the weaklings who decided to free you. So your surgery saved an officer of the Third Reich. That's your job as a physician. I still don't understand how they had agreed to allow a Soviet doctor to work on one of our officers. You were lucky. You should still be rotting in the barracks."

Vladimir and Slava remained silent, looking down at their feet, their insides boiling. *How does he know about the surgery?* The man's continued barrage seemed no longer to be directed at Vladimir, but more generally at the subhuman enemies that the great Aryan nation was forced to fight. Finally, he stopped and returned to his seat. Vladimir glanced around and saw that the eyes of all the passengers in the car were fixed on them. Some of the soldiers made crude remarks, cursing at them. He did not see those behind him, but knew that they were now the center of everyone's attention.

A moment later, the man in black returned. "When we arrive in Slonim, I personally will escort you to see the commandant. We'll see what, in fact, will be done with you. If I had it my way, you would be shot."

Vladimir did not look at the man. He felt as if he was being squeezed between the train's wheels and the track. The horse's ass finished what he wanted to say and once again stomped back to his seat, swearing in German. Vladimir took Slava's shaking hand and pressed it to his chest and held it tightly. She felt his heart thud. They sat silently, staring out the dirty window as the train rolled slowly through the countryside. The morning sun once again broke through the clouds as it had done since dawn.

"Look, Slavochka, at how the birch trees glisten as the sun rays hit the white bark. Notice the fresh snow nestled on the branches of the pines. I haven't seen anything this beautiful for over a year. An artist could not draw anything this magnificent. Life is beautiful, especially you. You fit in perfectly in this picture. I love you because you enhance the beauty of this earth."

Slava smiled and kissed Vladimir's hand. "Keep talking, Volodya. I do feel better, but what about him? Can he really cause us trouble with the local authorities?"

"I don't think so. We have our orders. We'll be all right. He is just an idiot that is trying to take the war out on us."

"Oh God, please make it so."

She turned to gaze out of the window to admire the view, still shaken by the incident. Suddenly she spotted an aircraft over the horizon of the forest, approaching the train. "Oh my God! We're being attacked!"

Chapter 3

THE TRAIN ground to a sudden halt, propelling the young couple against the wooden seat back in front of them. Vladimir struck his left shoulder. Slava hit her head. Bullets spewed from planes. Shards of window glass and splinters from the wooden veneer lining flew randomly about. Slugs whizzed past Vladimir and Slava. German soldiers stationed on the sides of the train and on a flat car had no chance to return fire as they jumped off to seek cover. The ear-splitting clamor went on unabated.

Somewhat disoriented, Vladimir grabbed Slava's hand as she screamed, "Oh God! Oh my God!" He pulled her out of the coach. He then quickly pushed Slava under the train car and dove underneath just as planes spit out another round of lead. The projectiles struck the frozen ground, throwing chunks of dirt and rock onto them. The bullets penetrated the roof and sides of the car. Slava laid face down on a frigid railroad tie. Whimpering, she covered her ears. Vladimir half-covered her body with his.

As suddenly as it started, the maelstrom ended. Slava's ears continued to ring. Soldiers scurried out from underneath the car. A few did not. Vladimir rolled off Slava's side, "Are you all right."

"I'm fine, thank God," her voice and hands trembled.

The couple carefully crawled out from underneath the train car. Chunks of dirt and ice covered their hats and the shoulders of their coats. As they brushed off the frozen snow that clung to the fronts of their coats, Slava, still in a daze, noticed the unsightly stain caused by the creosote coating the rail ties. "For crying out loud! Look at my coat. I probably won't be able to get this off. Now I'll have to wear this dirty coat."

The man in black, who now stood near them, yelled out, "Woman, this is the least of your problems. You can thank your damn Soviet pilots for this. Now get on that train!"

Just like old times, Vladimir thought. *Under attack again. This war will never end.* As Slava placed one foot on the step and grabbed the metal railing, Vladimir pulled her back to allow some soldiers to carry out one of their fallen comrades killed in the car by the spray of bullets. When the passage cleared, they made their way back to their seats. Slava brushed off pieces of glass and wooden splinters from the seat with her black leather glove. Further up the aisle, by the toilet, the couple viewed a medic attending to a wounded soldier. "Maybe I can help him," Vladimir said to Slava.

"Just sit still. Don't bring any more attention to us than we have to."

"But what if he needs my help? No, let me at least look at him." Vladimir said and a made a move to render that assistance.

The man in black blocked his exit, "Get the hell back in your seat."

Vladimir sat still, not really surprised by the rebuke. He remembered Major Kimmer, the SS officer from the camp. It was a matter of life or death for the German officer. Yet Kimmer did all he could to dissuade and prevent Vladimir from doing the surgery. He could not bear that a Slavic doctor would touch an officer of the Third Reich, let alone perform an intricate operation involving the brain. *This fool has the same mentality.* Vladimir could see the hatred in the man's eyes. *Fine, if the bastard doesn't want my help, good! Arrogant pig!*

Splatters of blood on the walls and windows were visible. Drops of blood stained the aisle. Placing his arm around Slava's shoulder, he felt a prick to his finger. Slava had small glass shards embedded in the right sleeve of her coat. He immediately pulled out the pieces. "Ouch! Actually, I feel some pain in the shoulder." Slava removed her coat, and Vladimir pushed aside the neck of the green woolen sweater and saw that her white blouse had a slight blood stain at her shoulder.

"I guess one of the shards penetrated the skin," Vladimir said as Slava unbuttoned the top button, pulling the blouse to the side for Vladimir to view it. "It's not bad at all. It stopped bleeding."

"Funny, I didn't even feel it at first."

"Yes, very funny all right, ha ha," Vladimir said sarcastically. "Does it still hurt?"

"A little, not bad," Slava said. "We were so lucky. Those bullets could have hit us. Look at the damage they have done to this car. We were in the direct line of fire. God was with us. Oh, Blessed Mother, please protect us and always be with us."

Slava crossed herself and tried to grin as she glanced at Vladimir. His sad eyes focused on her. "This was hard on you, wasn't it?" she asked.

"Not anymore than for you. You know, when I was a captive all I thought of was you and what it would be like once were together again. I prayed for freedom—freedom from the damn soldiers, freedom from the horrors and senselessness of war, and just plain freedom to walk out, smell the fresh air, see beautiful flowers and the magnificence of trees in spring with their vibrant green color or in autumn as their leaves are in an array of gold and red colors. My thoughts were always of beauty and peace. But look at us now. An hour into our journey and we're in the midst of war." Vladimir hesitated for a moment, reflecting on what transpired. "You're right. We were lucky. Let's hope our luck holds out."

Continuing to gaze into Slava's hazel eyes, he lifted her hand and kissed it passionately, "I don't want anything to happen to you, my darling."

Slava clasped his hand firmly and pressed her lips against his cheek. "Don't worry about me. I'm tougher than you think."

Vladimir grinned and put his arm around her shoulder, "Ouch," Slava said, laughingly, "You squeezed my cut."

"Oh, sorry."

Smiling, Slava gave Vladimir another squeeze on the hand and turned her head to peer out of the newly cracked window to see another body being pulled from under the car. She shuddered at the sight. *That could have been us.* Her heart raced as she thought of the death surrounding them. *How did Volodya survive this war? Is he used to death around him? Look how calm he appears, even with the threat from that awful, nasty man.* She sidled closer to Vladimir and laid her head onto his right shoulder.

They sat huddled together in silence, each with his or her thoughts, waiting for the steam engine to come to life. Finally, after a delay of at least a half hour, the train began its rhythmic clacking, and Slava once again glanced out the window.

"We're lucky our window is still intact. Several had been shot out."

"I know. I feel the cold air," Slava said. "It seems we have been traveling for hours."

"We are going awfully slowly. Maybe they're expecting more trouble. Or maybe they want to make sure the track ahead has not been damaged."

No sooner had Vladimir spoken, the train came to another abrupt stop. Gunfire erupted ahead once again. Soldiers scurried out.

"Should we get out?" Slava asked, her voice tense.

"Let's wait here. It appears to be ground fire." Vladimir glanced at the man in black. He was gawking out of the window, spewing a string of obscenities as he pressed his fellow passenger into the side of the coach.

"What is it this time?" Vladimir had the courage to ask a passenger across the aisle.

The man's face turned red and a fanatical gleam lit his protruding eyes. Through his pressed lips he blew out two hard breaths. Finally, with a snarl, he roared, "Bandits! Sons of bitches. People like you. All of you and your kind must be destroyed!"

Vladimir quickly turned away from the hateful individual. Gunfire continued somewhere ahead of them. Vladimir turned to Slava who sat trembling, looking as though she was about to cry. "What bandits? What's he talking about?"

Slava, breathing shallowly, answered quietly, "He's talking about our partisans. The Germans call them bandits. You haven't heard of the role of partisans in this war?"

"Well, no. Remember I have been confined all these months. I really don't know anything that's happening around us. Who are these partisans?"

"They are men, and women, who had escaped from the Nazis and hide out in the forests. Some are former soldiers that either deserted or bolted from enemy encirclements and were unable to reunite with their units. Many are people that fled the towns held by the Fascists. Some are Jews."

"So what do they do, attack trains?"

"Yes, they attack trains, destroy tracks, blow up bridges. They do anything to harass and disrupt the invaders and their supply lines."

"Good. That must drive the Nazis absolutely crazy."

For a moment, they remained silent. Slava turned to Vladimir and whispered, "Well, it's good. On the other hand, we most likely will be in deeper trouble if the Soviets win. I mean, you were captured by the enemy. Stalin decreed that any soldier who surrenders is considered a traitor and will be executed. I'm probably not in any better shape, since I worked for the Germans, even if they forced me to do it. I would still be considered an enemy sympathizer."

Vladimir's mouth sagged. He fell into deep thought as if in a trance. A lone tear made its way from his sad eyes. *Oh God, again I should have kept my mouth shut,* Slava thought. *He is obviously very sensitive about this subject. I can certainly understand. After all, it is our motherland. The thought of him being considered a traitor must be tearing him apart. Maybe someday we'll be able to return safely. But he needs to comprehend that there is no return now.*

"Volodya, I'm so sorry that I brought up such an unpleasant topic. I didn't mean to. Please forgive me. War changed everything. It will never be the same as it was. We can only look to the future. For now, we must escape. We are caught between two evils and must survive." Vladimir slowly nodded his head in agreement, his eyes staring out of the window into space. "Volodya, you can't look back. I left my parents, my brothers, and sisters. You left behind your mother and your sisters. At least we are together."

"I know. I know. Everything has changed." Vladimir took a deep breath and forced a grin, muttering, "Maybe Slonim will be the break we need from the war."

Chapter 4

THE FIGHTING intensified. Vladimir flung his arm around Slava and pulled her to him. She flinched with each loud shot. Her lips pressed together, her jaw clenched, and bright eyes widened. *How can I alleviate her tension?* Vladimir thought. He gently stroked her cheek. "We'll be all right. Just relax."

Slava immediately cracked a smile. "Just relax! Just relax! Now that's funny. Gunshots are popping all around us. Who knows if one will come right through this window, and you say just relax?"

"Well, there is no use in worrying about it."

"All right, if that's what you want, that's what I'll do. I'll just relax, ha ha."

Vladimir squeezed her right shoulder. "Ouch, you touched the glass cut again. Remember, that's my big war injury." Slava laughed at herself. Vladimir grinned. "That mystery man must think we're absolutely crazy, giggling our heads off while a battle rages around us."

"He probably thinks we're hysterical. Maybe we are?"

Suddenly a nearby explosion rocked the ground beneath the car. The coach swayed as if in an earthquake. Slava threw herself onto Vladimir's chest, hugging his neck. Vladimir felt not only her terror but also his own.

"That was a bad one," Vladimir commented. "It must have been a grenade."

"I still think we should get out of here," Slava said. "We're sitting ducks."

"Here, switch places with me. I'll sit by the window. I still think it's safer here than underneath the train with small arms fire around. Besides, that man probably won't let us get off."

Slava changed places with Vladimir. The fighting deepened and then suddenly stopped. After a few minutes, the soldiers returned, discussing the battle. Slava tried to overhear and later relayed what she heard to Vladimir. The Germans only had a few losses while the bandits lost several men. One soldier laughed uproariously describing how, when a few of the partisans wanted to surrender, they were shot on the spot as they raised their hands. Another soldier commented that the other was a chump saying, "Yes, the bandits lost a few men, but most ran back into the depths of the forest, only to strike the next train."

Vladimir's mind focused on the partisans. Vladimir whispered, "Tell me, where do partisans get their weapons? Many of our soldiers didn't even have a weapon when they advanced in an attack. They were instructed to pick up one from a fallen comrade, if he had one."

"I heard they steal them from wherever they can—from dead Germans, from their armories, from farmers, anyplace they can get weapons and ammunition. And food, for that matter."

"How do you know about the partisans?"

"I picked up bits and pieces from the Germans in the office in Vitebsk. The partisans are a big problem for them. But I heard much more from the local women I worked with. I believe that some of their husbands were partisans."

Once again, the train resumed its journey westward. It traveled only a few meters before it again came to sudden stop. A spray of bullets struck the car. One penetrated the wooden side of the car and whizzed past Vladimir. The couple crouched down behind the seat backs. The man in black fell to the floor. Vladimir saw his body sprawled out on the floor. *Was he hit? I hope he's dead.*

"Let's get out of the car!" Slava screamed.

Vladimir hesitated and held Slava back. Their car no longer seemed to be the target. He looked over at the man in black and saw him move his head toward them. "See what your kind does," he snarled as he stood and sat back in his seat. *That's funny,* Vladimir thought. *As though his kind didn't cause all this.*

"Slava, let's stay put. The shooting has stopped. Those might have just been some stray or departing shots. Take some deep breaths. It will be all right. Remember, just relax."

"Oh, be quiet with your relax."

They sat back in their seats. A commotion ensued among the soldiers when they were ordered out of the cars to help replace damaged rails. "They must carry extra rails with them," Vladimir said. Slava nodded. Only the man in black and the couple remained in the car. Slava's eyes swung to him. Brushing off his mud stained black coat, he spewed profanity—his face crimson with rage. "Too bad," Slava whispered in a chuckle, "He's still alive." Vladimir drew in a deep breath.

As they waited, Slava, crossing her leg, took off one of her boots and rubbed her foot to warm it. Vladimir helped her rub it. He picked up her boot and breathed into it. "This may help," he said, grinning.

"Thanks," Slava said. "Aren't your feet cold? You don't even have boots, only worn-out shoes with a big hole in the sole."

"You know, I feel lucky to have these. My feet are a little cold, of course, but I guess I'm used to it."

After half an hour, the soldiers filed back into the car. Their usually impeccably clean uniforms were filthy, first from taking cover under the train, then from lifting rails and replacing them. The men looked tired, grumbling about the "damn bandits."

"They were expecting them," Vladimir said. "That's why I saw all those soldiers positioned on a flatbed behind the coal car and armed men in the cars and caboose."

The train resumed its journey, traveling even slower than before. Vladimir sensed that the soldiers seemed on edge, their eyes glued to the surroundings. Vladimir dozed off.

Luckily, no other incidents occurred. Slava stared at the endless rows of birch and ash trees as they passed. Her mind drifted to her home and parents in Vitebsk. She missed them dreadfully. In silence, she prayed for their safety. Then the mysterious town of Slonim loomed in her mind. *What's it like? Will we survive there?* She turned her head away from the window and watched Vladimir for several minutes. The last seventeen months had taken their toll on him. He lost much of his light brown hair. His trademark rosy cheeks were ashen pale. *Poor Volodya, you have endured so much. I thank God that you're alive and are mine.*

The train lurched violently and Vladimir opened his eyes. Slava threaded her arm around his and planted a kiss on Vladimir's cheek.

"I liked that. What were you thinking about?" He smiled.

"I was thinking that I'm so blessed to be with you again. I missed you so much. It was total hell when you were away, not knowing whether you were dead or alive or if I'd ever see you again."

Vladimir grinned and looked into Slava's sparkling eyes. He felt warm inside. "I know the feeling. I love you, Slavochka. I always will until the day I die. Just wait; we'll have a happy life together."

They both sat silently, gazing out the window. There was not much to see other than trees and more trees, with an occasional village. Once again Slava's hand was in his. He gently stroked each one of her fingers. Vladimir could not shake the man in black from his mind. *Who in the hell is he? Why is he here?* He glanced across the aisle at the man who appeared to be sound asleep. His head was thrown back and his mouth agape, drool flowed from the right side. His hat lay in the muddy aisle.

Looking out the window, Slava's mind floated to the partisans. *How fortunate we were that no harm came to my family for all those months.* She turned toward Vladimir, whose eyes were shut.

"You're not asleep, are you?"

"No, just resting my eyes."

"Do you remember a soldier named Igor who was a medic under your command?"

Startled by the question, Vladimir opened his eyes in bewilderment. "Yes. What the devil? How would you possibly know of him? He deserted just before we were ordered into the trenches outside of Smolensk at the very beginning of the war. I was so disappointed with him. He turned out to be a coward. How would you know him?"

"Igor came to our house."

"What!" Vladimir said in a loud voice waking the man in black. The man griped, then turned away from Vladimir and resumed snoring.

"He came to our house!"

"Shhh, quiet. He became a partisan. Somehow he knew I was your wife. We had two German officers visiting at the time."

"What! Are you crazy? What are you telling me, you had a deserter in our house, and the enemy came for a social visit?"

"Shush. Keep your voice down. Yes. It wasn't our choice. The Germans just showed up. Their visit scared us to death. Father looked as if he would have a coronary. But they brought delicious food. It turns out all they wanted was to socialize and hear me play the piano. They were lonely for their families. That's all."

Vladimir's face flushed red, and his sunken cheeks puffed out.

"Before you get too upset, let me explain. If I didn't have such good rapport with those two German officers who I worked for, I wouldn't have been able to deliver your diploma and other medical certificates to Minsk so that you could be released. So you should be thankful that I kept them interested. But again, I had no control over it, and I had to go along with it to survive. The men were perfect gentlemen. I was constantly uncomfortable with them, but they never touched me. Thank God."

Vladimir sat back, took a deep breath and exhaled. "You better explain all this to me. I don't understand. What's Igor's connection with those officers?"

"Igor had been watching our house. I saw a man peeking through our front window. He saw the holstered pistols that the officers had laid on the entry table. When I went onto the back porch to see who was at the window, he grabbed me, put his hand over my mouth. Only after I promised that I'd be quiet, let me go."

Vladimir's breathing became heavy and forceful as his rage built. He could not believe what he was hearing. The thought that Igor assaulted his precious wife sent lightning bolts throughout his body. *Oh God, Volodya looks furious,* Slava thought. *I should not have told him about Igor.* "I can't get over this, he assaulted you!"

"Volodya, calm down. That is so unlike you. You're generally easygoing. Let me explain. Igor scared me at first, but he didn't hurt me. He said he respected you, his Captain, and because of that he kept the other partisans away from our house. They would have taken every piece of food that my father had stored. It was because of father's food supplies that we did not die from hunger as so many in Vitebsk did."

Vladimir's fury began to ebb after listening to Slava. "So why did he come?"

"He wanted me to slip him the weapons. He wanted to kill the officers. I absolutely refused. He was a fool. Do you know the repercussions that would have followed? I and my parents would have been hanged on their specially constructed gallows and left for days to rot as a lesson to the populace. We would not have been the only family hung. They would have rounded up many innocent people, stringing them up as well. They do that. I've heard that for every German soldier that is killed by someone locally, tens of dozens are slaughtered in retaliation. Imagine how many would have died if two high ranking officers were shot?"

"I can only imagine," Vladimir said, still deeply upset but calmer now. "How did you get rid of Igor?"

"I refused his insane demand and finally talked him out of it. He settled for some food and quickly left. As he descended the back steps, he warned me that he will no longer be able to protect our house from other partisans, so we best be on our guard."

Vladimir closed his eyes, shook his head, remained silent a moment, then said softly, "Igor was a lazy worthless bastard anyway. God, when will this nightmare end? Do you think your parents are safe from the partisans now?"

"I don't know. I'm so worried about them. Father will take out his hunting rifle, one that the Germans don't know he has, and start shooting if anyone tries to break into the house. That would only lead to an arrest by the Nazis and probably my parents' death. All firearms should have been turned over to the Germans. I hope that they somehow try to escape to their relatives in Latvia, as they had planned."

Suddenly a booming explosion swayed the train from side to side. The train kept rolling. Both Vladimir and Slava stiffened. "Oh God! Not again," Slava yelled out. "We're under attack again, this time from the back!"

Vladimir took Slava's hand. "We'll be all right," he said forcing himself to remain calm so not to add to Slava's obvious fright. "Slavochka, don't worry. The train's still moving. The explosion was behind the train. As long as the track ahead is intact, we can make it to Slonim."

Chapter 5

THE TRAIN picked up speed. The forests began to thin. In places, cannon fire had downed several trees. Eventually, vast stretches of snow-covered fields came into view. Black blotches from burned fields bled through the snow. As the train crept along, someone's battle-ravaged house and two crumbling barns caught the eyes of the young couple. Stone chimneys and foundations nearby gave evidence to, what was once, a village. Yet among the ruins, an unscarred house stood its ground, defying the war.

"Are those actually bombing craters in that field?" Slava asked.

"They are. We're viewing a battleground."

"Those are burned-out trucks and tanks in the distance. This gives me the creeps. It's just plain eerie." Slava pulled in a deep breath and was slow to exhale.

"I certainly recognize them, even in that state. Those are German Panzer tanks. Believe me; I've seen my fill of them. You know, we were chased by them, only escaped by running deep into a forest. Later, after we were captured, they forced us to push those monsters out of the mud."

"That's horrible! Such a nightmare." Slava said and then remained silent, her eyes studying the wasted countryside.

Vladimir sat quietly, leaning over Slava, also staring at the landscape.

"The whole scene is surreal, isn't it?" Slava said, after a brief silence. "It's as though we're traveling on another planet, one that we're not a part of. But, sadly, we are. You know, all those burned-out houses remind me of our neighborhood in Vitebsk after you left. Our home and our neighbor's house were the only ones left standing. My father absolutely refused to follow Stalin's order to burn the house, crops, fruit trees, sheds, food, whatever, so that the Germans didn't get anything. My father said, 'Never will I burn down the house that I built with my own hands and destroy the stores of food we worked so hard to accumulate.' And he didn't."

"I wonder why the Nazis didn't commandeer the house and take away the food."

"I firmly believe that Major Raake protected us. He liked me."

"Oh, he did, did he?" Vladimir grinned.

Slava caught the humor and smiled. "Yes, he did." Vladimir still didn't like hearing about that officer, but kept quiet. In his heart he believed that nothing improper occurred between his wife and the German.

"Anyway, I would leave for work in the early morning and think I had stepped into another world. I can still see the devastation in my mind. I can smell the acrid smoke, soot, and ash. It was simply hell."

"Ruins lives. That's what war does. Ruins people," Vladimir said with a tone of disgust.

"Do you think that all of Slonim will look like this—wreckage everywhere?"

"I hope not," Vladimir said. "But then, who knows. Look there, that looks like a big lake, partially frozen over." He studied the panorama for a minute. "Strangely, with the scars of battle, that scene with the lake, the crisp snow covering the ground and clinging to the trees gives me hope that we'll find beauty where we're going."

Slava glanced at the windows on the left side of the car. "We may soon find out whether or not Slonim has much damage. I think we must be approaching its outskirts. The houses are becoming denser." Vladimir gazed in that direction, but all the while he keenly felt that jerk's eyes, burrowing with hatred right between his shoulder blades. The thought occurred to him that for all he knows, the man might be a fraud, even a coward. He smiled at the thought of a childhood fairytale of Baba Yaga, a witch, a sorceress. *Baba Yaga would not waste her time with that bastard.*

As a child, he believed that if he ventured far enough into the woods, Baba Yaga would entrap him and devour him. Baba Yaga, not just the wolves, was what terrified his young mind. But after his tortuous life as prisoner of the Nazis, he embraced her now, and in his mind the Nazis were the demons, and Baba Yaga was no longer the figure of dread—she was perhaps a figure of justice. Someone, somewhere, would have to destroy the Nazis. He laughed out loud at the crazy thought that he had.

"What's so funny?" Slava asked, startled at his outburst.

"Oh, nothing really. I'm just being silly. I thought of Baba Yaga, that's all."

"That's weird."

Vladimir decided to quickly change the subject. "It's not Slonim yet. I happened to see a sign along the tracks that read 'Albertin' a few meters back, just a small village."

Feeling uncomfortable looking across the aisle with the man in black seated on that side, Vladimir noticed a row at the very front vacated by two soldiers who left the car. It had a window still intact. "Slavochka, let's move to those seats over there," nodding at the seats. "There seems to be more to see on that side."

Slava readily agreed. She, too, did not feel comfortable sitting so close to the surly German. Vladimir retrieved the suitcase from the overhead shelf and they moved to those seats. They heard the German speak, but the click-clack of the train on the rails obliterated his words.

Gazing out the window, Vladimir said, "So far, everything looks intact. I see no battle scars. Most likely, Slonim is standing as well."

Moments later, the town of Slonim appeared. Along and near the tracks were wooden houses with high pitched roofs, surrounded by rough board fences, same as in Albertin. A wide river popped into view through the barren trees, displaying the main area of Slonim on the opposite bank. Slava immediately focused on the beautiful Catholic cathedral in the distance with its large central tower narrowing to a point topped by a large cross. Below the large tower she saw four identical, but much smaller towers, also crowned by crosses. Being Catholic, her heart skipped a beat hoping to be able to attend that imposing church, especially since the communists closed the churches in Vitebsk.

Other large buildings pleased the young couple. Vladimir enjoyed the bright sparkle in his wife's eyes. "I think I'll like it!" In excitement, Slava rapidly rubbed her hands together numerous times. "It looks much bigger than I had imagined. I thought it would be a tiny village like the one we just passed. There are many substantial buildings, all seemingly white with high-pitched red roofs."

"I think the city looks great."

"This all used to be Poland," Slava said. "Isn't the Polish flag red and white?"

"Yes. Do you think the buildings are painted red and white on purpose?"

"That's interesting. You may be right. Anyway, Slavochka, I'm so glad that you seem excited about Slonim."

"Volodya, my darling, as long as we're together, I would be happy in a hole." Vladimir leaned over and kissed her several times on her cheek with his lips finally landing on hers. His smile broadened and both sets of eyes drifted on to the town that would become their new home.

"So far, everything looks deserted," Slava said. "I haven't seen much life. But then Vitebsk looked deserted, there wasn't much life visible with the Germans occupying the city."

Suddenly, the man in black approached them. "We're almost at the station. You will follow me to the city administration. I'll see that they send you to one of our cozy labor camps in Germany." A malicious smile appeared on his face. Both Vladimir and Slava tensed. The huge pit returned to their stomachs. Their excitement for Slonim quickly vanished.

Vladimir tried to gauge if he was joking. But his sadistic smile faded, replaced by his usual cold stare.

"Could they really do that?" Slava whispered to Vladimir, her lips quivering after the man laughed wickedly and returned to his seat.

"Don't worry, Slavochka. They can do anything they want, but I was assured by the commandant that we were to stay and work in Slonim. Let's try not to pay attention to this man. He just enjoys watching us squirm."

The man, once again, stood over them holding on to the back of their seat as the train came to a stop at the depot.

"All right, get out. Your days on this earth are numbered."

Chapter 6

THE DINGY white stucco walls and fading red roof of the Slonim train station loomed ahead, separated from the train by two sets of tracks. Slava shivered as she stepped down onto the platform. Heavy steel-gray clouds threatened snow. The dreary frigid atmosphere matched the mood of the young couple.

Vladimir wrapped his right arm around Slava's shoulder and they followed the man in black. "Look at that beautiful station!" Trying his best to be cheerful, Vladimir pointed to the depot. Slava was not fooled. She saw his attempt to assuage her fears from the vile threats made by that appalling man leading the way. "It's so striking, especially with those long, narrow windows topped with arches. There are seventeen just on the first floor alone. And did you notice that water tower behind us? It has a small building built underneath it. I have never seen that before. I wonder what's inside."

"Enough already. Your scheme to distract me from what lies ahead is not working. At this point, I really don't care what that station looks like or how many windows it has. Just think. We might end up dead or in a forced labor camp!" The man turned his head and gave them a smug grin, pleased to hear that his earlier comments upset them.

The couple exchanged a quick glance. He spoke Russian, even though his prior conversations with them had only been in German.

"Slava," Vladimir said softly, "We'll be all right. Just wait and see. They need doctors here. Otherwise they wouldn't have given me money and sent me here."

Slava had heard Vladimir's assurance several times already, and each time it seemed to mitigate her anxiety, at least a little. Nevertheless, an awful knot in her stomach still persisted. She knew that her husband's assignment was made by the German army medical personnel, but she wasn't sure whether the SS had approved. *They have the real authority. I am certain that man is SS or a member of the Order Police, dressed in civilian clothing as they often are.*

Two workers inside the train station in soiled and tattered suit jackets mopped the wooden floor of the cavernous open interior. Several men in green German uniforms milled about. At the other end of the depot, two more men, these in black uniforms, half-dragged a civilian out the door obviously against his will. Along the side wall, only one of the four ticket windows was open. The large clock above the door struck twelve as their escort led them out of the front entrance.

Past the steps and along a cement walkway, they were hurried toward a horseshoe-shaped cobbled drive blanketed with muddy snow. In the center of that semicircle, their eyes were drawn to a huge, sprawling horse chestnut tree whose bare branches took up a large portion of the grassy open space. To the left, across a snow-dusted field, a clump of wooden houses, topped with high-pitched gabled roofs, spewed out smoke from their chimneys. Beyond were more fields scattered with naked trees. Straight ahead, toward the river below, clusters of other houses dotted the landscape. They were surprised to realize that the depot stood at least two kilometers from the main part of town. An occasional vehicle or a horse and cart drove by, but generally there was little life. In the midst of this calm scene, there was no peace for the couple.

"Wait here!" The man's face turning red with anger, barked out the command to the couple, as they stood outside of the front entrance of the station. "There should have been a car waiting for us!" He screamed the words out with much irritation, pacing back and forth, glancing in the direction of downtown. Aggravation obvious, he bellowed, "Well, I really don't give a damn if it isn't here. I can use the walk. Let's go."

They maneuvered past mud-caked military vehicles. Soldiers sat behind the wheel of some. Local women loaded other vehicles with provisions brought by the train. The scene with the military vehicles, his empty stomach, and now the order to follow the man into town reminded Vladimir of the endless forced marches, without food or water, which he endured the year before. He remembered his extreme exhaustion that left him barely able to walk as they were herded along in a column of thousands.

They turned right and trudged silently along the muddy roadway toward the town. Slava wrapped her light-brown woolen scarf around her neck and tucked it underneath the rabbit-lined collar of her black wool coat. A few minutes later, she pulled it higher still to cover her mouth and nose trying not to breathe the frigid air. She glanced at Vladimir and saw him lift up the lapels of his coat. His five foot eight inch frame had suffered from malnourishment at the hands of his captors. His jaw was stubbornly clenched. Deep, dark circles underlined his blue eyes. He showed extreme stress, yet a usual charismatic smile played on his lips as he tried to appear brave when intercepting her glances. She sidled closer and wrapped her arm around his.

"Volodya, what you said made sense," Slava broke their silent walk. "They wouldn't have sent us here unless they needed you. They could have thrown us in one of those awful cattle cars you told me about. They could've easily shipped us off to work camps from Baranovichi instead of bringing us here."

"That right. That's exactly what I think."

"I don't know what that man is all about. You really think that he just wants to toy with our nerves?"

"Sure, that's all it is. He's a sadist." Vladimir comforted Slava even though the man's apparent hatred for them made his own heart race, his breath catch. He realized that no matter what encouragement he gave, fear overwhelmed her thoughts. Her almost perpetual smile had faded long ago. Her usually sparkling hazel eyes were now dull. Her normally upturned lips were pursed and turned down.

They passed two streets that turned right toward the tracks, both dotted with dilapidated houses with visible outhouses behind sagging fences. At the intersection of the second street from the depot, in a small house, Vladimir spotted a curtain pull back in the window. A gray-haired woman scowled at them and abruptly snapped the curtain back. A large two-story stone and concrete structure loomed at the third intersection. Pointing to the building, their tormentor spoke, "That, you pigs, is the jail. That's where you'll be until we ship you out." He snickered coldly, enjoying his own wit. Slava exhaled heavily.

"Don't let him get to you," Vladimir whispered. "Pay no attention to the fool."

"How can I not? I try so hard to ignore what he says, but his comments just get worse."

"He's enjoying your stress," Vladimir whispered even though his heart banged so hard against his chest that he thought it might break through. "That's his game. We'll be all right."

The road twisted to the left toward the river. An occasional truck drove by splattering a mix of snow and mud on the group. Each time, their escort lifted his fist up and yelled obscenities at the long gone driver, while at the same time brushing off his black coat. "Where is that dammed car?" He grumbled. "I'll have their heads!"

Vladimir and Slava exchanged fleeting looks and hid their smiles. The man in his rage made for a comical figure, slapping his hips, shaking his arms in the air. Then the thought of what might await them ahead again crept into their minds, wiping any smile from their faces.

Ahead, a long bridge over a wide river emerged. They saw yet another bridge was in the distance. "Look at that," Vladimir said. "Are there two rivers here?"

"It looks like it," Slava answered. "Look on the left, there, in the distance. Both rivers seem to unite into one."

After they crossed the long bridge and approached the second bridge, Vladimir pointed to the right. There, buildings and houses were cordoned off with many strands of barbed wire. A few soldiers supervised old men and women as they removed the makeshift fence. A tall barrier lay parallel to the bridges and wound along the banks of both rivers. Except for the people dismantling the fence, the area seemed deserted. "What do you make of that?"

"That probably is or was a Jewish Ghetto. It looks like the Jewish area in Vitebsk that the Nazis surrounded with a barbed wire fence. They forced all Jews that did not evacuate, as ordered by Stalin, into the compound. They were not allowed to leave and had to fend for themselves. I do think, however, that they were provided some rations for food and coal. We were not allowed to help them, not even with food. Then one day, we heard that all of them were gone from Vitebsk, and the area was left abandoned. The Nazis appropriated everything from their houses and businesses."

"What happened to the Jews?"

"We all assumed that they were taken to Germany to work."

Vladimir shook his head. He felt in his heart that they were probably dead.

After they crossed the second bridge, they saw more of what appeared to be a ghetto. It hugged both banks of the river with more to the left than to the right. In front of several substantial looking houses, with second floors tucked away underneath the high-pitched roofs, several workers, bundled in caps and heavy coats, were moving furniture onto army trucks parked at the curb.

"I bet that no Jews live there now." Slava said. "They'll probably begin relocating non-Jews into the area." She hesitated, swallowed and commented, "Oh God, I hope we don't get one of those houses. I'd hate to live in a place where the people were forcibly evicted from their homes." Then she remembered, "That is, if they leave us in Slonim." Vladimir remained quiet, his lips pressed into a thin line.

A block past the second bridge, they turned left onto a cobblestone street. Many storefronts stood vacant and boarded up. Most had faded large black letters scribbled on the boards spelling out the word, *JUDA*. Vladimir sadly realized that those stores once belonged to Jewish merchants.

Weak from hunger and knowing that Slava was even more so, Vladimir wondered if they could stop for a moment to purchase a loaf of bread. In a narrow store that they passed by, he had spotted a few loaves of bread on shelves behind a counter. Salivating profusely with the thought of sinking his teeth into the crust, he felt pain in his abdomen as though someone squeezed his stomach. He decided he'll have to brave it and ask the man in black if they could stop for a minute and buy some food.

"No! Come on, speed up. I don't have all day."

The thought of eating something made Slava do something that she ordinarily would not have done. She ran up to the man in black, grabbed his arm, "Please, can't we just buy something to eat. Please."

The man jerked his arm away from her. "No. Your hunger is not my concern."

Vladimir knew it was useless to pursue the subject any further. He pulled Slava back and gave her a reprimanding look. Trying to change the subject, he asked, "How much further is it?"

"You'll see it when we get there."

They walked past three older women wearing heavy cotton scarves on their heads. A younger woman with a fur hat rode past them on a black bicycle. An old man with a heavy coat and a knitted cap covering his ears rode his bicycle toward them. He was followed by a man on a cart packed with old lumber and doors and pulled by an ancient-looking nag. Behind him sped a Mercedes with its horn blaring, warning the old man to get out of the way. The horse panicked and bolted to the left forcing the auto to swerve and barely avoid a collision. "Oh my God!" Slava cried. "That was close." Moments later, more military vehicles passed in both directions, including what appeared to be a staff car with attached small red and black Nazi flags on each side of the hood.

Approaching them, two rather sullen men in uniforms unfamiliar to Vladimir walked past their German escort and stopped the young couple. Vladimir immediately spied a red Polizei patch on the arm of the beige overcoat.

"Papers! State your business here," the young-looking, pale-faced policeman demanded in very broken Polish. The man in black stopped, pivoted around, grunted, and rapidly flashed some sort of document to them that neither Vladimir nor Slava recognized. With an arrogant and authoritative manner, he abruptly waved the men away without ever uttering a word. One of the Polizei began to speak, decided otherwise, and reluctantly said something to his companion in a language that neither Vladimir nor Slava understood.

"See, I told you he is SS," Slava whispered to Vladimir. Nodding agreement, Vladimir suddenly felt weak at his knees.

"And a coward," he added, feeling better by saying that.

At the end of the long block, they spied a plaza ahead. A massive stone building with a clock tower emerged to the right.

"Probably that's the building we are going to," Vladimir told Slava. He turned out to be correct. As they entered the stone-paved wide plaza, they walked past the side of the building and turned to the right.

A few more steps and their unwanted escort pointed to the large two-story baroque-style building. The lump in Vladimir's stomach doubled in size as he looked at the cold, stone edifice. *Well, I guess this is it. This is where, at least for now, our fate will be sealed.* Slava sidled closer to him.

"We go there. That's City Hall, home of the military and local administration. From there you'll be shipped out," the German laughed sadistically.

Vladimir peered up at the massive structure. The building looked somber, even oppressive, Vladimir thought, with the gabled center portion protruding a meter from the rest of the building. Tall narrow windows of the two floors appeared forlorn and gloomy. The couple doggedly followed the man in black past the armed Polizei and up four brick steps to the iron and glass doors.

Chapter 7

PAST THE doors, German soldiers dutifully stood guard. A rifle dangled from the shoulder of each. The man in black flashed his identification. Clicking his heels, the guard immediately straightened his shoulders and motioned them to pass.

"Follow me!" His brisk, deep voice echoed in the wide tiled hallway. They strode down the hallway, past an oak door. The word, *Mayor*, in gilt letters on the frosted glass window of the door caught Vladimir's attention. Across the hall, a similar door with a blank frosted glass window had black letters poorly scratched off. At the foot of an elaborate staircase, yet another German guard, standing at attention, stopped them from proceeding up the stairs. "State your business here."

The man in black flashed his credentials again. "I demand to see the commandant immediately."

"Commandant Weinheimer is not available. He left the building."

"Find him. Tell him Lieutenant Adler of the Order Police needs to see him now!"

"Sorry, Lieutenant, but we cannot leave our posts. You may proceed upstairs and talk to one of his assistants."

"To hell with that! Have someone find him immediately!"

"Yes, Lieutenant."

The guard by the stairs shouted orders to one of the soldiers to find the commandant without delay.

That soldier hesitated. "I don't know where he is. Besides, I can't leave my post."

"He's in his quarters for lunch. Go get him."

"I can't leave my post."

Adler turned abruptly and marched to that guard, holding his papers in his right hand. He shoved his credentials into the soldier's face. "You do not want any trouble from me, you idiot. Move it!"

The guard grabbed his helmet hanging on a hook by the door, handed his rifle to the other soldier across the hall, and ran out of the building, leaving the door ajar. The other soldier shut the door.

Vladimir and Slava, still standing by the stairs, glanced at each other. "I think we're in big trouble," Slava whispered, chewing her lip.

Vladimir took Slava by the arm and edging closer to the peeling light-blue wall of the hallway, leaned against it.

"Do not lean against the wall," the guard by the stairs said. "You are leaning on the property of the Third Reich."

The couple jumped away from the wall. Adler stood a few feet away, staring at the front door, fuming at the delay. At that moment, three Polizei came through the door, nodded their heads at the lone guard, glanced at the direction of the missing sentry, shrugged, and entered the door opposite the mayor's office. Their uniforms were identical to the ones worn by the men that stopped the couple earlier.

"Who are those men?" Vladimir whispered to Slava. "They are obviously not Germans."

"I saw similar uniforms in Baranovichi," Slava replied quietly. "I asked the same question of a man passing by. He told me that those men are German sympathizers. They are brought in to do the wicked work for the Nazis. They are called police, under the authority of the Germans, and are controlled by the Order Police, which in turn is controlled by the dreadful SS, Hitler's elite force, the Gestapo. In these parts, the police are most likely Latvians. All Germans, including high command officers, are terrified of Hitler's special goons."

"Why are they so terrified?"

"Because they are Hitler's henchmen. They do his dirty work, and he has given them implicit authority to do what they want."

In that case, we may be in trouble. If Slava is right, a regular army officer's order would make no difference. Adler may actually have an upper hand. Oh God!

Adler paced smartly up and down the hall, back and forth, back and forth. Vladimir and Slava stood silently, their insides tied into knots.

"I don't know why we have to wait for him here," Adler declared, almost to himself. "These pigs got me all upset, and I can't think straight. We'll just go upstairs and wait for the commandant in his office. It better not be long."

At that instant, Adler turned and glared at Vladimir. Spittle ran down the left side of Adler's mouth, his eyes ablaze with anger. *What is his problem? He is taking this personally for some reason.*

Vladimir took Slava by the hand and squeezed closer to the wall as Adler pushed past them, shoving them on purpose, as he stomped on the first two steps of the stairs. At that moment, the door opened, and a short, thin officer in an expertly tailored brown uniform with golden epaulettes walked in, followed by the soldier sent to find him. The frown marring his features belied what Slava felt were kind eyes on his square face. Adler quickly pivoted and waited for the officer to approach him.

"I am Commandant Weinheimer. What is the meaning of this—ordering my soldier from his post to rudely track me down?"

"I don't have much patience, as you can see. And I do not have to explain. Let's proceed to your office."

"Who are you? What do you want?"

"I'm Lieutenant Adler of the Order Police. Now let's go to your office."

"Address me properly and don't give me orders."

Adler's face turned the color of a beet. "Don't you realize that I am part of the SS and we have authority over local German administration?"

The commandant wanted to respond, but decided against it. He drew in a deep breath and exhaled. "Follow me upstairs to my office." The major glanced at the couple huddled together off to the side. "Is this the doctor and his wife that we have been expecting?"

"Yes, this is the scum, the Soviet prisoner that is not fit to live, let alone be allowed to work as a physician within the Third Reich."

Weinheimer gave Adler a disapproving look but remained quiet. He turned to Vladimir and Slava and motioned for them to follow. Vladimir felt a little better about the situation. He decided that the commandant showed his suspicion that Adler was a waste of oxygen.

The guard, who seemed to enjoy the conversation, lifted his shoulders and saluted by projecting his right arm in the air and bellowing "Heil Hitler" as the four of them began their walk up the wide marble staircase. Neither Weinheimer nor Adler returned the salute.

A large dimly-lit hallway, leading to several doorways, greeted them at the top of the stairs. They approached an office with an open door and heard women chatting in a Slavic language, not loud enough for Slava to discern. The conversation ceased as the major approached. Several soldiers in green uniforms, sitting behind desks with typewriters, occupied another open office. Their prattle and laughter quickly vanished as the major passed the door. Across the hall, open double doors led to a spacious conference room. Inside, an intricately carved oak table stood surrounded by several old battered and mismatched chairs. Each step down the long hall constricted Vladimir's chest. His head throbbed. Slava walked so closely to Vladimir that it appeared they were fused at the hips. He could feel her tension. *Well, let's get it over with,* he thought to himself.

At the far end of the hallway, Weinheimer briskly entered a windowless inner office. A lieutenant with a similar uniform jumped from his chair and stood at attention as the party filed past him into the outer office. The couple's eyes blinked to adjust to the brightly-lit overhead light fixture. Two tall open-draped windows opposite the door added to the brightness of the room. A highly polished walnut desk, free of clutter, and a brown leather chair took up half of the intricate red and green Persian rug, which covered most of the light oak floor. A fresh coat of light green paint covered the walls. Four leather side chairs, evenly placed from each other faced the elaborate desk. A photograph of Adolph Hitler hung behind the desk, while a map of Europe was stretched on the opposite wall. A gilded framed oil painting of what appeared to be a Spanish woman holding a flower bouquet hung on the wall opposite the windows.

"Sit down."

Vladimir and Slava sat down, as told. Adler remained upright even after Weinheimer sat down.

"I want these two executed," Adler demanded as his index finger pointed at the couple.

"And why is that, lieutenant?"

"These people are our enemies. He was a Soviet prisoner of war, for God's sake. Why are we rewarding him with this position?"

"Listen Adler, you have your orders, and I have my orders. They are from high command in Minsk. He is to open a medical practice in this town. The population is in desperate need of doctors."

"Damn the population. Who in the hell cares? All of them eventually will be annihilated. You know our führer's plan. I want these people shot immediately. As an officer of the Order Police, I am ordering you to do exactly that, Major."

"Adler, I've heard enough!" Weinheimer said, breathing heavily, his cheeks reddened. "You do not have authority in this matter. The order came from Minsk, sanctioned by the SS, and unless I receive new orders, they stand. The doctor stays in Slonim. Now, is there anything else?"

"You listen to me. As a member of the Order Police, I am ordering you to obey my command."

"No, you must take it up with Minsk. That is all, Lieutenant."

Adler's face, already red, now turned crimson. The veins in his neck protruded. His nostrils flared. Vladimir thought the man would explode. He leaned into the desk, placed his fists on it and stared at Weinheimer, who in turn sat silently, staring up at Adler. Finally Adler spoke, "This is not over with yet. I will take it up with my superior at the SS and see to it that you are relieved of your post!" He abruptly turned and stormed out of the office, leaving the door open. He was heard to yell out, "Heil Hitler," as he stomped down the hall.

Weinheimer's face paled. His hands trembled. He took a deep breath, and pulled out a cigarette from a gold case sitting at the corner of the desk next to a framed photograph of his family. He took an ivory cigarette holder out of his breast pocket and with precision, placed the cigarette into it. The flame from the match flickered wildly as he lit the cigarette. After a few puffs, he forced a smile at the couple. "Smoke?" He asked as he offered the cigarettes to Vladimir and Slava. Both refused.

Weinheimer took a few more puffs, exhaling with force, watching the smoke as it rose toward the window. "Herr Doctor Moskalkov, I'm sorry you had to hear that. You must excuse the man. Do not concern yourself any longer with him. I had a telephone call regarding Herr Adler. He is bitter and angry. He left Baranovichi without permission after he was informed that both his father and brother were killed a few days ago on the Russian front. He has taken the loss rather badly it seems. He became incensed when he found out that you were released from the camp and given this assignment. Still, that is no excuse for his behavior. Actually, I think your luck in this matter is highly unusual and unbelievable. But orders are orders, and my orders are to allow you to stay in Slonim on the condition that you work for the population as a physician."

Up to this point, Vladimir and Slava listened to the struggle between the two Germans, their insides ready to burst upon hearing the words *executed* and *shot*. After realizing that Adler was not getting his way, a wave of relief filled the young couple. Vladimir took a full, deep breath. *We escaped the bullet this time.* For the first time since arriving in Slonim, Slava grinned broadly, her eyes ablaze with brightness.

"My instructions from the medical command in Minsk are clear. You are to open, as soon as possible, a clinic, specializing in ear, nose and throat. From here on out, you're on your own. It shouldn't be too difficult. With the Jews gone, there are empty buildings and houses. You need to buy your own medical instruments and supplies. One thing must be clear. You are not to treat enemies of the Third Reich such as communists, partisans, or partisan sympathizers. Nor are you to treat Jews. If you know of any Jews, you are to report them immediately, or you will be severely punished, most likely by death. Do you understand?"

Slava and Vladimir nodded affirmatively.

"Do you have any questions?"

Anxious to leave, Vladimir quickly shook his head indicating that he had no questions.

"Fine. Then that is all. You are dismissed."

"I do have a question, after all," Vladimir said. "I was told that you will provide me and my wife with documents indicating our status here."

"Yes. Go two doors down on the right and see one of the corporals. He will provide you with temporary documents. Anything else?"

"No, thank you," Vladimir said.

"Thank you very much," Slava said and gave Major Weinheimer a sincere smile. He returned her smile.

"Good afternoon," he said.

They walked to another office, which was rather large with two metal desks facing each other. Two soldiers in green German uniforms sat behind their desks. A large portrait of Hitler hung between them. One of the soldiers with a look of authority motioned to both to sit down on a chair at the side of the desk. He began to immediately write on a preprinted form information concerning both Vladimir and Slava. After finishing and stamping the forms, he instructed each of them to stand in front of a camera in the back of the room.

"I'll have your documents in one-half hour. You can wait in the hallway until I call you."

When they returned to get the papers, Vladimir asked where they could buy some food. The corporal glanced briefly at the other soldier in the room. Seeing that he was busy with someone else, in a low voice he said, "You know, we don't sanction people selling food in the black market.

But you might try the market square a few blocks away. After you leave this building, turn to the right and again to the right and follow that street until you'll see a square. They usually leave about this time of day, but there may still be a vendor there."

"What about a place to live?" Slava asked before they left.

"You need to see one of Lieutenant Hartman's assistants. He is in charge of housing. His office is at the other end of the hall to the left."

"Can we just go and find a place on our own?" Slava asked timidly. She feared that if the Nazis assign a place to them, it would be one of the houses taken away from a Jewish family. She knew she would feel terrible about benefitting from their tragic loss.

"I wouldn't advise it. Private rentals are not allowed in most occupied areas; however, so far, Commandant Weinheimer had not made his position known on this subject. So, I advise you to see Lieutenant Hartman. Come back tomorrow for your food and coal ration cards. I don't have any here today."

The couple thanked him and hurriedly left the building. The hunt for something to eat became their first priority, and they thought they could see about a place to live later. After a five-minute walk, they approached a large gothic stone structure. Past the building, the square loomed ahead. As they entered the cobbled-stoned square, they glanced back at the building, spying the Star of David embossed in the stone. "That's a synagogue," Slava said. "It looks so old."

Vladimir nodded, glancing at the structure. They were now on the large cobble-stoned square, bordered on three sides by houses and buildings. The massive synagogue took up the shorter side. Their hearts sank as they observed horse and handcarts leaving. Vladimir ran after the straggling one, calling out for the old woman to stop. She turned toward him and yelled out, "Everything gone. Be back tomorrow."

"Watch out!" Vladimir shouted at Slava. She jumped out of the way when an old man on a rickety black bicycle almost collided with her in the middle of the square.

"He must be blind," Slava said.

"That was close. Are you all right?"

"I'm fine, don't worry."

"Good. Did you see the potatoes in that wire basket attached to the handle bars. I wish we could have at least one. We could eat it raw."

"Volodya, we'll eat soon enough. We need to look for a place to live. I really want to avoid getting a house from the Nazis, if possible."

Chapter 8

SNOWFLAKES RELENTLESSLY tumbled out of the ashen sky. The frantic pace of the snow was offset by the quiet and gave Vladimir and Slava a feeling of temporary peace. Famished and with no place to go in an occupied town, they, yet, were filled with strange euphoric freedom. As the clumps of moisture struck their faces, they took deep breaths and exchanged beaming smiles. Vladimir pulled Slava towards him and hugged her. Neither said a word, allowing their nerves to settle. They were alone in the square with only an occasional pedestrian or a bicyclist.

"The snow makes everything so beautiful," Slava said. "We're lucky the wind is calm.

I'm glad my mother made me take the boots." She glanced at Vladimir. We need to find you some boots! The snow will stay on the ground probably until spring."

"I'll be all right. I'm used to it. A little moisture is nothing. Besides, I can't complain about these shoes. I'm fortunate to have them," Vladimir continued. "Even though they are a bit tight, it was miraculous that the German officer even gave them to me to wear—not only the shoes but this suit and hat as well. He didn't have to do anything for me. Yet he arranged my release. I'll never forget him!"

"Yes, but you saved his life. I am sure he'll never forget you either."

"I know. It amazes me that amidst tragedy, we found such luck. I just can't get over it."

"God was watching over you."

"He watched over both of us."

Vladimir's eyes glazed with a faraway look. For a moment, he looked mesmerized by the falling flakes. Slava realized that his mind was elsewhere at that moment. *It will take some time for him to get over all the death and destruction he witnessed. He lived in hell.* The thought of what her husband went through brought tears to her eyes. She tried to blink away the tears, and reflected on just how vulnerable they were in their emotional state.

"Well, Slavochka, the new life beckons us. Let's hurry on to it!" Vladimir said smiling and grabbing her arm. "Let's make the best of it."

"So what do we do now?"

"Well first, I insist on looking for food," Vladimir said. "Even if I have to knock on doors, we'll find something. Let's try that street ahead of us. Maybe we'll find a store."

"Excellent. Let's go."

The couple scrambled across the plaza and entered the street. About halfway down the block and across the street, they spotted a food store. Excitedly, they hurried across the street.

As they entered the shop, a plump middle-aged, round-faced woman seemed startled at their appearance. She was just removing a white apron bordered by intricate red stitches from her dark blue, snugly fitting dress. Absently, Slava noted that it was a pretty apron, with intricate red stitchery lovingly applied to its borders. "Yes, what do you want?" She asked in Polish, revealing her crooked teeth. "I'm ready to close."

"We would like to buy some bread and anything else you might have available to eat," Vladimir said.

"I only have bread, grain, and dairy products. Let me see your ration cards."

"We don't have any yet."

"Then I can't help you. I can only accept ration cards. This is an official government store. You're not from here, are you? Where are you from anyway?"

"We're from Vitebsk," Vladimir answered in Russian. He was much more proficient with Russian and hoped she would understand him. He continued until he noticed a blank expression descend on her face. He switched to Polish. "We only arrived in town this afternoon. Both my wife and I are famished. We need at least a little bit of food. Can't you make an exception for us? We have the money to pay you."

"No, no, no. I'm not allowed to sell food here without rations. You need to find someone at the black market," the woman answered in what was a combination of Polish and Byelorussian.

"Please, the vendors on the plaza are gone," Slava said in Polish. "We know no one in Slonim or even where to go to find someone to sell us food. I'm ready to faint from hunger."

The lady crossed her arms around her impressive bosom. Cocking her head to the side, she carefully studied the couple, wrestling with her thoughts. Pressing her lips together, she smoothed one hand over her light brown hair, pinned into a tight knot. A bobby pin held a green ribbon tied around the knot.

"Listen, I can't sell you anything. I have to account for each loaf, bag of flour, whatever. However, I'll lock up the store, and you follow me to my house. I live only a few blocks away. We'll find something for you to eat. Then, in the morning, there will be vendors selling their products for you to purchase."

Vladimir's and Slava's eyes met in disbelief. How kind and unexpected was the offer. *What luck*, Slava thought. The woman slowly ambled a few steps from behind the counter over to a wall, removing a red knitted hat, a brown woolen scarf, and a tattered gray fur-trimmed coat from a hook. Vladimir offered to help her with the coat. She readily obliged, handing it to him and pushing her arm into the sleeve. She then stuck her plump fingers into her pockets looking for something.

"Let's see, where did I put the key? Oh yes, silly of me, it's in my purse. But where is my purse?" The lady muttered to herself as she began to search behind the counter, opening and closing several drawers. At that instant, Slava noticed a black handbag adorned with a large brass clasp peaking out from underneath a chair beside the counter. Vladimir could not keep his eyes from the loaves of bread on the shelf. The urge to grab a loaf and bite into it became overwhelming. *Control yourself.* The thought of attacking the bread was sidetracked when he heard Slava point out the purse to the lady.

"Of course, I usually leave it in the drawer here. I forgot I left it under the chair. Ah yes, here's the key," she mumbled, slowly rummaging through her bag, and clutching the key. "We can go now."

Thank God, Vladimir thought. *Can this lady be any slower?* The couple stepped outside with the woman and waited for her to lock the door.

"Oh my, I forgot to cover the bread. Wait here, I'll be back in a second." The lady slipped the key in her coat pocket and went back inside the store. Vladimir and Slava continued to wait impatiently outside the door. Vladimir glanced through the window and saw her neatly and very deliberately stretching a white cloth over the loaves. She walked out, and in an attempt to retrieve the key out of her pocket, dropped a wadded green knit glove and a white handkerchief onto the ground. Vladimir quickly picked up the items and handed them to her. She nodded and stuffed them back in the pocket. This time, in the process, she dropped the key further down to the bottom. Again she fiddled in the pocket and finally pulled it out. It took several attempts to lock the door. At first, she could not find the keyhole. Then once the key was in, the lock seemed to stick. She jiggled the key for a few seconds before the lock clicked. Vladimir gritted his teeth.

"Ah, all right," she stated triumphantly. "Now it's locked. This always happens to me. There is a knack to locking this door. Well, let's go that way," pointing down the street, away from the square. "By the way, they call me Agata."

"We're very pleased to meet you," Slava said, introducing herself and Vladimir. "It's so generous of you to do this for us. You're a godsend."

"No problem. I've been hungry before. I know how it feels." *That must have been a long time ago judging from her weight now. No, lady, you don't know how it feels.* Vladimir thought of the emaciated faces and bodies of people who had died of starvation and how close he, himself, came to death from hunger. *That was real hunger—weeks of no nourishment. Breathing skeletons, that's what we were.*

"So how is it in Vitebsk?" Agata continued. "I'm sure the Germans had occupied it. You know, they have been here since July of last year. It was awful at first, especially for those unfortunate Jews. But now life could be worse, I suppose. As long as you do what they say, you're allowed to live unharmed. Whatever you do, don't get involved with any partisans. If you do, they'll hang you and make an example of you." *I hope no patient ever comes to me and admits that he is a partisan. I doubt anyone would.* Vladimir thought. *They probably have their own doctors in the forests.*

As they plodded along, Agata talked incessantly, not even waiting for a response to her questions. The more she chattered, the slower she walked. Vladimir thought of some way to keep her quiet, hoping to move her along faster. He knew Slava needed nourishment quickly.

"How far did you say your house is from here?" Vladimir asked hoping that Agata would concentrate all her efforts on reaching her home as soon as possible.

"Really not far at all from here. Nothing in Slonim is too far. My house is on the outskirts by the forest. It's down this street, then on the last street to the right."

As they walked, the cobbles were replaced with dirt and stones. Some sections showed deep ruts carved out by wheels. The street narrowed. Steep-roofed wooden houses, bordered with rough-hewn fences, became less dense. In yards, chickens, with an occasional pig or goat, pastured in dormant vegetable gardens.

"There, we'll turn right here, and I'm the third house on the left—the one that's missing a few bricks of the chimney. My husband built the place himself. He died in 1939, shortly after the Soviets took over this part of Poland. That occupation was hard enough on us. There was so much panic and anxiety."

Vladimir was curious about the Soviet presence in Slonim. He wanted to question her but did not dare to delay the walk to the house.

"Then the Germans invaded last year," Agata continued. "Thank God my husband didn't live to see their occupation. He would have been devastated again. I think he probably would have joined the partisans. Oh God, I shouldn't say the word so loudly. They'll think I'm a supporter."

"There must be a strong partisan movement here," Slava said. "Do they bother the residents?"

"It's very strong. The Germans don't know how to quell or defeat them. I try to have nothing to do with the partisans, but sometimes I can't help it. Since I am so close to the forest, they sneak around at night and steal my vegetables. Last month, my one and only pig had disappeared. I am sure the partisans stole it. But maybe it was someone from town. With these hard times, there are plenty of thieves. The people are desperate. You had better be careful."

"Is it dangerous just walking around town?" Slava asked, looking around as though she expected to find a partisan or thief lurking about.

"It could be. But most of the crime is theft. You better lock everything up tight."

The sagging wooden gate creaked as Agata pushed it open and they entered a snowy path to the front door. A corroded tin roof covered the front porch. Once again she fumbled with the lock. A few seconds later, the young couple followed Agata into the front room. It was small. Slava gazed around. An opening immediately to the left of the front door led to what probably was the bedroom. Next to that door, a reddish-brown sofa covered with a colorful carpet, depicting a scene of a horse in a pasture, occupied much of the space. Another picturesque carpet hung on the wall over the sofa. At an angle, next to the sofa, sat a worn, lumpy velvet oversized chair. A cast-iron pot belly stove stood at the opposite corner. Slava's eyes stopped on an elaborate and highly polished walnut buffet sideboard next to the wall opposite the sofa. A narrow aisle bordered by the furniture led to the kitchen visible beyond.

"Let me light the wood stove as it's very cold in here, isn't it? It will warm up in no time," Agata said as she threw her coat, hat and gloves onto the chair and reached into a wooden box next to the stove to pull out some straw. Underneath, various lengths and thickness of tree branches stuck out of the box.

"Here, let me help you," Vladimir said. "I'll start the fire."

"Good. Slava, follow me into the kitchen. Take a seat at the table, and I think I'll fry up some eggs. I have five hens, you know. I had more, but they gradually disappear one by one. Oh yes, I also have some pickled green tomatoes. Everyone here has a small garden, and we can eat our vegetables. That's how we survive in such perilous times."

"That sounds really good," Slava said as she sat down on a stool next to a heavy homemade wooden table, her eyes on the black kitchen stove. "May I help you with something?"

"No, I'll light this stove, and we'll be ready to eat soon," Agata said as she stoked a few pieces of coal into the stove. "Coal is so hard to obtain. The rationing is limited, so I have to be very careful and use it sparingly. I use wood for heating. Sometimes, I go into the forest myself for fire-wood, but usually a neighbor brings me some. I slip him a few marks. Although, the Germans say that the forests belong to them, and we're not allowed to take anything out of them. But, so far, no one is enforcing that rule, thank God. By the way, if you need to use the toilet, it's outside, through that door," pointing to the back door.

The fire in the stove glowed and Vladimir joined the ladies in the kitchen. His eyes immediately found the highly polished cooking stove to see what treat awaited them. He gulped as he saw Agata break open an egg and let the contents spill into a heavy iron frying pan. He had not felt the taste of an egg since he left for war. Two more eggs followed into the pan. *God, the aroma is overwhelming!* His stomach growled. He glanced at Slava who sat looking exhausted. Her eyes, also fixated on the pan, seemed luster-less. Her face suddenly turned pale as the white blouse she wore. *Oh my God! She's going to faint.*

Vladimir grabbed hold of Slava. "Agata, quick, I need some water!"

Agata glanced at Slava, dropped the spatula into the pan, quickly grabbed a cup and poured some water from the teapot sitting on the stove.

"Oh, the poor thing! I'm such a fool. I should have immediately offered you something to drink. The water in the pot is good. I boiled it this morning. I don't trust the well water without boiling it."

Slava recovered slightly as Vladimir told her to drink the water. Touching her parched lips to the rim, she slowly sipped the contents of the cup. A few minutes later the color came back to her face.

"You were dehydrated, Slavochka," Vladimir said. "We should have found us something to drink long before now."

"You better have some also," Slava said weakly. "I don't want you collapsing on me."

"Oh my! The eggs! I forgot about them! They'll burn!" Agata screamed and pulled the pan away from the heat. "Phew! There're all right. I got them just in time, maybe a little crisp."

"I'll eat them anyway," Vladimir said. "Even raw would have been good enough."

"That would have been all right," Agata said. "My mother always used to say that if you want to sing well, you must eat raw eggs."

"That's funny," Slava said. "My mother used to say the same thing."

Vladimir was pleased to hear Slava's voice speak out.

Agata slipped the eggs and the pickled green tomatoes onto a porcelain plate edged in faded gold leaf. She also took out half a loaf of black bread from a cupboard, and cut them each a slab.

"Oh, I also have some delicious currant jam that I've saved since last fall. We can have it with tea as a dessert."

Vladimir and Slava devoured their food. It was gone in an instant. Slava was embarrassed at her manners, especially when Agata sat staring at them with pity. But they needed to eat. Over tea, Agata's curiosity became overwhelming. She wanted to know everything about them and why they had not eaten for so long. Vladimir had told Slava earlier that it would be prudent not to let anyone in Slonim know that he had been a prisoner of war or that he served in the Soviet army. It would only lead to more questions, he thought.

"The Germans decided that the population needed a doctor, and they hurriedly ordered me here," Vladimir explained.

"You're a physician, then?"

"Yes. Right now we have to find a place to live and a place for a clinic."

"Do you have any suggestions?" Slava asked.

"With the Jews gone, there are plenty of vacant houses. Half the population is gone, although, the Germans are relocating many of the homeless in the area into formerly Jewish homes. It's a shame. I had a good friend who was taken away this past July, and I haven't seen her since.

Rumor has it that there is a mass grave outside of Slonim. I'm afraid she is probably there."

The couple saw Agata's eyes water. The three sat there quietly for a few moments. Vladimir broke the silence, "Do you know what time it is?"

Agata looked at her watch. "Oh, I forgot to wind it this morning. Let me go in my bedroom. I have an alarm clock there. From the bedroom she called out that it was almost four o'clock."

"We better go and try to find a place," Slava said. "I wish we knew where to start."

"You can get a list of housing from the German commandant. As I said, they have a lot available. Or just walk up and down the streets and look for a 'rent' sign. Those places belong to the Poles. Actually I saw one not far from here. Do you remember where the cobbled street ended?"

"Yes," said Vladimir.

"Well at that point you'll find a street to the right as you're walking toward the square. Take that street; it's a curvy and hilly street, as so many are in Slonim. I believe I saw a fairly nice house for rent as you walk for at least four blocks toward the south."

The couple wholeheartedly thanked Agata for her kindness. Slava offered to pay her for the food. She vehemently refused their offer and said that she was insulted at the thought. However, she did say it was always good to know a doctor and smiled. Agata looked disappointed that they were leaving. She obviously wanted to talk. But they now felt invigorated, ready to tackle the task of finding a place to live. As they walked out of the door, Agata shouted to them, "Once you get ration cards, come visit me in the store."

"What a nice lady," Slava said. "I already feel better about living in Slonim."

Chapter 9

PIERCING GUSTS of wind stabbed at the freezing faces of the young couple. The snow underfoot crunched with every step. Clouds hung low. Soon the dreary day would give way to dusk. A touch of glumness crept into Slava's mind. *How will we ever be able to find a place to live this late in the day?* Overcome with concern, she glanced at Vladimir who answered with a warm smile. His eyes had that twinkle of excitement that she loved. *Look at that. I'm worried sick, and Volodya seems unconcerned.*

"Do you feel all right, Slavochka? You gave me quite a scare back there."

"Oh, I feel fine. I'm just nervous. Where do we go from here? Don't you think it's a little late to look for a place now?"

"Look, little one. Don't worry. We still have time to find a place. It's only a little after four and we still have a few hours of daylight. Let's check out the house that Agata told us about. We'll find something."

They followed Agata's directions and turned right at the point where the dirt street turned to cobbled stones. At this point, stone sidewalks began. Though the street and side-walks on both sides were cobbled, the paving rocks were rough and difficult to walk on, especially with the slick layer of snow. Many of the stones were missing, some crumbling to gravel. Their pace slowed.

Every house they passed, including Agata's, had the names of occupants printed next to the front door. "That is the work of the efficient Germans," Slava said. "They know exactly who lives where, and they keep good records."

An occasional bicyclist or a passer-by made an appearance, each looking over the young couple with curiosity and suspicion. Vladimir stopped a woman, bundled up in a heavy coat and scarf, to ask whether she had seen a house for rent. "There, there," she pointed in the direction they were heading. She quickly moved on, avoiding any more conversation. In the distance, Vladimir spied an old man and woman sitting on wooden crates in front of a crumbling brick house. The man weakly waved them over. Vladimir and Slava approached. A faded green box, holding two loaves of bread, sat next to him. Next to the woman, another box contained dried mushrooms. The old man shivered in his worn, shabby coat, battered boots, and a tattered hat. The woman, covered with a heavy black coat and woolen scarf, greeted them with a warm generous smile thus exposing her missing front teeth.

"Would you like to buy a loaf? Or maybe some mushrooms?" The woman asked in Polish. Vladimir felt his heart leap with joy at the prospect of bread for later.

"Yes, we would," Slava blurted out anxiously, glancing at Vladimir for his approval.

"How much do you want for both loaves?" Vladimir asked of the woman.

The woman did not answer immediately. She appeared to be sizing up the young couple to see what she could get out of them.

"Two marks each."

The price seemed steep, but Vladimir had no notion how much bread could cost in occupied German currency. Slava, somewhat familiar with the specially printed marks for occupied territories, knew that price was outrageous.

"Your price is too high. How fresh is the bread?" Slava asked.

"I baked it myself this morning. It will be good for several more days if you keep it covered. And it's a good price. But since you want both, I'll sell you the two for the price of one."

Slava sensed that the price was still high, but did not object. The old man said nothing. He sat silently, shivering. The lifeless, grey eyes on his leathery face seemed fixated on the ground. The pleading expression on the deeply wrinkled, thin face of the hunched woman, tugged on Vladimir's heart. Feeling sorry for their plight, Vladimir handed the woman the money. She snatched the bills out of Vladimir's hand and handed him the loaves.

"Are you sick?" Vladimir asked the old man. "Or are you just cold?"

"I can't seem to warm up. I'll be all right."

"You shouldn't be sitting out here on this cold, damp day. You should go back in the house."

"It's just as cold in the house as it is out here," the woman said. "But now that we have a couple of marks, I'll see if I can buy some peat bricks. Our ration cards just don't last for the coal we need."

"You can buy peat coal, then?" Slava asked.

"It's probably illegal, but this fellow gathers the peat from the forests and makes bricks out of it. He even delivers it if we have the money."

"What about firewood from the forest?" Vladimir asked.

"We were told that all of that belongs to the Germans. We are not supposed to take even a mushroom from there. But I know a lot of people who do, and they are not hung or shot. We're just too old to gather our own wood."

"Let's give them an extra mark," Slava whispered to Vladimir.

Vladimir readily gave the woman an extra mark. She appeared stunned at the gesture. Her eyes welled. She rose slowly and stretched out her hand in appreciation.

"Would you like to come in? I can make a pot of tea. Unfortunately, I don't have anything sweet to go with it."

Vladimir and Slava appreciated the kind gesture. "Thank you, but we must be going. We are looking for a place to stay," Vladimir said.

"Come back and see us. Hopefully, we'll still be alive."

Vladimir and Slava walked away with heavy hearts. They felt sorry for the old couple, but knew that the elderly people were not alone in such a predicament. Life, under the German occupation, with its shortages and rationing was extremely difficult, especially for the sick and feeble. "Once our clinic is set up, and I'm able to obtain medications, I'll come back and help them," Vladimir said. "Unfortunately, I don't think that old man has much longer to live."

They broke off a piece of a loaf to eat while they walked. The rest Slava placed in her little suitcase. "This bread tastes as if it has sawdust in it," Slava said.

"It probably does." Vladimir said. "At least it'll fill a void in our stomachs. Flour must be hard to obtain." Slava nodded, her mind still on the old couple.

"I see a sign in the window," Vladimir said after they had hiked another block in the slippery snow. "That must be the place for rent."

The house with a tall peaked roof looked in decent shape. An ornate wooden door at the end of a wide porch seemed welcoming. A note attached to the door directed the couple to a house across the street for information. Slava stayed on the porch while Vladimir inquired. A pleasant thin woman with long blondish hair wound around her head to the door. She greeted him warmly and seemed overjoyed to show the house.

"Let me get my boots and coat, and I'll be right there. I know you'll like the place."

A minute later, she joined them holding a key in her hand.

"I hope you need a furnished house, because this one is fully furnished. I even left the sheets, towels, and kitchenware."

Oh that's wonderful, Slava thought. *That solves that worry for me.*

The small house appeared immaculate. The smaller of the two bedrooms contained a cot, the larger one held a big oak bed flanked by a couple of tables. A dresser topped by a large mirror stood across from the bed. A bluish-green bedspread with bold floral pattern covered the double-sized mattress.

"I like the house," Slava whispered to Vladimir as the woman went into the kitchen. "How much do you think she wants?"

"I'll ask. I like it too. We could, if necessary, use the front room and leave the small bedroom for a clinic until we find a more suitable place."

"Come and look at this kitchen," the lady said. "I think I have provided everything necessary to cook with. I even have an icebox for you."

"How much is the rent?" Vladimir asked.

"Fifty marks per month. That includes electricity. There is a little coal left in the metal bin next to the kitchen stove."

The couple eagerly agreed to rent the place. The woman hurriedly stuffed the marks into her coat pocket and cautioned Vladimir that coal was rationed as was firewood and that he should use the heat sparingly. "I hope you have warm sweaters."

By the time the landlady left, fatigue from the long day overwhelmed Slava and Vladimir. Slava pulled back the bedspread, sheet, and blanket and both collapsed onto the bed even though it was early evening. Snuggling for warmth, they quickly fell asleep in each other's arms.

Suddenly, Slava's shrieks awoke Vladimir. "Something is biting me!" Vladimir jumped out of bed. Startled from deep sleep, he searched for the lamp next to the bed, almost knocking it to the floor. Slava stood next to the bed, her night gown shed, scratching profusely. Vladimir saw red blotches over her left arm, shoulder and side. He began to feel his own body itch. Small red bumps appeared in a cluster pattern on both of them. The irritated skin had swollen sacs of pus in blister-like formations.

"My God, what caused this?" Slava sobbed. "It looks terrible, and the itching is unbearable. It hurts to scratch."

"I'm afraid that we were dinner for bedbugs, those nasty tiny insects that come out at night and gorge on humans."

"I know what they are. But I've never seen them before or had them eat on me. How do we get rid of them?"

"We can disinfect the bed, the frame, the mattresses and bedding. We could get other furniture, but they could be in the walls, behind the molding, anywhere."

"We can't stay here! We can't be a meal for them every night. What can we do? We need to find another place. We need to tell the landlady. She better give us our money back."

"Slavochka, relax. Take a breath. I agree. I'll go talk to her first thing in the morning."

"What time is it anyway?"

Since a German guard had long taken away his, Vladimir picked up Slava's wrist watch laying on the night-stand, "It's four in the morning."

"Well we can't go back into this bed," Slava said with disgust. "Ouch, ouch, this is really painful. I couldn't sleep now anyway."

"I'll light both stoves," Vladimir said. "We'll boil some water. Maybe, we can eat some of that wooden bread with a cup of steaming water."

"Wooden bread, wooden bread," Slava started to laugh. Vladimir joined in.

"We needed that, Slavochka. I feel better already, don't you?"

They sat down huddled together on the plush sofa, waiting for the house to warm up, Slava squirming from the bites. She imagined that the bedbugs had also infested the couch and were nibbling on her yet again.

Vladimir lit the bulky stove through the fuel door on its side and Slava filled the tea pot with water from the faucet. After about twenty minutes they heard the water boil. They sat down at a rustic old table flanked by heavy wooden stools and each ate a piece of bread with the hot water. The white porcelain cups came from a glass cupboard hanging over the table.

Vladimir looked at Slava's watch and said, "In about an hour, I'll go and break the happy news to the landlady that her house is full of bedbugs. Then we'll leave and look for another place and both of us will scratch ourselves bloody."

"It's discouraging to walk up and down the streets looking for a place. Maybe we should go see the Germans after all and ask for a house, but not one that was in the ghetto."

"Sure. That's the plan. You know, I've been looking around more carefully and just wondered why the landlady has such a finely furnished house. I mean, except for one room, it's completely furnished. The closet is full of linens, blankets, and extra pillows. This kitchen is fully stocked with dishes, pots and pans. Where do you think she got all this stuff?"

"Slavochka, maybe they had it from before the war. But more than likely, they picked it up from the surplus left by the poor souls that were shipped off."

"You mean like the Jews."

Vladimir nodded. "It hasn't been quite an hour, but I think I'll go see the landlady. After that, we'll go talk to the Germans. Although, I really hate the thought."

Chapter 10

THE MORNING sun had yet to arrive. A low layer of gray clouds hung over the city. Already bundled in his coat due to the cold house, Vladimir put on his hat and walked across the dark street. A cold, bitter wind almost swept the hat off his head. The landlady in a pink robe and a purple scarf, which covered her hair, looked surprised to see Vladimir at her front door. Embarrassed, she apologized for her appearance.

"Yes, what is it? Is something wrong?"

"The house is lovely and we really like it. Except that my wife and I were severely bitten by bedbugs."

"What? It can't be. I cleaned that house immaculately. Are you sure you didn't bring them in with you?"

"Of course not! Very regretfully, I must tell you that we can't stay in that house. Even with a new mattress, the bedbugs hide in the frame, baseboards, or even the walls. They lay millions of eggs in any secluded crack or crevice, and they are so difficult to control. I'm sorry but I must ask for my money back."

"You paid for a month. We had an agreement. If you don't want to stay, you don't have to stay. It's your problem. I will not return your money. Now, good day to you. Let me know if you need anything else." The landlady, a thin smile on her face, began to close the door.

Vladimir placed his foot through the door threshold, "Madam, let's be reasonable. We only have a limited amount of money. I must set up a household and a clinic with what I have. You do have a very clean house, and it's wonderfully furnished. But as I said, bedbugs are almost impossible to eliminate. Sometimes even DDT does not work. Why don't you keep a portion of the rent? Even though we only stayed last night, I am willing to pay you for a week. I believe that is more than fair."

Suddenly, from the other side of the door, an older, stocky woman with short white hair, a black sweater covering her flower-patterned dress appeared at the door. "I heard the conversation. Give him back his money. It's the right thing to do. He's new in town, and you know very well that if the Germans find out they didn't get their housing from them, they may cause a problem. Besides, did I hear him mention the word clinic? Are you a doctor?"

"Yes, I've been sent here to open a clinic."

"But mama, it's so hard to rent anything around here because the Germans control everything. We need the money."

"Sophia, give him back the money. In the long run you'll feel better. Besides, we may need to ask this fine doctor to help us someday. As a matter of fact, doctor, I need to see you soon. I have a problem with my breathing, especially at night."

"I'd be happy to help you. Hopefully, I'll have my clinic open in a few days. I just don't know where it will be."

"Give him back the money, all of it," the mother sternly instructed her daughter. With a meek look, Sophia reluctantly complied. "Wait here. I'll get the money." She closed the door while Vladimir stood on the porch. A minute later, she returned and handed the money to Vladimir. "I hope you're happy."

Once again the couple set out wearing all their clothes on their backs. Vladimir carried Slava's small battered suitcase. Slava walked silently. *This is sickening*, she thought. *I liked that house. Everything we needed was furnished. Where would we find such an arrangement? Where would we find what we need under this miserable occupation?* She looked upward and noticed Vladimir's smiling face glancing at her. Taking her hand, he squeezed it.

"Don't worry, Slavochka. We'll find something even better. Those tiny bugs might have done us a favor, and as my grandfather always said, 'Everything happens for the best.' We were not meant to have that house."

Vladimir and Slava again found themselves in front of the same soldier guarding the staircase leading up to the German administration offices. He recognized them and waved them through after they told him that they wanted to see a Lieutenant Hartman who they understood to be in charge of housing.

The housing department office was located at the other end of the hallway from the commandant's. A greenish-colored counter cut the large room in half—on one side were German soldiers mixed in with some local workers while the other half was filled with civilians needing homes. The couple complied with instructions to take a seat along the wall and await their turn. After almost an hour, they were summoned not to the counter as others had been, but to a small drab office on the side. Behind a gray metal desk sat a German sergeant. Reading a book, he raised his narrowed blue eyes and looked sternly at the couple above his round wire-rimmed glasses, motioning them to sit down on wooden chairs.

"You arrived in town yesterday, yes?" Anger laced the question.

"Yes," Vladimir answered nervously.

"So where did you spend the night?"

Oh! I have to be careful here. I could get that landlady in trouble. "It was late and after we met a nice lady, she offered us a place to stay for the night. We were not aware that one day later would make a difference."

The impish looking man with cropped sparse, sandy hair pursed his lips and looked closely at Vladimir. Anxiety twisted Vladimir's stomach. Interrogations conducted by German officers while in their captivity flashed through his mind. The German continued to glare at Vladimir. Then his gaze turned to Slava. She sat uncomfortably resisting the unbearable urge to scratch the bedbug bites. A look of pain crossed her face and the Sergeant caught it.

"What's wrong with you?"

Vladimir hoped that she did not say anything about the bedbugs. Again, the landlady could get into trouble.

"Nothing, I'm just not feeling well, that's all," Slava said. "I need a good night's rest."

"You look sick, Frau Doctor. Maybe you should see your husband here for help." The man cracked a grin, obviously pleased with his sense of humor. Neither Vladimir nor Slava were in the mood for humor and did not respond.

The soldier's tone changed again. "There is no excuse for you not to have checked in with me yesterday. I was expecting you. You do not know how close you came to an arrest. In a few minutes, a squad would have been sent out to search for you. If they had found you, the consequences would have been drastic." Vladimir's head pounded. Slava's muscles in her jaw clenched and her stomach jumped. "I'll let it go this time, but don't do anything like this again. If you're told to do something, you need to do so immediately, understand!" A sense of relief swept simultaneously through Vladimir and Slava as they nodded their heads in unison.

"Yes," Vladimir said.

"Now, I have your papers here. My superior, Lieutenant Hartman, told me to give you a choice of two places. One is a single family home not too far from the plaza. The other is a building with two apartments. Both sides are empty so you can choose either one. Both places are well kept, and of course, they will be fully furnished for you."

Slava felt relief that she will be given a furnished place. Vladimir's ears perked up when he heard that one of the buildings was a duplex. "Sergeant, how are the apartments arranged in the building you referred to? I mean are they side by side, one story or one apartment on top of the other?"

"They are side by side. There is a separate entrance from the street. Why, does it matter to you?"

"Yes, it may be a good solution for us. I have been sent here to set up a clinic and treat patients."

"Yes, I know. That is why you're getting special attention. Why do you think I'm bothering with you here? I have my orders to give you accommodations. And that is all. How you survive here is up to you."

"Thank you, but I was thinking that we could organize a clinic in one of the apartments and our living quarters can be in the other. That will be extremely convenient for my patients and for us."

"I suppose. It matters not to me. All right, you can have both sides."

Slava's facial muscles relaxed, and she was able to form a timid smile. Vladimir took a quick glance at Slava and beamed back. The soldier buried his nose in an endless stream of paper, writing furiously on half-sheet papers. After he finished the paperwork, he gave them ration cards.

"Go back to the office where you received your temporary identification papers and wait for your permanent ones now that you have your address. Give the corporal these forms. Then come back here. It appears that Lieutenant Hartman wants to escort you personally to the house." *Why does an officer want to escort us personally? What's going on here?* Vladimir suddenly became concerned again.

The couple followed the precise directions. After they received their permanent forms, Vladimir and Slava returned to wait for the officer. As they waited, they studied the two documents each received. These were of heavier weight paper, meticulously folded into thirds. The pinkish-colored half sheet contained the word *Personalausweis* in German and the Polish and Byelorussian translations typed below on the outside fold, indicated a special certificate with personal information. As they unfolded it, they viewed their photographs attached in the upper left-hand corner with the word *Slonim* and the number *6153/A* typed underneath. "Oh, I hate my picture," she blurted out. "I wish I could retake it."

"You look fine, darling. How can you take a bad picture?"

"You're so sweet, but I hate this picture. I look like I spent a year in a prisoner of war camp." As soon as she said it she regretted it. Vladimir gave her what she thought was an odd look. "I'm sorry, dear; I didn't mean anything by it. I know how much you suffered."

"Don't feel badly, I knew what you meant. Believe me, you look lovely."

The document included the last name, first name, father's name, occupation, date of birth, place of birth, current place of residence, religion, distinguishing features, and the date of issue. For occupation, Vladimir's document indicated *Physician*, while Slava's listed, *Nurse*.

"We told him I will be your assistant, and after asking me about my education, he gave me the title of nurse. It's a shame I didn't finish medical school. If only the Germans hadn't invaded last year."

"Well, yes, if they hadn't, we wouldn't be here. We would lead normal lives back home."

It was Vladimir's turn to regret his comment when he spied Slava's eyes well up. "Slavochka, don't worry, we'll make normal lives for ourselves once again."

"Do you think that Slonim will really be our new home? Won't we ever go back to Vitebsk?"

"Who knows what lies ahead? One thing is for sure, wherever we are together, that is our home."

Slava swiped at the tear on her cheek with the side of her index finger and focused, along with Vladimir, on the other card that dealt with their employment. The light green document was entitled *Beschaftigungs-Nachweis*. Oddly, they thought, the work permit contained the same information as their personal identification card, including once again listing their religion: Catholic on Slava's, and Orthodox Christian on Vladimir's.

They put the cards away and continued to wait. Fifteen minutes later, a short, heavyset man with grayish bushy eyebrows and a smooth round face entered the room. His brown uniform looked rumpled. He walked past them with an air of authority into the office and immediately walked out as he spotted Vladimir and Slava.

Chapter 11

LIEUTENANT HARTMAN's lips stretched into a broad and pleasant smile. With a wave of his hand, he motioned for Vladimir and Slava to follow him. They had no idea what to expect, but Hartman's friendly demeanor put them at ease. Would they finally be allowed to settle down and live as normal a life as possible under the occupation and in this new town? Slava could not wait to see the place assigned them. *What's it going to be like? Will we be able to live there?* She could not get there soon enough, but Lieutenant Hartman's short legs did not move at a quick pace. He carefully descended each step as if it were his last. *His stomach is in the way. He can't see his feet.* Slava thought to herself in amusement. Once in front of the building, Hartman told the couple to wait. He had ordered a car for the three of them. As they stood impatiently by the stone curb, the Lieutenant had a barrage of questions for Vladimir.

"So where are you from?"

Vladimir barely finished his answer before he asked, "You're a doctor, aren't you? Where did you go to school? Is your wife from the same place? Were you an army man?"

Vladimir answered all his questions up to the last one. A queasy, unsettling feeling suddenly gripped Vladimir. He knew that if he answered that question, more questions would follow. He did not want anyone to know of his army or prisoner of war past. *Who knows how this soldier would react or how the townspeople would accept us if they knew I was in the Red Army. It is better to keep that information to ourselves. The commandant must know why I'm here. Hopefully no one else does. I have to avoid the subject.* "I'm just a physician, here to help the local civilians. Do you think if I were in the Soviet army, I'd be sent here?"

The Lieutenant gave a jovial laugh. Laughter seemed to come easy to him. "You're right. You wouldn't be here, would you? I just assumed that since you are from Vitebsk that you might have been in the Red Army. I should never assume things, should I?" Hartman grinned. Vladimir returned the grin.

"Is the house far from here?" Slava asked, trying to change the subject. She remembered that Vladimir and she decided not to talk to anyone about the recent past.

"Not too far. We could walk, but I'd rather not, if I don't have to." Hartman laughed again.

That's obvious, Slava thought, glancing at his rotund form.

"You are lucky. I've given you a house in the best part of town. I have been through that house, and it's very nice. The houses in that area remind me of the houses along my street in Münster. I really miss my hometown. Though, it really isn't the city. It's mostly my family that I yearn to see." Slava thought that she noticed his eyes film with moisture as he longingly spoke of his kin. "But enough about me,"

Hartman once again laughed heartily. His rounded cheeks crunched up and puffed out even more with each chuckle, like those of a squirrel storing nuts.

Finally, a dark-gray Mercedes sedan, an iron cross painted on the front door, rolled up in front of them. The driver, a young, impeccably uniformed soldier, stepped out of the driver's side. His appearance was in sharp contrast to the slovenly lieutenant. The driver saluted then circled the vehicle and swung open the rear door for the couple, while Hartman seated himself in the front passenger seat. Projecting a disciplined bearing, the driver avoided eye contact and seemed to frown at the ground as though Vladimir or Slava did not exist. He did not utter a word or crack a smile, obviously annoyed with their presence. After the passengers were in the vehicle, he slammed the door shut and resumed his position behind the wheel, waiting for further instructions from Hartman.

With the motion of the vehicle, Slava sat back against the cold stiff leather of the seat. Her breathing slowed, her body tensed at a jolting memory of the first and last time she took a journey in a car. Reflecting back, she visualized the incident when German soldiers, on the second day of their occupation, entered her home in Vitebsk and searched for Jews, weapons, valuables, and food stocks. She and her parents had hidden a Jewish family in the cellar, the trap-door to which was covered by a Persian rug and topped by the dining room table. The Nazis shuffled next to the cellar door, and it would have been only a matter of time before they found it. She remembered the cold sweat that poured off her parents and herself. They must have looked guilty, especially after they were asked repeatedly whether they were hiding any Jews.

As one of the interrogators began questioning Slava about family background and what friends she had who were Jews, a German officer abruptly entered the house. He immediately ordered the soldiers to put everything back that they removed from the house and leave. At first Slava felt relieved. However, the relief was short-lived. In the next instant, her heart fell to the floor. Her brain went blank. The officer ordered Slava to come with him. He escorted her to his waiting car, similar to the one she was in now, except that the top was down. She was then driven to a converted warehouse by the railroad tracks, made into an office by the Germans. There, the officer guided her to the office of the commanding officer, Major Raake.

Slava had inadvertently met him the day before. At that time, Slava made the mistake of questioning why the German invaders had detained Jews behind a quickly constructed barbed wire compound in downtown Vitebsk. It was then that she gave herself away as being fluent in German. He demanded to see her identification papers and remembered her the next day. Raake wanted her to work for him and implied that if she refused, she and her parents could end up in a forced labor camp in Germany.

"Slava, you seem far away. What's on your mind?"

"Volodya. Riding in this car brought back some distasteful memories. The last time I rode in a car, my whole life changed."

"Perhaps now it will change again, but for the better."

The car proceeded southwesterly past the market square, turning left toward the synagogue that the couple had seen the day before. The driver steered the car past the structure and the shops lining the street, then easterly over a bridge that spanned a river. Remains of a barbed wire fence stood in sections along both sides of the bridge. The lieutenant pointed out the river, the bathhouse, and the flour mill. He did not stop jabbering. *What is he, a tour guide?* Vladimir thought. Vladimir could see the driver's irritation at the casual warmth of the lieutenant. He kept clearing his throat to give the man a warning to shut up. Hartman did not heed the hints.

"That was the Shchara River we just crossed."

He continued with the tour of the town. He pointed out the steeples of St. Andrew's Catholic Cathedral in the distance and even admitted that the Nazi policy discouraged large gatherings for religious services in occupied territories. *That's a strange thing for a Nazi to admit. You can tell that if he is truly a Nazi, he is not very dedicated to the cause. Probably just another unfortunate man swept up into war just as I had been.*

Slava intently studied the houses along the way, wondering which one was assigned to them. As they drove on, the houses became more substantial in appearance. Fewer were sided with aged wood, but instead with stucco. Rather than cobble stones, cement sidewalks lined the streets. The car turned left onto Commander Street. Here the houses sat a distance apart and were well maintained.

A swirl of first impressions raced through both of their minds. Slava's heart raced with the prospect of residing in one of the houses along the street. In the next block, the houses diminished in size but were still sizeable. After passing a few more dwellings, the car came to a stop in front of a classical style building with a solid cement porch with two steps leading to two intricately carved doors. The portico was bordered by white columns holding up a massive beam. A wooden carving of an oval, inset with a rose, graced the area above the doors. *This can't be the place, it is so beautiful*, Slava thought with excited anticipation.

"Well this is it, numbers 48 and 50," Hartman pointed to the house with a broad grin. "I told you this is a better part of town. There aren't that many vacant houses left in town and even fewer in this district. You would think that with the resettlement of Jews there would be more of them empty. They were resettled to other areas."

Vladimir caught Slava's glance. They rolled their eyes. Slava's thoughts tumbled in her head. *Who is Hartman kidding? Resettled! Next he'll say it was for their good. Does he really believe that nonsense? Or is he just deceiving himself? Surely, the local population does not believe that. But then how would they know if the Jews were shipped off, never to be seen again? But I saw what happened in Vitebsk. I know better. I know that Volodya knows what happens to the Jews in the hands of the Germans. He saw his best friend executed right in front of him.*

"Fires from battles destroyed so many of the houses. Many had to sleep outside, so we moved those people into the houses vacated by the Jews. You see, we try to be humanitarian," Harman giving them a slight wink. Both Slava and Vladimir bit their lips. Vladimir knew better than to argue with Hartman. After all, he still was their enemy, no matter how friendly he appeared. The lieutenant kept babbling his twaddle, while both Vladimir and Slava could not wait to get out of the car. Yet they could not walk out while Hartman chattered away.

Finally, the lieutenant, said, "Well, let's go and look at the place. You're probably anxious to see it." The couple walked briskly toward their new home. Hartman lagged behind, searching in his pocket with his fat fingers for the keys. "Wait till you see the inside. You'll love it. As a matter of fact, I'll be most appreciative if I could visit you some time. We can have schnapps, ja?"

Slava's exhilaration ebbed momentarily as she reflected on Hartman's words that he plans to visit them. *Now another German wants to socialize with us.* In Vitebsk she became familiar with German visits. She recalled the nervousness and discomfort she, and especially her parents, felt when Major Raake and his aide appeared uninvited for social visits. They would ask her to play the piano for them and kept returning for more entertainment. The atmosphere was strained. They had to watch every word they uttered. They needed to smile or laugh at the appropriate time and to be careful. Always be careful. However, Slava now came to realize that the strange socialization led to a significant benefit to both herself and to Vladimir.

She remembered the kindly, elderly German train worker who, on a stop in Vitebsk, had sought her out and delivered a crumpled message from Vladimir. Her heart almost stopped when she heard from him. He was alive and he needed her help. It was another German, Major Raake, who arranged for her travel from Vitebsk to Minsk to present Vladimir's diploma to the enemy's chief medical officer in Minsk so that he could be released from the prisoner of war camp. This brought them to Slonim. *You never know how this jovial lieutenant might be of assistance to us in Slonim.*

"That would be fine. We would like your company." Vladimir gave her an incredulous glance that Slava understood to mean, *"What are you doing?"* But he caught on quickly and said, "Yes, do please come over and visit us. We'll see if we can find some schnapps." Slava expected him to approve. She knew Vladimir enjoyed people and talked to anyone, even his enemy. Realistically though, what option did they have?

The lieutenant unlocked the door, and Slava crossed the wooden threshold. As she stepped into the front room, a surge of warmth overcame her. "Oh, Volodya! Look at this large room. Look at the tall ceilings. I already love this place."

Vladimir grinned and wrapped his arm around Slava's shoulder and squeezed her toward him. "I like it too, my sunshine. Let's look around."

Hartman planted himself in one of matching brown overstuffed chairs. "Go on, explore your home. I think I'll just sit here for a while."

Not wasting time, the couple complied. As they meandered through the living room, they noticed several small gouges in a portion of the walnut parquet floor. There might have been more scratches, but two mismatched faded oriental rugs covered the rest of the floor in the living room and dining room. A wide open archway separated the two rooms. Robin-blue wallpaper with a large marguerite daisy bouquet pattern plastered the walls. Once fashionable, it was now discolored and in several places came unglued from the wall. *A little glue will fix that,* Slava thought. Royal blue drapes, adorning the narrow double windows, hung limply to the floor. White sheers peeked in between the drapes.

"Oh look, Volodya, just like at home in Vitebsk, there is a small ventilation window inside each window pane.

That will give us air without opening the whole window." Vladimir nodded with approval, his beaming face full of excitement, matching hers, as he proceeded into the bedroom and bathroom area.

Impatient, Vladimir finally walked off to explore the rest of the house on his own. Slava proceeded to take in every small detail, in exuberant examination of the premises. Hartman continued to recline and amused himself by watching the young couple explore the house. He chuckled at Slava's habit of gently running her thin hand over the surface of each piece of furniture. She touched the sofa, each of the two overstuffed chairs, end tables, mahogany side board, dining table, and each of the six matching high back wooden chairs. He laughed out loud when she suddenly did a double-take at the sight of an old Victrola standing at the corner of the dining room.

"Oh, look at this Victrola just waiting for us to play music!" Slava exclaimed as Vladimir came out of the kitchen. "It's just like the one back home. One can imagine happier times when this music box was the life of this household. It's too bad that I don't see a piano."

"Slava, you're just asking for too much. A piano yet!"

"I know, I know. I'm just joking. What's in the bedrooms? I haven't seen them yet."

"You'll like them. Everything is great. You need to look at that huge fenced yard in the back. There's even a barn."

The yard and the barn did not interest her at the moment. She strolled out of the dining room into a small hallway leading to the two bedrooms. Ahead, as she passed through the archway leading into the hall, she spotted the open door of the bathroom. Small octagon-shaped black-and-white tiles covered the floor. Larger black-and-white square tiles lined the walls halfway up to a ceramic wainscot. Above the tiles, the light green floral patterned wallpaper hung loose in several places. A porcelain oval washbasin with two faucets stood between the claw-foot tub and the toilet. *Whoever lived here before had money.* Mismatched pieces of furniture decorated the bedrooms, but everything they would need seemed to be there.

In the kitchen, glass doors on the white cabinets above the porcelain sink allowed Slava to view a stack of dishes, bowls and cups. The table, two chairs, an icebox, and a fully equipped stove were similarly arranged as in the kitchen of the house with the bedbugs. At that comparison, Slava could almost feel the parasites crawling over her body. She shuddered and prayed that none would be there. *That will ruin everything about this house.* She would be at a loss of solutions if any were found on the premises. Foregoing the exploration of the covered porch and the cellar off the kitchen, she hurriedly marched back to the bedrooms and lifted the mattresses to see if any evidence of the bloodsucking creatures existed. Her visual inspection did not reveal any.

Chapter 12

CHEEKS FLUSHED with excitement and with sparkly eyes, Vladimir hurriedly finished exploring their new living quarters. He expected that the space next door would accommodate his clinic, and he could not wait a minute longer to discover its layout. He determined that no matter what it looked like, he would make it work. For a long, miserable year, he had been cooped up as a war prisoner and had no opportunity to practice medicine. Throughout that time, his only thoughts had been of Slava and the survival for both of them. Starvation, disease, and the harsh and cruel treatment under the hands of the Germans in the prisoner of war camp reduced the prison population to a fraction of what it was at the beginning of the year. He dwelt on the figure of approximately forty thousand in the camp when he trudged in, but only maybe five hundred survived at the time he walked out. There had not been much he could do to help his fellow prisoners. Typhus fever ran rampant, even hitting him. He did survive but was left too weak to be of much help to his fellow prisoners. Even if he had been physically able, he could not do much without medical equipment or medications.

Vladimir fought off the dreaded disease and regained what physical strength he could. Then a few weeks before his arrival to Slonim, fate once again interceded. In an instant, his life spun around once more. They came for him. He believed he would be executed as they marched him out of the barracks. Instead of a bullet to his head, the order came that he must perform a delicate surgery on a German officer. No German doctor was available. He had no choice. He shuddered yet again, as the words, "Either he lives or you die," resonated in his mind. Under extreme stress and poor conditions, Vladimir carried out the needed surgery, a severe middle-ear infection that affected his patient's brain. The officer lived.

Like a gift falling from heaven, Vladimir was set free and assigned to Slonim. In a strange way, even under the threat of death and weak from malnutrition, Vladimir looked back at the operation and realized that it felt good to do what he was trained to do. He needed the challenge. He craved contact with patients. Now his future waited for him next door, along with the opportunity to be someone again—the sooner, the better.

With those thoughts in mind, Vladimir approached Hartman and asked if he could see the space next door.

"Of course. Here are the keys. Both sides of the building are yours. I told you that you are very fortunate. Well, make yourself comfortable. I will leave you now."

"Thank you very much," Vladimir said, as he extended his hand to shake the officer's. It occurred to him that he had no idea where to even look for medical instruments.

"Before you go, can you tell me where I could purchase medical instruments and equipment in Slonim? Would that even be possible?"

"As far as I know, there are no stores that sell such things. Even in Münster, I wouldn't know where you can buy medical equipment," he said, grinning from ear to ear. "Oh, wait! There is a store owned by a Pole on Paradna Street that sells all kinds of used stuff. It's like a pawn shop. Who knows, you might find something there. Or, you might ask the Materials Officer at the administration building.

"You know, we Germans are smart. When we first arrived here, we secured the public buildings, factories, and stock. That prevented the population, and I hate to admit this, even our German soldiers, from plundering. Actually the Nazi Public Welfare Organization has provided clothing and other living supplies to the city administrator for the use of the local population. So if you need something, you should go there first." *And how much did they take away from the people and the country and cart off to Germany?* Slava thought, overhearing the conversation between the two men. She knew better, she saw it in Vitebsk. She remembered that the contents of factories, buildings and homes, not evacuated or destroyed, were inventoried by the Nazis, item by item, and shipped to the Rhineland. Vladimir also strongly suspected there was very little of value left for the local administrator that would benefit the occupied populace. Besides, he would rather not deal with the German administration, if possible.

"Well, good-bye. We'll see each other again, I'm sure."

The Germans left. Slava continued her inspection of her new home. Vladimir hurried next door to plan his clinic. The layout was identical to the other side, except reversed. The front room would be his reception area. The dining table, if moved to the side could be used for his desk. The sideboard would be used for instruments and supplies. The kitchen was ideal for storing medications and boiling water for sterilization. One of the bedrooms would become the surgical room and the other the examination room. His heart pounded with enthusiasm. If he could start the next day, that would not be soon enough. He began to compile a list of necessary supplies in his head.

While planning the layout, he allowed his mind to wander. Memories of years of struggle to get his medical degree heaved to the surface. He thought of his sporadic primary education, not being able to attend school regularly because of his usually drunk shoemaker stepfather. His father had died a hero in World War I the year Vladimir was born in 1915. As a little boy Vladimir had to work in a village shop as an apprentice shoemaker with not much time for school. After the stepfather died, he fled to the big city of Vitebsk. As a child of thirteen he worked in a shoe factory getting paid for each piecemeal of leather. He, at that age, was able to financially support not only himself but his mother and his three sisters. Vladimir smiled when he remembered that at that job, some adults were envious that he made more money than they did. He was quicker and better at it. Looking back, he marveled at how he managed his time and accomplished everything. He worked, attended school, finished gymnasium (high school) with honors, passed a grueling examination for Feldscher (physician's assistant) school, and the even harder and more grueling examination for medical school. And now he would have his own clinic. *Fate is amazing. Thank you, God, for how you have protected me and given me this.*

Vladimir's thoughts drifted back to the present. There was no time to waste. They had to get supplies, not only for the clinic, but also food and household items.

Vladimir ran back next door to the residence side. Slava had just sat down on the green velvet sofa, taking in their new home. "This is just unbelievable, isn't it? I wonder who owned this house."

"Yes, what luck! This is exactly what we needed."

"Here, sit down next to me," Slava said, still scratching from the bedbug bites, her welts increasing in size and becoming more painful. "We can do so much with this place. By the way, did anyone say what the rent was?"

"You know, that was not even discussed. Maybe they don't plan for us to pay. Wouldn't that be nice? Slava, let's go. We have lots to do."

Chapter 13

PARADNA STREET, seemingly the main shopping street of Slonim, was lined with many small shops and even a few department stores, though almost half were boarded up. Passing by a hardware store, Vladimir thought that he might inquire regarding medical instruments. An elderly man with bushy white hair and a waxed handlebar mustache appeared startled when the couple entered.

"Oh my, I didn't expect anyone today," the man said in Polish. "I was just ready to go to lunch. But business is business. I can go later. What can I do for you?"

"I'm looking for medical tools such as scalpels or anything like that."

"By your accent when you speak Polish, I can tell you're Byelorussian. Am I correct?"

"Yes, that's right."

"Oh. When the Soviets grabbed this Grodno region in 1939 from Poland, they moved some Byelorussians here. Of course, there were many that lived here for generations. Are you relocating here?"

"Yes, I'm a physician and will be opening my practice shortly."

"I'm really glad to hear that. I'll be one of your patients. You see, I have this problem with my arthritis. Can you do anything for me?"

"Maybe. Please come see me later in the week. If I find what I need, I should be prepared to see patients by then. My clinic will be at number 50, Commander Street. It's only a twenty-minute walk."

"I'll remember that. Unfortunately, I can't help you with any medical supplies. That would be hard to find. As you may know, the Germans take anything worthwhile out of here." He shook his head, as though in despair, then stared at the floor for an instant, stroking his mustache. "Wait. My friend, Sygmund, may have something that you need in his store. He has all kinds of junk, although he hates it when I call it junk. There might have been a doctor who sold him his equipment." Vladimir perked up at the possibility. "Go see him and tell him Rafael sent you."

Sygmund's store was indeed a collection of sad and eclectic merchandise—from torn clothing and battered shoes to old radios and phonographs. The couple walked around the musty place searching for what they needed, while at the same time, looking at items for the house. There was no one in sight, nor could Vladimir see anything resembling medical equipment. His hopes began to dwindle as he looked around, but nevertheless, he doggedly continued searching because something may lie underneath the disarray of items stacked on top of each other.

"Hello, anyone here?" Vladimir yelled out.

A slim wrinkled-faced man with long gray hair protruding from underneath a stained black beret rose slowly from behind a wooden counter. He rubbed his grey eyes with a heavily veined hand adorned by a deep purple amethyst ring.

"Oh, I didn't hear you come in. I was too busy looking for something back here. What do you need?"

I doubt that. He must have been asleep on the floor behind the counter. "I understand that you may have medical instruments for sale."

"Why? Are you a doctor?"

"Yes."

"Well in that case, I'll point you in the right direction. Follow me to the cellar."

Vladimir could not believe his ears. *That's unbelievable. Could it be?* Slava noticed his eyes alight as they followed the hunched man with a pronounced limp to the back of the store. They turned a corner and came to a grimy light-blue door. The man opened the heavy, squeaky door. Above a staircase, he twisted a knob on an electrical box illuminating the dimly lit interior.

"You go down and look. I think I have a few items down there that you could use. If you find what you want, bring it up. Stairs are hard on me."

Vladimir and Slava carefully made their way down the creaky wooden steps. The walls of the musty cellar were lined with shelves made of old lumber. Down the center assorted industrial tables, set between the crumbling brick pillars holding up the floor above, were piled high with merchandise. Toward the end of one row, Vladimir spied a metal examining table with two open drawers. Bubbling with excitement he pointed out the table to Slava, who had already noticed it.

A surgical table stood next to the stone wall of the foundation. Both tables were upholstered with extremely cracked matching dark brown leather. A small plaque with the word *Doktor* and a white gooseneck lamp lay on top of the metal surgical table. A heavy-duty scale leaned against yet another table.

"We don't need anymore light in this cellar," Slava joked. "Your excited eyes are bright enough to light up the city."

"Slavochka, I can't believe our luck. Let's keep looking around."

Going through disorganized shelves from the top to the bottom of each section they discovered a dusty doctor's bag tucked away behind a box of rusty nuts and bolts. Underneath was a stainless steel sterilization box.

With avid anticipation, Vladimir yanked out the bag, placed it underneath one of the light bulbs and rummaged through it. Two stethoscopes, one battered from use, the other in excellent condition, lay on top of a rolled up red cloth. Wrapped in the soft cloth were three scalpels of various sizes, needle holders used in stitching, a hemostat to clamp blood vessels, forceps for baby deliveries, a retractor to pull wounds apart, and a pair of surgical scissors.

At the bottom of the bag, Vladimir spotted a roll of cat-gut sutures, straight and curved needles, syringes, and two bottles of medicines. "This is fantastic, but what I really need for my ENT practice, I don't see."

"You mean the otoscope and the head mirror?"

"Yes. It would be hard to see inside the ear or the nose without them."

"Well, you could just look up their nose, look important, and guess," Slava chuckled.

"Slavochka, get serious, I really need those two items, and I don't see them."

"Well then, Volodya, let's keep looking."

They searched every shelf, every box, and even shoved aside some of the stored old furniture. The needed items were not there. With his feet already on the stairs to exit, Vladimir noticed through the open risers a dusty cardboard box stored on the floor underneath the staircase. "Slava, wait! There is a box under the stairs. I want to look at it."

Vladimir crawled under the stairs, and pulled the box out. Slava hung on to the wooden railing a few steps up and watched. Vladimir rummaged through the box, pulling out some rags, then let out a whistle. "Oh my God! This box has some medical instruments in it. It must have sat here a long time. Unfortunately, I couldn't use them, they're too rusty."

He kept looking deeper in the box. "Look at this! I can't believe it, here's an otoscope!"

Vladimir extracted the cone-shaped otoscope. It had a little rust on it, but he knew he could clean it up. "Now only if it would work."

When he switched it on, there was no light. "Maybe all it needs are new batteries."

"Did you find the mirror that you need?"

"No, there's none here." Vladimir said, disappointed. Taking the otoscope, the medical bag and the metal box, he began to ascend the stairs. "Let's see how much this is going to cost us."

The couple placed their find on a wooden counter. Sygmund sat at a heavily scratched metal desk set along the wall next to the counter. He removed his reading glasses, placed them on the desk with a negligent expression on his features, as though he was bothered, and slowly rose and approached.

"We found a few items that might work," Vladimir said. "The instruments in the box are old, but I can probably clean them up. I don't know if this otoscope works or not. It looks pretty bad. I'm also interested in the surgical and examining tables you have."

Breathing heavily as though he could not fill his lungs, Sygmund looked at the couple and cracked a slight smile. He looked in the bag, and then briefly delved through the box. "I remember these, only a few months ago, I think in

July, I bought these items from Dr. Siegel. I felt sorry for him and paid him more for these instruments than I ordinarily would have. He came to me, his eyes swollen as though he had been crying. The next day he and his family were gone. He was my doctor, and a very good, kind-hearted one. He needed cash. I'll tell you what. You give me what I paid him and I'll let you have them. But I don't remember who sold me this otoscope. It does look in bad shape."

"Do you have batteries so we can try it out?"

"Batteries are impossible to get under the damn occupation. I'll give you the otoscope for free. You'll have to find the batteries yourself."

"Thank you for that, but how much for the other stuff?" Vladimir asked.

"Let's see," Sygmund thought for a moment, went back to his desk, opened a drawer and pulled out a ledger book. He turned several pages then answered, "Thirty-five marks."

That's all he paid him for all these tools. That doctor just gave them away. "Does that include the examining and the surgical tables? Also I would need the lamp, the small doctor sign, and the scale."

"No. I had those before from another doctor that was removed. Give me another thirty marks and take them away."

Slava whispered to Vladimir, "We can't pay that much. We need money for food and who knows how much the rent for the house and clinic is yet."

Vladimir nodded and addressed the shopkeeper. "I'm just beginning my practice. I need those instruments and tables. Since we have our work permits, I'll be seeing patients tomorrow or the day after. I should start making money shortly. May I pay you next week? I promise to have your money then." Slava gave Vladimir an anxious look as if to say, how can you be so sure?

In an instant the old man's black eyes became razor sharp as he intently studied Vladimir and Slava. Vladimir could see the anguish in his face as he tried to make a decision whether to extend credit to them. In an attempt to help persuade him, Vladimir said, "These items are no good to you just sitting on the floor or on the shelf. How often do you sell medical equipment anyway? You may never have the opportunity again."

The shopkeeper pursed his thin lips, looked at the couple again and nodded in agreement. He prepared a short contract providing that full payment must be received within thirty days or the items returned. He further made the point that he would not charge interest.

Relieved, Vladimir asked the man if he knew anyone that could help deliver the tables. "No, there are no young men around with the war and all. That, my good doctor, is your problem now. I hope you have a strong back, although both you and your wife look as though a brisk wind could blow you over."

Before leaving the store, Slava grabbed the bag and Vladimir tucked the metal container and the cardboard box under each arm. "That was just incredible," Vladimir said. "It's too bad that we couldn't find a head mirror."

As they trotted down the street toward their house, Slava asked Vladimir how he proposed to bring the tables back to the clinic.

"Don't worry. We'll find a way."

Chapter 14

A GENTLE, but frigid breeze accompanied Vladimir and Slava as they lugged their newly acquired equipment home. After unloading, they scampered out to the square hoping to catch the market merchants. The morning sunshine gradually conceded to silvery, snow-laden clouds, darkening the sky. Even though many vendors were already packing to leave, the couple found a few that still remained, anxious to sell their wares. Vladimir and Slava purchased ten brown-shelled eggs, an already dressed skinny hen, some home-canned mushrooms, pickled green tomatoes, toothbrushes, coarse soap, baking soda, and a box of matches.

While at the market, Vladimir spotted a man and his wife loading the last of their unsold goods onto a cart attached to a miserable-looking old gray stallion. The man seemed strong for his age and his wife looked as though she could lift the horse. He approached them and politely asked if they could help him move two heavy tables out of the basement of Sygmund's store. At first, they only shook their heads with matching sneers of annoyance. But when he offered them ten marks, they suddenly warmed up and readily agreed to meet him the next day.

Once at the house, Vladimir hung the hen in the cool cellar. The useless icebox had no ice. Slava began to light the stove using the kindling and bits of coal stored in the nearby metal bin when Vladimir climbed out of the cold cellar. He took over the task of lighting the fire while Slava placed a pan with water and eggs on the burner and a tea pot to boil water. Both Vladimir and Slava collapsed on the kitchen chairs, with elbows on the table, their heads cupped by their hands and anxiously waited for their meal. The wait seemed endless, taking forever for the steam to finally rise from the pan. Their stomachs ached and growled. With the impatience of the hungry, they allowed the eggs to boil only a few minutes and quickly devoured six soft boiled eggs and the rest of the wooden bread purchased from the old couple. Since they had no tea, a cup of hot water flushed down the meal.

"Now that we have the ration cards," Slava said. "Let's go to Agata's store in the morning. Oh, Volodya, I'm so excited. I can hardly wait to see what tomorrow brings."

Chapter 15

VLADIMIR AND Slava walked quickly, almost at a trot, to reach Agata's food store. As they came around the corner, Vladimir suddenly stopped. "What's the matter?"

"I want to go into this building."

"Why, what do you mean? The store is all boarded up."

Vladimir pointed up toward a window. When she looked up, she noticed a sign that read, "Doktor Ostrovska, OB-GYN."

"I see, you're having female problems," Slava laughed.

"You're always joking around. Let's go meet her. Maybe she has a head mirror that she's not using."

"I know. I caught on."

Steep, narrow stairs on the side of the building led to the second floor. Vladimir allowed Slava to lead the way while he closed the outside door behind him. "How does a pregnant woman make it up the steps?" Slava asked, not expecting an answer from Vladimir.

"The doctor visits her," Vladimir answered, nevertheless.

The staircase led to a door indicating Dr. Ostrovska's office with bold black letters painted on the frosted glass. Vladimir turned the brass door knob and walked into a narrow room lined with armless wooden chairs. Two women sat across from each other. Both studied the couple as Vladimir asked whether they knew if the doctor was available. One of the ladies wearing a black scarf around her head said, "You have to sit down and wait for her. She is here all by herself, the poor thing."

"Yes, she works all the time," the other woman with graying hair and a shabby coat chimed in. "I don't know when she ever sleeps."

The couple sat down next to the woman with the scarf. The women continued to stare at them, making Slava uneasy. *Their curiosity of who we are is killing them,* Slava thought.

"How long do you want to wait?" Slava whispered to Vladimir.

"I don't know what to do. Maybe we should leave and try again later."

"Let's wait a few minutes and see what happens."

"Are you in such a hurry that you can't wait?" The woman with graying hair asked. "I've been here for ninety minutes. I waited for this room to clear out and now my turn is next."

"Of course," Vladimir said. "I'm a new doctor in town and I just wanted to meet her."

The woman's dour expression changed instantly. Her face lit up with a toothy smile. "Oh that is wonderful. We need doctors badly. What kind of doctor are you?"

A good one, Vladimir laughed at himself at the thought and was dying to use that phrase for fun, but decided against it. Instead, he told them his specialty and the location of his office. The woman wrapped in the scarf rose and walked a few steps to the inner door and knocked. "I'll try to get the doctor for you."

"Oh, we shouldn't bother her," Slava said. "She's with a patient."

Suddenly the door opened and a middle-aged petite woman in a white lab coat looked out. "Is there a problem here? I'm with a patient." Even though she must have been irritated, she seemed pleasant, her gray eyes sparkling, her narrow face framed by blondish hair.

"This new doctor here, wants to meet you, Dr. Ostrovska," the woman with the scarf said. "We didn't think he should wait as if he were a patient."

Ostrovska twisted back toward her patient and told her she'll be right back. She closed the door behind her and approached Vladimir and Slava. After introductions, they explained their plans. She seemed genuinely pleased that a new doctor arrived. They chatted briefly and agreed to meet frequently to discuss medical issues that might arise and to refer patients when necessary. Finally, Vladimir asked if she had an extra head mirror or knew where he might find a head mirror and an otoscope, or at least some batteries.

Dr. Ostrovska shook her head from side to side. "I have a head mirror, but I use it. I don't have an otoscope."

"I know where you can get one," the woman with graying hair said, eager to help. All turned toward the woman.

"Where?" Vladimir asked in anticipation.

"I was a cleaning maid for a Jewish doctor. When they took him away…" The woman hesitated. "Well, I didn't think it was wrong. I confessed to the priest, and he only gave me a penance of five Hail Marys. So it can't be too bad." *Get to the point, where can I find those items?* Vladimir waited, his heart raced. "Well anyway," the woman continued. "When they took away the doctor and his family, oh, it was a terrible sight. My heart bled for them, they were such good people." *Please, lady, what about the items?* "I managed to take a few items from their house. I knew that if I didn't take them, the bastards, oh dear Lord, I'm sorry for swearing. I now have another sin I need to tell the priest."

Patience, patience, Vladimir told himself. "Please continue, were you able to take some medical instruments?"

"Yes. I took his medical bag and threw some more items in an old shoe box. A head mirror? That's a round mirror with a hole in the middle, is that right?"

"Yes, exactly," Vladimir said, his heart racing faster. "Did you see one?"

"I sure did. I still have it in my apartment, under the bed. If you wait here, I'll go get it. I'll just give it to you if I could become your patient."

"Yes, of course."

"Good, I'll be right back; my apartment is just a block away."

The woman pulled her dark blue coat off a rack in the corner. Vladimir helped her put it on, and they heard her make her way down the stairs.

Dr. Ostrovska told them she had to go back to her patient. "Let's get together soon," she said. The couple sat down and waited. The remaining woman's curiosity did not subside. She continued to ask questions about their background. Suddenly, the door to the examination room opened and Ostrovska approached Vladimir and handed him two batteries. "Try these batteries on the otoscope you have. You can keep them. One of these days I may have to borrow something from you. Well, I better get back to work. It was a pleasure to meet you."

Vladimir studied the batteries that the doctor placed in his hand. "This is unbelievable," he told Slava. Slava pressed closer to him and squeezed his arm, her eyes as bright as Vladimir's. A few moments later, the woman, out of breath from the walk up the stairs came back with a head mirror.

"There you are, doctor. What's your name anyway? I need to know so that I can come and see you. You see, I have this condition where it's hard for me to breathe through my nose. Maybe you can help me with that."

Vladimir exchanged names and gave her his address.

"That was totally remarkable," Slava said. "Who would have thought? And I really liked Dr. Ostrovska. I'd like to get to know her better."

"I'm sure we will."
"Now, can we go get our rations?"
"Yes, Slavochka, I'm certainly ready."

Chapter 16

WITH FROZEN and numb toes, they reached the store. Vladimir's socks were soaking wet inside his worn-out holey shoes. He badly needed a pair of boots, but money was in short supply, and he imagined that boots would be hard to find. He hoped that soon he would earn enough at his practice so that both he and Slava could find and purchase the desperately needed boots, shoes, and clothing.

The warmth of a rusty pot-belly stove inside the store welcomed them, as did Agata. She greeted them with a bear hug, as if Vladimir and Slava were long lost friends.

"I'm so happy to see you. I've been wondering how you were getting along. Did you find a place to live? Were you able to get your ration cards?

Grinning, Vladimir pulled the cards out of his pocket and handed them to her. "We have them and we're ready for everything you can give us."

"We're pleased to see you as well," Slava said, still reeling from the massive embrace that knocked the wind out of her. "We can't forget your generosity the other day. I'm sorry that I fainted. I feel so embarrassed."

"You were just weak from hunger. You look much better today. Well, let me have you're your cards, and I'll give you the rations."

Agata took great pride in taking products off the shelves and placed them on the counter. Their mouths watered as she provided them with a large loaf of heavy rye bread, a kilogram of buckwheat grain, one-half kilogram of flour, one-fourth kilogram of butter and a liter of milk. Then, smiling broadly, Agata reached under the counter. "I have something for you, Slavochka." She pulled out a piece of German chocolate candy wrapped in colorful foil and handed it to Slava. Still grinning, she offered another piece to Vladimir. "These chocolates are rare. Anything that is a little bit of luxury…. Oh, I shouldn't say anymore. This world has flipped on its edge." Slava understood what she meant. Somehow she obtained the chocolate under the noses of the Nazis. If they were anything like the ones in Vitebsk, these chocolates were only reserved for German officers. *One of these days, I'll ask her how she managed to get them.*

Agata's conversation, coupled with the magnificent, rich smell of the chocolate and the items sitting on the counter for some reason brought to Vladimir's mind his family back home. *I wonder if they are still alive. If so, do they have enough to eat?* He had not seen his mother or his three sisters since he was mobilized into the Red Army days after the German invasion into Belarus on June 22, 1941. Slava assured him that they were probably all right since they fled to Jazwino, the village of his mother's birth. *Hopefully, one day I'll see them again.*

"Oh, Agata," Slava said. "You shouldn't. Keep the chocolates for yourself."

"No, no. I want you to have them. It'll please me so much. Here, take them. I insist. Please do not disappoint me."

"Thank you so much for everything." Slava touched, once again, by her generosity approached her and gave her a firm hug, kissing her on the cheek."

Before they left the store, Vladimir paid three marks for the products. Unable to hold off any longer, Slava quickly popped the chocolate into her mouth. Vladimir smiled watching her close her eyes as she savored the taste. Even though he had a weakness for chocolate, he handed his own piece to her. He wanted Slava to enjoy it. Slava refused to accept it and insisted that he eat his. But he forced it into her hand. Slava placed the little morsel of chocolate in her coat pocket with the intent of sharing it that evening.

Agata found a tattered green cloth bag in the rear of the store for them to carry the items. She also told them that next time they needed to bring their own bags. She suggested a name of a woman that can sew them for a mark each. She also directed them to other stores to purchase rations of cooking oil, canned goods, meat, and sugar. They thanked Agata, inviting her to visit. "Just let me know when," she said, beaming.

On the way back to the house, the lingering taste of chocolate reminded Slava of the boxes of chocolate that Major Raake had brought to her parents' home. She often wondered if he had a romantic interest. However, she was fortunate that he turned out to be truly a gentleman and did not push his feelings on her.

Slava heard Vladimir whistle. He always whistled when content. But for the first time since they reunited, he not only whistled but she heard him softly hum a familiar song as they walked. She listened and felt at peace.

Upon return, Vladimir informed his wife that he must leave again to meet the people that were willing to move the medical tables from Sygmund's store. "Oh, Volodya. You must be tired from that long walk carrying a load of groceries. Please be careful. You still don't have all your strength. Don't strain yourself. Maybe, you can find someone else to help out. Give him a couple of marks, but don't you overdo it."

"All right, all right. I'll be fine. See you soon with the tables." He grabbed his coat and hat from the couch where he left them and opened the squeaky door.

"Wait, you didn't give me a kiss."

On the way, two Latvian policemen walked intentionally across the street toward Vladimir. He saw them approach, and his heart jumped beats. They detained Vladimir and demanded to see his papers. At first they acted gruff. But after studying the documents, Vladimir sensed that their disposition softened when they read he was a doctor.

Once at the store, he found the leather-faced burly man and his equally leather-faced large-boned wife waiting with their arms crossed. The man spoke in Byelorussian in a croaky stern voice, "I looked at those stairs and those tables down there. That's a job. Hell, we don't think we can do it for ten marks."

Vladimir expected that. "I'll add another five marks, but I need the tables loaded and then unloaded at my place. Do you agree? Can the three of us move the tables, or do you need more help?"

"What do you think, Anna?" The man addressed his wife. The woman grinned widely and nodded, exhibiting a lone tooth on each side of her upper square jaw. "Boris, tell that skinny runt of a man that he will only be in the way. We don't need his or anyone else's help."

As they plowed down the aisle, knocking a stack of merchandise off a counter, Sygmund yelled out, "Hey, dammit, be careful." Vladimir picked up the fallen goods and returned them to the table, then hurried to catch up with Boris and Anna as they stormed down the steps. Boris grabbed one side of the examining table while Anna grabbed the other. They lifted the table as if it were a feather. Vladimir attempted to help Anna, but she shoved him away. They were slowed by the steps. Sweat poured from their brows as they cleared the last step. They yelled to Sygmund to open the back door, but Vladimir ran around them and flung the wide wooden door open as they charged through it and pushed the table onto the waiting horse and cart in the alley.

They wiped their foreheads with the sleeves of their coats, almost in unison. Taking a deep breath, they rushed back into the store, down the stairs, grabbed the surgical table, which appeared to be much lighter than the examining table, and loaded that on the cart as well. A half meter of the table protruded from the cart. "You better perch yourself next to the load to keep it from falling," Boris said. "That way you give us directions."

"Wait, we also need to take the lamp and the scale."

"Wait a minute!" the old woman said. "That will be another five marks."

"Look," Vladimir said. "I'll bring them up myself. "There is still room left on the side for the scale, and I'll carry the lamp."

"You put the scale on there; it will cost you five marks."

"I'll give you two."

"Take it, Anna," said the old man. "Hell, I'll go get the scale for you. It probably weighs more than you do."

Once everything was loaded, Vladimir wondered whether that old horse could pull the three of them and both tables. The man assured him that the horse would do fine. If there is a problem, his wife can get out and walk. "The load seems stable enough," Vladimir said. "I think I better walk also. I'll trot along and show you the way."

"Do what you want if you don't believe me," the man growled, now irritated.

Halfway to the house, two policemen in an army vehicle stopped the party. The three were immediately accused of stealing. Without inquiring further, the policemen were ready to arrest everyone in sight. Boris was ordered off the cart. He got off, but his face turned red as a beet. Vladimir saw his hand clinch into a fist. The old man's chest filled with air like a balloon. Vladimir knew he had to intervene before Boris belted one of the policemen. He quickly pulled out his papers and stepped between Boris and the accusers. He explained as quickly as he could that he is a doctor who bought the tables from Sygmund. He showed them the contract for the instruments, tables included. "These fine people were helping me move the tables to my new clinic."

The policeman's suspicious gaze left Boris as he grabbed the papers from Vladimir. He took the documents and both men studied them intently. They argued between themselves in Latvian. *God, I hope they can read them. The contract with Sygmund is in Polish. The identification and work cards are in German, Polish and Byelorussian. And they are Latvians.*

They evidently knew German, at least enough to read the official documents. One of them even spoke and read Polish. The policeman handed the papers to Vladimir without saying a word. He motioned for them to continue and strode back to the vehicle. Boris breathed hard, hatred lurking in his eyes. Anna laughed. "Boris, look how fast they backed off. Two of them together are not as big as you. But how many times did I tell you to control yourself?"

"Anna, I can't take it anymore. If you had no need of me, I would be with the partisans this very moment. Those foreign pigs that the Nazis recruit to do their dirty work need to go. Look what they've done to the Jews. I told you what I saw—with my own eyes. I saw them chase the Jews out of their houses only to shoot them down in cold blood. They're scum, I tell you, and we need to kill them all. Thank God for the partisans."

"It's enough. We already lost our boys. And who knows if our daughter is alive with them. No. I can't lose you. Get that nonsense out of your thick, stubborn head. You're too old, a man in his seventies. So settle down, climb back up that cart, and let's go."

Relieved that the incident did not escalate out of hand, Vladimir guided the old couple to his new clinic. When the medical equipment was quickly unloaded, Vladimir paid them the seventeen marks. "Nice place you have here, man." Boris said. Vladimir heard the resentment in his voice. "Well, I guess we might come to see you if we have to. Right now I can't think of any reason."

"Boris, don't jinx it. Now you're healthy as an ox. Who knows what will happen tomorrow?" She looked at Vladimir for the first time with some approval. "Doctor, get ahold of us if you need anything. Good-bye now."

After they left, Slava grabbed Vladimir's arm and physically pulled him out of the clinic telling him he must eat.

"While you were gone, I prepared that chicken. We'll get busy and set up your clinic later."

"I can't just yet. I need to get medications for the clinic. A small supply of sulfa drugs, aspirin, and bandages are vital to our opening tomorrow. I saw a pharmacy near the square."

"You have to eat something before you collapse."

"I'll be all right. It's getting late, and I need to see if a pharmacy will give me what I need before they close. You go ahead and eat without me. I'll be back soon."

"Here, at least take this chicken leg to chew while you're walking." Slava ripped off the leg, including the thigh bone and gave it to him. She also handed him a handkerchief that she bought from a vendor at the black market.

"All right, thanks." Vladimir kissed her and ran out of the door, biting a big chunk out of the chicken leg.

Chapter 17

THE PHARMACIST, a short elderly man with a long gray bushy beard, with a fringe of gray hair surrounding his bald round head, had already heard of Vladimir. "We need doctors badly here. There are only two doctors left in this city. Although, I'm surprised that they're even still here. Not only were the Jewish doctors taken away, so were some of the non-Jews. I was afraid the bastards would take me too. It seems that anyone with an education is an enemy and a threat to the German occupiers. They want to keep us dumb. They closed the schools, you know. You better be careful, yourself. As soon as they don't need you or you cross them, it will be good-bye to you." Astonished by the candid conversation, Vladimir felt uncomfortable. *If he keeps talking like this to every stranger that comes through the door, he'll soon be eliminated. And so will I, just for listening.*

"Of course, maybe the scum decided that they need to provide medical care to the population since you're here. But you know—"

Vladimir cut him off. In his mind, the conversation became too dangerous. He was conditioned to the soviet system under Stalin where even the walls had ears. *The Nazis can't be much different.* "I am indeed pleased to meet you. I am sure we'll work well together. But I'm in a hurry now, and I need to talk to you about a supply of medications and other items for my clinic."

"Of course, of course, no problem. I need to see the card."

"The card. What card?"

"For me to dispense any medications, you first must get approval from the Germans in City Hall. They control everything here, and I guess I should consider myself lucky that they gave me the privilege to continue working in what used to be my store. Now they are the owners, and they pay me to work here. Listen, go see a Lieutenant Hartman. He is a good soul, and he'll be quick about getting you what you need."

"Lieutenant Hartman! I know him. I'll run over there right now before they close. Can you wait for me?"

"Sure, they promised me a shipment of supplies that's arriving from Germany today. I'll be here anyway."

Lieutenant Hartman smiled broadly and seemed pleased to see Vladimir. "Of course, I'll give you the document for your purchase. Just tell me what you need. Did you find the medical instruments?" Hartman took out a half sheet of a green paper from the top right drawer of his badly scratched desk. "Now, what do you need?"

"I need aspirin, sulfa drugs, alcohol, cough syrup, ointments, ether, local anesthetics, sedatives, bandages. Oh yes, muslin cloths for the open ether anesthetic."

Hartman meticulously wrote down each. He then signed his name with a flourish and stamped the document, showing his vast authority. "Since it is for your clinic, I gave you an extra ration. But remember, you will need to pay the pharmacist. I hope that won't be a problem. Please be careful how you use the supplies. I've heard rumors that some of the medications may be cut off for the occupied territories. Until then, don't worry. By the way, are you settled in?"

"Yes, we're making progress, I'm just anxious to get the clinic opened."

"Well, one of these days I'll come and visit you. I'll bring some schnapps."

Vladimir, once again felt uncomfortable with a visit from a German. Hartman seemed sincere and for some reason wanted to carry on a friendship. However, after the brutality he endured at the hands of the German guards he did not trust any man in uniform—at least not yet. *Why does he want to come over? We're still enemies. They are the masters here and we live under their mercy. This wasn't the first time he invited himself. What does he really want?* "Sure, Lieutenant, we would be pleased to see you. Come over anytime."

The pharmacist sat next to the stove reading a copy of Slonim's newspaper. Upon seeing Vladimir enter, he stood and ambled on to the counter. "You're back already? That was fast. I still didn't get that shipment. I shouldn't be surprised. They've been promising more supplies for a month now. They told me it will be in today for sure. I'm running out of medications. So I sit here and read this paper that comes out sporadically. It used to be a fine newspaper when a Jew owned it. Now, the Germans took it over, hired inexperienced people, and tell them what to print. It's all Nazi propaganda. But at least it is something to read."

Vladimir, once again, became inpatient with the pharmacists rambling. "I hope you still have enough supplies to accommodate me? Here's the card you needed."

The pharmacist studied the list. Then he looked at Vladimir suspiciously. "How did you ever talk them into giving you a double supply?"

"Why? Is that unusual?"

"I'll say it is. Someone there must like you." He immediately fell silent. His smile disappeared, as he quickly went about his work pulling items off the shelves and onto the counter. "I don't have enough of some of the medicines. You can come back after I get that new shipment." He began writing down the items and when he finished, he priced them and submitted the bill to Vladimir. "That comes to one hundred thirty one marks, doctor."

Vladimir could see the sudden change in his demeanor. *Oh God, now he thinks I must be a German collaborator or something. Maybe Hartman didn't do me such a favor. I better straighten him out.* "Listen, I don't know why I received such an amount. Maybe Lieutenant Hartman decided that my new practice will need it. Maybe he doesn't want to see me very often, begging him for more medications. Please don't think I'm for the Germans or work for the Germans. I'm just trying to survive this war, just like you."

Vladimir could see the muscles in the pharmacist's face relax a little. A slight grin parted his thin, chapped lips. "No, no. I didn't think that at all. I was just surprised at the amount. But, I suppose you will need it."

"Great. I'm glad we cleared that up. I don't want to start off on the wrong foot. Actually, I need a big favor from you. I only have a few marks left, approximately thirty. I'll give that to you. But I will begin accepting patients tomorrow. I am sure I'll have a few in the next several days. All the income I'll bring in, I'll give to you until the bill is paid. Can you wait a few days for payment in full?"

"I shouldn't do it, but I'll take a chance because I know you'll have no trouble at all getting patients in this town. I'll take your thirty and the rest you must pay me in four days. That's when the Germans check every piece of inventory and expect a full accounting from me. Please, don't disappoint me. If you are late with the payment, I might be arrested."

"Thank you, thank you. I promise to have the money by then, or I'll return the drugs."

"All right, but please don't let me down. I'll be in deep trouble. And so may you for that matter. They control every aspect of our lives. For example, did they tell you who you could or could not treat?"

"Yes, they certainly did. They warned me not to treat Jews and partisans. If one were to come to see me, I must inform the Germans immediately."

"You see. That's exactly what I mean."

"Well, we must be careful, that's for sure. You know, I would have a problem, though. I might not be able to identify a Jew or a partisan unless they told me they were one. Anyway, I'll have my account settled with you soon. If my practice takes off, we'll see each other quite often."

"I'm sure. You will be busy. The problem though is that there is not much to spend your money on as long as we are under the tight control of the Germans. On the other hand, they have allowed peasants and merchants to sell their goods in the market. Oh well, good luck to you and welcome to our town, such as it is now."

Vladimir thanked the pharmacist, took a box of supplies and worried if he, in fact, will indeed have patients and be able to pay back, not only Sygmund but now also the pharmacist, as promised. *Time will tell. I never owed any money to anyone before. It's not a comfortable feeling with this lump in my gut. But I will not let the pharmacist down. I must pay him first.*

Chapter 18

VLADIMIR STRENGTHENED out and with a quiet satisfaction looked around him. The clinic appeared ready for business. After returning from the pharmacy, he and Slava toiled into the early morning hours to get everything in shape. The little sign with the word *Doktor* that he found at Sygmund's store would be the finishing touch, could wait until morning.

That morning at eight o'clock, Vladimir nailed the sign to the building next to the door. He found two rusty square nails and an old hammer in the cellar. He stepped back into the street to see if the plaque hung straight and could be read from there. As he did so, two women approached him.

"You're the new physician, aren't you?" One of the women asked as she came up closer.

"Yes, yes, I am. My, word gets out quickly."

"Well, people have been talking. We are very happy to have you here. I need your help. My ear is driving me crazy—it's been unbearable pain for a week now."

"Come in and let me look at it. You will be my first patient in Slonim."

"May we also come in?" Another woman, holding a squirmy toddler in her arms, was quick to ask.

"Yes, of course, come in," Vladimir said with a hint of excitement.

Vladimir anxiously began treating his new patients. Before long, the waiting room filled with people. Slava was there to greet them, asking them to take a seat and listed their name on a notepad that she and Vladimir had purchased at one of the stores. The overwhelming response so early in the day surprised her. She, as did Vladimir, assumed that, if they were lucky, perhaps they may see one or two patients that first day. Vladimir believed that it might take at least a month or more to keep the eight seats he arranged along the wall in the waiting room filled. They were unprepared. Slava hurriedly brought in additional chairs from their home to seat the many people standing. Some waited outside in the cold wind that began that afternoon.

While Vladimir treated the patients, Slava set up a work area at the mahogany dining room table and took control to keep order. Everyone clamored to see the doctor as soon as possible. Vladimir saw the patients according to her list. At first, Slava felt overwhelmed. *How can Volodya see all these people today? The poor thing, he will be totally exhausted. He still doesn't have all his strength.*

Vladimir needed her help in the examination room, but someone also had to manage the patients. She thought of developing her own triage program. The more serious cases, those that required the most immediate attention and could be handled by Vladimir during the visit, would receive the first priority. Those who could wait, she wanted to assign a later date and time. She mentioned her idea to Vladimir as he finished with a patient and came out to call the next name on the list.

"No, not today. Although it's a good idea." Vladimir said to Slava in a hushed tone so that only she could hear. "I'll see all these people. It maybe a long night, but I'll do it."

Slava thought that was impossible. It was already mid-afternoon, and how could he treat the twenty-eight patients still waiting? The door never seemed to close. However, Slava had never watched Vladimir work, and she underestimated how efficiently he handled the patient load. His face beamed as he saw his patients. He appeared truly pleased to see each and every one. *He looks like a child in a candy store*. Vladimir wasted no time going from one patient to another. The more complicated cases took longer. She became concerned when he spent almost half an hour with one, but generally he was through with each person in ten to fifteen minutes. The patients seemed to love him. They praised him highly to her. And she was thrilled when most patrons before leaving paid her for the treatment. She scrambled to find a box. Not finding one, she took a small drawer out of the buffet and used it for a cash box.

"It's really cold in here," an elderly lady grumbled. "My feet are frozen."

Slava suddenly realized that her feet were cold as well. In all the excitement, neither Vladimir nor she remembered to stoke the stove. Vladimir had done so before he went out to hang the sign, but the coal burned out many hours ago.

"The stove needs to be refilled. I'll do it right away."

"Here, let me take care of it for you," volunteered a kindly looking man with a red nose who had been sneezing while awaiting his turn.

"Thank you, the stove is in the kitchen and there is probably enough coal to fill it up."

"No worries, I'll get it done. Just make sure I'm called when my turn comes if I'm still away."

The kind man lit the stove and soon warmth filtered into the clinic. A few minutes later, Vladimir took the man in. Darkness had fallen hours ago. The wind rattled the windows. Only a few patients now remained as the rush ebbed. Slava thought that they might be through with the long, grueling day. Suddenly the door flew open and a middle-aged man in stained pants, muddied shoes and a torn jacket walked in holding a small pig in his arms. He marched toward Slava and with his heavily bearded face almost in her face, barked out in a brash, booming raspy voice, "Are you in charge here?"

Slava backed away from his garlic breath and nodded in the affirmative. "Well, tell the doctor that this pig is for him. But first he's got to earn it."

Slava recovered from the intrusion and smiled sweetly at the man. "Oh, how cute that little one is."

"Listen miss, you shouldn't look at an animal whether it's cute or not. The pig is for food. It's valuable. You can eat it now or let it grow and get fat and eat it later, or trade it at the market for something else. But don't you get attached to it, understand?"

Tired and hungry, Slava was irritated by the man's attitude and did not appreciate his brusque lecture. She had to overcome her annoyance. A pig was obviously a wonderful payment, and she appreciated the offer. She continued to smile and politely thanked the old man for the animal. *What am I supposed to do with this pig? I guess I can put it in the barn for now and let Volodya worry about it later.*

"Is the pig weaned? It doesn't need milk, does it?"

The man did not hear her and again stuck his face next to Slava. She repeated the question. "No, just give it a little grain. If you have milk, mix it into the grain. But listen, young lady, I'm not giving you this pig yet. The doctor has to earn it first."

"What is your problem?" Slava asked, just to carry on a conversation. She heard tell of so many illnesses this day that in reality was not curious at all. "I'm going deaf that's all. I feel as if there is a tree stuck in my ear. And it will be a miracle if he can help me."

Slava wrote down his name and asked him to wait his turn. He listened to her and sat down and held the pig firmly in his lap as it kept wiggling. Slava felt drained. As the excitement of the day wore off, all she could think of was how wonderful it would be to be home where she could eat and collapse into bed. Vladimir also appeared totally exhausted as he took in yet another patient. She glanced again at her watch and saw the time was almost nine o'clock in the evening. Her stomach sent shooting pains begging for food. At least, no one else came through the door. The man with the pig appeared to be the last patient. She took it on herself to lock the door. *I've decided. We are officially closed for today.*

Finally, Vladimir, in a tired voice, asked the man into the examination room. He managed to produce a tired-looking smile. Slava threw Vladimir an angry look for overdoing it. Earlier she had insisted that he take a break, go next door and eat something. "The patients can wait for a few minutes," she told him. *But did he listen? No!* She determined that this cannot go on every day. After all, this was the very first day, and it would get worse in the days to come as far as the volume of patients. But then, Vladimir had asked her many times to go rest. "I can handle it by myself." She also refused to leave.

The grump with the squirmy piglet approached the door. "No, no," Vladimir said. "I'm sorry but you can't bring the pig in here. I need to keep the examination room as clean as I can."

"Well, what am I supposed to do with this pig then?"

"Here, let's take it to the shed outside. There is nothing in it and no way for the animal to get out. It'll be all right there."

"But I'm not giving you the pig yet. You have to help me first."

"Please, leave the pig in the shed. I'll show you the way. You can pick it up after our visit."

The man followed Vladimir to the shed, their shoes crunching on the frozen ground, a bright full moon lighting the path. After inspecting the shed to satisfy himself that the piglet could not escape, he agreed to return to the examination room.

Slava was now alone. She glanced at the overflowing cash box. The sight of all that money bolstered her energy. Her heart pounded at the sight. She had never seen such an amount of small bills before. She hurriedly counted the income for the long day. The tally was one-hundred-ninety-seven marks, and perhaps one pig. *Oh my God! Volodya and I never really discussed how much to charge for services. People just gave what they could. Isn't this amazing? Thank you, Jesus, for providing this to us. Thank you, thank you. Volodya was right with his philosophy. If he treated his patients well, the money would flow in.* When patients asked about the fee, Vladimir's response was "pay what you can." Several people walked away without paying, but promised to come back with payment. *We made enough money today to pay off not only Sygmund, but also the pharmacist,* Slava thought with a happy smile.

Soon the patient walked out of the examination room followed by Vladimir. "He did well by me," the man told Slava. "He did something to my ear, and now I can hear. Now you can keep the pig. I'll tell all my friends about your husband."

After the man walked out, Slava ran up to Vladimir, almost knocking him over with her hug. "Look at that bundle of money."

"Did you count it yet? Although at this point I don't care. I need to sleep. I'm so tired, I can't think straight."

"Let's eat first, and I'm ready to collapse, myself."

"You did well, today, Slavochka. Thank you for your help. I thought I could do it all, but it would have been difficult without you. I love you so." Vladimir squeezed Slava's hand and kissed her on the cheek.

"Volodya, we have a pig in the back. Shouldn't we feed it or something?"

"I'll go check on it. But we have nothing to feed it with. Do we still have a piece of bread?"

"Yes, we do. Are you asking for yourself or the pig?"

"For the pig, of course! I'll mash the bread with some water. That should hold him until we figure out something tomorrow."

"If tomorrow is anything like today, there won't be much time for anything else but to see people. By the way, what was wrong with that man with the pig? Was he really going deaf?"

Vladimir laughed. "His ears were plugged with wax. He had never cleaned them out before, and he didn't know what hit him."

As the days, weeks, and months sped by into the summer of 1943, Vladimir had seen many patients and administered treatments from simple colds to serious infections. On numerous occasions, Vladimir made house calls. Generally, he tried to avoid conditions that were outside of his specialty of ear, nose and throat. But when on call for the obstetrician, he even delivered babies. He often met with Doctor Ostrovska and with the other physician, Doctor Savitski, a general practitioner, to discuss cases and on occasion to socialize. For the most part, he referred the obstetric and general surgical patients to them.

For those patients that required surgery, Slava scheduled certain mornings and then assisted him. The patients loved both Vladimir and Slava. The money accumulated. So much so, that they hired a receptionist within the first two weeks to help out. Much later, the woman admitted that she had been stealing cash out of the box. Neither Vladimir nor Slava had suspected it. They actually were not too upset because they had more than enough to live comfortably, as comfortably as they could under the German occupation, and enough to give to some desperately needy people including the old couple they first met in Slonim who sold them the bread made with some sawdust.

The patients not only brought cash, but also brought animals or other goods as payment. The Moskalkov backyard became a barnyard with pigs, calves, sheep, ducks, geese, and chickens. Vladimir fattened them with grain and milk that he obtained at the market by trading animals for the supplies. The animals were also used as barter for shoes, clothing, and household goods. Some animals were taken to a butcher who prepared meat for them. The butcher was paid for his services with a large portion of the meat for himself. The couple worked hard, but they were content. Their home was filled with song and laughter. They dressed well and ate well. The Germans, for the most part, left them alone. The Moskalkovs liked Slonim and its people. But war continued to rage around them. They knew that at any moment their lives could be disrupted yet again.

Chapter 19

SCORCHING HEAT and humidity enveloped Slonim for a majority of August 1943. The second Sunday of the month proved to be no exception. Most residents cooled themselves on the banks of the two rivers flowing through the town by splashing around in the murky waters. The Moskalkovs reluctantly spent that Sunday entertaining Lieutenant Hartman in their home.

Hartman did not come empty-handed for the visit. He brought with him a half-liter of schnapps and by the end of his stay almost single-handedly consumed the entire contents. "Ah, this is fine, really fine liquor. It came from Germany, you know," he boasted. The alcohol he drank, combined with the sweltering heat both inside and outside the house, resulted in heavy perspiration beading on his now beet-red face. Slava had offered him two handkerchiefs just so he could wipe his brow and nape. When he finally left the house late in the evening with his clothes sticking to him from the sweat, he staggered out the door in a happy mood.

That had been his now third unexpected visit, and each time it confounded Vladimir and Slava as to why he wanted to socialize with them. The conversation seemed awkward, although he never ran out of things to say, jumping from one topic to another. He gossiped about people that neither Vladimir nor Slava knew and expanded on the history and brilliance of the people of the Rhineland.

Hartman appeared jovial and laughed freely, especially at his own pointless jokes. When the bottle was half gone, he broke out into a song. He even knew an old Polish ballad, which surprised the young couple. *Where did he learn to sing in Polish?* Slava wondered. At that visit, out of politeness, Slava asked him to stay for dinner expecting him to refuse. After all, he had devoured most of a ring of pork sausage. Slava had sliced the fatty meat as an appetizer to go along with the schnapps. "Of course, I'll stay," Hartman readily answered, astonishing Slava with the response. "Home-made dinner would be fantastic. Your kind invitation is most welcome."

While Vladimir continued to entertain the lieutenant, Slava excused herself, went into the kitchen. and began peeling potatoes. She decided that dinner would consist of lamb chops, mashed potatoes, sliced tomatoes, and cucumbers.

His visits remained a mystery. Was he a spy? But what did they have to reveal? Was he just bored? Or did he truly like to be with them? For whatever reason, Vladimir's heart rate raced each time he visited. Slava noticed how strained his demeanor became. The sight of a German uniform, especially in his home, set him on edge. He had complained to her several times how uncomfortable he felt, that the local people must think that they are in bed with the Nazis. On the other hand, he found the visits useful. Through these visits they were able to keep somewhat in touch with the outside world.

His tongue loosened with liquor, Hartman blabbed about the buildup of German troops around Slonim. "We'll chase those criminals out of the forests," he vowed, referring to the dreaded partisans that the Germans could not eradicate. He actually mentioned a figure of three hundred thousand troops. Vladimir also learned from Hartman that the United States and Britain joined the Soviet Union as allies. Hartman laughed at the notion. "Britain is weak. We have been pounding it with bombs all these months. America is too far. They really have no will to fight. Why should they? They will not make much of a difference to the Third Reich."

Through Hartman's bravado, Vladimir sensed his uncertainty and worry. Hartman let slip out a little later in the evening that the war for the Nazis wasn't going as well as they planned. He admitted that many of the German soldiers were developing a defeatist attitude, and he himself was not sure of the outcome anymore.

This information planted a lump in Vladimir's stomach. If the Germans are pushed out of the region, then the Red Army would move in. As a true son of his country, he thought he should feel allegiance to his motherland. He felt he needed to cheer at the prospect. Normally, once the

Soviet Union chased the enemy from his homeland, he could return home to Vitebsk. Yet, Vladimir realized how that particular outcome would be catastrophic for them. *We truly are without a home.*

If he were to fall into Soviet hands, he would be executed—and for more than just one reason. He remembered fellow inmates in the prisoner of war camp discussing Stalin's unreasonable and unbelievable decree. Soviet prisoners of the Germans were dubbed as traitors for merely being captured. Once they returned to the Soviet Union, execution or, at best, brutal labor camps in Siberia would be their fate.

Vladimir shuddered at the thought. He realized that he, undoubtedly, would be shot. Having been taken by the Germans as a prisoner of war concerned him, but saving the life of a German officer would mean certain death. He would not be able to conceal his past. All they had to do was question his release and the reason he ended up in Slonim working as a physician with approval of the enemy. *I would be considered a traitor. A traitor? A victim of circumstance. That's what I am. Fate has so many twists and turns, and who would have ever dreamed that I would be in this situation? I don't really work for the Germans. I work for myself. But that distinction will make little difference to Stalin's henchmen. They'll execute me on the spot. And Slavochka could be shot as well for working for the Germans, even though she had no choice. No, I need Hartman around to let me know when the Red Army advances toward Slonim and somehow figure out a way to escape.*

Chapter 20

THAT EVENING, as Vladimir and Slava prepared for bed, a loud knock at the door startled them. It was not that it frightened them. It was just the unexpected noise. Patients frequently came to the residence at all hours of the night with emergencies. Vladimir twisted the switch to illuminate the porch and opened the door. There stood a tall man with graying hair. Large bags under his eyes were the most notable feature on his narrow ashen face. A slightly soiled white collar protruded from underneath his black shirt.

"I'm so sorry to bother you this late in the evening. I wouldn't have come except that my friend is desperately sick. She needs your help right away. Would you come with me? It's only about a twenty minute walk."

"What's wrong with her?"

"She has extremely high fever and terrible abdominal pain. She's vomiting and screaming from pain. I am very worried."

"Yes, I can see that. Come in and please sit down here," Vladimir said, pointing to a chair. "I need to throw on some clothes and grab my bag. I'll only be a minute."

"Doctor, before we go, there is something I should tell you. I believe God would want me to warn you first. Are we alone?"

"Yes. My wife is in the bedroom but she'll be unable to hear."

"Well, you must know that my sick friend is Jewish. Some of my parishioners and I have been hiding the woman and her two children since last summer. I'm sure you realize that if the Nazis find out, not only will the family involved be killed, but also all those kind people that hid her for all these months. So will I and unfortunately, so will you if you treat a Jew."

Vladimir had always dreaded this moment. He tensed. An unwanted decision had to be quickly made. *Why did he have to tell me? It would be simpler not to know.* He heard stories from his patients that some Poles and Byelorussians in the region hid Jews, particularly the children. He often wondered what he would do should he be confronted with this particular situation. He and Slava had discussed it. They apprehensively decided that he would have no moral choice but to treat all people in need. That was the Hippocratic Oath he took. They must take the chance. The German commandant's face and words flashed through his mind, "You can not treat Jews, and you must report any Jews or anyone helping the Jews." *Should I discuss this with Slava first? After all, once again, our lives could be disrupted. Disrupted? We would lose our lives is more like it. We would lose everything we had worked for. Our life here is now stable and we live well. It could all change in an instant over one sick*

person. No, Slava doesn't need to know. I've disregarded com-
mands before. That's not new to me.

He recalled an incident from the first days of his mobi-
lization into the army. A pair of sunglasses saved him then.
He disobeyed his commanding officer's orders and barely
escaped a bullet to his head. The officer forbade him from
going to a village outside the camp to obtain additional
medications for his wounded soldiers. The suffering, the
moaning of those wretched souls convinced him he had
to do something to alleviate some of the pain. He could
no longer watch his patients suffer needlessly. So he took a
chance and ignored a stern order and successfully retrieved
the medications under the nose of the advancing Germans.
Incensed with his insubordination, the officer pulled out his
weapon, stuck the barrel to Vladimir's forehead determined
to pull the trigger. At that instant, an airplane circled above
them. The commander glanced up to see whether it was
a German aircraft, but squinted from the bright sun. The
simple gesture of Vladimir offering his sunglasses to him
saved his life. The officer pulled back the weapon, cursed
at Vladimir, and ordered him to go back to his patients.
I've taken chances before. I have to do it again. A woman needs
my help.

"Well, father, I guess we are going for a walk," Vladimir
commented softly and nervously. "I'll be right out. Please
make yourself comfortable."

"I pray that I made the right decision coming to you. I've heard that you are a kind, caring man. You now have the power to inform the Germans or their lapdogs. We are now in your hands."

"Father, don't worry. Your secret is safe with me."

"Thank God. I've been told it would be."

Vladimir told Slava that a patient needs his help and he had to go. He did not want to cause worry that he will treat a Jew, particularly now that Slava was pregnant. She gave her typical response when he left at night, "Please be careful. There are always bandits and hooligans out this late at night." And as was her habit, she made the sign of the cross in the air as her husband left the house. Vladimir knew that she would not sleep while he was gone, waiting for his return. He knew she would lie awake, praying to her favorite saint, Anthony, asking that no harm would come to him.

As Vladimir walked out of the bedroom, the priest stood up. As he did, Vladimir noticed a dirty sock showing through a large hole in the sole of his shoe as he uncrossed his legs. He thought of a pair of shoes he bought at the market that were two sizes too large. The softness of the dark brown leather attracted him to them, and he hoped that they would fit him if the wore two or three pairs of socks. Even so, they were still uncomfortably large.

"Father, I have an extra pair of shoes that are really too big for me. I wonder if perhaps you could use them."

"Oh, thank you, my son. I really need a new pair. By the way, Doctor Moskalkov, my name is Father Aleksandr."

"I'm pleased to meet you. I'll go get the shoes. They're in the bedroom wardrobe."

Vladimir explained to Slava why he needed them and returned to the priest. The shoes fit well and elicited a half-smile from the priest, the first one that evening.

As the men ventured off into the dark night, the priest holding his old shoes in his hand and Vladimir carrying his medical bag, the man volunteered that he is of the Franciscan Order and conducts services at the beautiful St. Andrew's Catholic Cathedral. "There were several Roman Catholic priests in Slonim, but I'm the only one left. There is also a Russian Orthodox priest. Are you religious?"

"I believe so. I believe in God and believe that he watches over us. At least that has been the case with me."

"That's good. We should all be religious now, especially in such difficult times. The Nazis per se don't ban religion, but they don't encourage it either. Notice that I'm the only Catholic priest left. The others were arrested for one drummed up charge after another. And why is it that there are so few physicians in Slonim?"

Before Vladimir could render his opinion, Father Aleksandr continued, not waiting for a response. "They do not want anyone around who has had an education and can think. They gathered up the lawyers, doctors, priests, professors and took them away. They left me alone for some reason. Maybe that means that they didn't believe I could think." The priest chuckled at his attempt at humor and proceeded to talk. He seemed to have much to say and hurried to unburden himself.

"Did you notice why there are practically no young people in Slonim? Well I'll tell you. In April of last year, the Germans forcibly rounded up all non-Jews, young enough to work and sent them off by train. I presume it was to work in Germany. They even provided a list of things they needed to bring with them—shoes, clothing, food for three to four days, a spoon, a bowl, and a cup. They could bring a musical instrument. Ha! As though they would have a good ole merry time playing music. You should have seen the youth huddled together carrying suitcases and pillowcases. Jews, they placed in a section of town that they segregated by barbed wire. You might have seen parts of that awful fence when you arrived."

"Yes, I saw it. It's all down now, isn't it?"

"Yes, finally most of the vestiges of that monstrosity, that monument to the cruelty of humanity, were removed. But that barbed wire plagued us for months and will continue to plague mankind for generations. I personally saw them drag people out of their houses and herd them into that ghetto—the Jewish quarter. Then in July of last year, let's see… we're still in 1943, right?"

"Yes, 1943."

"Yes, yes then. Last year in July, I personally saw the Nazis round up the Jews and herd them out of their compound. This time, they were told not to take any of their belongings except the clothes on their backs. Some were led out into the fields. Gunshots were heard afterwards. There is evidence of mass graves out there. But most were shoved into filthy cattle cars, jammed in like sheep, and taken away. Jews made up half the population of Slonim in July. I'd say, about fifteen to twenty thousand. Now they're all gone except the very few that we had managed to save by use of tunnels or by smuggling them out on service vehicles entering the ghetto. Most were children, but now they have no parents.

Vladimir listened to the priest's sad account, the atrocities leaving him speechless. The priest continued, "Thank God for so many locals risking their lives to hide them. In the meantime we try to assimilate them into the Christian faith for their survival. Some don't even know how to speak Polish or Byelorussian or Russian. But they're learning. We taught them to make the sign of the cross, either left to right, the Catholic way, or right to left, the Orthodox way."

Vladimir had heard from his patients and others of how the Jews were rounded up and taken away. But he did not realize how widespread the operation to save the Jews had been.

"We're almost there," said the priest. "Oh, dear God, Sweet Mother in Heaven, here comes a patrol. What time is it anyway?"

Vladimir glanced at his new gold-colored Swiss watch sporting a brown leather band that he had traded a calf for on the black market. The luminescent hands sparkled in the dark night. "It's 9:40. We still have time before the curfew of ten o'clock. And I am allowed to be out all night if on a medical call."

"But I'm not. And I so wanted to walk back with you. I want to tell you about a Jesuit priest and two sisters who were killed not too long ago for hiding Jewish children."

"Are you talking about Father Sctark?"

"Why yes. You've heard about his brutal death. Then you realize how dangerous it is for all of us. Oh Jesus Christ! They're stopping. They hassle me every time. I think it's just because I'm a priest."

"They stop everyone. I get stopped frequently, even though many already know who I am. They just want to show their authority."

Chapter 21

THE BRAKES squealed as the truck slowed and stopped next to the men. Inside the cab were two Latvian policemen. Six others sat on wooden benches in the bed of the vehicle. Vladimir had been stopped on numerous occasions and thought he was used to the routine, but as always, a cold chill swept through him. His breath became shallow. *Am I this stressed because I'm going to see someone I'm not supposed to?* He felt weak at his knees. *What's wrong with me? They'll just look at my papers and dismiss me. Maybe one of them will even recognize me and let me go on, with no questions asked.* Somehow this time he knew that was unlikely. He had never seen these men before and realized that many questions will now be asked. He had to lie to save himself, the priest, and ultimately, the Jewish patient he had yet to see and the family hiding her. There was much at stake.

Always before, upon examining his documents, the routine questions followed: Who he was? Where was he going? Name of patient? As he thought of the answers he must give, the knot in his stomach turned into a boulder at the thought of the Jewish patient waiting for him. *I have no idea who she is. I don't even know where I'm going.*

"Come here!" Shouted the policeman seated in the passenger seat of the truck. Both Father Aleksandr and Vladimir approached as ordered.

"Papers!" Vladimir pulled out his identification card and his work permit, while the priest seemed to fumble in his pockets with a concerned look as if he had forgotten his papers. *God! He better have his papers. He also better come up with a good excuse where we're going. We could say we were just out for a walk. We still have ten minutes before curfew. But then, I'm carrying this medical bag. That won't work.* "Produce your documents now!" The policeman yelled at the priest, relishing his authority.

Aleksandr reached in his back pants pocket and tried to pull out his papers. They seemed stuck as he had a difficult time retrieving them. The policeman began to lose patience. Finally the papers came loose, and with a visibly shaking hand, the priest passed them to the man. Guilt or fear plastered his face. Vladimir quickly assessed Aleksandr's apparent distress. His heart pounded faster at the thought that his companion's demeanor would mean a gruesome interrogation by the Gestapo.

Too absorbed on the papers, shining his flashlight on them, the policeman seemed not to notice the priest's unusual nervousness. Turning his light first on Vladimir, then on the priest, he asked, "Why are you here?" His glare drilled a hole through Aleksandr.

Trembling, the priest replied, "I went to fetch the doctor because one of my parishioners is very sick."

"Name of parishioner."

In a barely audible voice, the priest answered, "Nina."

"What was that, speak up man."

In a louder voice, the priest said, "Nina."

"Last name also, you fool. That's a common name here."

"Peretzkaya."

"Her address?" The priest hesitated. "What is the problem here? I asked you a simple question. Do you want to answer these simple questions at SS headquarters?"

The priest continued to appear in a daze, but at the mention of SS, he suddenly became more animated. "No, no, of course not. I'm not feeling well myself. Actually after the physician examines Nina, I was planning ask him to help me as well. You must excuse me."

"Look, priest, I repeat my question. Where does this woman live?"

"553 Yablina Street."

"Both of you get in the truck."

Vladimir's heart stopped when he heard the command. Blood drained from his head. *They're going to interrogate us at the SS. Oh God! That is never good. I may never see Slavochka again. I'll never see my baby. But then, I haven't seen the Jewish woman yet. So maybe, they'll let me go. But yet, I was on the way to treat her. The priest better not blab.* "We'll take you to the patient." Upon hearing those words, he felt a great sense of relief, although his breathing remained shallow. He will not be taken to the Gestapo after all. *But then what if they go into the house and discover that his patient is Jewish? That might even be worse. I hope the priest knows what he's doing leading them there. If not, that will be the end for us.*

Vladimir pulled himself up onto the tall bed of the truck. Aleksandr had difficulty getting on so Vladimir helped him. They sat down opposite each other, by the open tailgate of the truck, both glum. In less than three minutes, the vehicle stopped in front of a small house. Light shone through the curtains of one of the narrow windows. Vladimir jumped down off the German truck and helped the priest down. The policemen in back of the truck continued to sit in their seats, but seemed to tighten the grip on their rifles. They scowled in unison as Vladimir looked up at them. Vladimir's relief that the policemen did not descend suddenly evaporated when the two men in the cab exited and approached Vladimir and Aleksandr.

"Thank you, gentlemen, for your courteous service of bringing us here," Vladimir said, hoping that his thanks will be all that is necessary, and they would leave without following them into the house.

"We did not bring you here out of kindness. We want to see this sick lady the priest told us about. The priest is hiding something. Go! We'll follow you to the door."

Bastards! This is not going to end quickly. I guess I'm stuck. Oh dear God, help us here. The priest knocked and a gray-headed man answered the door. His hazel eyes widened, and he took a deep breath as he saw the two policemen on his porch. Then he spied the truck with its occupants parked by the curb. The man's quickness and appraisal of the situation impressed Vladimir as he watched the man begin to play a role.

"Oh, thank God, Father Aleksandr. I see you must have brought the doctor. And also more help if we need some. Good." He turned his attention at Vladimir. "Doctor, I am so pleased you came," the man spoke loudly, loud enough for the policemen to hear. "My wife is extremely ill. She has a very high fever, severe headaches, diarrhea, and is vomiting nonstop. Now I'm afraid for myself that I'm coming down with the same thing. It hit me all at once." The man began coughing. In the background more coughing was heard. "I hope that you gentlemen don't catch whatever it is that my wife and I have. It's probably very contagious. I hope it isn't something really nasty like tuberculosis or something like that. As a matter of fact, Father, you would be wise to wait outside."

Is this fellow for real or is he acting? That cough doesn't sound like tuberculosis. At that moment, Vladimir noticed one of the policemen with them give a quick sign to leave to the other by nodding his head toward the truck. The other policeman did not hesitate as one of his feet was already pointing away from the house, ready to walk away.

"I guess this looks legitimate. We'll let you do your doc-toring," said the first policeman and followed the other into the truck. The patrol quickly drove away.

The man at the door, with a satisfied smirk on his round unshaven face, introduced himself as Leon.

As Vladimir and the priest entered the small room, clut-tered with mismatched furniture, a frail woman with short blonde hair and penetrating green eyes approached them. She stuck out her hand as Leon said, "This is my wife, Nina. She is the one that helped with the coughing—an act for the police, of course."

"Hello, Nina," Vladimir said, as he shook her hand.

"Doctor, we heard so much about you. It seems that you and your wife are big news here in Slonim. Thank you so much for coming. Our very sick guest desperately needs your help. We had no choice but to take a chance and ask you to come. Please follow me. Father Aleksandr, you may come too if you wish."

"No, I'd like to stay. I so wanted to walk the doctor back to his house, but the curfew, you know. It's getting close to ten o'clock. I'd better be home by then. Aleksandr said his good-byes, and Vladimir followed Nina into the back porch through the kitchen. She brushed aside a colorful, mud-stained rug from the floor and lifted the trapdoor into the already dimly lit cellar. Vladimir followed her down the wooden steps.

Chapter 22

A DARK-HAIRED woman lay on her side in a fetal position, the knees pulled up to her abdomen. At the foot of the bed, a sheet and blanket slipped down to the floor. A grimace of pain distorted her pale face as her blue eyes focused on Nina and Vladimir as they descended the steps and approached her.

Beams braced the floor above, the underside serving as the ceiling. Frayed electrical wires hung loosely about. Rocks and dirt formed the floor between the jagged walls of the stone foundation. Stale air and a strong smell of vomit permeated the otherwise cool cellar. Two small dark-haired children, their hair matted, sprung up from an adjoining cot. Their puffy eyes drilled into Vladimir's face. *Will you help?* Their eyes begged.

"Hanna, this is the doctor we told you about, Dr. Moskalkov," Nina said. "He'll help you."

Vladimir smiled politely, "Where does it hurt?"

Hanna rolled onto her back. The movement prompted a scream. "My stomach! Oh, doctor …the pain …unbearable," Hanna gasped through the pain. "I… usually…can take it. But this… this is bad."

Vladimir touched her sweat-beaded forehead. It was burning. "You do have a fever. How long have you had this severe pain?"

"I …I don't know."

"I'd say about two days, maybe less," Nina volunteered. "Her temperature keeps getting worse. I have been checking it and it's up from 38 degrees Celsius (100.4 F) to 39 (102.2 F). That was an hour ago. She has not kept food down for two days. Throws up at the sight of it."

Vladimir carefully studied his patient as he listened to Nina. He removed his blood pressure monitor and stethoscope from his bag.

"Hanna, I'd like to listen to your heart and lungs and measure your blood pressure." She nodded, half closing her eyes. Her heart beat was rapid, but seemed strong. Her lungs were clear. Her blood pressure, though, was extremely high. "Now Hanna, I'm going to press on your abdomen. Tell me where it hurts the most."

Vladimir lightly touched her upper stomach and Hanna flinched. She grimaced with pain, but kept quiet. As he gently touched another spot, she yelled out, but as he came closer to the lower right corner of her abdomen, Hanna screamed. When he lifted his hand from that spot, her cry escalated.

"Oh my, I hope the neighbors didn't hear her scream." Nina interjected. "I don't trust them. They would be the first to turn us over to the Gestapo."

Vladimir didn't respond to Nina's concern. He suspected appendicitis. She had all the classic symptoms of appendicitis: fever, pain in the right lower side, extreme sensitivity to touch, and afterwards withdrawal of pressure, swelling and rigidity of the abdomen. He had to make a quick decision. From the pain exhibited by his patient, he was afraid the appendix might have already ruptured. In that case, under the present circumstances, that could be deadly.

"Hanna, I suspect that you have an inflamed appendix. You need surgery immediately. It really should be done in the hospital."

"Oh God no, no!" Nina wailed. "That won't do! Do you realize what would happen? They'll know she's a Jew. The hospital is in total German control. We'll all be killed. You must do the surgery here."

"Calm down, Nina. I realize that. What should be done and what needs to be done sometimes are two different things. We'll do it here and now. Usually my wife assists me in these matters, but there's no time to get her. I'll need your help. For starters, would you boil a pot of water for me?"

"Of course," Nina replied and ran up the steps.

"Hanna," Vladimir said turning again to his patient. "What we should do and can do is at odds with each other. I really should at least have you on a table, such as the one in the kitchen, but it would be better if we don't move you. We'll get it done here, don't worry."

Vladimir inspected closer the light source in the cellar. It was totally inadequate for an operation. However, on a hanging bulb above, there appeared to be an extension outlet to plug in yet one more lamp. "I'll be right back," he told Hanna and ran upstairs.

Nina and her husband were lighting the coal stove underneath a pot of water. They turned to Vladimir as he ascended the rickety steps. "We need better lighting. I could use a lamp with an extension cord to plug into the ceiling bulb."

"I understand," said the husband, a moment later he pulled out an extension cord out of a kitchen drawer and quickly left the room.

Vladimir placed his bag on the table and began removing instruments to drop into the water once it begins to boil. He searched his bag for retractors, but they were missing. He had a scalpel, forceps, and enough cat gut and silk sutures, "Damn, no retractors," he said almost at a whisper. But Nina overheard, "Is that a problem?"

"It could be. I have to think of something else we can use." He began to look around the kitchen for ideas. He spotted a silver table spoon in the sink. "Do you have another one like that?"

"Yes, why?" Nina was puzzled, but pulled out a drawer and took out another spoon.

"If you don't mind, I'll bend the two spoons at right angles. You should be able to bend them back afterwards without breaking them."

"All right. But what are you going to do with my spoons?"

"I don't have a retractor with me to pull the layers of skin and muscles apart. The two spoons working together will work as a retractor."

"Sure, go ahead and bend them." Vladimir quickly bent the spoons and dropped them along with the other instruments into the pot as the water began to boil.

"Nina, I'll need you to assist me in the operation. Do you think you can handle it?"

"I'll do anything you ask."

At that moment, Leon walked into the kitchen from the cellar. "I plugged in the cord and lamp, and it's ready to go." Leon looked into the pot, as was his habit to look to see what was cooking and spied the bent spoons.

"What the hell? What are those spoons doing there? And who bent them? Those were passed on in my family from the days of the magnates of Poland."

"Don't ask so many questions," Nina said, irritated. "We needed to bend them. He needs them to pull apart muscles. You always ask too many questions."

"What the hell?" Leon muttered. "All right, now what?"

"Let the instruments boil for a few more minutes, then let them cool and we'll begin, Vladimir said. In the meantime, I'll prepare Hanna for surgery. Leon, I'll need your help holding the lamp over the incision."

"I can do that, but I won't watch."

"He is so squeamish, he can't even kill a chicken for dinner," Nina retorted. "I have to do it. For a big guy, he's too soft."

"What do you mean?" Leon was offended.

"You don't have to watch, Leon, just hold the lamp steady over the area of the incision." With that said, Vladimir walked down the splintered steps and thought of the ether drip that he'd have to do. He realized that it would be difficult to concentrate on the operation in the body cavity and yet monitor the drip all at once. He needed yet another person to assist, and he wondered if he could trust either Leon or Nina with the assignment. *Too bad Slava is not here to help. Perhaps the older child can hold the lamp, although I hate for him to see his mother cut up. Someone should also be monitoring the blood pressure while the either is being inhaled. Damn! We'll just have to take a chance on that.*

"Hanna, we'll be ready to take out that inflamed appendix. With the ether, you won't feel a thing, all right? Afterwards, you'll feel much relief."

"Yes, doctor. Ow, it …really hurts," Hanna grunted.

"I know. Stay strong. It will be over soon."

Vladimir ran back upstairs and drained the water out of the pan, pulled out the instruments. Flinching at the heat, he laid them out on a clean towel that Nina had provided.

He scrubbed his hands at the kitchen sink and requested that the husband and wife do the same. He then carried the instruments wrapped in the towel back down and set them on a nightstand next to the bed. Leon and Nina followed him down. He had no choice but to show Hanna's oldest boy, who looked to be about eleven, how to hold the lamp over his shoulder and told him not to look while he worked on his mother. He proceeded to give instructions to Leon to observe how he gave Hanna the two drops of ether into gauze over her nose and mouth and unless he instructed him otherwise, to repeat the procedure every three minutes. Leon appeared horrified at this responsibility, but was determined to follow directions. The boy readily agreed to his task, and Nina stood by to assist with the operation itself.

A few minutes later, Hanna lay unconscious on her back. Vladimir inserted his hands into rubber gloves and made the first incision of approximately twelve centimeters (three inches). He cut through the skin. Next he went through a very thin layer of fatty tissue and muscles. Nina faithfully used the spoons to pull apart the layers as Vladimir instructed. Sweat appeared on her forehead, but she did not flinch once. Vladimir was also amazed at Hanna's son, who followed directions perfectly. Leon conscientiously timed the drops of ether, even after Vladimir made an adjustment in minutes for the drops.

Vladimir nimble fingers entered the abdominal cavity. At the large part of the large bowel he observed the infected and inflamed appendix that looked ready to burst. He quickly clamped an area behind the appendix, cut a piece of cat gut and tightly tied a portion of the bowel behind the appendix. With scissors, he snipped off the grossly inflamed appendix. After removing the culprit and placing it an empty jar, he cleaned the area and oversewed the outer area of the bowel. From inside out, he closed each layer of the abdomen using silk sutures for the skin.

"There, all done," Vladimir said, almost to himself. "Leon, stop the drip. We'll let Hanna wake up. She'll be just fine."

In a while, the patient woke up weak and groggy. Vladimir sat by her side, monitoring her blood pressure, while the rest of the people in the household stood around.

"Hanna, are you all right?" Nina asked, concerned.

Hanna mumbled something that no one understood. "She is doing just fine," Vladimir said with a tired voice. "Hanna, you should be all right now. I'll leave you for now, but will return later to check on you. I gave Nina some medicine that you should take for a few days. If we don't run into a problem with infection, you should be healed in a week, and I'll take the stitches out."

"Thank you doctor," Hanna whispered softly. "I don't know how to repay you."

"Don't worry about paying the doctor," Nina said. "Leon and I will figure out how to pay Dr. Moskalkov."

"Don't worry about that now. We'll work it out." Vladimir said yawning as he snapped shut his bag after dropping his now cleaned instruments into it. "I'm going to go now, but I'll be by late tomorrow."

Vladimir left the house, looking cautiously around. He wanted to avoid a police patrol if at all possible. Even though he was allowed to remain past the curfew, he did not want to be stopped and then have to lie to explain where he had been and why. The overcast sky rendered the night pitch black and the few streetlights that there were, were extinguished in case of air raids. Walking on the uneven stony sidewalk became precarious. Vladimir stumbled a few times. The roadway would be smoother, but he wanted to stay closer to the houses lining the street in case of a patrol. He would be less of a target, and he thought he would be able to slip into the shadows and not be noticed as quickly by the men.

Almost home, Vladimir began to relax somewhat as he rounded the corner from one street onto another. Suddenly, he felt his heart contract at the sight of narrow slits of the headlights as a truck approached. He briefly panicked, contemplating what he should do. He knew he was too exhausted to cope with the patrol this late in the night. He had to think fast. He jumped an adjacent short fence into someone's front yard. He stumbled into a freshly watered vegetable garden. He heard the squishing sound as his shoes sank into the soil and compost and then enveloped his ankles. A dog began to bark. Fortunately, the dog gave up quickly. His heart beat rapidly as he crouched behind the wooden fence. He heard the patrol approach slowly.

For a moment, his heart pounding harder, he thought it had slowed to a stop next to him. He heard voices in the vehicle. *Did they see me? Please, please keep going.* The truck moved on, away from him. Relieved, Vladimir peered over the fence. The coast was clear so he jumped the fence back onto the sidewalk. It turned out to be more difficult than he thought, and he barely made it over as the mud and dung weighed him down, ripping his trousers on a nail sticking out in the wood.

His shoes squished as he walked. His socks were caked with mud. He looked for a branch or a twig to scrape off the muck, but the dark night made finding anything impossible. He felt his medical bag; the mud lined it as well. *What a mess.* He scraped his shoes on the jagged rocks of the sidewalk, as he walked, knocking much of the mud off. When he finally came home, he left his shoes and socks on the porch as he entered the house. Slava flung herself into his arms in vast relief.

"Where have you been so long? I've been beside myself. I ran out of prayers. I had to keep repeating them. Oh my God! I'm so happy to see you!" Slava exclaimed as she showered Vladimir with kisses. "What happened to your shoes and socks?"

"Slava, I had to perform surgery at the people's home. It took a while."

"Well, what did you do, leave your shoes and socks there?"

"No. I got my shoes, even my socks muddy. I'm too tired to explain now. All I want is to sleep."

Chapter 23

THE APPROACHING Red Army was closing in on the German occupied territories. The way it looked, the war in Slonim may soon be over. At least those were the rumors circulating around the city. Vladimir and Slava knew that the advancing Soviet troops were more than a rumor. After guzzling down yet another bottle of schnapps, Hartman, in his visits, had lamented the fact. The Moskalkovs had lived and worked in Slonim relatively peacefully for sixteen months, thankful for a home in the midst of maelstrom. Now their future was again uncertain. *What does fate have in store for us this time?* They knew that colossal changes awaited them. They had already experienced so many uneasy adjustments in their lives. But the biggest change, consuming their thoughts at the moment, was the upcoming birth of their baby. And they could barely wait.

Despite the cold, bleak, wind-driven days of February, their hearts were warmed by the advent of a baby. When the time came to give birth, Vladimir asked two other doctors, Drs. Ostrovska and Savitski, to deliver the child. The delivery at the house went well. The moment his son made his way into the world, Vladimir grabbed the baby, wrapped him in a baby blanket, and floated from room to room with him. "I have a son! I have a son!" He babbled, overwhelmed by joy and excitement.

His contagious elation prompted Dr. Ostrovska to say, "Look at that boy, look at his long, thin fingers. He's going to be successful in life." Slava beamed with pride at those words.

They named their son Victor. They chose an international European name, not knowing where their son might end up. Victor was duly registered with the German administration and a German Birth Certificate was issued. Being devoutly Catholic, Slava wanted a Roman Catholic baptism, but they could not find a Catholic priest as even Father Aleksandr had now disappeared. No one seemed to know or would say what happened to him. Vladimir contacted the only remaining clergyman in Slonim, a Russian Orthodox priest, who agreed to baptize Victor. The doctors that helped deliver their son agreed to be Victor's godparents as both were of the Christian Orthodox faith.

As lifeless gray tree branches sprouted to vibrant green leaves in the spring of 1944, the Red Army continued its push west into Belarus and toward Poland on its way to Berlin. Vladimir and Slava witnessed the exodus of trains filled with German soldiers and equipment streaming out of Slonim, heading west. Vladimir recognized Soviet reconnaissance planes making more frequent flights overhead. They saw some locals packing up what they could carry into suitcases or pillowcases preparing to make their escape. Some hung onto railroad cars or left in horse and carts or trudged on foot, fleeing Slonim out of the Soviet advance. What Slava and Vladimir saw left a lump the size of a boulder in their stomachs. *What shall we do? We can't stay here. Yet can we go to Germany? Where can we hide?*

During his last visit, Lieutenant Hartman moaned that the end was near, and he, most likely, would be leaving with his detachment. "How long will it be before the Soviets get here?" Vladimir asked Hartman, with a catch in his voice.

"Probably by mid or late summer, your people will be here. Hopefully, we'll be pulled out before then. You're probably very excited, aren't you? Who would have thought that the rag-tag Slavs could defeat our mighty army?"

Vladimir did not answer. His mind wandered toward that probability. He knew he would be executed, as could Slava, yet at the same time, he could feel a sense of pride that the Red Army, after all the casualties, lack of supplies, weapons, and the general ineptness he had witnessed in the early months of the war, was now, indeed, able to, defeat possibly the best army in history. In reality, he surprised himself with his pride that he, too, was Slavic and had the strength to endure hell and still survive. He was also hopeful, unrealistically so, that no harm will come to them, and they will be able to return home unscathed.

Several more weeks passed and more trains were dispatched by the Nazi high command to evacuate their troops. More and more residents, mostly those that worked for the Germans, left. Mid summer came and Slonim was already morphing into another city. The strict discipline that the Nazis instilled on the population, by fear of torture and public hangings, began to break down. Food supplies, always meager, became even more so. For some, thievery became a way of life. Many of the couple's farm animals were stolen. Their days in Slonim were numbered and somehow they had to find a way out. Vladimir made arrangements with a local butcher to take all the remaining animals in the backyard. In return he asked for two boxes of smoked sausages.

As he approached his home from the butcher, Vladimir's heart fell to his knees upon spotting a German army vehicle in front of their house. He recognized the open Mercedes Benz as one used by the commandant. One soldier sat behind the wheel, the other stood next to the vehicle with a machine gun in his hand. Vladimir ran up to the house and walked in, breathing rapidly. He recognized the commandant's assistant, a tall, lanky officer sitting in the living room chair. Holding Victor, his wife sat glumly across. Both stood when Vladimir entered.

"The commandant wants to see you," said the officer. "Come with me now."

Vladimir glanced quickly at Slava. He saw her face turn ashen and her eyes widen. "What's this about?" Vladimir asked.

"You need to talk to the commandant. Your wife already asked that question more than once. I'm here to take you in."

With no choice left for him, Vladimir followed the officer to the car. *What now? Am I being arrested? What would he want from me?* The soldier opened the back door and waved him in. The officer walked around to the other side and slipped in next to Vladimir. He gave the order to the driver to proceed, and within a very long ten minutes, Vladimir found himself on a wooden chair in the outer office, waiting for the commandant. After thirty minutes, Vladimir was summoned into the office, his insides trembling. He stood meekly next to a burgundy leather side chair by the desk and waited for permission to sit. The commandant did not look up. He kept writing on a form as though Vladimir didn't exist. Finally, he put down his gold-plated fountain pen and raised his eyes to Vladimir. "Sit down, Herr Doctor."

Vladimir sat down; a headache was splitting his skull.

"You and your family are to leave Slonim within two days," the commandant said with a sneer. "I'm making arrangements for your travel."

Stunned as if a sack of cement fell on his head, he asked. "Where are we going?"

"I don't know yet, but somewhere in Germany."

"And if I choose not to go?" Vladimir surprised even himself how boldly he asked that question. The commandant appeared startled. His face turned from one of apathy to a scowl.

"You have no choice in the matter. You obey or you, your wife, and child will suffer serious consequences. Personally, I don't like the whole idea, but unfortunately we need doctors to tend to all the scum that are fleeing the Soviet dogs and polluting our fatherland. But I suppose, we also need them to rebuild our country."

Vladimir swallowed hard. He tasted bile in his mouth as he asked, "What can we take with us?"

"Take whatever marks you have accumulated, but they'll probably not be of any use. Take whatever you can carry. I would suggest if you have food, take that. There will be none on the many days you'll spend on the train. Maybe even none once you reach your destination."

With that he rose suddenly. Vladimir did as well. "Be here tomorrow at 1600 hours sharp, and my clerk will give you travel papers and tickets. Heil Hitler!"

Vladimir did not acknowledge the salute. He walked out and almost ran all the way home to give Slava the stunning news. *Here we go again, being moved to only God knows where.*

Slava reacted as Vladimir had expected; at first with disappointment and fear, and then with an optimistic attitude. "Well, that is actually good news. We wondered how we will escape the Soviets. This is our opportunity. The Blessed Virgin Mary is showing us a way out."

"What about living in Germany itself? We are not Germans. They will look upon as their enemies to be used by them. Who knows what bastards we will run into? If they find out I was in the Red Army, they may finish me off as well. We may be running away from one pack of wolves into the arms of another pack of wolves."

"Vladimir, that is so unlike you. You are so frustrated that you haven't even thought this through. Granted, we had not lived in Germany, but we have been here, in Slonim, under their strict and restrictive administration. And as long as we obey or at least pretend that we do, life here has been bearable. Look at this house, look how we lived here. For us life was more than bearable compared to the rest of the population. And who knows, we may be better off in Germany. I believe that Germany is going to fall soon. Life for us may even get better."

"Slavochka, I love you so. You are wonderful to be so flexible. I was more worried about you and Victor. I think that my problem is…" Vladimir's voice cracked and he walked over to the window and stared out.

"What is the problem, dear?"

Slow to respond, Vladimir turned and faced Slava, "We will be taken further away from our home. I will never see my mother or my sisters again. I am leaving the land that I love, not the government by any means, but my homeland where my grandmother and grandfather are buried." Tears began to run down his cheeks. He wiped them fiercely with his sleeve. "I'm sorry. I've noticed that with what I went through, tears seem to come easily to me. I'll get over it."

"I know you will. It'll take time for you to forget the horrors you suffered in that camp."

"I know. I'm tough and I'll be all right, maybe just a bit emotional once in a while. So with that off my chest, I guess we better prepare to leave."

At 1600 hours, Vladimir had his papers in his pocket. They were to leave the next day at 1553 hours from the Slonim depot headed for somewhere in Germany. Until then, Vladimir chose to treat a few more patients while next door, with great sadness, Slava packed. She placed her underwear, a couple of dresses, a skirt, blouse, black boots, and her coat in one of the two battered brown mid-sized leather suitcases that Vladimir had bartered for on the black market. She packed Vladimir's second suit, boots, underwear, shirts, and pants in the other. Victor's clothing and extra cloth diapers were spread out between the two suitcases. Slava decided to travel in her gray suit trimmed with black velvet. She placed two thousand marks, hand-kerchiefs, additional diapers, toothbrushes, tooth powder, combs, bar of soap wrapped in wax paper, and some medications into a roomy black leather handbag purchased on Paradna Street. *Thank God, this bag is so roomy*, she thought. *But it's a bit heavy. That's all right. I'll be able to carry it just fine.* Vladimir was to carry the travel documents in the inside breast pocket of his dark blue double-breasted suit.

His personal items along with his diplomas, family photographs, birth certificates and anything else that fit were packed in a newly-purchased backpack. They planned to take only the hats on their head and shoes on their feet. To leave more room in the suitcase, Vladimir decided to wear or carry his coat, even though the weather was frightfully hot. Whatever clothing, shoes, and household goods that they were unable to take with them were given away to friends and patients.

Before departure, Vladimir met with the butcher who handed him two mid-sized wooden boxes filled with sausages, made mostly of pork. Vladimir struggled to carry the bulky boxes home. He tried to find an efficient way to carry Victor, two suitcases, a backpack, a burlap bag, a large handbag, and the boxes the whole distance to the train station. *I got it! Slava and I can take turns carrying Victor. Slava can handle the handbag and I'll have the backpack. For the rest, we'll use the stroller, which we can leave behind at the station. We'll be all right.*

Three hours before departure, the stroller was loaded with the boxes of sausage. The suitcases were stacked on top. He topped off the pile with his precious medical bag that he just didn't have the heart to leave behind. Slava hauled out a mid-sized burlap bag with sewn on handles overflowing with a loaf of bread, cucumbers, tomatoes, peaches, and apples. Thrown in at the bottom were a couple of knives, spoons, forks, and bowls rolled up in three kitchen towels.

A deep sense of melancholy overcame Vladimir when it became time to lock the door to his clinic for the last time. Inside were the medical instruments and equipment that he was so proud to possess. Also left behind the now locked door were his dreams of his own clinic.

When he returned to the loaded stroller to tie down the load, he noticed that the front axle looked bent. The wheels sat at an angle. He was afraid that would happen, but hoped the stroller would hold up. *Don't panic, don't panic. We have to find another way. I need to tie ropes around the boxes for handles, and we'll just have to carry everything. We'll make it.* As he finished making handles for the sausage boxes, he heard a horse and wagon approach. He turned to see Boris and Anna.

"Get in! We came to take you to the station." Since helping Vladimir deliver the surgical furniture, they had become his steady patients, supplying egg-laying hens over the months as fees. Vladimir found out that they only looked tough on the outside. Their health, especially, Anna's, was not as good as both pretended it to be. She looked gaunt, and he knew that cancer was eating away at her.

"Let's load up." Boris and Anna grabbed the suitcases, boxes, and bags and threw them on the cart. Anna insisted that Slava sit next to Boris on the bench, while she and Vladimir were to dangle their legs from the back.

"How did you know that we were leaving?" Slava asked.

"Are you kidding? The whole town knows. I'll bet there will be more than a few of your friends and patients to see you off at the platform."

"Actually, I was hoping you'd come earlier," Slava said. "We had some clothes to give you."

"Well thanks, but we don't need anything. Besides, none of your clothes would have fit us, you skinny people." Anna chuckled at her comment. "Anyway, are you ready to go?"

Slava and Vladimir looked at the house with the comfortable furnishings. Vladimir gazed with sadness at the little sign on the wall that read *Doktor*.

With heavy hearts, they turned away and climbed up on the cart. They both thought, almost simultaneously, *what awaits us now?*

Chapter 24

PANDEMONIUM AND din awaited them at the old station—the same railroad depot from which Vladimir and Slava stepped off the stone curb and made their way into Slonim more than a year before. At that time, they both had a sinking feeling caused by the uncertainty of the unknown as they made their way down that asphalt street and over the bridge into town. Little did they know that Slonim, even under German occupation, would turn out to be a haven. The cruelty of the Nazis that so many of Slonim's residents had endured had barely touched them. They were fortunate. Their lives, at least for a short period of time, seemed almost normal in the midst of the struggles and horrors of war.

Now, again, the station represented a new upheaval. Once more, they faced an intense mental stress as their life was yet again uprooted. They were not alone. So many panicked people clamored for escape. They looked for a route out of town, a train perhaps, a buggy, just a horse.

Unable to bring his horse and cart closer to the station, Boris had to stop at a distance to drop the Moskalkovs off. He realized that it would not be an easy trek for the family loaded down with their belongings. He had no choice. Vladimir took Victor from Slava and helped her descend from her perch. Once she alit, he handed Victor back to her and quickly pulled down their belongings. With tears streaming down her cheeks, Anna hugged Slava and then Vladimir and wished them the best of luck. She then kissed the five month old Victor on the temple. Boris also got down and made his way to the back, leaving his old horse unattended. As he tried to help Vladimir with the luggage, the cart began to roll away.

Dumbfounded, he spun around just in time to see a thin older man, dressed in a soiled suit jacket and a tweed cap, carrying a bundle over his shoulder, pulling the horse and cart away. Luckily he could not go far due to the crowd, and Boris with clenched fists gave chase, yelling obscenities. The crafty man dropped the reins and disappeared into the throng. Boris grabbed the reins and managed to back the horse and cart back a few feet. People yelled at him to watch what he was doing as they scrambled out of harm's way. Meanwhile, Vladimir stood guard over their baggage.

"We better get out of here," Boris shouted to Vladimir in his booming, gruff voice. "There'll be others who'll want my horse and cart. This is madness. Look how many are fleeing the Red Army. Well, I'll welcome them. We'll be rid of the Germans and their sympathizers."

Some individuals overheard, even in the bustle. One of them yelled out to Boris, "You fool, you old man. Once the Soviets come, life will get even worse if we survive."

"Oh shut up and mind your business," Boris shouted. "I wasn't talking to you." Boris sidled up closer to Vladimir and placed his big hand on Vladimir's boney shoulder. "I know they want you to go to Germany and told you that you have to. Of course they would. A good doctor is needed everywhere. But if you want to stay, we'll hide you until the Nazi scum run away with their tails between their legs."

"It's not that easy," Vladimir answered Boris. "We really don't have a choice. It's complicated."

"Well, in that case, we'll say our goodbyes. Come on, Anna, let's go. Let's leave these misguided people."

Vladimir smiled, "Thanks for all your help, friend. God be with you!"

"And God be with you! Oh hell! Anna, here hold the horse. Whip anyone that touches it. I need to say goodbye to them properly."

Vladimir noticed a glistening of tears in his eyes as the crusty, gray-bearded man in a sweat-ridden straw hat gave him a bear hug. Vladimir felt almost crushed. His frail body still had not fully recovered from his ordeal as a war prisoner under the Germans. Boris then turned to Slava and did the same, squeezing the breath out of her. Then he rushed to join Anna on the dilapidated splintery seat of the old cart. "Wait," Slava yelled out to the old couple. She turned her attention at Vladimir. "Volodya, you don't really want to lug that medical bag with you. It's so heavy, and I'm sure they'll have instruments for you. Why don't we give it to Boris and Anna. They can trade it for something."

Vladimir understood. With everything they had to carry, that bag would be difficult. He sadly agreed and quickly took out the medications and handed the bag full of instruments to Anna. Anna's face lit up as she eagerly grabbed the bag.

They waved good-bye to the old couple as they slowly inched through the crowd. Boris was heard yelling to those in his way to step aside. With Victor held firmly to her chest with her left arm and the overloaded handbag dangling from its straps on her right forearm, Slava picked up the lighter of the two suitcases with the right hand. The straps of the handbag slipped down her arm to the wrist where they settled. It pained Vladimir to watch her struggle, "Here, let me carry the other suitcase. I can carry a suitcase and a box of sausages in each hand."

"No, it's too much for you. You still have that food bag to carry. I'll manage. I'll let you know if I can't."

Vladimir knew from previous experience that arguing with Slava was of no avail, so he acquiesced. Her stubborn streak had come out, and it would only be a waste of time to insist. After strapping on the backpack, he grabbed the rope handle of one of the boxes of sausages. With the same right hand, he lifted the suitcase. The box slid to its side and lay flat against the suitcase. He repeated the procedure with the other box and the bag. The weight was heavy and cumbersome, but he knew that the provisions would become indispensable.

The family fought and pushed their way through the throng of frantic people, some pulling their children by their hands, carrying their own few possessions.

Vladimir's back and arms ached. He knew that Slava struggled as well. They stopped several times to shift the load, from one arm to another. This procedure jostled Victor and made him even more fidgety. In one of the brief moments that they rested, Slava stroked his hair and quietly sang, rocking him to sleep.

There were many familiar faces in the crowd—patients, neighbors, store clerks. Some smiled and some even offered to help, if they could. But, they also had their arms and backs packed with their belongings, searching a way to squeeze through. Their panicky flight bewildered Vladimir. Why were so many bolting from the Soviets? He and Slava had no choice but to leave. *Surely not all of these people would be punished or executed. What did they do to warrant such dread? Or are they like me, anxious what would happen to them. Many are probably searching for freedom, to get as far away from Stalin and the Godless communists. I guess I can't blame them for trying to get out. But where are they going? Where are we going? Why would it be better fleeing into Germany, into the hands of the enemy?*

As these thoughts played out in his brain, Vladimir intermittently turned his head to make sure Slava was fine and behind him, following in his wake. Slowly, they were carried with the crowd towards the railroad depot. Six armed soldiers, positioned at the main entrance of the station, were now in view, three on each side of the doors. Many more soldiers were at both ends of the depot holding the crowd back, keeping anyone from the tracks.

Unable to move any closer, Vladimir and Slava put down their belongings, keeping them at their feet. They needed the respite. Suddenly they heard a familiar voice call out their names. They turned and saw their old friend, Agata, the first person that helped them in Slonim. Agata pushed her way through the crowd calling out their names. Finally squeezing through, she rushed up to the family throwing her arms around Slava, then Vladimir. With tears flowing down her checks, she shoved a wrapped bundle at Vladimir. "Here take this. You'll need it. It's a piece of smoked ham. Don't object. I want you to have it. God bless you. I will miss you so." She wiped the tears from her face and turned abruptly, disappearing into the crowd. Vladimir and Slava were touched with Agata's gesture.

"I'll miss her a lot," Slava said. "She was a good friend."

The crowd around the station had not budged. "We're running out of time," Slava sighed, a frown on her face. "We'll never make it."

"We'll make the train somehow. I'll try to push forward. Let's try it."

It was to no avail. The mass of people around them prevented any further progress. They were caught in a shoving match ahead. By way of a domino effect, they actually lost ground, their belongings almost trampled; only saved by Vladimir's quick action of jerking them towards him. Slava noticed Vladimir glancing, once again, at his watch. She saw him purse his lips. *He will never admit it, but he's worried. If we don't get in soon, we'll miss the train. Then I don't know what we'll do. Oh, mother of Christ, dear Jesus, help us board that train on time.* Slava understood that their travel documents were only for this one train. They were warned that no other passenger train would be available for them. They left three hours before the departure to make sure that they would make it in plenty of time. But this crowd was a surprise.

Vladimir glanced at his watch again, as if time would stand still for a little while. He began to lose hope of catching the train. *Maybe it will be delayed?* He thought. The scheduled departure, only fourteen minutes away, would be difficult to make with this crowd. The soldiers took their time examining documents at the door. He knew the Germans prided themselves on precision and would not delay the train. They were so close, yet so far away.

Suddenly, the crackling sound of gunfire hushed the crowd. Slava felt her blood drain away from her face.

Chapter 25

"OH MY God! Gunfire! They're shooting at the crowd!" Slava shrieked, her voice shrill, her face white. Vladimir assessed the crowd. He just happened to witness one of the soldiers at the end of the depot raise his rifle and fire twice over the heads of the throng. Vladimir flinched. Gunfire still never failed to have this effect on him.

"It's all right, Slavochka. It's just crowd control. One of the soldiers shot in the air, not at us."

"Oh God, no! They're so trigger happy, scared and angry. They could easily shoot at us. With the Red Army near, why not just take it out on us? I've seen it in their faces, especially the past week. They're demoralized and frustrated. Who knows what they'll do to us?"

Vladimir saw fear in her eyes, as she clutched Victor even more tightly to herself. "Slava, you always worry about something that may never happen. No matter how they feel, they are still disciplined troops, and I seriously doubt they'll just start shooting. Just relax, everything will be fine. We are the lucky few that have travel documents, and hopefully we'll be on the train soon. We'll be all right."

"You always say 'just relax' or 'we'll be all right.' Look at us. How are we supposed to relax?"

"Here, let me have Victor," Vladimir said. "I'll hold him for awhile. Rest your arms."

"No, he'll just wake up. Actually, I'm surprised that those gunshots didn't awaken him."

At that moment, a crisp German voice rang over a loud speaker. "Only those civilians with travel papers from the commandant are allowed to enter the station and the train. All others must clear the area." The message was repeated in broken Polish. "Clear the area immediately or our soldiers will sweep you away."

After living under German occupation, the people knew better than to disobey a Nazi mandate. These were not idle threats. Almost all complied. The throng left the immediate vicinity of the depot and moved back onto the street, past the long horseshoe drive leading up to the station. Vladimir at first didn't understand why they still hung around. Then it occurred to him. These people wanted to find a way to get onto a freight train where security was less stringent. Needing a source of labor, the Germans actually encouraged the younger people to catch those trains into Germany.

As the way toward the entrance gradually cleared, the Moskalkovs picked up their possessions and made considerable progress toward the station's front entrance. A few pushy individuals attempted to test the guards and try to get through. Using their weapons, the soldiers knocked them to the ground.

The Moskalkovs were almost at the entrance, relieved that they would soon be allowed to enter the station. Suddenly, the rumble of heavy military trucks with blaring horns made their way up the street, turning onto the drive in front of the station. People milling around on the street scrambled out of the way, yelling obscenities. Awakened by the commotion, Victor began to cry. He was hungry, but Slava was in no position to feed him while in line.

After the trucks stopped with screeching brakes, intermingling the oppressive humid summer air with a heavy smell of exhaust, soldiers began to jump off. Rifles or machine guns and rucksacks hung off their shoulders and backs. They waited in formation near the trucks until given the command to march forward. Once ordered, they made their way down the central sidewalk toward the entrance. The waiting passengers scrambled to get out of the way. Vladimir grabbed Slava's arm and pulled her to the side, bumping into someone behind them. Studying the soldiers, he agreed with Slava that indeed there was a look of defeat about them. They no longer seemed as tall and as proud. An air of dejection clung to their faces. Instead of sureness and arrogance in their step, their formation now appeared sloppy and tired.

Vladimir's eyes picked out a familiar face. Lieutenant Hartman lumbered down the sidewalk. Burdened with a larger than normal rucksack, he had a pistol strapped to his side. He noticed the Moskalkovs and gave them a quick wave of his right hand. Both Vladimir and Slava smiled. He returned a lop-sided grin. He then seemed to straighten up and hold his head higher as he marched past them. Slava called out, "Goodbye, Lieutenant, good luck to you." Hartman's wide grin stretched from ear to ear, exposing his cigarette-stained teeth. He did not say a word, only nodded his head. Strangely, Vladimir hated to see him go. Over the course of a year, when Hartman seemed to befriend them, he actually began to look forward to the man's visits. He enjoyed the historical and philosophical talks. Hartman became their window into the war and the world. Notwithstanding the Nazi propaganda, especially with a few drinks, the man gave them the straight scoop as far as he knew it. Vladimir's eyes followed Hartman as he went through the door. He turned out to be a friend. Vladimir knew he would miss him. *War creates strange bedfellows.*

Finally, all the soldiers passed through into the station and the line of passengers regrouped. "What time is it?" Slava asked Vladimir.

"We have four minutes. Don't worry, we'll make it. We're so close now. Besides, it'll take some time for all those soldiers to board."

Slava kept rocking Victor and speaking softly to try to get him to stop crying but to no avail. He was hungry, needed a diaper change, and nothing else mattered to him at the moment. Finally, they were second in line.

Visibly irritated at Victor's incessant weeping, a middle-aged couple with three older children, laden with suitcases and backpacks, stood before them. They were not German. They spoke Russian, and judging from their somewhat fashionable and expensive garments, Slava surmised that most likely the man worked for the Germans in some high capacity. But then, Vladimir and she were also well dressed, yet did not work for the Germans.

The soldiers at the door were reviewing identification papers along with travel authorizations. It appeared the family in front of them had a problem. The man raised his voice as he and his wife became agitated. Slava overheard that they could not find one of their children's identification cards. The guard would not let the boy through. The boy and his siblings began to cry. The father, his narrow face red, blurted out, his voice rising with every syllable, "What do you mean; we can go through, but not our son? Can't you see he looks just like his sister? He is our boy. Listen here, you, I know all your superiors. You will be in big trouble. Now let us through! You hear!"

The guard was in no mood to put up with the man. He grabbed his rifle, leaning against the side of the stucco building. With a hand on each end of the weapon he began to push the family out of the way. The man now irate, yelled obscenities at the soldier, again threatening to have his head. *Oh this is bad. The man is a fool to argue with them.* No sooner had Vladimir thought that, the soldier used the butt of his rifle to knock the man to the ground, splitting his upper lip, perhaps breaking his jaw. His wife screamed, the children squealed. "Now get out of here!" The soldier yelled at the family, pointing the rifle at the man on the ground.

The other guard pointed his finger at Vladimir and barked, "You're next, show me your papers."

Vladimir and Slava approached, both breathing shallowly from the incident played out in front of them, praying that the soldier will not take his anger out on them. The guard studied them carefully, making a point of comparing the photograph to their faces. Victor kept up his barrage of bawling.

"Keep him quiet!" The soldier growled at Slava. Slava rocked her infant son more vigorously. Victor cried louder. The soldier began to lose his patience. He shoved the documents back to Vladimir, almost punching him in the stomach. "Go, get out of here," pointing to the front door. Vladimir and Slava scampered as quickly as possible through the entrance, Vladimir banging the box of sausages against the sash of the door.

The station was practically empty. Through the large windows leading out to the platform, they saw the standing crowd of passengers, mostly uniformed soldiers. Vladimir and Slava glanced at each other and both exhaled in unison as no one seemed to be boarding yet. They scurried across the worn floor toward the platform. As they made their way out the rear door, a man in a gray suit holding two suitcases pushed past them back into the station and commented with a sneer, "What's your hurry? You're not going anywhere. No one is."

Chapter 26

PASSENGERS BEGAN filtering back inside the station. Slava saw the rush for seats and quickly turned back and slid into the nearest vacant seat for herself and Victor. She placed her small suitcase in the adjacent seat, saving it for her husband. Vladimir lingered behind wanting to get the attention of the man to find out what was happening. "Why aren't we boarding?" Vladimir shouted out. Not responding, the man plowed deeper into the station and plopped down onto a wooden bench. He appeared exhausted, his face flushed with exertion. A woman, lugging more bundles than Vladimir thought possible, overheard him and volunteered the information.

"The tracks need repair. Bombings, you know." Sweat ran down her face, her colorful yellow and white summer dress was drenched from the heat. Not a breeze flowed through the large open arched windows of the stuffy depot. The woman shook her head from side to side in disgust. "It may take hours, maybe even days. This is miserable, absolutely miserable, and I'm so hot," the woman complained as she scurried to find a seat.

Like all the passengers, Vladimir and Slava were hot and thirsty. Wearing layers of clothing to save room in the suitcases, they were both overdressed for the humid July weather.

Vladimir sat down next to Slava. She was finally able to feed Victor. He laid down his load and forcibly exhaled as he took off the backpack, setting it down between his feet. He retrieved one of the two Polish Army water bottles that he was surprised to find on the black market. It cost him two hundred marks, but he thought it would be well worth the cost in case of an evacuation. Months earlier, he felt that they may be facing an evacuation, particularly after his conversations with Lieutenant Hartman. He held the bottle up for Slava to take a drink before he gulped two swallows for himself. He repeated the procedure, then screwed the cap back on and placed the bottle back in the satchel. Not knowing where he would find clean water to refill his containers, he was determined to save as much as he could.

"Phew, as soon as Vitya (diminutive for Victor) is finished, we better change him. He sure needs it," Vladimir said with a slight smile, twitching his nose.

"It's your son, the smell should be sweet to you," Slava laughed out loud, the first that Vladimir heard from her that entire day.

"Of course it's sweet," Vladimir returned the chuckle. "I hope we brought enough diapers."

"We'll do fine," Slava said. "We'll have to wash them out on the train. I brought soap."

As Slava nursed their son, Vladimir studied the interior of the large station. The peeling faded lime green paint on the plaster walls masked how splendid the old building must once have been. Yet now, the white wainscoting had been ripped off the walls, the short pieces still left were gouged with large splinters readily visible. The covers of the overhead lamps were missing as were many of the light bulbs. The wooden floor was scuffed and badly needed varnishing. *In war not only the people suffer, but beautiful buildings are neglected and left for ruin and scavenging. Who knows, this station may not even survive until the end of the war,* remembering hearing that the Nazis demolished cities and towns as they retreated.

Fed and changed, Victor was happy, cooing as the parents fussed and played with him. He giggled when his mother moved his arms and legs up and down. His little mouth puckered up as he peered at his proud parents.

Finally, in the late afternoon, an announcement called the passengers to board.

Chapter 27

THE TRAIN loomed before them. Steam drifted out of the black engine. Once again destiny thrust the Moskalkovs westward. Where were they going now? What would become of them? All they knew is that they must go. They must strive to survive even if it takes them deeper into enemy territory. For now they had yet another life dependent upon them. They had Victor.

It seemed just yesterday, but in fact, twenty months had passed, since the last time a similar train carried them to some unfamiliar place. At least then Vladimir and Slava knew their destination—Slonim. Now, as they nervously stood on the platform, they felt they were about to be hurled into a vortex. Just the thought of more war awaiting them clenched their insides. Both were wound up like a tension spring. Slava's temples throbbed as blood rushed to her head.

Clutching their tickets, they were swept up with the wave of the crowd once the boarding order sounded, propelling them toward the open doors of the cars. Their destination was a class C green-colored coach. In the confusion and ensuing frenzy of fellow passengers, Vladimir and Slava finally made it inside, barely able to push their belongings through the rushing crowd of desperate humanity around them. Inside, hard wooden benches lined the sides. The center of the coach was bare of seats, left purposely empty for freight and luggage. Luckily, they found a place to sit, squeezing in between other passengers. There was barely enough room for two of them, let alone for their baby, Victor. Vladimir stashed the sausage boxes, the burlap bag and the backpack under their seats. He shoved the suitcases in front of them, slightly pushing other passengers' bundles back. The woman across the aisle grunted, shot him a nasty look and pushed a portion of the pile back toward Vladimir, leaving just enough room for a narrow aisle. Vladimir shrugged fatalistically, *what else am I supposed to do?*

That settled, he glanced on either side of the bench to see if perhaps someone could squeeze over a little to give them more room. No such luck. The passengers were so packed together that they barely had enough space to move their elbows. "We'll just have to hold Victor carefully on our laps," he told his wife disappointingly.

"No problem," Slava said. "It'll be all right with you, won't it, my joy, my little prince?" Slava crooned softly, bouncing her tiny son on her knee. Afterwards, she snuggled and rubbed her nose on his soft belly. "You're going to have fun, going on a train ride." Victor smiled a toothless smile. Craving attention, he swayed back and forth, wiggling his little body and cooing. Both parents laughed at his silly sounds.

"Here, let me have him," Vladimir said, stretching out his arms. Slava handed the baby to him, and the father laid him across on his lap. He then proceeded to exercise his son's little legs and arms, repeatedly kissed his bare feet. Slava withdrew a baby bottle filled with water from her handbag, handing it to Vladimir for Victor. The baby earnestly sucked on the rubber nipple, grasping firmly his father's finger, both parents proudly watching and smiling.

As his infant son slept in his arms and the train rocked away with a steady rhythm of metal wheels grinding on metal track, Vladimir began to take stock of his surroundings. His nostrils were by now accustomed to the reek inside the coach from the jam-packed, perspiring passengers and their food provisions in the heat and humidity of late July 1944.

This moving rectangular box, with its constant sway, would be their home for at least a number of days. Vladimir and Slava discussed the length of the trip on several occasions. They would have to traverse the full length of Poland, about five hundred kilometers and then, depending on how far they would be taken into Germany, could be another hundreds of kilometers. If they went no further than Berlin, the total kilometers from Slonim would be 940.

The train plugged along at a snail's pace, stopping in both large and small towns. A whole night seemed to go by, yet they had not reached the large city of Bialystok, only 131km from Slonim. Vladimir's heart sank with the thought that the trip may take not days, but a week or more. *I hope we'll have enough food. We should. We're probably better off than most of these people.*

"Do you think we have enough provisions for this journey?" Slava asked as if reading his mind. "If this is full speed, we're crawling."

"It's uncanny how you do that. I was just thinking that and here you say it. Don't worry, we'll be just fine."

"Here you go again with your 'don't worry.' Next you'll say, 'just relax,' won't you?" Slava grumbled, teasingly.

Vladimir grinned, "You think you know me so well, don't you?"

"Of course I do, you're my soul mate after all. Anyway, have you noticed how this car had been shot up? It reminds me of the train from Baranovichi to Slonim. And just like there, I see a couple windows covered by cardboard and a couple more with no glass or cover of any kind. At least our window and the ones across are not covered. We can look out."

"In this weather, that isn't all bad," Vladimir said. "We'll have some ventilation from the bullet holes and the open windows. Can you imagine how cold we'd be in winter?"

In the car, almost all the men wore fedora hats. A few had caps, but all wore suits. With the excruciating heat, some took off their jackets, as had Vladimir. Early on, most of the women had on a head cover of some sort—hat or a scarf. But after a few hours in the stifling car, those came off too.

There were a dozen or so children, ages two to the teenage years. Victor was the only infant. It didn't take long for these children to grow restless. Complaints of "I'm hungry" from them grew louder. The language in the coach was mainly German, although words in Russian, Byelorussian, and Polish were frequently heard. There were no smiles, no laughter. The passengers sat with stoic or vacant expressions, lips turned downward, eyes tired, almost lifeless in despair. When Vladimir or Slava tried to make eye contact, there was no response—their glances slid away.

Vladimir studied his fellow passengers. He understood their state of mind. The Russians, Byelorussians, and Poles were escaping the Soviets and the harsh communist way of life under Stalin. They must have held important jobs under the German occupation to be granted permission to travel by passenger train. They, he thought, hated the occupiers, but chose to survive and cooperate with the regime. They knew that Stalin would punish anyone who held a job under the Germans as a traitor. Their fate was either execution or confinement in a gulag in Siberia. To escape the likely fate, the refugees abandoned their way of life, their countries, land, homes, and families.

The Germans traveling on the train, on the other hand, were running away in defeat. Under Hitler's policy to repopulate Eastern Europe with Germans, thousands settled in occupied lands. Over the period of occupation, they invested time and money into building themselves new lives, acquiring lands and homes. Now, all was lost. *Life will not be easy for them back in Germany either with this raging war. They will face defeat and hardship there as well.* Then there were those numerous Germans who had settled in Russia years ago, even hundreds of years ago, invited by Catherine the Great. They made homes along the Volga and other locations in Russia and lived among the Russians. They too, were now fearful for the suspected retaliation for Hitler's actions in Russia. *Some of them may also be on the train, even though they may not speak German but Russian.*

"You're so deep in thought," Slava said. "What's on your mind?"

"Look at the people here. Look how miserable they look. The Germans are running away with their tails between their legs and the rest of us are in no better shape. It's an awful feeling. It tears me up to leave our homeland."

"Oh, Volodya, it may be only for a short time, and we'll be able to go back."

"No, my little one, I'm afraid that would be impossible. I suspect that I'll never see my mother or sisters again. I will never feel the Belorussian dirt between my toes where I grew up. I will never see the tall grass and soaring birches swaying in the breeze. Actually, I see them now in my mind waving 'good-bye.' Are we fools for leaving? Should we have stayed and faced the consequences? We know what

Stalin has in store for us, but we don't have a clue what Hitler and his henchmen will do to us."

"You're just emotional right now. It's understandable. I may never see my parents again, but we've been over this before. We have no choice. It's life versus death for us."

Vladimir glanced at a woman on the other side of the car staring unseeingly into space behind him. Her deep blue eyes had tears rolling down her wrinkled cheeks. He watched her for a minute, and then his eyes drifted to the open window where the morning light illuminated strands of birch, fir, and pine trees. His eyes welled up, a tear making its way down his sweaty cheek. He caught himself, angry for showing so much emotion. *I'm strong, tough, and can take anything that is dished out to me. So can Slava.*

"The moment for feeling sorry for ourselves has passed," Vladimir said to his wife. "I always believed that everything happens for a reason. Anguish makes us stronger and tougher. Something good will come of this." The words buoyed him. He needed a pep talk for himself. Suddenly he felt as if he could take on the world.

Smiling, Slava leaned over and kissed Vladimir on the cheek. "We are certainly not alone. Have you looked out the window as the train plugs forward? Look at all the pitiable souls lugging their precious belongings bundled together in sheets and pillowcases, going to only where God knows. They trudge along on both sides of the tracks pulling their wagons westward. It's been like this since we left the station."

"Yes, I've noticed. What a sight. A few more fortunate have a horse and cart. And look at that German column of cars and trucks trying to make their way through that crowd, probably running over the people. What a mess?"

"What a migration of people. Oh, Volodya, see how lucky we are. We're cramped, hot, and miserable, squeezed together on these hard oak seats, but at least we don't have to walk."

"And we have food that should last us," Vladimir said. "Speaking of which, let's eat some of that ham that Agata gave us."

Vladimir retrieved the small package from the bag. With his pocketknife, he sliced two generous portions, using up one-half of the total. He gave a slice to Slava and began chewing on his piece. Gradually, many in the car began pulling out a portion of their supplies. Hard boiled eggs seemed to be the most prevalent as the aroma of eggs mingled with sausages, ham, dried jerky, and, of course, body odor. Slava saw a family eating fresh tomatoes, so she proceeded to pull one out of the bag. She also broke off a chunk of bread.

"We're almost out of water," Vladimir said. He took his metal canteens, and made his way to the water reservoir, a large metal jug with a spout at the bottom. The container sat on a table in a small compartment across from the restroom. In normal times, there would have been a samovar for tea and the table lined with glass mugs. But with this refugee train, those items were absent.

The water was warm but looked clean. Vladimir filled the first canteen, but the water ran out before he could fill the second one. A woman waiting behind him began yelling in German that he took all the water. Vladimir offered to share his water.

"I don't want any of your germs," she yelled out. He quickly turned and walked away from the angry, sweaty woman. She followed him, yelling obscenities, until her husband grabbed her arm and led her back to her seat. Everyone turned to stare. Somewhat embarrassed, he was stopped by another woman, pulling on his arm as he walked by.

"Don't feel bad or think anything of it. We're all hot and irritable. This is hard on everyone here. She's just taking out her frustration on you."

"Thank you," Vladimir said as he returned to his seat. While he was gone, his neighboring fellow passenger slid over and occupied half of his space. On his return, she reluctantly slid back to her spot allowing Vladimir to sit down again. Vladimir smiled at her as he approached, but she did not return a smile, her face expressionless.

"What in the world? What was that about?" Slava asked with concern.

As Vladimir explained, Slava glanced toward the angry woman, who now sat motionless staring at the floor.

"I just hope they fill the jug soon."

"I'm sure they will," Slava said. "Hopefully, we'll be able to get out and walk around. Victor needs some fresh air, don't you, my baby."

"Who knows what they will decide to do. They did at the first stop, but I didn't want to leave my seat and lose it."

"We'll have to take turns. Assuming, of course, that we'll be allowed to get out."

Chapter 28

THE DOOR to the coach squeaked open. An old, stooped man sporting a bushy white mustache and a goatee ambled through, limping noticeably. Slava studied him for a moment. Her eyes focused on a brass emblem depicting a winged wheel fastened to the collar of the man's pale blue uniform. All conversation in the coach ceased as the conductor began checking tickets and travel authorizations.

Rising to grab his suit jacket from the rack above the seat, Vladimir withdrew the documents from the inside pocket and sat down waiting for the conductor. He knew that his papers were in order, having been checked numerous times before they were allowed to board the train; nevertheless, the fact that someone else was to check them yet again, using his authority, made him uneasy. He felt a slight twinge in his stomach as the man approached. Vladimir handed him the papers. The old man barely looked at them or Vladimir or Slava. Without a word, he made a check in red ink from his fountain pen on the tickets and slowly proceeded to the person sitting next to Vladimir.

That person was a well-groomed German woman in her early forties, traveling with her two teenage daughters. She and the children were dressed impeccably in obviously expensive clothing. The first few hours of the journey, she wore her blue straw hat exposing a part of her short auburn hair. When she finally had enough of her hat, she took it off and carefully laid it on top of her overcoat stored in the rack above. Slava noticed the styled locks of her hair. She appeared unfriendly and obviously felt uncomfortable sitting next to Vladimir. Vladimir surmised that she hated the fact that he was a Slav. Hitler had tried hard to ingrain in the German minds that the Slavs were subhuman and should thus be exterminated. He understood the frustration of the German people. They were the one now being chased out by the despised Soviet army. They were the losers, and that is a very hard lump to swallow.

After having rubbed elbows with each other for hours, Vladimir tried to engage the lady in a friendly conversation. He knew he would soon have to learn to live among the Germans soon, so he might as well begin to communicate with at least this neighbor.

When she happened to look in his direction, Vladimir decided to break the ice. "We are certainly in a tight fit here," he commented in his broken German. She stiffly nodded and turned her head away. Her attitude was not unexpected by both Vladimir and Slava, so they decided to keep to themselves.

Meanwhile, a little boy kept circling the inside of the coach around the stacked luggage, irritating the passengers who had to move their feet out of the way to let him through as he came around by them. On his fourth circle, he stopped to view Victor. The baby, slouching on Slava's lap, waved his arms excitedly each time the boy walked by.

"How old is your baby?" The boy asked in German. "What's his name?"

Slava answered and then proceeded to comment on how well dressed he looked in his tan leather shorts and a frilly white shirt. She then asked whether the children seated with their parents across the coach from them were his brothers and sisters. "Yes, we had to leave, and we're going to stay with my grandmother in Germany. She lives in a tall building in Berlin."

"That's nice. You'll be able to visit her soon. You're probably very anxious to see her."

"We sure are. Although, my father is not very happy about it. I overheard him tell my mother, 'Who wants to live with a mother-in-law?'"

Both Slava and Vladimir laughed out loud. Vladimir continued chuckling after eyeing his son. The baby's eyes were fixed on the boy. His lips stretched in a toothless smile, his mouth looking as if he wanted to say something. When the boy was ready to leave, Vladimir said, "Come back again and visit with us."

After hearing Slava speak fluent German, the formerly unfriendly neighbor warmed up and struck up a conversation with the Moskalkovs, especially with Slava. As the two women conversed, Vladimir caught in the middle, suggested that he exchange places with Slava.

Her name was Helga. The woman planned to reunite with her husband, a civilian engineer in the employ of the Third Reich. "He is waiting for us in Berlin." She began to sob, complaining how badly her life has turned out. "I don't think our army will be able to stop the Soviet advance. I'm so afraid they will be in Berlin. My husband wrote to me that Berlin and most of Germany is being bombed by the British and Americans, those bastards!" She paused as she pulled a white linen monogrammed handkerchief out from the pocket of her light gray skirt. She wiped her eyes and nose. "What are we getting into? What's going to happen to us? Germany is out of food and fuel and our enemies are at our doorstep."

"We're in the same boat," Slava said. "As my husband always says, 'we have to be strong.' Somehow, we'll all survive. Trust God." Vladimir sat listening to the conversation, or at least as much as he could understand, holding Victor in his arms. *That's really strange that we are in the same boat,* he thought. *How ironic. By circumstance, we will be subjected to the German enemies. I suppose now, my homeland is my enemy as well. I suppose when they bomb a city, as Helga had mentioned, the bombs will not discriminate as to who is a German or who is not. What a predicament.*

"That's all we can do," the woman continued. "I am so ashamed. If anyone from the Party heard me say this, I would be arrested as a defeatist or traitor or something. I am just simply terrified."

She continued to wipe tears from her eyes and fell silent, staring into space. Slava put her arm around the woman's shoulders and embraced her. "We have no choice but to go on. We'll make it. God is watching over us."

"If only that were true. I don't believe it anymore."

Slava did not know what else to say. In her mind she thought to say, *Well, you reap what you sow.* Of course, she never uttered the words. Always diplomatic, she tried to say the right things without confrontation.

After a moment of awkward silence, the woman asked Slava who they were, eyeing Victor and actually smiling at the baby.

"We are also trying to get away from the Red Army."

"But why? You are from there. What are you afraid of?"

"You need to know the ruthlessness of Stalin to understand. We know what fate awaited us if we had stayed in Belarus or Poland."

"Well, maybe I don't understand. You are going into Germany. That must be even more frightening. After all, we are your enemy, and the whole country may yet collapse."

"I sincerely pray that we are not going from the frying pan into the fire. I guess…" Slava hesitated. Vladimir glanced at her, curious to hear what she was about to say. "I guess we don't know exactly what awaits us, but we certainly do know the outcome had we stayed."

Suddenly, brakes of the train screeched to a halt. Passengers nearly tumbled from their seats. Helga's hat flew off the rack and struck Vladimir on his head. While Vladimir handed the hat back to Helga with her apologizing profusely, Slava eyes darted out of the window. Soldiers scurried out of the train seeking cover in the tall green grass of the adjacent fields. No sooner had Slava cried out, planes began strafing the train.

Chapter 29

THEY WERE sitting ducks. Caught in a flurry of gunfire, Vladimir and Slava instinctively dove onto the filthy floor of the narrow aisle. The barrage came from planes overhead. German soldiers returned fire. For Vladimir and Slava, it was déjà vu. They had been through this before. Slava pushed Victor toward the boxes under the bench and covered him with her side, shoulder, and arm. Vladimir tried to shield both of them with his own thin body. Helga and her children fell on top of Vladimir and Slava, while the woman on the other side of them inadvertently kicked Slava on the shoulder while she slid down into the aisle.

Passengers screamed in panic as a spray of bullets peppered the train car. Shards of splinters and glass fragments from the windows flew indiscriminately in all directions. Squashed on the floor by the other passengers, Vladimir thought his family would be protected, yet he worried about those at the top of the pile such as Helga and her children. The intermittent screams of pain confirmed his fears that there would be wounded, perhaps even loss of life. *We just can't get a break—one thing after another.*

In a matter of what seemed hour-long minutes, the grinding thunder of airplane engines and the resound of weapons finally stopped. With screams and moans, passengers began to get up. It seemed to take forever for the family on top of the Moskalkovs to disentangle their arms and legs and pull themselves off. Still penned down, Vladimir heard Victor cry. Assuming that because his son was crying he must be all right, he called out to his wife, "Slava, are you all right? You're not squashed, are you?"

"I'm fine. It's just a little hard to breathe, especially in this heat."

"We should be up in a minute. Poor Victor. The racket really frightened him." Vladimir said. "He won't stop crying." *Come on, lady, get off of me!*

"I don't blame him," Slava said. "The attack is almost too much to take. I am also ready to cry. We could have been killed! Oh God."

Finally, Helga and her girls managed to arise. Vladimir quickly darted up and helped Slava to her feet. She lifted Victor up gently while still on her knees and handed the baby to Vladimir. The father took his son and cuddled him to his chest, while Slava straightened up and stretched, wincing as she rubbed her shoulder. Rocking the baby, Vladimir quietly hummed a tune that he knew would calm him. Slava took out a baby bottle of water and held it to Victor's mouth. Their tiny son enthusiastically sucked on the rubber nipple.

A blood-curdling scream erupted in the car, causing Victor to cry again. A woman discovered her husband's lifeless body lying next to her in the aisle. A stray bullet pierced the roof and struck the man. She and her daughter huddled again in their seats, keening. Slava looked in their direction. The woman's sobs brought on her own tears.

Luckily, there were no other deaths in the car, but there were several people wounded by flying glass, including Helga's daughter. "Oh God, oh God!" Helga cried out. "You've been stabbed with the glass. Oh God!"

"Let me help you, I'm a doctor," Vladimir offered. He handed Victor back to Slava and began examining the back of the girl's left shoulder. A narrow, pointed piece of glass pierced her frilly white blouse, leaving a blood stain. He had no idea how deep the fragment entered. "Hopefully, it's not too deep, just a superficial wound. I need to cut the blouse around the shard."

"Yes, of course. Please do what you can. We have other blouses."

Vladimir gently separated the fabric and exposed the wound, still oozing blood. He slowly pulled out the piece. The fragment pierced the skin and muscle about three millimeters deep. He turned to Slava and said, "Could you get the iodine and a small piece of gauze out of my backpack?" Slava pulled out the bag and fumbled in it until she found what was needed.

Vladimir took the items and told the child, "Now, young lady, this is going to sting. You are a brave girl, aren't you?" The girl nodded, then let out a scream as Vladimir applied the iodine to her wound and quickly covered it with gauze, holding it down firmly to stop the bleeding. "See, that's all it was," showing the shard to the girl. "You will not even need stitches."

As Helga kept up her thanks, he brushed away her words of gratitude and went on down the aisle to see who else needed help. Three more people had similar wounds.

When he returned to the seat between Slava and Helga, a couple of railroad workers entered the car. They quickly scanned the car, saw the dead body and started dragging it out. The deceased's wife and daughter followed them out, only to return a half hour later to resume their seats. The train had yet to move forward.

The couple sat silently. Even Victor was quiet, playing with a rubber toy. They felt extremely sorry for the poor woman and her daughter. *What are they going to do now?* Slava thought. *What did they do with the body? There must have been others on this train. Surely they had a place for them and will take them to the next station.* Suddenly, their son began to cry and the parents knew he was hungry.

Slava looked tired and frazzled as she fed Victor. When she finished, Vladimir said, "I think it's time to take out a sausage. I've been thinking about biting into one for hours."

"That's a wonderful idea," Slava said. "Here, hold Victor. I'll get it." She slid the box from underneath her, halfway into the aisle, untied it and pulled out a stick of a pork sausage which she broke in half. One half she returned to the box and covered it up. She split the remaining half and handed his share to Vladimir. As she did so, she noticed the looks on the other passengers' faces. They were watching her eat. She felt uncomfortable and guilt suddenly overcame her. She felt guilty that they were so well prepared. Nevertheless, she also realized that they were in no position to offer any of their food supply to the others. Lieutenant Hartman had advised them to take care of themselves. He told them to haul as much food as possible, not only for the trip, but also for Germany as provisions there were scarce.

With that advice in mind, Slava decided to ignore her guilty conscience. She needed to overcome her feeling of guilt for the sake of their survival. Vladimir had often told her that in war, the everyday niceties that we live by in society are unfortunately often discarded. It becomes every man for himself. She shuddered at the thought, but knew that was the way it was.

Suddenly, Slava felt a light tap on her shoulder. "Excuse me. Do you, by chance, know what the reason is for the long holdup?" The formerly unfriendly woman to Slava's right asked, after fashioning a crooked grin. Her friendly demeanor did not fool Slava. She saw how her neighbor covertly eyed the box of sausages. Slava's previous attempts at friendliness had been ignored, as the woman scowled and turned away, refusing to even acknowledge her. Yet now, even as she knew that Slava would have no better knowledge than she herself had as to why the train had not moved, the woman had extended a peace branch.

"No, I have no idea. Perhaps the train is damaged."

"Oh that would be simply awful. By the way, I'm Maria and this is my husband Rafael." Rafael's forced smile exposed the only two teeth in his mouth. And this fine lad is our son, Yan. You must be Polish as well, since you speak it so well."

"Actually, I'm Byelorussian. We spoke Polish at home since both of my parents are Polish." Slava reluctantly introduced herself and Vladimir.

"You have such a beautiful baby. What's his name?"

Slava told her and wondered if the neighbors will now give them any peace. Suddenly the train jerked forward. It quickly picked up speed as the wheels squealed along the metal tracks. Slava turned back to her own little family as her neighbor focused on her own. The train finally settled to a smooth run for an hour, when it again screeched to a stop, throwing some passengers out of their seats.

Chapter 30

THE TRAIN stood motionless. No steam escaped from the massive rusting black locomotive. An hour dragged by, then another. Travelers were allowed to leave the train and wait outside, but few left, afraid of losing their possessions or seats to stowaways or other passengers. Bored and restless, some children repeatedly made their way up and down the aisles, pushing each other, annoying fellow passengers, except for little Victor. Propped up against his father's chest, the baby enjoyed watching them run past him, gumming his mouth and clapping his little hands.

"Hold on to my seat," Vladimir said to Slava. "Victor and I are going to go for a walk outside, get some fresh air."

"Are you crazy? It is pitch black out there now—no moon or stars. Better not go. You'll be pushed aside or the train will suddenly take off, and you'll be unable to get on. Why don't you just go for a walk with him inside the train? I know they won't let you in the cars where the soldiers are, but at least you can walk up and down in the C-class coaches. Maybe you can find out why we've stalled so long."

Vladimir turned to gaze out the window. He realized that Slava was probably right. *She always seems to be right.* In the dim light emitting from the train car, he saw some unsavory looking characters hanging around who could quite easily rob him or even take Victor. "All right. We'll take a stroll up and down the train as far as we can go, won't we, Victor?"

Slava's eyes followed her loved ones walk down the aisle toward the door. Unexpectedly, all the lights inside went out—total blackness. Vladimir hurriedly struggled to rejoin Slava, bumping into passengers and baggage. Slava shouted out his name to guide him, stretching out her arm to catch him. He found his wife and plopped down next to her, taking her hand and gently squeezing it to give her comfort. Some of the smaller children began to cry from fear, but everyone continued to sit in darkness. Before long, both the father and the baby dozed off. Slava, though, could not sleep, worrying as usual. Suddenly, she felt with the back of her legs, the sausage box slide from under her seat. She immediately suspected one of her neighbors and instinctively, pressed the back of her legs against the box, the box kept inexorably sliding slowly, away from her toward the neighbor. "What are you doing?" She demanded loudly. "You're taking our provisions." The box quickly slid back into place.

Vladimir awakened and leaned down to feel for the boxes. Everything seemed in place.

"Oh, I'm sorry," Maria said meekly. "I thought that was one of our boxes. I made a mistake."

"You don't have any wooden boxes," Vladimir said.

"I couldn't tell in the dark. Sorry."

Vladimir and Slava realized that they would not be able to leave their seats or their belongings for a second without one of them keeping guard.

They continued sitting in darkness for probably another hour. Finally, as suddenly as they went out, the lights came back on. The whistle blew, and they felt hot steam snaking through the open windows, adding to the clamminess in the train. All three were drenched with sweat. The train wrenched forward and continued its journey. A few hours later, the ancient conductor make his rounds once again, looking more disheveled than before. With an angry snarl, he began checking the passenger's travel documents. When he came up to the Moskalkovs, Vladimir again handed him the documents and asked him about the long delay. "Bandits. They blew up a large part of the track ahead. We brought in a train from the other direction to replace the rails. Hopefully, it will be clear all the way into Germany."

"Where are we now?" Slava asked the conductor in German. He seemed pleased to hear her speak with fluency. She had no accent.

"Young lady, we are not far from Bialystok."

"That's only about 140 kilometers from Slonim. You mean that we have been sitting in this train for more than a day and we're not even in Bialystok?"

"Young lady, you should be glad you're alive and well. We are in an area fraught with partisans. They disrupt our trains almost every day. Then lately, it became a habit of

the Soviet pilots to strafe our trains. But not to worry, the
repair train came through without a problem. We should
be able to make it to Warsaw without any further incident."

"How far is Warsaw from Bialystok," Vladimir asked.

"It's about 175 kilometers."

"How long will that take?"

"With two short stops for water and coal on the way
from Bialystok, it usually takes about three hours, sometimes four or five. Well, enjoy the ride." The conductor
abruptly turned and went on to ask Helga for her documents. Helga shoved them at him. She overheard the conversation and did not hesitate to show extreme annoyance
at the long delay.

"How could it possibly take so long to arrive in Warsaw?"
She snapped at the conductor. "By now we should have
been in Berlin!"

"It may take us a week to reach Berlin. I'm not here to
explain things to you. If you don't understand the danger
of this trip, then you're a fool. Good day, madam." Irritated,
the conductor went on to the next passenger and barked
that they should have had their travel documents ready
for him.

A full moon peaked out in between the dark clouds. The
young couple turned their heads to watch the landscape
slide by. Tall trees lined the sides of the tracks. A little later,
the moon reflected brilliantly off the still waters of a slow-
moving river. Slava continued to look out for a few more

moments. Sleep had finally overtaken her and she joined Vladimir's deep slumber. They awoke promptly when the train began to reduce its speed. Thick trees still lined the track. As the train crawled along, the outskirts of Bialystok came into view under the moonlight. Small shacks nestled within thick clumps of trees and brush lining the track, eventually changed to larger homes, then four or five story buildings. The city seemed deserted, with only an occasional light seen in a window. A half-tumbled fence made of wood and barbed wire came into their sight. "That must have been the Jewish Ghetto," Slava said. Vladimir nodded. Visible also in the compound were factories and tall apartment buildings—then a cemetery.

The train came to a stop at the Bialystok, Poland station. At night, the back of the station seemed dingy, although it displayed beautiful columns of brickwork. Swastikas were painted on the brick walls. A wide overhang above the platform provided cover for a multitude of people carrying bundles of all shapes and varieties. Anxious to walk out, Vladimir grabbed their two canteens, expecting to fill them with water. He also hoped that he would be able to find food to buy, particularly fresh vegetables. Again Slava cautioned him to be very careful. He stood in line with several fellow passengers, waiting to exit. The doors stayed sealed. They heard shouts and banging on the doors from the outside, as people on the platform tried to break into the car. He glanced back to check on his family just in time to see

Slava push back a man attempting to climb in through the open window behind her. Vladimir hurriedly rushed back, joining his family to protect their spot on the train.

Suddenly the crowd outside began to disperse after whistles and gunshots signaled the arrival of police. A few bodies lay on the ground. Vladimir was not sure whether they were shot or trampled. As the platform cleared, the doors opened; however, no one was allowed to get off. Instead, a man in a dirty gray railroad uniform brought in two buckets of water and filled the passengers' water supply. After about an hour at the station, the train once again jerked forward and the Moskalkovs were on their way toward Warsaw. "Volodya, we are so blessed that we're in the train. The stream of people trying to escape has not abated. They're walking, and like us, they don't know where they're going. They're just going."

Chapter 31

"We must be approaching Warsaw," Vladimir told Slava, in a tired yet somewhat eager tone. Gazing out of the window, she nodded. Through the leafy trees, she spied a cluster of small cottages with their thatched cone-shaped roofs. These were a prelude to larger houses, some made of brick, but most were wooden or covered in white stucco topped by high pitched red roofs. Closer to the center of the huge city, the scene changed to very dense, multi-storied apartment buildings dotting the avenues.

Vladimir and Slava would have liked to explore the capital of Poland, but they knew that would be impossible. Nevertheless, Vladimir was anxious to exit the car and feel the solid ground beneath his feet. As the train finally stopped at the busy station, they saw the typical Nazi flags and posters hung throughout the platform. This display of Nazi propaganda was similar in all the previous stations that they passed, even the smallest rural ones. The typical throngs crowded the platform along multiple tracks. A large military presence kept the crowd from rushing the trains. Vladimir sat for a few minutes studying the huge depot. "Slavochka, if they allow us to get off here, I think I'll go and see about finding us some food."

"Oh no!" Slava said in a worried voice. "Just sit still. I know it's something that's hard for you to do, but just sit here and don't be restless. You can't take the risk of not being able to get back on. We have water here. Granted it tastes like mud, but it's drinkable. And we have plenty to eat."

"I'd love to find some more bread and maybe a few vegetables. I'll stay close to the station. Don't worry."

"Honey, please, I'd rather you wouldn't."

"I'll be all right, really."

Slava learned that, at times, when Vladimir had determined to do something, she had better give in, because he would probably do it anyway.

"Don't be a fool. You're so stubborn at times. You really want to take a big chance?"

"It won't be a chance. I'll be close by."

"All right then, but come right back."

"Of course."

As Vladimir walked off, Slava hoped that the authorities would turn him back. Instead she soon saw him make a dash toward the platform entrance of the station. She sat playing with Victor, nervously glancing out the window for Vladimir's return. Minutes seemed like hours to her. She again checked her watch. Twenty minutes had passed and there was still no sign of him. The few other passengers that got off, after seeing Vladimir leave, all seemed to have returned, all empty handed, but still no Vladimir.

The whistle blew. Slava's heart began to pound harder. *Please, God, please. Let Volodya return this instant.* Fewer people were now hanging around on the platform. Slava thought maybe she should take the baby and jump off and search for him. *We have to be together. Where in the hell is he? Jesus.*

Suddenly Slava saw Vladimir sprinting through the door of the station and then across three track platforms. The whistle blew again and the train started to move. She briefly saw Vladimir running up closer with something clasped in his hand, but then she lost sight of him. The engine picked up speed. Slava's head felt like bursting open, her heart pounding, trying to escape her chest. *Oh God! Oh God, no.* Her eyes were peeled on the door, repeating prayers to Saint Anthony, her favorite saint. A minute passed, then another. Suddenly the back door of the coach flew open. There was Vladimir, out of breath, but with a smile of accomplishment on his face. The other passengers stared at him, bewildered by his sudden appearance in the car. Then their eyes focused on the loaf he held in his hand.

As Vladimir sat down next to Slava, she was beside herself with anger. "Do you know what you put me through? I thought I'd never see you again. What took you so long?"

"Slovochka, look what I was able to find," Vladimir said proudly holding the dark bread up to her. "Take a whiff of this. Listen, I knew when the train would leave. I asked the conductor exactly when. I knew I'd be back in plenty of time. I would have had plenty of time, had I not been stopped by the soldiers. While I showed them my papers, one of them kept eyeing the bread. I thought for sure he'd take it away, but I lucked out. The other soldier told him to hurry it up because they were late for something. He even pulled him by his sleeve to get him to go. Then it took some time to get back in the station. The guards were extremely careful with my papers."

"I can't believe that you took such a stupid risk."

"I'm sorry, sweetheart."

"Don't sweetheart me. I'm still angry with you." Slava turned away from Vladimir and looked straight ahead, her face red.

Vladimir tried to take her hand, but Slava pulled it away. "What happened to all the people on the platform? They were gone when I came back."

Slava did not reply. Vladimir's feeling of elation and triumph, of finding, what he considered to be a trophy now quickly dissipated as Slava gave him the silent treatment, which he hated. He realized now that he really shook her up. He felt guilty for putting her through that and sincerely regretted it.

"Another train came and took them all away," Slava finally answered Vladimir's question after she cooled off a little.

"Where in the hell did you find that loaf of bread? An angry voice from across the coach yelled out. "I walked all over and around the station looking for anything to eat."

Slava felt embarrassed. Everyone's eyes were fixated on them. One woman with her arms crossed even stood up to get a better look. Vladimir shrugged and quietly answered, "I must have gone a little further than you. By a bus station, a little old lady had a loaf to sell." The man waved his hand at him in disgust and looked away.

Slava sat silently staring out into space while Vladimir held Victor. "Slavochka, my sweetheart, forgive me. I'm sorry to put you through this worry."

Slava turned toward him, "Don't you ever do that again. First of all, you could start a riot on this train by finding something they don't have. Secondly, I don't know what I'd do without you. Don't leave my sight."

"All right, I won't." Vladimir leaned over to kiss her, but she turned away, still cross. Vladimir sat back studying Victor as he slept. The baby looked so content. *Ah, to be a child again and not have worries and responsibilities.*

A few minutes later, Slava nudged him, offering her cheek by pointing to it with her finger. Vladimir understood and leaned over to kiss her. As he did, she moved her head just in time for their lips to lock.

The train picked up speed. It seemed to travel faster than they remembered since they left Slonim. Their neck muscles felt sore from gawking out the window at the scenery and villages along the way. Before long, the train stopped at a station.

"Where are we?" Vladimir asked Slava. "I didn't see the name of the station. All I see are more of the Nazi flags and their propaganda. This place seems deserted—no one except for a couple of policemen by the entrance. And I don't see the usual presence of armed soldiers."

"I noticed a railroad signal about a kilometer back. The word *Kutno* was painted on it. We must be in Kutno, Poland."

"Kutno, Kutno," Vladimir said softly. "We're getting closer to Germany."

Slava felt twinges in her chest when Vladimir mentioned Germany. She hugged Victor closer to herself. "You know, Volodya, I almost wish we could stay in this coach forever. At least we know where we are. I dread Germany. What do you think will become of us?"

Suddenly, a contingent of armed German soldiers marched onto the platform, their leather boots resonating on the bricks. They approached the train. Vladimir assumed that they would board to check the passengers. The military presence at the stations always gave Vladimir a pit in his stomach. There was no knowing what to expect of them. The sight of their uniforms still repulsed him. He expected the soldiers to enter their car. They had been through this on many stops; nevertheless, each time he worried. With the appearance of the soldiers, both Vladimir and Slava stiffened, not murmuring a word. Awakened from sleep by the commotion from the soldiers, Victor remained quiet watching them take their time and carefully examine each passenger's documents, including the Moskalkovs. Fortunately, their documents were found to be in order and the soldiers finally exited.

Not forgetting her earlier question, Slava asked once again, "So what do you say? What will happen to us in Germany?" She knew Vladimir would have no answer, but she wanted some kind of reassurance from him.

Vladimir turned and looked into Slava's fatigue ridden eyes. His mind also dwelt on Germany. He hesitated for a moment, then spoke, first clearing his throat. "We'll be all right. Somehow we'll survive. They obviously need doctors. Otherwise, why did they take us? Don't worry." Vladimir expected Slava to comment, "Here you go again with your 'don't worry.'" She didn't. She sat still running her fingers through Victor's hair, while the baby cooed from the pleasure of it. She lifted him up for a hug when her son unexpectedly stuck his finger in her ear.

"Ouch. Vitya, be careful."

Vladimir chuckled. "We should have trimmed his fingernails before the trip."

Several hours passed before the couple saw a large city approach. Beautiful and colorful large buildings presented a brilliant contrast from the endless forests interspersed with rivers, lakes and small towns. The depot sported a sign indicating this city as Poznan.

"I wish I could get off and just walk around the place," Vladimir said. "This appears to be a magnificent place."

"Don't you dare! Besides, the conductor told us while you were in the toilet washing up, Victor, that we are not allowed off the train until the final destination."

Vladimir sat restlessly watching Slava walk around the coach with Victor. They both realized that the baby too, was fatigued from being cooped up in the coach. When Slava had her fill of walking around in circles, Vladimir took over until Victor fell asleep.

After what appeared to be an endless stop in Poznan, the whistle blew twice and the engine chugged forward once again. The train kept a steady pace for little more than two hours, then it slowed as it approached a much smaller town. Vladimir noticed that his German neighbor lady became animated. Before that moment, she and her daughter sat quietly almost the whole trip, not moving about much and only talking to each other in hushed voices. Suddenly she looked at Vladimir. "This is Rzepin," she said beaming. "We're now only twenty kilometers from the German border. It's just wonderful that we made it." Vladimir nodded and returned her smile. At the same moment his heart sped up and perspiration beaded his forehead. Overhearing, Slava's breathing quickened. It was ironic, Slava thought. She did everything she could to avoid being forcibly sent away to Germany while in Vitebsk and in Slonim. Now they were about to enter Germany, voluntarily. *What a turnaround! What are we doing? What does God have in store for us?*

Chapter 32

THE TRAIN pulled slowly into the Rzepin station. As it came to a stop, two armed soldiers burst into the car. With bravado and a show of authority they demanded to see the papers of every passenger. After studying one of the passenger's documents, they ordered him to accompany them off the train. The man began to argue. Without hesitating, the ruffians dragged him out of the seat and began to remove him. His wife and children screamed out. The wife stood up, swearing in Polish. One of the soldiers pushed her back into the seat and slapped her on the head, calling her Slavic scum. Slava's hands trembled from the incident. Would they be next? A few minutes later, the soldiers returned and took away the wife and children. No one knew the reason.

"Welcome to Germany," Vladimir whispered to Slava, scowling. Immediately afterward he regretted what he said. He realized his comment did not help calm Slava's nerves. Slava looked frightened. "Slavochka, I was just joking. Those people probably didn't have the travel documents or maybe they did something wrong. Nothing is going to happen to us."

Slava took some deep breaths. "God, I hope so," she said, with much sadness. "But then, with the German soldiers, you never know when they'll decide you're doing something wrong."

The soldiers returned and continued their methodical examination of documents. It seemed they were trying hard to find any excuse to take a passenger off the train. Finally, they made their way to their German neighbor, Helga. With a friendly, almost flirtatious tone, smiling sweetly, she handed their documents to one of the soldiers and while doing so, stroked his hand. Grinning, his gruffness mellowed and he barely looked at her papers. However, his stern, intimidating demeanor returned when he stood before Vladimir. Vladimir already had the papers in his hand and tendered them to the tall soldier. Both Vladimir and Slava sat still, barely breathing, while the man examined the documents. He carefully studied their photographs and compared the likeness to each individual. A vise tightened even more around Slava's chest as he studied her face for several long seconds before looking at the photograph again. Finally, without saying a word, he handed the documents to Vladimir and went on to the Polish family seated next to Slava.

After the soldiers left the coach, the familiar click and clack of wheels on the rails continued. After several hours, the train slid to a sudden stop. The lights went out. The sun had set hours before and the moon hid behind the clouds. In the distance, Vladimir and Slava heard what they thought was rolling thunder. But as the continuing noise became louder, closer to the train, they realized that the din came from the dreaded drone of airplanes, lots of them. Slava grasped Vladimir's hand.

"What shall we do?" Slava asked. "We can't just sit here. Once again we are helpless."

"Not much we can do. Hopefully, they pass over us."

They sat silently as the planes flew overhead, away from them. Mere seconds later, the low sound changed to what sounded like whistles and screech. Those were followed by thunderous explosions in the near distance. Vladimir stuck his head out the window and was amazed by what he witnessed. He turned back and looked into Slava's tired eyes.

"What did you see?" She said, anxiously. "You look frightened. Here, hold Victor, I want to look."

Slava turned around, stuck her head out the window as had other passengers, and witnessed the horizon on fire. A massive cloud of black smoke rose above huge red and orange flames. "Oh God! Saint Anthony, help us all." She repeatedly crossed herself after she turned back around again. Some children in the coach began to sob. "Volodya, what have we done? We're traveling straight into an inferno. It appears that the earth is on fire."

Vladimir, resolutely locked his jaw as Slava knew was his habit when he worried. "Well, Slavochka, at least we are safe. I admit that's quite a sight. Never had I seen a firestorm as widespread as that. And I thought it couldn't possibly be worse than what I saw on the battlefield. Fate guides us, and for some unknown reason we are meant to be here, sitting on this benighted train at this present moment."

"If that's what you think, I suppose it makes it easier to go on. Anyway, whose planes were those? Were they the Soviets?"

Before Vladimir could answer that he did not know, Helga, through a river of tears, swore at the British. Vladimir and Slava turned towards her. "Those are British planes. I received a letter from my cousin in Berlin that they are subjected to constant air raids—the British bombard at night, the Americans in the morning. The bastards. They have no regard for the innocent people below."

It's funny hearing her say that, Vladimir thought. *As though the Nazis have regard for anyone in the territories they occupy. So, those were British planes.* He could not believe it himself. He tried to suppress a tinge of some perverse pleasure in seeing Germany burn. He had gone through a lot of punishment by the Germans and it was bittersweet feeling that they were getting a taste of their own medicine. *Strange, though, we are going to suffer as well, same as the Germans. A real paradox. Life is indeed strange with all its twists and turns.*

The lights came back on. The train resumed its trudge further into Germany. "That must be Berlin then, ahead of us?" Slava asked Helga.

"Yes, yes. That is where we're supposed to get off. What are we going to step into? Oh my God." Helga sounded hysterical, also crossing herself and hugging her daughters as they huddled and sobbed.

"Do you think they are going to tell us to get off in Berlin also?" Slava asked Vladimir.

"I have no idea."

"Well, I hope they take us far away from here."

As the train approached Berlin, a horrific panorama greeted their eyes. Huge parts of Berlin burned. From the eerie light provided by flickering flames, the couple viewed the horror of buildings resembling dragons spewing fire in all directions. A little further they saw charred structures, skeletons of themselves. Yet other buildings looked intact except for some blown out windows. Shivers ran throughout both Vladimir and Slava. Their eyes watered as they inhaled the acrid smoke with each breath. Slava placed a handkerchief over Victor's mouth to keep smoke out. She reached in the bag and pulled out one for Vladimir and herself. Slava wanted to turn away from the ghostly scene but could not. Mesmerized by it, as though she was in the middle of a nightmare, she kept staring out at the destruction.

They came to a standstill at the Berlin station. Fortunately, the area around the depot seemed spared. A stern voice from the platform announced in German, then Polish, then Russian that only those passengers ticketed to Berlin were allowed to leave the train.

Breathing seemed more difficult the longer the train remained at the station. Their eyes burned and all three coughed incessantly. Everyone anxiously waited for the train to move out. It had to be better outside of Berlin.

Fortunately, the stop in Berlin was short. Steam intermingled with the acrid air as the train jolted forward. Many of the German passengers exited in Berlin and now there was more room to move around or stretch out. Before long, the air, though humid and muggy, became easier to take, but they continued to cough, to expel the smoke out of their lungs for some time.

The engine seemed to crawl along and when the early glow of daylight appeared in the eastern sky, it picked up speed and whizzed past the Potsdam station, not stopping for coal or water until reaching a small town with an old wooden station to refuel. The train stalled at the stop for several hours. Vladimir took Victor and tried to get off and walk around on solid ground. No one else followed him. He made his way down the three steps, actually touching German soil, when a gruff voice, seemingly coming from nowhere, yelled obscenities and ordered him back on the train. Vladimir quickly complied. One of the passengers with a smug smile told him as he reentered the coach that the conductor had told them that no one was allowed off the train while in Germany. Vladimir remembered what Slava told him, but he just had to touch the ground. He did not intend to go far beyond the steps.

The train again picked up a steady sluggish pace, slowing only in the late afternoon as it approached the city of

Magdeburg. Here the air once again smelled acrid, although not as bad as in Berlin.

After a long stop, the train moved on. The sky turned dark, not a star or the moon in sight. The engine chugged along for a few hours more until it suddenly came to a standstill and the engine shut down. Once again, the lights went out. "Oh God!" Slava said. "Not again. The bombers are back."

"They're only hitting the cities. Didn't you notice that none of the countryside was bombed, only the larger cities?"

"How far do you think we are from one?"

"I don't know."

Chapter 33

Nazi flags and posters indicated, "Hanover." "Do you think we'll get off here?" Slava mumbled to Vladimir. She looked exhausted as she sat with her eyes closed. "We've been on this train far too long. It seems like a never ending journey."

"It can't go on much longer. In the meantime we need to enjoy every minute of this fabulous train experience."

"Oh, you're certainly funny, ha ha! It's obvious we're so tired we are just plain silly. After all we must have covered close to a thousand kilometers in these five days."

"Is that all? It feels like a lifetime. But remember, Slavochka, try not to worry. Everything will work out."

"Here you go again with your 'don't worry,'" Slava began to laugh almost hysterically, almost leading to tears, from sheer fatigue and tension. Vladimir joined in with a much needed belly laugh. Even Victor, hearing his parents laugh, surprised them with a loud laugh of his own.

After waiting hours for the train to refuel, the locomotive jerked forward. The now very familiar clink of metal wheels on metal rails resumed. Slava yearned for the clanging to disappear. Though dreading what lay ahead, the need to remove herself from the hard wooden bench and the constant sway of the coach was almost overwhelming. Soon the sun peaked out. The train slowed, approaching yet another smoky town with parts of its industrial sections lying in ruins.

An abundance of military and police presence greeted the passengers at the station of the town of Soest. After the train stopped, an elderly, drained-appearing man made his way into the coach. He wore a military style uniform, and his bushy white hair protruded from underneath a battered helmet. He announced that everyone should gather their things and exit the train. Vladimir and Slava were stunned and sat as though frozen. It took them a minute for the words to penetrate their numbed brain. They could finally get off. As they gathered their possessions, their insides tied into knots. Praying to both the Blessed Virgin and to St. Anthony, Slava followed Vladimir down the length of the coach and then the metal steps. Allowing Vladimir to carry the bulk of their belongings, Slava held Victor, her heavy oversized handbag and one of the leather suitcases clenched in her hands.

Once they descended, another elderly soldier in an ash-soiled uniform, ordered the passengers to line up and wait on the platform of the depot. Following directions, the family stood amid the crowd consisting mostly of German refugees. Looking around, Vladimir concluded that, unlike in their coach, most of the passengers on the train were Germans. They too, now were homeless in their own land.

That's what happens when you leave your country and occupy someone else's land, Vladimir thought bitterly to himself. *Nazi greed turned into Nazi failure. We wouldn't be here with our legs trembling.*

Several minutes passed and the couple placed their possessions on the worn, though spotless, brick platform and waited. And waited. As the early August sun beat down on them, the humidity seemed as stifling as in Slonim. Vladimir wore his winter coat when he left the train, not having the space to pack it away. The wait continued. Soon the coat came off and joined the rest of their luggage. Vladimir wiped the perspiration from his face and felt sweat roll down his body. Victor was hot and fidgety even as Slava fanned him with her hat. Finally a soldier, a mere boy who looked too young to shave, walked up to the crowd. Clad in a loose-fitting uniform hanging on his scrawny body, he commanded with as much authority as he could muster, that they follow him.

"Do we have to walk far, young man?" A concerned German lady asked. "My feet are swollen from travel and are killing me."

"You're going to have to walk a distance. We have no gasoline for our buses."

Even though exhausted from the many days traveling without adequate sleep, the Moskalkovs were determined to sustain the long walk. They picked up their luggage and trudged along with the others. "Hurry up! Hurry up! Keep moving," the young soldier hollered.

They toddled along in the midst of other passengers through narrow winding streets for at least two kilometers. Vladimir and Slava took in as much of the town of Soest that they could absorb. They marveled at the three-story buildings packed together with their variety of facades and ultra-steep roofs. The white stucco sidings interspersed with painted brown half-timbers created a scene from a fairytale.

A solid, red brick, utilitarian two-story building, which seemed to serve as an administrative center for processing refugees, loomed before them. The Germans were dealt with on the first floor, while all others were directed to the second. Since most of the refugees were German, their line was lengthy, winding through the foyer, outside, and around the building. The line for the second floor was much shorter; however, there were fewer clerks processing the refugees, and it took two hours before the Moskalkov family found themselves in front of an old highly polished wooden counter. Across the counter stood a very thin middle aged woman with brown eyes and short black hair wearing a quasi-military uniform

"Papers, please," she said in German, a faint, soft voice, breaking as she covered her mouth to cough. She didn't even glance their way as Vladimir laid out all the documents provided to him in Slonim. The round hanging lights overhead flickered and then went out. The woman seemed unconcerned. The tall arched windows provided adequate light. She read over the documents briefly.

"You're a doctor?"

"Yes."

"Good. We badly need doctors. I'll assign you to a refugee camp in Castrop-Rauxel. You and your family stay in the barracks overnight and tomorrow at precisely 7:08 a.m. the train will take you to your camp. Soest is only an assembly point where all refugees are brought, then we reassign you to different camps. Now as for you," she turned her attention to Slava, "What kind of work have you done?"

"I assisted my husband in his medical clinic."

"Education, please."

"Four years of medical school."

"Did you graduate?"

"No. The war interrupted my education. I only had one year to go."

"Fine, you will work as a nurse, when needed. But since you have an infant, it will not be expected of you to work," she informed Slava, quickly scribbling on half a sheet of paper. When she finished, she handed it to Vladimir. She followed the same procedure with another piece of paper. "How old is your baby, boy or girl and name?"

"Five months old, almost six," Slava said. "He is a boy, named Victor."

"Oh yes, I see his birth certificate here. It's nice to see a German one."

Neither Vladimir nor Slava made a comment. They knew that it would not have been a German birth certificate had the Germans not invaded their homeland. The woman scribbled some more on yet another half-sheet of paper.

"Go to the room next door, to your right, as you walk out. Give these forms to the lady there. She will fingerprint and photograph you."

In that room, the woman, dressed in the same brown uniform as the previous clerk, curtly nodded to Vladimir and Slava. She appeared extremely annoyed. She mumbled under her breath, but loud enough for the couple to hear, that too many foreigners were entering Germany. "Put your thumb and index finger on the ink pad," she ordered. "Now put your thumb and finger here," pointing to a form for each one of them. "Stand there, in front of the camera." Vladimir and Slava complied and each had their picture taken. "Now you need to come back at precisely three o'clock to get your papers, understand?"

"That's fine, thank you," Vladimir said. "But where do we go from here?"

"Oh, this is ridiculous! Must I answer every stupid question around here?" The couple was astonished at her irritated response to a simple question. "You should have been instructed by the last clerk. Go back to her. That is not my job."

"She said that you will give us further instructions."

Her wrinkled checks puffed out and her face red-dened. "Wait here." She stormed out of the office in a huff to confront the other lady. A heated argument ensued. In the meantime, the line outside her room grew longer. She returned, red-faced. "Now go back to that woman and she has to tell you where to go. As far as I'm concerned, you can all go to hell. They tell us that they need workers, but what are we going to do with them afterwards?" Still fuming, she pointed with her wrinkled, arthritically deformed, index finger to the next person in line. "What are you waiting for, get in here," now directing her anger at them. With fear in their eyes, the family with two boys entered the room as the Moskalkovs exited and once again got into line to obtain further instructions.

Chapter 34

THE ANCIENT brick barracks of what was once a slave labor camp reeked with stagnant, still, putrid air. With her patched black socks visible above her highly-polished frayed brown shoes, their guide led the Moskalkovs to a room on the second floor. She was a fragile, elderly woman, wearing a drab, worn military-style uniform similar to the ones worn by the clerks. Surprised, Slava realized that they would not be alone as they walked in. Parents with their two preteen daughters already occupied the room. "You sleep here tonight," the German woman snarled. "You share the room. The toilet is at the end of the hall."

Vladimir smiled and said hello to the family dressed in ragged, soiled clothing. A pungent smell of body odor permeated the room. They appeared astonished to see the well-dressed, stylish Moskalkovs, eyeing them up and down. The father said something in answer to Vladimir's greeting, but neither Vladimir nor Slava understood the language. Two chipped metal bunk beds, placed on opposite side walls, took up most of the tiny room. The father, lying on the upper bunk, snapped his fingers and waived his finger motioning to the girls to get to their side of the room. Lying on the bunks assigned to the Moskalkovs, the girls immediately scurried to the parents' side of the room and sat down on each side of their mother. She placed her arms around the girls and continued to gawk at the couple and their baby as they laid down their possessions on the green, worn linoleum floor between the bunks.

With their neighbors' belongings wrapped in blankets and pillowcases lying on the floor, there was barely enough space to walk between the beds. The woman, seeing the situation, looked apologetic and quickly tried to gather what she could closer to her bunk, leaving a little more room on the floor. Vladimir now had space to shove their food provisions and suitcases under their bed. Slava laid her large handbag on the lower bunk, and Vladimir threw his backpack on the upper.

Slava gave the neighbors a friendly smile. The mother returned the smile exposing a large gap in her mouth where at least three teeth should have been. She said something to Slava, pointing at Victor, then placing her hands together and leaning her cheek with her eyes closed on them. Slava nodded and grinned again, understanding that the baby was sleeping. Vladimir tried to strike up a conversation in Russian, Polish, Belorussian, even broken German, but to no avail. They only shrugged their shoulders and shook their heads indicating that they did not understand. Slava wondered if perhaps they were Hungarian or Romanian.

Barely able to keep her eyes open from exhaustion, Slava studied the bed. A sheet, a pillow, and a blanket were provided. She could only guess how clean they were. *Those girls lay on the beds, and who knows who else might have slept on these sheets and pillows.* "The bed might be infested with lice or bed bugs," she said to Vladimir. "Don't use the pillow or the blanket."

Vladimir nodded and pulled himself up onto the upper bunk. He bent over the bed and looked down just to see both Slava and Victor already fast asleep, the pillows lying at the foot of the bed. *We're so mentally drained and physically exhausted.* He turned toward the wall, closed his eyes. He almost dozed off when he realized that they might oversleep the time given to pick up the identification and work documents. He lay in bed, his eyes shutting down, but fought the overwhelming urge to sleep. An hour later, he heard Victor cry. Slava awoke and began to feed her son.

"I really need to take a catnap now," Vladimir, told Slava, bending over the bed. Can you stay awake while I do? And don't forget, we need to be back to get our papers at three o'clock."

"Sure, I got my second wind. When you wake up, I'll snooze a little more if Victor lets me. I won't forget. We'll make it."

Afraid that the neighbors might ransack their luggage, Vladimir and Slava took turns in retrieving their identification papers from the administration building. Once both were back in the crowded room with their neighbors, they carefully studied the issued documents.

"What a terrible photograph," Slava said after reviewing the Foreigner Identification Card. "I look so tired, like a real refugee. My assigned number is 11163. With a number, I feel like a prisoner. And look at the official stamp, the fascist eagle with a swastika in its tail. Just the thought of having to carry around this document with a swastika again as we did in Slonim makes me sick."

"I know what you mean. Me too."

"And the second card has the same horrible picture with the same number, my place of birth in Vitebsk and that I can work as a nurse. It also shows that we came from Slonim, by way of Bialystok. Let me see yours." As Slava examined the documents, the youngest girl slid next to Slava on the bunk and took a look at the papers as well. She smiled and said something in her language. The mother yelled at her, grabbing her arm, and pulling her back to their side of the room. Both parents seemed apologetic for their daughter's behavior. Slava tried to explain that she didn't mind.

Examining Vladimir's documents, Slava commented, "You also look exhausted in your photo. Your number is 11164. Look, they even warn us in these papers that we must carry them at all times or else be arrested. And your work card lists you as a physician. I hope that means you won't have to dig ditches."

"I will if I have to, but I don't think so. Did you notice the general appearance of many refugees we had seen? They seemed malnourished and sickly. Some are walking skeletons and they'll be prone to illness. The Germans are very meticulous and must be extremely concerned about disease and its spread among their population. I think I'll have plenty of work."

"Yes, it's very sad. Life is so hard for all of us now, some definitely more than others."

The Moskalkovs thought the night would never end. When morning finally came, they picked up their belongings and waving goodbye to their roommates headed back to the train depot. There followed other passengers, burdened with the precious baggage representing a former life, onto yet another third class coach. "Off we go again," Slava said. "I hope we'll at least get a room to ourselves at the new camp. I never thought anyone could snore like those people we were with, whoever they were. At night, it seemed like a train ran through our room."

Vladimir laughed. "I was lucky. I slept like a log."

"Ah, so, you probably added to the racket," Slava teased.

The crowded coach held Russian, Belarusian, and Polish refugees. Squeezed by the neighbors on both sides of the bench, Vladimir decided to get up, joining the many other standing passengers. He held Victor, who seemed to be studying a little girl with a red bow in her yellow hair. No one spoke. The only sound was the hypnotic rhythm of metal wheels on metal tracks. The low gray clouds hung over the isolated, wooded countryside, making the day seem oppressive. Here and there, clearings of fallow fields were interspersed with sleepy villages. An overall feeling of dejectedness clung to the ongoing journey.

Vladimir stood deep in thought. He missed his home, his mother, and sisters. He thought about the three clinics he worked for in Vitebsk where he shuttled from one to another, making more money than an average doctor. His gaze roamed the foreign landscape. Everything appeared different—the houses, the villages, and even the few trees appeared sinister looking. He craved the sight of the birches of his homeland. Their magnificent white trunks all lined in straight rows like soldiers, their leaves glistening in the sun. He missed the fresh smell of the Belorussian country-side. He understood that everything, including the culture and customs would be different, totally foreign to him. He knew he would have to become proficient in German. *Oh well, I should not look back. We only have what lies ahead.*

The train stopped at Unna. Again, the typical Nazi flags and posters were displayed at the station. No one was allowed off the train. Before they left Soest, a bowl of meat-less barley soup was served in the camp's mess hall. Nothing else was provided, not even a crumb of bread. With only that small, nonnutritious breakfast that morning, Slava felt hunger pangs. "Shall we split a stick of sausage?" She whispered into Vladimir's ear after standing up to join him, grabbing the luggage rack above their seats with her hand for support.

"No, I think we should wait. Everyone is starved."

"You're absolutely right. We can wait until it's more appropriate."

The train rumbled out of the Unna station and an hour later, stopped at Castrop-Rauxel. The conductor, a white-haired, wrinkle-faced old man wearing a spotlessly clean pale-blue uniform ordered them off the train. On the platform and in and around the depot stood several young boys proudly displaying their green uniforms inscribed with police insignias sewn onto their sleeves and chest. "The country is now run by old men, women, and young boys," Vladimir commented to Slava as they walked through the depot and onto the street.

"They need the younger men on the battlefields," Slava said.

Laden down with their possessions, they were taken by bus to the former labor camp six kilometers from the station in Ickern, a town that was consolidated into Castrop-Rauxel. The weather remained hot and muggy. Finally the gates to a fenced compound came into view.

Chapter 35

THE EARLY August sun failed in its attempt to peek through the thick clouds. The day continued to be gloomy and oppressive. The tired couple followed the crowd of refugees past two glum old men wearing loose-fitting brown uniforms. Standing guard at the open gate, they seemed barely able to hold their heavy rifles. The purple sunken eyes of the guard on the right caught Vladimir's attention. *The discoloration under the eyes is due to visible blood vessels from severe fat loss. I've seen at lot of this problem lately. The Germans are not getting enough to eat.* The old man noticed Vladimir studying him and turned away.

The camp appeared to have been put together quickly without much effort in its construction. Small concrete foundation blocks held up wooden rectangular structures with low-pitched roofs. A short overhang covered the wooden step leading to a door in the center of the barracks. Chunks of siding and asphalt roof tiles were missing here and there while boards or cardboard covered some of the windows. The condition of the camp was not what Vladimir or Slava would have expected from the meticulous Germans. *The war has taken its toll even on the mighty Germans. They're running out of material and energy to keep this camp up,* Vladimir thought.

The teen-aged policemen, guiding the refugees from the station, now herded them toward a more substantial two-story brick structure. Vladimir surmised that the building was at one time a residential house, and the barracks were quickly erected on its grounds.

As they waited in a long line to enter the building, a woman called out the name, "Moskalkov." Both Vladimir and Slava were startled to hear their name singled out. With trepidation, Vladimir raised his hand and took a step out of the line. A slim brown-haired woman in her forties, wearing a similar brown uniform as the women in Soest, approached the family and instructed them in perfect Russian to follow her. *Oh no!* Slava thought. *What's this all about? Why did they take us out of line? Are we in trouble?* A knot tied her stomach as she and Vladimir picked up their belongings and followed the woman around the line and through the door into the hallway of the building. The woman proceeded up a wooden staircase holding on to the highly polished walnut handrail, to a room converted into an office. Slava eyed the protruding veins on Vladimir's temple indicating his extreme stress.

The woman walked around a gouged oak desk and picked up a piece of paper and some colored cards. She introduced herself as Hilda, assistant administrator of the camp. Vladimir and Slava nodded and attempted a smile as they stood motionless. "Herr Doctor, we need to get you started to work as soon as possible. We are prepared for you. Here is a note stating that you are attached to the Castrop-Rauxel camp and here are your ration cards. Carry that note with you along with the documents they issued you in Soest. Do you have any of the occupation marks?" Vladimir indicated that he had the money used in Slonim.

"Fine, give them to me." Vladimir reached into the breast pocket of his suit jacket and Slava into her purse retrieving their wallets. Hilda called out across the hall to a room with its door wide open, "Angela, come here." A large-boned girl in her late teens ran in. Flashing a quick smile at the couple said, "What can I do for you, Frau Hofmeier?"

"Take these and exchange it for our marks—hurry. I'll meet you at their designated house."

Angela took the money and was heard running down the stairs. Vladimir looked concerned. "Don't worry, Herr Doctor, you'll get your money back. Hopefully, it will be enough for you to buy food for at least two weeks. After that time, you will be paid for your service. Your pay will be determined later and should be enough to buy food and coal, if you can find it. Now follow me. I'll take you to your assigned house." Vladimir and Slava felt the world lift off their shoulders. *We're going to get a house?* Slava couldn't help grinning with the news of this sudden and unexpected development. Also smiling, Vladimir noticed that her weary eyes again had the sparkle in them that he had not seen since they left Slonim. The woman walked up to Victor, "Coochie coo, coochie coo," she said, rubbing his tummy with her index finger. "Nice baby. You must be very proud." She did not wait for an answer but walked hurriedly out of the office, followed by the Moskalkovs.

Slava looked around the camp grounds trying to determine where their house could possibly be. All she saw were grungy barracks. Instead, the woman headed straight for the gate and out of the camp. They made their way on a narrow path across a grassy field and to a street lined with apartment buildings. Shops occupied the ground floor of several of the buildings—a bakery, a small café, a tailor's shop. An abandoned gas pump of an auto repair garage could be seen in the alley.

After allowing some pedestrians and bicyclists to pass, they walked across the street and made their way to an intersection. Turning left, away from the camp, they approached the next block then turned left again onto a narrow street lined on both sides by small brick houses setback only a few feet from the sidewalk. Most had vegetables growing out of window boxes. Even though carrying her son, a heavy handbag, and a suitcase, Slava seemed to be floating on air from the prospect of their own house.

In the middle of the long block on the right side of the street, Hilda led them up to a tiny blonde brick house with yellow shutters. Evidence of picked-over vegetable gardens covered the bare ground on the sides of the house. Hilda picked out a key from the batch she was holding. She unlocked the door and walked in, followed by the Moskalkovs. "This is where you will stay until further notice." She glanced at Vladimir with a serious face. "I'll give you two hours to rest or go to the grocer for your rations." She reached in her uniform pocket and pulled out a small piece of paper. "These are the addresses of the grocer, the butcher, and the milk store. The stores are close to each other, about three or four blocks from here. I advise you to hurry. This time of day the lines are still long. They run out of supplies rather early in the day. By the way, you were given the same ration cards that the Germans get. The same ones my family gets. You should consider yourself very fortunate." Vladimir caught the look of disapproval from Hilda.

"As for your rations, note that there are various stamps with different denominations from 10 to 500 grams. Also the colors are different. The blue ones are for meat, white for sugar, yellow for dairy products. Eggs, oils, breads, and other groceries such as marmalade and imitation coffee are green. It seems complicated, but believe me, you'll learn quickly. Now where is Angela? You need the money before you can buy anything that is rationed. Well, I need to get back. The girl should be here soon."

Vladimir thanked Hilda, who looked gratified that she accomplished a great task. She said a curt good day and as she began to walk out, she called out, "Oh yes, remember, in exactly two hours from now I want you in my office, and I will take you to the camp hospital. We Germans are very precise with our time. Understand?" Vladimir nodded and told her that he would be there. She again turned to leave and paused by the door. "Oh, and one more thing. You will hear sirens. The sirens are not for exercise. They are real. Everyone must, not should, but must run to the nearest shelter. Bombers fly over us frequently, almost daily. So far, we haven't suffered from many explosions, but you never know. The cellar in this house is not approved as a shelter so you cannot stay here. You must take your baby and run down the block to the corner apartment building we passed. There is an air raid shelter sign on the front door. You enter and run down to the basement stairs in the back and underneath the main staircase. Understand?"

"Yes, we certainly will," said Slava, concerned. With the excitement of the house, she forgot, for a moment, the destruction she had seen in some of the cities they passed on the train. "You need to take a practice run, and while there, register your names with the superintendent of the building."

She finally left and the couple began exploring their residence. It was much smaller than their place in Slonim—a front room, one bedroom, an adequate kitchen, and a bathroom off of the kitchen. The boarded up, glassless window of the bedroom made the room look dark, the only light a narrow stream between two boards. The furnishings were plain but appeared comfortable consisting of a sofa, a stuffed sagging chair, a bed, a dresser, and a scratched wooden kitchen table with three matching wooden chairs.

"This is great," Vladimir said.

"This is more than great," Slava answered. "It is wonderful. We'll live like royalty compared to the poor people stuck in those barracks we had seen."

Worried about his money, Vladimir pulled back the pale blue flowered-patterned drape of the front window and peered through a delicately embroidered but tattered sheer. He felt relief when he saw Angela strolling lazily up the walk. Vladimir opened the front door and the girl ran up the steps. "I have your money for you," she said, smiling sweetly. She handed him an envelope. Vladimir thanked her and after she left, he counted out two hundred thirty marks."

"We got only a fraction of what the occupied marks were. I wonder how much this will buy. But in the meantime, Slavochka, let's have some of that sausage we had lugged around. I'm starving."

Using a knife she found in the kitchen drawer, Slava sliced a large piece of sausage for each of them and they quickly gobbled it down.

Vladimir saw the line outside of the store. As he joined the string of women awaiting their turn, he felt their eyes fall on him. *I hope I don't stand out too much, although I'm the only man here.* The women looked hostile, and Vladimir felt out of place. He was a stranger among them and now he was here to partake in the doling out of the meager food supply they themselves felt entitled to buy. Vladimir understood their anger. He imagined, even though he was well-dressed, maybe too well dressed, that they assumed he was one of those German refugees from the occupied eastern lands. Those refugees were not welcomed because the locals were forced to share their homes and now their food with them. He realized that he better keep silent and not give away that he was even something worse than a German refugee in their minds—a despised enemy from the Soviet Union. There was muttering as some of the women swore at him, while others began to ask questions where he was from. He nodded and remained silent knowing that will infuriate them even more, but it still would be better than letting them know that he was not German.

Eventually as the line proceeded toward the entrance, the women concentrated on getting their rations and left him alone. He still felt uneasy. *It's a good thing that Slava isn't here instead of me. It would really upset her. Unfortunately, next time, she'll have to go through this herself because I'll probably be at work. But then, she'll probably charm them and get along very well.*

Inside the grocery store, Vladimir handed all his ration cards to the extremely arrogant clerk behind a long wooden counter. She wore a spotlessly clean white apron over her light brown dress. A black net covered a portion of her gray hair. She studied the cards for a moment, and then looked

Vladimir over from top to bottom, her nose held high in the air. "What do you want?"

"I'd like everything that these cards will allow me to obtain in this store." She heard his accent. She smirked sarcastically and studied Vladimir even more intensely. Then she examined each card carefully, holding them up to the light, checking it to see whether they were forged.

"You want everything right away?" She laughed again, looking around at the other clerk for support. "I can't give you everything all at once. The card supposed to last you a full month. You can't carry it all and some will spoil. You're a foreigner, aren't you? How did you get these cards?"

"I came here to work and they gave me these cards." The woman shook her head, her sagging chin flaying. "This is highly unusual, but I guess I need to accommodate you. Do you have money to pay for the groceries?"

"Yes." Vladimir said, beginning to lose his patience, yet there was nothing he could do about it. He was a foreigner in a foreign land and he had to take the abuse. Instead, Vladimir smiled warmly. "I'll follow your kind advice. We only arrived today and please give me what you think I should have at this time."

"All right, then. You need to come tomorrow for more. That's how normal people do it."

Vladimir smiled. "Yes, thank you, we'll do that."

The lady softened her tone and something akin to a smile appeared on her face. She turned around to the shelves lining the wall behind her and grabbed a bag of sugar, bag of nuts, a tin of cooking oil, a small bag of flour. She placed these on a counter. She then proceeded to remove a larger bag of cornmeal, a small container of margarine, a small jar of strawberry preserves from the shelves, and added those to the pile on the counter. A half-bar of soap, a tin of baking soda, a can of corned beef, and a tin of coffee were added to a now substantial mound of goods. The couple later learned that the coffee was not real coffee but a poor imitation made from roasted barley, oats, and chicory mixed with chemicals from coal oil tar.

The clerk took out a pair of scissors and snipped out the portions she needed from the white, yellow, purple, and green stamps, leaving the cards in a jagged shape. She added the cost of each item on a cash register and demanded seventy-five marks from Vladimir. "You need to go to a milk store for milk, cheese, and eggs, and the meat store for meat. Where is your bag?"

Vladimir remembered that they had to provide their own bags in Slonim. Prior to leaving the house, he grabbed a pillowcase from one of the pillows on the bed. At the store, he pulled it out and began placing the groceries inside. "That doesn't look good," the woman commented. "A pillowcase is for a pillow. We in Germany are very proper and expect others to be so as well. You better find a grocery bag. The clothier next door has some available."

With a friendly smile, Vladimir assured her that he would. Without returning the smile, the clerk waived him out of the door. A woman in the back of the line heckled him.

Slava sat on the faded gray rug in the front room playing with Victor as he lay on a small blanket. She heard Vladimir's knock. Quickly rising, she unlocked the door and embraced her husband. Vladimir beamed when he saw his family. "Look what we received. We now have more to eat than our sausages."

Slava grinned as she helped him unload the items onto the oak table. "You know, I was thinking…"

"You were, well what do you know?" Slava commented, displaying her playful side.

"Yes, Slavochka. I was. And I'm relieved that you appear happy."

"Well, why not. We're all together. We have our own house, food. If the bombs don't get us, we'll do all right. And, as I told you, every place is a wonderful place as long as we're together. Now, what were you thinking about?"

"There is a backyard here and a shed. As soon as I get paid, maybe we can buy a goose or a chicken."

"Well, it will have to be on the black market, then. And we'll probably have to find something valuable to trade for it."

"We'll find a way." Vladimir glanced at his wrist watch. His favorite one was taken away by a German guard shortly before he became a war prisoner, but he bought three more in Slonim to be used for trade, if necessary. "I better go to work."

"Is it time already? You didn't have a chance to rest."

"I'll be all right." Vladimir kissed Slava, and then stooped down on the floor, rubbed Victor's stomach and kissed his cheek, then the bottom of his feet. "All right. I'm off. See you when I get back."

Chapter 36

FAMISHED AND exhausted, his muscles aching, Vladimir returned a few minutes after ten o'clock in the evening. "I was so worried," Slava said, flinging herself into his arms. "How are you holding up? I fretted so much that I was beside myself."

"Everything is fine. I saw a lot of patients and tried to avoid the Germans. Slava, I didn't eat at all and I'm starved. Actually, I don't know if I can even eat now. I just need to fall into bed. They want me back at the clinic at 5:30 in the morning."

"Oh no, you don't. You must eat. You won't make it otherwise. Hurry then, you can jump into bed right after you have something. You poor thing, how will you ever rest up?" Vladimir wearily complied. Washing his hands, he plopped down on a chair at the table and quickly gobbled down his food.

"I'm dying to know what happened to you today."

"Let me wash up and get ready for bed first," Slava waited in bed while Vladimir took off his suit and changed into a pair of pajamas that he had lugged all the way from Slonim.

"How were you treated?"

"Slavochka," he sighed. There is a lot of resentment of me by the German staff, but the refugees and laborers that

I treated really appreciated me. You should have seen all the hugs I received from my patients."

"Oh, and were any of them that were young and beautiful females that I should worry about?"

"Don't be silly."

"I'm just kidding. I'm glad that they feel you made a difference in their lives. How was Hilda? Was she still somewhat friendly?"

"She was the same as before. I think that she would like to be more open and friendly, but feels that it is expected of her not to be," Vladimir mumbled the words as he stretched out on the bed, covered himself with a sheet and instantly dropped off into deep sleep.

Slava lay next to him, unable to sleep. She took a short nap earlier while Victor slept and felt somewhat refreshed. She was never one to fall asleep quickly anyway or be able to take naps. She envied Vladimir for his ability to turn his mind off and sleep, almost at any given time or any place. She lay awake for an hour, wondering over and over what this strange land held for them.

Suddenly a horrible, eerie nerve-jarring reverberation destroyed the peace and serenity that Slava felt just as she was about to succumb to slumber. The wail of the sirens froze her to her bed. Her heart started to beat erratically. Vladimir jumped out of bed, "Hurry, get your clothes on. We have to go." It dawned on Slava what the ruckus was all about and she, too, flew out of bed.

They grabbed the sleeping Victor, covered him in a blanket, and rushed out of the house to the shelter. There was no time to lock the door. The unsettling racket of flak guns cracked the air. Black cottony puffs of smoke lingered in a lit reddish sky as they headed for the corner of the street. They ran into the building, around the stairwell almost falling down the stairs to the basement. The place was a long narrow room. The walls, lined with aged stone and patched with concrete, were the foundation of the building above. Old galvanized water pipes and black electric wires hung below the wooden beams. Rough wooden benches lined the walls and mismatched chairs of all varieties stood in the center.

Filled with people, Vladimir looked around and saw two vacant spots along the wall. As they approached, a stern-looking woman in a pink bathrobe shook her finger at them saying those spots are for someone else. They tried to sit down at another place, only to be rudely informed that those seats were also taken. After another attempt, they found two places in the chairs set out in the middle of the room.

The sirens continued to wail for a few minutes and then suddenly stopped. The tattoo of flak guns continued unabated. The low thunder of numerous propellers added to the turmoil. Vladimir braced himself for bombs to plunge down to earth, but there were none. The flak guns quieted and the drone of the planes became fainter with each second.

The Moskalkovs remained seated for several more minutes. Vladimir decided that it was safe now to go home. He made a motion to Slava to leave. "Are you sure?" Slava asked as they rose.

A young woman, wearing a light summer dress, sitting next to them with her two children, grabbed Vladimir's sleeve, wagged her finger at him and told them they must remain in the shelter until the siren sounds again. She informed them that if they were caught outside of the shelter, they would be arrested. With all eyes in the cellar upon them, the couple sat back down and waited with the others for that all-clear siren.

After sitting quietly for a few more minutes, Slava turned her attention to the woman next to her. She appeared in her forties, looked pleasant enough, and did not show any concern of the evening's raid. She was dressed in a light-green robe with her hair covered by a small scarf. "How often do the sirens go off here in Castrop-Rauxel?"

The woman gave Slava a hard, suspicious look as if put out by the question. Taking a deep breath and after studying Slava for a few seconds, she finally drawled. "In the bigger cities, they hear sirens every day. That's because they bomb them daily for one reason or another. Just to be cruel, I guess. Here, we don't get bombed as much, but the sirens do go off quite often because they fly over us on the way elsewhere. We, poor people, have to suffer." *As though, the Germans don't cause terror in the minds of the conquered,* Slava thought. *Is she for real or is she so brainwashed and unaware of what their bombers do to innocent people?*

"We have our oil plants and coal mines and they can strike us at any time." She turned away from Slava, her face solemn. She wrapped her arm around her small son, awaking him. He cried out in protest but promptly fell asleep again.

"Thank you," Slava said.

"Where are you from? I know you're not from here. What are you doing in this building?" Her tone turned suddenly sharp and nasty.

I should have kept my mouth shut, Slava thought. *What should I say so not to be yelled at?*

Slava tried to formulate an answer when suddenly the all-clear sirens went off and everyone rose to exit. The woman seemed to be in a particular hurry and rushed toward the steps. Vladimir looked at his watch. *We lost almost two hours stuck down here. It'll be a rough day tomorrow.*

Chapter 37

Hilda looked stern as she met Vladimir at the door of the hospital. "I see you finally made it. Didn't we tell you to be at the hospital early?"

Vladimir looked at his watch. The hands on his Russian-made steel watch, for which he traded a piglet on the black market in Slonim, showed 5:10 a.m. "Isn't it still early?" He asked the woman, surprised that she criticized him when her instructions to him were to be there by 5:30 a.m. She looked frazzled, eyes reddened from fatigue.

"Never mind. We needed you earlier."

"What is the trouble?"

"We're overrun with sick workers, and then some new refugees were admitted throughout the night. I know there will be many more. This is just starting. They're overwhelming us with these eastern people and we can't keep up. Some of them may even have typhus. We'll be out of bed space if this keeps up. On top of it all, our regular physician is too sick to come in." Vladimir had met the white-bearded doctor. He appeared ancient, pale, feeble, and barely able to move around. If he did come down with something like typhus, most likely he would not survive it at his age. "We're expecting another doctor soon, but until then, it's solely up to you to treat the patients. I hope you know what to do.

It may become a desperate situation. If it is indeed typhus, we could have a city-wide outbreak with not enough grave-diggers to bury the dead."

Hilda shook her head and raised her arms in despair. Vladimir thought, *how dramatic she is. She is almost hysterical.* At that moment, the door flung open and two women pushed a gurney, a frightened wide-eyed child lying upon it.

"Where should we take this one?" One of the women asked Hilda.

"Oh my God! Another one. This time a child. Take her to the intake ward. If there are no available beds, leave her in the aisle on the gurney until the doctor here examines her." Both women studied Vladimir. One smiled and nodded at him as they wheeled the child down the hall.

Hilda turned her attention once again to Vladimir. "You see what I mean. Where in the hell am I supposed to put them if they keep rolling in?"

"Nevertheless, we have to isolate those suspected of typhus the best we can."

"You must be joking," Hilda forced a laugh. "Don't you understand, with all the refugees they keep sending us to house and feed, where the hell can I find a place to isolate them?"

"I understand. We'll figure something out. And maybe, it won't be as bad as you think. Let's take it one step at a time."

"That's mighty easy for you to say."

Vladimir remained silent for a moment while Hilda repeatedly shook her head, her cheeks sucked in. "But, if I may say so, I am also concerned about the supply of medications that I saw yesterday." Vladimir was almost afraid to ask that question. It could be a tipping point where Hilda may go over the edge. He had to ask and hoped that Hilda remained calm.

"Yes, what about it?"

"I didn't see much of anything. With typhus, we'll have patients with respiratory problems. I didn't see any sulfa drugs on the shelves. In the early stages of the disease, I had found that sulfa helped. You showed me the pharmacy closet yesterday, and, quite frankly, it looked bare."

Hilda stiffened up, clenching her jaw. She took a deep breath. "Look, Herr Doctor, just do your job here." Her voice became squeaky and loud, veins swelled on the temples of her forehead. She pointed her index finger at him and shook it as she spoke. "You must realize that there are shortages in everything now, including—" Hilda suddenly stopped in the middle of her sentence and twisted around abruptly to see if anyone could have overheard.

Vladimir knew why. Just like under Stalin, Hitler's henchmen were still everywhere and they punished those who said anything that showed a defeatist attitude or criticized the government, the definition of which was extremely arbitrary. It was obvious that Germany's glory days were numbered, that the war was lost, but yet, no German had better complain about the government or any shortages. They would be punished. "Our brilliant medical researchers have come up with a vaccine," Hilda said, trying to calm her voice and raising its level in case anyone listened down the hall. "We should be able to get it shortly." *Just as in the Soviet Union,* Vladimir thought. *I've heard that story before. Shortly never comes.*

"Anyway, enough conversation. Go to work."

"Yes, certainly, right away. Oh, and just one more thing. If there is such a vaccine that would, indeed, be remarkable if it works. But in the meantime, we need to make sure that the patients and the rest of the population in the camp are bathed and their clothes boiled to get rid of the lice. As you know, the louse's sticky eggs or nits cling to bodies and particularly to clothing. Everything needs to be disinfected." Vladimir hoped that his order did not overwhelm her as she seemed already overburdened from the moment he arrived.

"Do you think that I was born yesterday?" Hilda answered belligerently, "Or that the Third Reich is not aware of what must be done?"

"I'm sure you have taken those precautions. Except the patients I saw yesterday…" Vladimir paused, concerned that he was being maybe a little too forward and should keep his mouth shut.

"Well, finish what you were saying."

He hesitated again. "Well? What is it? Spit it out."

All right then. It needs to be said otherwise there really could be an epidemic. "I observed that the patients I saw yesterday were filthy. Typhus is a disease of filth, particularly when humans live together in close quarters such as in prisons or labor camps. The people I examined yesterday were badly in need of a bath and their clothes reeked with sweat."

"Of course, what do you expect?" Hilda's face turned crimson. Vladimir could see her boil and expected an angry response, but she kept her voice down. "Listen, this is not a spa but a work camp and is now being taken over by eastern scum families. They come here in rags, already covered with sweat and filth." Vladimir was not surprised by her bigotry. He was a refugee himself from an occupied land. He expected that as long as he and Slava lived in Germany, their status as eastern scum would be held by most Germans and that it should not bother him. Once again he realized how fortunate they had been, dressed well and traveling by train when so many came exactly as Hilda described—shoes with holes after walking for long miles, with only what they could carry. Of course they were dirty and smelly. But now they should be given the opportunity to clean up. That was even more important reason for them to bathe and have their clothing boiled to eliminate the danger from typhus.

"People work and get dirty. The refugees come here filthy, most wearing rags. They bring in the lice." Hilda continued, her voice becoming louder. Vladimir thought back three days ago in Soest. There, he, Slava, and Victor were checked for lice. If these other refugees came through Soest, they would also have been checked. "We take every precaution to delouse the population," Hilda continued. "Haven't you noticed the shaven heads? That is a proven way to keep lice out of the hair."

Vladimir had enough of this conversation. He felt that he needed to see his patients, particularly to examine the child that awaited him. Hilda's statement about shaved heads bothered him. If they thought that was a big precaution, he needed to explain. "Yes that is good, but in medical school I learned that it is questionable that head lice cause typhus. We must be predominantly concerned with body lice."

"Herr Doctor, we know what to do. We are not idiots. I will continue to request more help from the commandant. We need more coal to boil the clothes. Now we're through here, go to work."

"Yes, of course. Thank you."

. Vladimir walked off regretting his conversation with Hilda. *I should have kept quiet. Hilda seems unstable, and I'm a nobody here. What's the matter with me, blurting out my opinion like that? I have to be more careful. I really don't know her, and she probably has the authority to send me to the coal mines. But it's obvious that they need me. Nevertheless, I need to say as little as possible. On the other hand, they want me to prevent an epidemic and I need them to do certain things before it's too late.*

Vladimir proceeded down the corridor, kept spotless by women laborers. He climbed the wooden steps, his hand on the highly polished brass handrail, his mind filled with the thought of the dreaded disease. *Typhus again. It just seems to follow me everywhere—all the way from Belarus to Poland and now to Germany. The Germans should have expected typhus as a consequence of war. Now they are concerned for their own people in Germany. They know that typhus kills in war conditions. Hundreds of thousands of their soldiers died from the disease during WWI and probably even more in this war.* He shook his head in disgust and turned the corner, opening a door to his assigned tiny office and stepping inside. He thought of Slava and Victor and wondered how they were faring in the house by themselves.

On the hook behind the door, hung the white lab coat and a heavily used stethoscope issued to Vladimir the day before. Down the hall, a washroom enabled him to thoroughly scrub his hands. A half-full box of cotton face masks along with newly sanitized rubber gloves sat on the shelf above the sink. When he finished, he walked back out to the corridor and with his quick step, ran back down the stairs to the intake ward.

As he hurried, he tried to remember all he could about the nasty disease. An infected common body louse transmitted bacteria called Rickettsia prowazekii from one person to another causing typhus. The bite of a louse was not the primary reason for infection. The scratching of a bite and thus forcing the louse's dusty, powdery fecal material into the wound was what caused typhus. A simple brush with the clothing of the infected person was enough to become infected, rendering the disease extremely contagious.

Vladimir shuddered as the memory of the disease came to his mind. He recalled how close to death he came from typhus while a prisoner. He felt lucky to have survived and would not have wished the suffering he underwent on anyone else. Fortunately, not everyone dies, but a significant portion of thirty to even sixty percent do. The patients slip into a coma and usually die of heart failure or pneumonia. *The Germans have every reason to fear the disease. If unchecked, it could be another Black Death of Europe.* But having endured typhus, he hoped that his body had developed enough immunity to it. At least, he counted on it.

He entered the small room with occupied beds lining the room, two on each side. His hands slid into the gloves and he pulled on a mask to cover his nose and mouth. Even though he thought he might be immune, typhus may become airborne, and he did not want to take any unnecessary chances. The gurney, left between the rows of beds, still held the small child. A woman in white nurses' uniform, white stockings, and black shoes was bending over the girl, placing a compress on her forehead.

As he approached the gurney, the nurse heard him and immediately straightened up, greeting Vladimir. The little girl had an incessant, gut-wrenching cough. As Vladimir examined the child, the nurse introduced herself as Ingrid. She began speaking rapidly, flaying her hands about. Vladimir knew some German, enough to get by and was able to generally understand the gist of a conversation, but he found her speech difficult to follow. He asked if she could speak slower. Her blue eyes seemed to smile as she shook her head in the affirmative and began speaking more slowly and precisely. "Would you rather that I speak in Polish?" Ingrid asked in German. Vladimir's face lit up hearing that she spoke Polish, a language in which he was so much more proficient. He nodded quickly in agreement. "I was assigned as your nurse, although there are several others that work in this hospital that will help you as well. Just let me know what I can do."

She spoke Polish without an accent. "Are you Polish?" Vladimir asked.

"No, I am German. I learned Polish because I grew up on the border. Everyone in our town spoke both languages. We used to trade back and forth. I had playmates on the other side of the border." Vladimir observed that she must be in her early twenties. She was very slim, fair of complexion, with light brown hair pinned into a bun, showing underneath her nurse's white cap.

"I think the girl has a very bad case of bronchitis," Ingrid said.

"You're absolutely correct."

The girl appeared frightened. "Do you know what language she speaks?" Vladimir asked the nurse.

"No, I don't know. She can't understand me in German or Polish."

Vladimir asked her name in Russian.

"Svetlana," she answered, between bouts of coughs.

"Good name. I'll give you some medicine to make you feel better. All right?"

The girl nodded. She remained calm for a few minutes, then again broke out in a coughing spell. When she finished she asked for her parents.

"They're probably waiting for you. Once you're in a ward, I'm sure they'll let them see you."

"I'm going to make the rounds now. Can you help this child?" Vladimir asked Ingrid. "Give her half an aspirin for her fever and a third dose of sulfa right away. Can you find a place for her?"

"Yes, I'll take care of it, Herr Doctor."

Vladimir left the room, walked across the corridor, and entered another ward. The ward was more crowded than it had been the night before. More beds were brought in, leaving barely enough room for him to examine the patients. He knew he had his work cut out for him.

Chapter 38

AUGUST, IN the depressed, war-torn nation, slowly turned into September. Vladimir seemed to work longer with each passing day, limiting his time with his family. Slava's task to find food was turning out to be a full-time job. She made a daily trek to stores pushing Victor in a baby buggy, hoping to obtain anything that might be available with their ration cards. Not much was available, not even on the black market. Fortunately, no bombs struck the city for several weeks leaving the Moskalkovs somewhat apathetic to the frequent sirens that went off when sorties of Allied bombers flew overhead or nearby on their way to attack larger cities. Then on September 11, 1944, their anxiety was renewed.

On that date, sirens wailed longer than normal, followed by a few moments of silence. The serenity was broken by the thunderous racket of anti-aircraft guns pounding away while the roar of multiple engines with their propellers amplified the cacophony. Targeted were the synthetic oil plants, located dangerously close to the labor camp.

The Moskalkovs, crowded together in the shelter with stone-faced individuals, struggled in vain to calm their pounding hearts. They trembled as they listened as a faint whistle would increase to a crescendo, then the horror-filled shrill scream of bombs as they plunged to earth. The inevitable explosions would then follow. *This is the real thing,* Vladimir thought as he grabbed Slava's hand, pressing Victor closer to his chest. Slava sat silently, her lips moving in prayer to Jesus, then to the Virgin Mary, over and over again. A woman screamed and another rebuked her, calling her a coward. The building shook. Their feet vibrated with the ground. Sitting helplessly underground, unable to escape, Vladimir felt trapped. *What if it's a direct hit? We're sitting ducks here.* More nearby explosions rocked the building. Slava kept praying, her breathing shallow, petting Victor's hair for comfort, thankful that he was incredibly sleeping soundly. How he could sleep through the racket was a mystery to her.

Dust and splinters from the wooden ceiling rained down. The two light bulbs in the basement swayed before the lights went out. More explosions followed. More swaying, more dust falling. Bits of concrete embedded in the stone foundation fell off the walls. Slava continued to squeeze Vladimir's hand, tighter and tighter with every explosion. Finally, their baby awoke from an extra loud boom and began to wail. In the darkness a woman yelled out, "Shut up! Can't you keep your child quiet?" Vladimir couldn't see her, but understood that her anger was laced with sheer fear. Suddenly, the ruckus stilled. It became eerily quiet. The lights eventually came back on and Victor settled down, his tiny hand grabbing his father's coat lapel. Everyone else sat silently as well, not knowing what awaited them.

The all clear siren sounded and the weary denizens of the bomb shelter came out into smoky sunlight. Looking around them, the Moskalkovs noted that the apartment building under which they hid, sustained only minor damage. Several bricks had been tossed from the chimney stack onto the sidewalk. Vladimir noticed a few cracked windows. Slava continued to pray as they walked back to their house, this time asking St. Anthony to have protected their house. With great relief she saw that their house still stood. Many cracks were visible in the walls and ceilings, but there were no broken glass panes.

No other bombs fell on Castrop-Rauxel until November, when the air raids were repeated with even more vengeance. More buildings stood in ruins, some were destroyed by fire. Their shelter building survived but sustained damage to the parapets. The ornate brickwork and glass from windows tumbled onto the sidewalk and street. After one of these bombings, the Moskalkov house sustained extensive damage to the walls and plaster as well. The two paintings of German landscapes, furnished with the house, were knocked off the wall, the glass and frames broken. Chunks of plaster from the walls and ceilings fell onto furniture and floor, causing thick white plaster dust to cover everything.

"Oh my God!" Slava sobbed.

As the days dragged on, food became scarcer. On his rare day off, Vladimir walked several miles out of town seeking out farmers with the thought of trading for food.

After being rudely chased away at the first three farms, he came across a farmer who was interested in a trade. Vladimir showed him his watch, one that he bought two months ago, and a pair of heavy woolen socks. After much negotiation with the old, pleasant man, Vladimir traded the items for two old hens and a goose. "If you give me your shoes, I'll bring the birds to you this afternoon. I'll even throw in half a dozen eggs. I have to go into town, anyway." Vladimir thought about it for a moment. He had another pair of shoes, but was hoping to trade them at a later date.

"I can't give you these, as they are my favorite. I'll give you another pair that I have at home, but I'd like another chicken and a dozen eggs in trade."

The old farmer frowned, not responding for a moment. Vladimir knew he was thinking hard about it. Still frowning he shook his head in the negative as though it was totally out of the question. Then suddenly asked, "Are they good leather shoes with no holes in the soles?"

"Yes, they are in good shape. Do we have a deal then?"

"No, not exactly. I can't give you another chicken, but I'll deliver the birds and will give you a dozen eggs and I'll even give you four potatoes if I like the shoes."

Vladimir felt fortunate at that point to find anything, so he readily agreed telling the man he will receive the watch, shoes, and socks when he brings the poultry and eggs.

When later that day the old farmer delivered the traded items in his horse and cart, complaining to Vladimir that he cannot find any gasoline for his truck, he placed the hens and the goose in a sack and rushed inside the house. "I didn't want anyone to see these birds. Keep them hidden from everyone; otherwise the government will take them to feed the soldiers."

Over the next few days the Moskalkovs ate the goose and two of the old hens. The birds were useless for egg production or for anything other than soup. The meat from the old, boney hens would soften up as it boiled in the soup. Slava added their last potato and some cabbage, saved over from a ration purchase.

On occasion, Vladimir surprised Slava with a stick of sausage, a small slab of bacon, pickled tomatoes, a jar of beets, or a potato. When she asked him where he got them, he would reply, "A patient, in appreciation, gave it to me." Vladimir's salary, though meager, allowed them to buy bits and pieces of food and clothing in stores and on the black market, but in November, very few accepted marks any longer. Barter was becoming the only way to obtain anything.

The parents were often hungry, but they made sure that Victor never went without. He came first. Slava thanked God every day for what He provided them. She knew that they had it better than even most of the Germans. They had spent every one of the marks they had, while they still could, for all the nonperishable food, shoes, and clothing they could buy. Now, they traded the clothing for food. *My husband is so resourceful*, Slava thought. *Somehow he manages to find food and provide what we need.* She remembered that her family had been amazed, while still in Vitebsk, at how Vladimir was able to bring them delicacies and wines when there were shortages there as well.

Coal for cooking or heat became scarce. Rumors flew that soon it will become non-existent. The Moskalkov house was always cold. They managed to get just enough coal to keep from freezing but not enough to be comfortable. Standing in line for food one day, Slava overheard a woman brag that she was able to gather almost half a sack of coal at the railroad tracks. She remembered that trains often drop bits of coal. Next morning, with Victor in the buggy, she took a stroll to the railroad tracks in search of coal. She was not alone. Many women were doing the same, but she was able to retrieve a few pieces. Looking down at her blackened hands, a melancholy mood descended on her. *How much longer can this continue? We're going to freeze before spring gets here.*

Unexpectedly in February 1945, Vladimir came home early. "What's the matter? You're home and it's barely noon. What is it, you look concerned?"

"They're moving us to a camp in Hamm. They need me there."

Chapter 39

A SOMBER panorama of destruction greeted the eyes as the slow moving train entered the outskirts of Hamm. Several burned buildings still smoldered. Factories lay flattened with only some tall brick chimney stacks visible here and there. "Oh my God," Slava said softly. "I never thought I would ever see such devastation. This is horrible. To where did they bring us?"

Vladimir, his jaw clenched, nodded. As he continued to stare out the window, he noticed tracks multiply from two to ten, then fourteen and then twenty. The train made several switches onto other lines reducing its velocity with each. Several women could be seen working hard, repairing rows of bomb-damaged tracks. "This is a big railroad town," Vladimir commented to Slava. "Probably a marshaling center. Did you notice those railcars, loaded with wire and iron rods, lying on their sides? Some of the factories around here must have been foundries."

The depot came into view. It had also sustained some bomb damage. But still looked well enough for Slava to be astonished by the spectacularly beautiful building. Its red-and-white deco design, accented by red circles in white background, had a row of narrow, but tall, arched windows. The engine came to a complete halt. Nervously, the couple gathered their belongings, once again loaded themselves down, and stepped off the metal steps. A giant pit in Slava's gut grew larger as the back entrance of the station neared.

They were instructed to wait inside until someone from the refugee camp came for them. As they entered, no one waited or paid any attention to them. After standing anxiously by the front entrance for several minutes, they decided to sit down. Now that he walked, Victor was not in a mood to sit quietly. He fidgeted to get off his father's lap. Vladimir let him down, and the boy wobbled from side to side as he began to run. Vladimir hurried after him, grabbed his hand, and together they walked stately around the lobby.

Still fascinated with the colorful building, Slava studied the interior of the station. The high barrel-shaped ceiling with many red hexagons, also in white background, matched the exterior. The rows of windows on both sides of the building gave the cavernous space an airy, elegant appearance.

After a leisurely walk around the perimeter of the building, Vladimir and Victor returned and sat silently for a moment. Grumbling that no one had shown up for them, Vladimir got up and restlessly began to pace back and forth to the door, glancing out the front doors and studying the face of each person entering. He finally sat back down again. Victor wanted to explore about again, so father and son circled the lobby several more times. After an hour's wait, a short lady in a uniform similar to Hilda's rushed in. She made her way directly to the Moskalkovs. "You are Herr Doctor Moskalkov?"

"Yes."

Without a smile or an introduction, she gestured for them to follow her. They all ambled down a sidewalk to a dark gray two-door Volkswagen automobile parked almost a block away, instructing them to get in. Vladimir glanced at the small interior and wondered how they'll all fit with their luggage. He shoved as much of the baggage as possible into the back seat, leaving a tiny space for Slava to sit and discovered that there was no room for one of the suitcases. "Ah, for heaven's sake!" The woman said, extremely annoyed. "Here, I'll open the front and you can slide the suitcase there."

The Volkswagen brought back unpleasant memories to Vladimir. He remembered how, while a German prisoner, he was forced, more than once, to push these vehicles out of the mud. As the woman lifted the hood, he recollected that the air-cooled engine was located in the back leaving a small trunk in front.

"Hurry, we don't have the whole day," the woman said impatiently, giving Vladimir a nasty scowl. Vladimir barely squeezed the suitcase into the compartment and quickly shut the hood. He then held Victor while Slava scurried into the tiny space in the backseat. As soon as she settled, Vladimir, holding his son, plopped down in the front passenger seat. He was barely in, the door still ajar, when the woman started the car, shoved the transmission in gear, jammed on the accelerator, and backed out. Vladimir quickly slammed the door. They sat silently, even Victor, as they drove through the city noting how some areas were extensively bombed.

Old men, small children, and women diligently worked in ruins cleaning up debris, enabling the streets passable. As they labored they sorted bricks, metal and other salvageable material. The energy displayed reminded Vladimir of an ant colony, each ant doing its duty for the good of the rest.

"How old is your baby?" Their driver asked suddenly, breaking the silence, as she glanced at Victor.

"He is a year old, actually this month."

The woman's lips quirked, but she made no further comment. She remained silent the rest of the way except to complain occasionally that she has to take a longer route, as some streets are impassible, and she is really late. She also muttered that she was using up precious fuel and that this may be the last trip for the car as there will probably be no fuel available for her, even though it's made from synthetic oil.

Finally, entering a small clearing, she turned into an unguarded open iron gate and drove up to a large brick building flanked by other two-story red brick buildings. In the distance, Vladimir spied low-pitched wooden barracks with a woman watching children play in the snow.

"You can get out and take your stuff with you."

The procedure was identical as in Castrop-Rauxel. The women in charge wore brown military-style uniforms and were just as irritated. It was yet another refugee camp. Except for the wooden barracks, the buildings were solid brick structures, and because of the placement of the buildings in a semi-circle, Vladimir surmised that it might have held a military garrison at one time. The administrator's name was Lisel and she reminded the couple of Hilda. With the same arrogant demeanor and spoke in the same domineering and superior tone of voice.

Lisel ordered Vladimir to follow her out of the building to the hospital while Slava and Victor were told to stay and wait. Left in the hallway on the second floor, Slava stood leaning against a heavily cracked wall when one of the ladies took pity and gave her a chair. After Vladimir came back, one of Lisel's assistants, a frowning older lady named Louisa, issued them ration cards with instructions as to which stores to use. Afterward, she told them to follow her as she waddled ahead on her swollen ankles. They followed her slow pace out of the camp, down the road to a two-bedroom brick house on a residential street a block away.

"You are to have a house that we have appropriated for you." Without going in, she handed them a key and turned to walk back. Then she stopped and, as Vladimir inserted the key in the lock, she called out, "Oh yes, I forgot. There are three bomb shelters back at the camp we walked out of.

You are to use the one in the basement of the hospital. Just follow the signs. We have air raids almost daily, the Brits at night and the Americans in the morning. Sometimes like clockwork, other times, who knows? Well, good day." She turned once again and proceeded slowly on her way.

It was with a subdued joy that Slava explored the house. She had no complaints. The house proved to be clean and surprisingly very well furnished, but the dire warning of the old woman still rang in her head. *Almost daily raids. Bomb shelter in the basement of the hospital.* The devastation that she had witnessed in Hamm still haunted her as well. "Isn't it great that we have our own house again?" Vladimir said with a broad grin.

"It's all because you're a doctor," she said. "We are definitely lucky as far as that goes, but will we get to enjoy it much—daily raids and all? That's crazy."

"We'll have to be careful, of course. We'll be all right."

Slava began to laugh. "Actually I'm happy to hear those words. "You haven't used them for a while, and, believe it or not, I missed you telling me that everything will be all right." With that, she went up to Vladimir, hugged him tightly, and kissed his lips. "Volodya, I love you so."

Vladimir kissed her back, "I love you even more." Holding her tight for a moment longer he kissed her again. "Well, let's settle in. Will you be able to find the stores? I won't be able to help as they told me to report to work in a few minutes."

Arriving at the hospital, he found out that once the bombings had begun, the second floor was no longer used. The patients' beds were crowded in on the first floor, with barely enough room to walk among them. The basement contained four makeshift wards, divided by partitions for nonambulatory patients. The remaining area served as a bomb shelter, furnished with a variety of chairs and wooden benches. The sole surgical room remained on the first floor with a decree that it could only be used in the hours between raids.

When the warning siren began its nerve-wrenching wail, Vladimir, as required, dashed with the others to the basement shelter, searching for his family, greatly relieved when he spotted them. He knew that if Slava were caught in town during the alarm she would use the closest shelter to her. Although, a few days ago, Slava admitted to him that when the bombing started at almost the same time as the sirens went off, with no time left to run to a shelter, she grabbed Victor and dove under the heavy oak dining room table.

Once, after a month working in the refugee camp hospital, Vladimir was caught in an unexpected early night raid. In the middle of an adenoidectomy procedure on an eleven year old child, he could not leave his patient. *What should I do? We need to be downstairs, but I can't take her down in this condition. Ten more minutes, ten more minutes.*

An elderly policeman stomped into the surgery room. "I saw the light. It should have been off and you should be in the shelter. Why aren't you?"

"I can't leave my patient at the moment."

"There is no exception. The order is firm, when the siren goes off, you must proceed to the shelter. Take your patient and go down this instant before I arrest you. You must take our rules and regulations seriously."

Vladimir could not believe his ears. *Is he joking? He's going to arrest me? I can't move the patient downstairs in this condition.* Suddenly, a bomb exploded near the hospital. The old building swayed, rattling the wooden window panes. The old man bent low as he scurried out of the room, leaving Vladimir to finish the operation and carry the little girl down to the basement.

That night, several casualties from the bombing raid were brought in to the already overcrowded hospital. Most were refugee residents of the camp, but a few were victims from the surrounding blocks, all were unable to seek shelter in time. Vladimir and three other refugee doctors from Belarus and Ukraine quickly examined them. In most cases, they required minor surgery for wounds caused by flying bits of masonry, metal, and glass.

As Vladimir approached one of the men lying on a cot in the first floor hallway, he thought that the man looked familiar. The man, moaning in pain, glanced at Vladimir and as their eyes met, each recognized the other. Vladimir's heart began to pound, his breath shallow. The man bleeding from his shoulder and arm was Adler, the man in black who enjoyed terrorizing them on the train to Slonim and pleaded with the commandant to execute them.

"You! You! No! Get away from me. Don't touch me. I want a German physician. I begged them not to bring me here. Don't touch me." As Vladimir drew closer, the man began screaming, hysterically, "Nurse, anyone, I want a German doctor!" There was no response from anyone. No one paid any attention.

"Well, what do you know, Herr Adler? What a surprise. Unfortunately, you are stuck with either me or some other foreign doctor."

"I'd rather bleed to death than have you touch me. Get away from me!"

"From the amount of blood I see, that's a very good possibility. You will bleed to death. You need to calm down and begin to understand that I can help you. Whether you like it or not, I'm here and I can save your life."

Adler seemed to calm down, taking deep breaths. His face contorted from the pain and the angst of the moment. "You need to allow me to help you," Vladimir said, his voice appearing calm and soothing even though deep inside he really did not care if the man died. He had caused them so much grief and pain.

Adler glanced at Vladimir, his eyes cloudy and distant. Then they closed and he nodded, conceding defeat before he passed out.

Efficiently, but with reluctance, Vladimir worked on him diligently removing shrapnel, cleaning the wounds, stitching them up and then bandaging them. It was difficult for him. He hated the man, but his job was to save lives and he took his physician's oath seriously. He hoped that he would never see this man again. Completing his task, Vladimir walked away toward the next patient. He was puzzled why Adler was in town and not fighting in the fields and forests as the other German men. *He must be one of those nasty henchmen that terrorize the public making sure that they comply with Hitler's insane directives. Or maybe he was sent here to make sure no one eats a dead horse left in the street.* Vladimir could not help but grin at that last thought and at the irony of it all. The man that despised him so much now succumbed and had Vladimir save him.

Exhausted, Vladimir finally came home. He was anxious, though, to tell Slava about who he treated. "You're not serious. Here, in Hamm? And in the labor camp? Why did you help that pig?"

"If I hadn't, he would have died. He had already lost so much blood that he passed out."

"Well, did he actually see you before that?"

"Oh yes. He was shocked and did not want me to touch him."

"Well, I don't know if I would have helped him. He is such a vile, despicable person. A man without a soul."

"Yes, you would have."

"Well, maybe. Before you fall asleep, I need to discuss something with you. I heard German women talking. They are petrified at the thought that the Red Army is so close to the German border. They pray that the Americans or the British get here first.

"I know, I've also heard the same," Vladimir said.

"They say that no woman would be safe. They describe such atrocities that the soldiers will inflict on the population. Do you really think that our countrymen would do such evil things?"

"I think the Nazis are purposely terrifying the population so that they will continue the fight. Though, there must be a terrific amount of hatred built up in the Soviets. Look what the Germans had done to our Belarus. We saw the cruelty first hand—the hangings, the shooting, random extermination of people, the warehousing of bodies in camps, and the raping of our own women. I am sure it will be unpleasant here. Millions have been killed or tortured at the hands of the Nazis. Lives had been ruined! Soviets will savor the revenge. Although, vengeance is a nasty thing; it's a human's solution to vindicate the evil experienced. Instead, more evil is inflicted. Slavochka, I'm so tired, I can't think straight. Maybe what I said makes no sense."

"Unfortunately, it does. But we have a huge problem that is really worrying me.

The war will be over soon. Hitler will give in. He's got to. We escaped from the Soviets, and now they are almost here. What are we going to do? They'll take us back and execute us."

"Slava, it will turn out all right. Don't worry."

"Don't worry! Don't worry! Here you go again telling me not to worry. Well, I am worried!" Slava waited for a reply, but Vladimir was sound asleep. Soon after, Slava joined him, and an hour later, the air-raid siren went off again.

Chapter 40

SLAVA WAS wrong. Hitler did not exhibit any intention of giving up even though the outcome for Germany appeared certain in February 1945. The Soviets were just east of Berlin. The British and Canadians were preparing to cross into Germany from the north, and the Americans were piercing the border from the south and west. Instead of winding down, the Germans intensified their efforts to defend themselves with everything they could muster. Any male that could carry a rifle and shoot, no matter his age, was mobilized to defend the country alongside the beleaguered and bedraggled troops.

"They're going to fight until Germany is totally flattened and its people annihilated," Vladimir commented to Slava as they observed the Gestapo rounding up old men and young boys, issuing rifles, preparing to send them into battle. Wearing black Gestapo-type uniforms adorned with gold braids and eagle patches on their sleeves, the boys looked excited by what they thought would be an adventure. They chatted and some even giggled as they boarded the trucks. "Look at that, Slava. Some of those boys can't be older than nine or ten, but see how enthusiastic they are. They will be extremely dangerous with a gun. They are foolish, brain-washed by the Nazi's. To them, it's a game."

"This is awful," Slava cringed observing the young boys. "They're sending children to do their dirty work and to a certain defeat. How many of them will be killed?"

The couple stood with a crowd of Germans on the bomb-damaged sidewalk, Vladimir holding his son on his shoulders. They watched the men and boys load onto trucks. Some of the old men could barely walk, let alone climb onto the beds of trucks. One decrepit-looking man hobbled up to the trucks using canes. The scene was pathetic. *Is it love of their fatherland, or is it heroism? This is a definite sign of desperation. It will not take long now,* Slava thought to herself. "Volodya, we have been here in Germany now for seven months. I think that by summer, if not sooner, Germany will be on its knees. Have you given any more thought to what would become of us once that happens? Surely, they won't send us back."

"I stayed awake at night thinking about it. But really, what can we do about anything? We'll just have to take it one step at a time. Everything will be all right."

"I've hope that the next words from your mouth are not 'just relax' like you're always telling me. Well, I don't think that I can 'just relax.'"

Vladimir laughed. "All right. Then let me tell you that I love you and I feel that everything will be fine."

"I like that better," Slava said, cracking a smile. "We'll take it one day at a time."

"Slavochka, my dear, you just worry too much."

The vicious fighting continued, made worse by the bitter winds and snows of winter. Experiencing intensive defensive efforts by the Germans with no moves to capitulate, the British and American bombing campaigns accelerated. A variety of special purpose bombs descended haphazardly from countless Allied planes, covering larger cities like a carpet. The Allies were punishing the defiant country. These projectiles falling from the sky included extra-loud concussion explosives designed to affect every cell in the body; phosphorous detonations that spewed hot spray, melting flesh from the bone; time-release bombs that exploded hours after they hit the ground, propelling shrapnel and later releasing invisible toxic gas.

Hamm was mostly subjected to the conventional exploding bombs. Most were the incendiary variety that on impact spit out fires resembling angry dragons. Areas of the city burned simultaneously, some uniting into one enormous swirling, howling fire storm incinerating bodies and destroying everything in its path. And as though that was not enough, the Allies dropped bombs filled with bits of concrete, bottles, trash, and garbage to totally demoralize the population.

The bomb shelter provided the only hope of escape. Unfortunately, even these shelters, at times, offered little protection. Buildings collapsed onto basements where residents huddled together, bodies trembling, anxious to survive yet another day. Occasionally, special missiles bored their way through roofs, past several stories striking the people congregated below.

Vladimir and Slava struggled to survive the onslaughts. They took seriously the tortuous wail of sirens. The never-ending alarms and the bombings that followed now ruled their daily life. How long can they go on like this, with their minds numb, their bodies cringing, their insides twisting and squeezing like a pretzel? They constantly struggled to shake off the unshakable feeling of doom. There were now rumors throughout the camp of swirling fire tornados in Berlin sucking the life of even those hiding in basements, tunnels, and under bridges, leaving ash as the only remains of human life.

They were edgy during and in between bombing raids. The next attack might be their last. The blare from the incessant warnings continuously reverberated in their ears. They seemed to hear sirens when, in fact, there were none.

They were no strangers to explosions with the accompanying devastation—Vladimir in battle, Slava in the destruction of Vitebsk and recently in Castrop-Rauxel. However, the couple had never experienced the degree of unremitting assault as was the case in Hamm. "One can never get used to anything like this," was Slava's answer to Vladimir when he attempted to comfort her by making the point that they had survived it before and they will again. He could not blame her when, at times, she seemed on a verge of hysteria. He too, felt the strain on his own psyche from the incessant sirens, the drone of countless propellers, the reverberation of flak guns, the scream of tumbling bombs followed by ear-splitting and earth-shaking explosions, one after another, one after another, each one jarring the soul.

The hopelessness around them that the Moskalkovs witnessed after the attacks was difficult to grasp as well. Crackling fires burned all around them. Buildings stood as skeletons in the acrid air. The atmosphere thickened to almost a velvet shroud of billowing black smoke and swirling, choking dust from what used to be brick and mortar. Awnings and metal balconies were ripped away, lying in the rubble with homes, leaving thousands of residents with no place to go. Light poles snapped like matchsticks with their wires strewn about and dead animals decayed in the streets. Trees burned with open flames, some lying across sidewalks and streets. The stench surrounding them was suffocating.

After a particularly severe raid, Slava, viewing the additional devastation, could not help but sob. "What new hell did we escape to when we left Slonim?" She screamed, letting her frustration out. "There'll be nothing left of this city and maybe nothing left of us. What's going on with this world?"

"As far as I'm concerned," Vladimir paused, inhaling deeply though his mouth. He choked and then coughed. His throat and larynx burned from the pungent air. "This whole war, this mad, insane chaos is as though it's the end of civilization. What are human beings capable of?" Slava remained silent, still sobbing. She also began to cough and looked at her son in his father's arms, his face pressed against Vladimir's coat. She reached in her handbag retrieving three handkerchiefs, giving one to Vladimir and tying one around Victor's mouth before she placed one over her own mouth.

Vladimir felt upset at his words. The last thing he wanted to do was to make matters seem worse for Slava. He realized that he needed to be more upbeat, if not for Slava, then for himself. "Do you know what, Slavochka? I don't actually believe what I just said. It may appear to be the end of the world, but it isn't. It's a trying time right now. But in the end these tribulations will only make us stronger. There will be resurgence. We are tough and we'll get through this. With a little patience, life will be good, better than we could ever imagine."

Still silent, Slava took Victor from Vladimir, and they both lumbered carefully over the rubble, trying to make their way around large and small craters while avoiding the snaking electric wires, which seemed ready to ensnarl them. Victor, though, wanted down. Slava was not about to let him run around in the debris. She gave him back to Vladimir. Vladimir told him to stay still and held him tightly to prevent his squirming. They finally made their way home, thankful that their house remained intact, except for additional broken and fallen plaster and a shattered window. Their hearts were heavy as Vladimir prepared to go back to work. "Be careful, my dear," Slava said, as she kissed him. "I'm sure I'll see you before long in the hospital shelter. Another siren will blare soon."

Chapter 41

"THE AMERICANS are across the Rhine!" "They're on our soil!" "They'll be here soon!" Slava heard the desperate talk at the black market. She felt a lump in her throat. Instinctively, she held Victor closer to herself, so tightly that her son protested. She had no clue what that news would really mean for them. Was it good? Was it bad? Regardless, it would be another change in their lives. She felt like running home, falling into bed and crying. At that moment she missed her mother and father. If only she could talk to them, hear her parents' voices of encouragement. *Thank God for my Volodya. Without him I'd be terribly lost.* She needed his comforting embrace. She needed to be held in his arms, smoothing her hair and telling her, "Everything will be all right." She felt that it would, but what did it mean with Germany defeated? She looked into Victor's smiling face as she put him down. She smiled back and sloughed off the thoughts for the moment.

"Victor, let's get serious about finding something to eat for tonight." Victor couldn't care less. He began chasing a lone pigeon that landed between the stalls of the vendors. Slava laughed watching her son run around in circles, although she was amazed that no one had caught and eaten the bird.

When Slava finally found a few carrots for sale, the woman with deep facial wrinkles refused to take her marks. "Money is no good. What do you have for trade?"

"I don't have anything right this moment."

"I'll take your gloves in trade."

"That's too much for just four carrots. What else do you have that we can trade?"

The woman reached into a box under the table and pulled out a half liter bottle of milk. Slava's eyes lit up. *Fresh milk!* Even powdered milk was now impossible to obtain. "Is it fresh?"

"Of course, it is. It's today's."

Slava took off her knitted gloves and handed them to the woman. She had more at the house since they bought seven other pairs in Castrop-Rauxel a few months ago specifically to be used for barter. "Please bring back the bottle," the woman said.

The food situation became even more dire as the days lingered. Ration coupons were still being issued, but the store shelves, for the most part, stood empty. On the days when Slava was unable to find any food to trade for, the Moskalkovs ate with the other refugees in the camp's community kitchen and felt fortunate to receive what they could. The meals were substandard, lacking taste and the quantity barely enough to sustain a person for the day—mostly watered down soup with a couple of thin slices of coarse bread. Occasionally, margarine would be doled out.

There was never tea, only a cup of hot water, but on certain days, ersatz, the imitation barley coffee, would be available.

The bitter winds and snows of winter gave way, in late March and early April 1945, to the first sprigs of green blades of grass and tiny buds on shrubs. The trees were gone, either burned or cut down for firewood. When the Germans were unable to stop the rapidly advancing American forces, the Nazi officials, together with German troops stationed in the vicinity of Hamm, pulled out in retreat, supposedly to defend Berlin. Citizens of the city were left to fend for themselves. Banks, post offices, busses, cable cars, trains, and all other services provided by the government stopped functioning. There was no fuel for automobiles, heat, or cooking. The city's mayor (the Burgermeister) became the ultimate authority figure. Once installed by the Nazis because he was active in the party, the man suddenly changed his colors, as the American forces were on the doorstep of Hamm. He declared that he never wanted to be a Nazi but was coerced into it. He tried to bring normalcy to the city, but it became an impossible task without the necessary resources.

With the approach of the Americans, all the remaining Nazi flags and banners were taken down. Instead, a huge sign hanging from city hall welcomed the conquerors. The mayor asked the local citizens to line up and greet the enemy troops as they arrived. Vladimir was given a day off, being told sarcastically by the administrator that if he wanted to see his allies he should go to City Hall to greet the Americans.

The Moskalkovs were astonished at the sight of banners of welcome on several buildings. Even an American flag was hung on a wall. Where this flag came from was a mystery. They watched citizens lining up as though waiting for a parade. "There is so much irony in this," Vladimir commented. "Welcoming the enemy that defeated them. Do they really think the Americans are going to be fooled?"

Slava did not hesitate to answer him as she had given it a lot of thought. "They are certainly going to try to butter them up, hoping they'll be treated well. Actually, if they are to be defeated, they would rather have it be the Americans. The Germans are deathly afraid of the Soviets."

Suddenly the roar of vehicles could be heard. The populace fell silent waiting for the Americans to materialize. Vladimir and Slava waited as well, with Victor in his father's arms. A nervous chill ran through Vladimir. He imagined Slava felt edgy as well. They should feel elated that their German enemy was defeated, at least in Hamm, yet they both feared what the Americans would be like? Will they send them back into Stalin's grasp?

A Jeep displaying flags on each side of the hood, one American and the other bearing the letters "First Army," turned at the intersection and headed toward the direction where the family stood. It was quickly followed by a convoy of Jeeps, trucks, halftracks, and many, many tanks. Being

American made, most of the vehicles were unfamiliar to Vladimir, but he could not help recognize the German automobiles, trucks, and the evil panzer tanks, all sporting the same colors and insignias of those of the American equipment. The sight of the Nazi vehicles brought back his days as a prisoner of war. He was thirsty, hungry, barely able to walk, yet forced to push or pull those evil machines out of the muddy, impassible roads of Belarus. A smile tugged at his lips, one of gratification, to see those same vehicles were now used by Germany's enemy as spoils of war to transport what appeared to be hundreds of soldiers sitting or hanging off of them.

The Americans looked relaxed, Vladimir thought. Their uniforms were so unlike the formal ones worn by the Germans. The soldiers were dressed comfortably, in loose-fitting fatigues with their shirts unbuttoned at the neck, their jackets open. If it were not for a few military insignias, Vladimir could not tell that they were soldiers. Their helmets did not appear as heavy as those of the Germans, each soldier wearing it as he chose, mostly slung to the side of his head. *What a difference from the meticulous Germans. Yet they're here. They are the victors.*

The soldiers' bearing also surprised Vladimir and left a deep impression on him. Many were smiling, even waving and not at all appearing to gloat at being the great conquerors of Germany. It was a refreshing change from the sober and strictly disciplined German soldier.

As the convoy filed past them on the way to the city center, the couple saw children yelling and flaying their arms about. At first they could not understand the commotion. Then they saw some of the soldiers tossing something into the crowd. Still holding Victor, Vladimir managed to stretch out and grab one of the items. He passed it on to his wife so that she could examine it. It looked like candy. Using her knowledge of the German alphabet, Slava read the word "Hershey." Unwrapping it, to her amazement she discovered a chunk of chocolate. She grinned with joy as she broke off a piece for each of them, then another and another until the chocolate quickly disappeared.

"I like these people," Vladimir said. "They are generous and appear friendly. Wouldn't it be something if, indeed, we could go to America?"

"Dream on, Volodya, dream on. But it sure would be something."

The American Army did not stay long. They left a small contingent at city hall, appropriated some of the houses for their staff, and then moved on towards Berlin. At first, life for the Moskalkovs did not change. Food and other supplies were still difficult to obtain. Luckily, Vladimir and Slava continued to trade items of apparel for food. Other refugees were in such desperate shape that they stooped to stealing from locals, particularly the farmers. Even though a minority engaged in theft, the local populace assumed all were thieves and despised the refugees more than ever.

The couple realized that once the men and boys come back from the front, violence against the refugees could erupt on a greater scale.

The refugees' state of health worried Vladimir. Many suffered from severe malnutrition. They began to remind him of his fellow emaciated prisoners held captive by the Nazis. At the same time, medicines and other supplies were being depleted. He concluded that unless something happened soon, many would die, especially the children. To add to his grave concern, ration cards ceased to be distributed by the Germans as there no longer existed a central German government. Besides, store shelves stood mostly empty anyway. The black market or a nearby farm provided the only source for food for the Germans. Surprisingly, meager amounts of food were still provided to the non-German refugees at the community kitchen by the local government due to a direct command from the US Army.

Toward the end of April 1945, a few packages containing food, medical supplies, and clothing arrived on US Army trucks at the refugee camp. The food was distributed to the refugees through the community kitchen as part of the meal program. The small allotment of clothing was issued to the neediest, but not enough to go around. This led to not only arguments, but actual fist fights, some brutal enough to seek medical attention from Vladimir or one of the other doctors.

A few weeks later, more shipments of food, blankets, clothing, and other supplies arrived. The supplies were provided by an organization called the United Relief and Rehabilitation Agency (UNNRA) created on November 9, 1943 at a multi-nation conference at the White House in Washington, DC to confront the massive refugee problem caused by the war. The food came mostly in powdered form in boxes—eggs, milk, and potatoes. There were some canned goods, of which Spam was the favorite among the refugees.

The German population was not provided with supplies and left to fend for themselves. Resentment toward the refugees went from bad to worse. Vladimir and Slava fearfully kept a low profile, trying to blend in as Germans when possible.

As Slava sat reading in a chair, the *Sailors' Chorus* from Richard Wagner's opera, *The Flying Dutchman* broadcast on the radio was suddenly interrupted with an urgent announcement. Slava's ears perked up, and she put her book down to listen. Stunned, she heard that Germany had capitulated. The war was over. Her mind still tried to absorb that statement when she heard the announcer state in a tearful voice and in a low tone that Hitler had committed suicide in his bunker. *Oh my God! Thank God. It's May 8, 1945, and at last this horrible, terrible war is over. I knew it would be before summer.* Leaning her head against the back of the chair, she shut her eyes. She felt deep emotions roiling inside her. She began to cry. They went through such an ordeal the last four years. *I wonder if Volodya heard. Surely, someone had the radio on there. Oh my God! It's over at last. But now what?*

Chapter 42

"Hitler is dead! The war is over! The war is over!" Hospital wards and halls resonated with shouts, hoots and hollers. Vladimir could not help but hear the commotion just outside the surgical room, and his jaw fell when he caught the words. It was finally all over. His heart skipped a beat, his breathing rapid and shallow; barely able to concentrate on the nasal procedure he just had begun. He glanced at his assistant, a young Russian refugee nurse. "Did you hear that, doctor?" The nurse asked, almost singing the words. She dropped the surgical scissors from her trembling hand, giggling as she quickly picked up the instrument and placed it in a sterilization container. Vladimir could see her eyes dance. He nodded, grinning beneath his mask. Her excitement was palpable. He tried as hard as he could to focus, but all he could think about was that he must hurry home and tell Slava. *Surely she hadn't heard.*

Vladimir remained at the hospital for a few more antsy hours. Throughout the day, the cheers and exuberant grins of the refugees continued. The few Germans he saw appeared downcast, uncommunicative, and tried to disappear from view. He wondered what went through their minds at the moment. *Surely they must be relieved, even though devastated by the defeat. They knew though, for months that this would be the ultimate outcome, but it must still hurt and embarrass the proud people. Rightfully so.* His grin widened at the thought.

Finally able to leave, Vladimir sprinted home. The unlocked door flung open as he rushed in, the force propelling it into the wall, startling Slava and Victor. They were sitting on the sofa, Slava reading the story of *Hansel and Gretel* to her son in German. "You obviously heard the news," Slava said as she shot out of the sofa just in time for Vladimir to grab her and spin her in a clasping hug. Victor ran to greet his father, locking his arms around Vladimir's leg.

"The war is over! The war is over!"

After the initial enthusiasm, their laughter and smiles faded. Thoughts of their own future began to creep into Slava's mind. Slava retreated to the sofa. As he often did, Vladimir played a game of catch with Victor, chasing him as he ran from room to room. Laughing and screaming from delight, his son tried to run past his father without getting caught, while Vladimir pretended to miss him as he squirmed by.

Slava watched them play, then cupped her face in her hands and, resting her elbows on her knees, stared at the floor. "Slavochka," Vladimir called out, looking her way. "I know what you're thinking. But at this moment let's just be elated."

"Oh, I am! I'm so joyful that the war is over. How can I not be?"

"Good. Think of what a relief it is."

"I know, I know. It's just that for so many months now, I had dwelt on what the end of the war would mean to us? We knew it would be over soon. It would be wonderful if we could go back home. But we can't. Will we be allowed to stay? Will they, whoever 'they' are, send us back to our certain deaths in the Soviet Union?"

"Slavochka, please. Here you go again. We'd covered this many times before. You're going to work yourself into frenzy. What happened to my always optimistic sweetheart? You're the one that has been upbeat, never complaining about our living conditions or our hunger or the loss of our homeland. I'm the one who usually whines about how homesick I am."

"What happened? I'll tell you what happened. Life happened. The war happened. Maybe I've become more realistic, or maybe I'm wary of the future. I miss Vitebsk also and want to return and know that we can't. Of course, as you had suggested, it would be great to go to America and live in a sane place for a change. But what are our chances of that. Nil, I'd say."

"Look we'd been very lucky so far. We'll take it a day at a time, and before you know it we'll be fine. We're not alone. I heard from a German official in the hospital that there are more than eleven million foreigners on German soil. How long do you think it will take to process that many people? Whoever is in charge will have a horrendous task.

Just think about the housing and the food they would have to provide. I can't believe that they would let us starve. The refugees will also need medical help. They'll need me. And during this time, we'll find out what becomes of us. Surely, they won't force us back to our deaths. They must know the Soviet government and how ruthless it is."

Slava sat quietly listening to Vladimir. Now in his father's arms, Victor kept pulling on Vladimir's nose. Slava smiled at her husband's annoyance with his son. Victor, though, thought it funny and giggled harder with every swat of his father's hand. The cackle became infectious, causing the parents to laugh. After which, Slava said, "Volodya, you have this knack of making me feel better. I'm sorry. I am optimistic that we'll be all right, but it's good just to talk about it. With the end of the war, there will be changes and we'll have to adapt."

A few weeks after the end of the war, the small American contingent withdrew from Hamm as the British army rolled into the city. Observing the men, the Moskalkovs concluded that there was a difference in their demeanor as compared to the Americans. More formal in appearance, they seemed rigid, no-nonsense individuals.

With the Allies as victors, Germany was divided into four zones agreed upon by Franklin Roosevelt, Winston Churchill, and Joseph Stalin at the Yalta Conference in 1944. The meeting tackled the issue of what to do with Europe and the mass of displaced persons after the war ended. Hamm, in the part of the Westphalia region of northwest Germany, fell into the British zone of occupation. The Moskalkovs immediately noticed that from the very beginning, the British took their job of administering the area seriously. They continued with the existing refugee camps as set up by the Nazi government, renaming them Displaced Persons Camps and added others as needed.

With the coming of the British, the German camp administrators suddenly departed. Once they left, squabbles, including fist fights among the refugees, escalated. Thefts and assaults became more prevalent. It came to a point that Slava feared for her safety. Fortunately the lack of leadership did not last long, as soon as the British soldiers and an officer in charge took over at the camp. With stern administration at the helm, arrests were made and some order returned. Food shipments began to arrive. The rationed food was doled out to the camps' residents. The community kitchen closed, and each family was expected to prepare their own meals with the provisions they received. The rations were pegged at 1,500 calories per day, twice the amount that the conquered Germans received.

Vladimir expected that the hospital would also be run by the British Army. He was right. One day, as he was leaving one ward to go to another, the front door flew open. Three British officers, armed with holstered pistols, entered the foyer. They were accompanied by two unarmed soldiers. The men glanced at Vladimir with a quick, measured look.

One of the officers, a tall, lanky man with graying hair protruding from underneath his military hat, walked up to him. "Good day," the officer said, raising his hand with a quick flick of his fingers. "I'm major Jeffery Jenkins, the new administrator of this facility. I take it you're a physician here since you're wearing a white doctor's smock."

Confronted with the English language for the first time, Vladimir shook his head and stated in German that he did not understand. "Jolly good." Jenkins commented and turned to one of the soldiers. "Perkins, would you step over here. It appears we need an interpreter." The erect soldier, thin and very young, towering a foot over Vladimir's five-feet-eight-inch frame, spoke German, and it turned out, he also spoke Russian.

Through the interpreter, Vladimir was told that they are medical officers and will handle the administration of the hospital. Vladimir smiled politely and said, "Good." He had mixed feelings about the news. It was probably beneficial to have the British take over. The hospital's supply of equipment and medications was almost non-existent. In addition, he hoped that better food would become available to patients to help with their recovery. On the other hand, he remembered his grandfather's saying, "Every broom sweeps its own way." There will be changes, hopefully for the better, but there will be changes, nonetheless. And with an influx of British doctors, will they still need him?

"I want to meet with the medical staff later this afternoon," the officer continued. "You will be notified of the time. You must all be present. Carry on."

Later in the day, Vladimir was informed by a nurse of the meeting. He arrived as instructed, to the formerly German chief administrator's office, at precisely five o'clock. His heart pounded. Will he be allowed to continue on as a doctor? He had never before set a foot in that office, something that had soothed him just fine. It was never good news when someone had to be called to the room. This office was larger than the other offices he had seen in the building, large enough to accommodate a sizable wooden desk and a conference table that had six chairs around it.

After being greeted by an attractive red-haired uniformed English girl, he understood by her gesture that he should sit down and took a seat at the pointed table. He slid in next to his friend, Bogdan Panasenko, a Ukrainian colleague. Both sat quietly as others came in. Soon fourteen people crowded together in the room. Most stood in the absolute, uncomfortable silence, anxiously waiting for the proverbial ax to drop.

Finally, after a long fifteen minutes, Major Jenkins walked in through the door, followed by the same officers Vladimir met earlier in the day. Perkins, the interpreter was last to enter. They made their way through the crowd and took a position behind the desk. Jenkins forced a quick smile, greeted the staff present and, through Perkins, told them that he expected them all to remain on the job. A weight lifted off Vladimir's shoulders. Jenkins continued with a series of rules and regulations. *Typically bureaucratic jargon*, Vladimir thought. *This could be worse than working under the Germans. They will probably micro manage everything*. The major told them about the new bulletin board in the upstairs hall on which their hours of work will be posted, including rotations for doctors on call. Everyone's ears perked up when he explained a schedule of pay and payments to be paid out in marks. "Don't worry about your money being accepted. In the British zone the German marks will be legal tender and will be accepted."

Vladimir felt satisfied and relieved. The rules and regulations did not faze him as he saw no problem working under them. As Jenkins was winding down, Vladimir's thoughts turned to his patients and the rounds at the wards he had yet to make before going home. He could hardly wait to tell Slava of the day's events. Then, out of the blue, he heard the major say, "Oh, by the way, some of you, perhaps more than a few, may not be with us for very long, and we'll have to make adjustments. Vladimir held his breath. *What did he mean? What's that all about?*

"I guess it's all right to inform you," Jenkins hesitated for a moment. He looked to the other officers, as if asking for their approval. They stood motionless, stone-faced. "It appears that the American president and our prime minister agreed to Stalin's demands at the Yalta Conference that his soldiers may enter the British, American, and French zones at any time, within any city and including this and other refugee camps, to look for Soviet citizens for the purpose of transporting them back to USSR." Gasps of outrage were heard throughout the room. Upon hearing the words, Vladimir froze inside. A shooting pain pounded in his skull. Bogdan's face turned crimson. He startled Vladimir when in his booming voice he cried out, "How can this be? How did this happen? What determines who is a Soviet citizen?"

All eyes were fixed on Bogdan as he asked the questions, then immediately shifted to the major for his answers. "Well, yes," Jenkins began, clearing his throat. "Good questions. I'll try to give you what I know, but please, don't ask me any more questions. Stalin wants his people back. He has a country to rebuild. He assured Roosevelt and Churchill that there would be no retribution against the Soviet citizens. I am sure he is a man of his word and that no one will be harmed." A groan was heard from the audience. Jenkins ignored the interruption as he went on. "As far as your question of who is considered a Soviet citizen, at this time I must admit that I'm bloody confused about that point. It has to do with which eastern border of Poland is the determining line. Corporal Perkins, you've studied orders, reports, and maps regarding that Yalta Agreement, would you enlighten us as to exactly who is a Soviet citizen."

Perkins stepped forward quickly, smug at being asked to show off his knowledge. "Yes, Major, I'll take a stab at it." Taking a deep breath, he began, "The eastern border of Poland, as it was agreed to after the Soviet-Polish war in the 1920s, is the now the demarcation line for the purpose of repatriation of Soviet citizens. From what I studied, the Yalta Agreement specifically determined that to be the line. That was the border at the time that Hitler's foreign minister, Ribbentrop, and Stalin's foreign minister, Molotov, entered into an agreement called the Non-Aggression Pact dated August 23, 1939. It divided Poland between the Soviet Union and Germany and moved the border of the Soviet Union considerably westerly."

"Perkins! You're going into too much history. How does this information precisely affect the people in this room?"

"Well, Major, the eastern border of Poland, as it was prior to August 23, 1939 is crucial in determining who is a Soviet citizen. If a person lived east of that border on or before August 23, 1939, then that person *is* a Soviet citizen. And conversely, if that person found himself to be on the western side of the border, then he technically is *not* a Soviet citizen for purposes of repatriation and would not be subject to Soviet authority."

"Borders, borders, I know about borders," Bogdan blurted out. "They change all the time in Europe, depending on who won. Where exactly is this border you're talking about? Does it affect the Ukraine?"

"Oh, yes, the old border went through Poland, Belarus, and the Ukraine. It's hard to describe exactly where it is without a map present, but as I recall, it is generally about fifty kilometers east of Wilejka, Nowogrodek, Baranovichi, Sarny, and Rowno."

"Well, I need to see this for myself. Where can I find a map?"

Annoyed at the lengthy explanation and the questions, Jenkins decided to put an end to it. "This is enough discussion on this subject. As medical officer, it is not my position to educate you on politics. I will warn you, though, that my orders are such that if I become aware of who is a Soviet citizen, under the Yalta Agreement I, as well as any other British or American officer, am required to turn that individual over to the Soviets." Hesitating, he mumbled, "By force, if necessary." He looked around the room, and seeing the many distressed faces, mellowed his tone. "If anyone wants a glance at a map with that line drawn, I'll try to have it on the bulletin board in a few days."

Vladimir felt deflated and powerless. His mind and body seemed in limbo struggling to comprehend the consequences to himself and his family of what he just heard. He was in Baranovichi, but not in 1939. In 1939 he and Slava lived and studied in Vitebsk, many kilometers from that Polish border. This fact meant that he and Slava would be subject to being rounded up and taken back to their deaths. He did not believe for one minute that there would be any leniency from Stalin, although he desperately wanted it to be so. He knew better. His hand trembled slightly as he brought it up to rub his forehead. He and Slava fell into that "Soviet citizen" category. *Didn't the British and the American leaders realize that they were condemning thousands, to death or hard labor in remote regions of Siberia? But then, why should they care, really? They have a huge problem with all the refugees that they're now stuck with. Sending these refugees back would be the easiest scenario for them*

The group was dismissed and Vladimir hurried off to see his patients. He tried to set the thoughts of what he had heard aside, but he wasn't able to shake them off. *How can I break this to Slava? It will devastate her.*

Chapter 43

SMILING AND bright-eyed, Slava met Vladimir on the porch when she saw him approaching. As he ran up the steps, she wrapped her arms around him and kissed him lovingly on his lips. He reciprocated, but his response to her affection was not quite as enthusiastic as she was used to. Concern and uneasiness showed on his face. "What is it? What's wrong?" Slava easily picked up on his mood.

Vladimir hugged her again, forcing a grin just as Victor ran up, nearly colliding with his father's knees. Vladimir lifted him up. Kissing his cheeks, he pressed his son to his chest. "Well, what's wrong?" Slava persisted.

Vladimir struggled to put into words everything that he heard. Words that would not make their situation sound quite as dire. How could he tell Slava of Stalin's far reach, even here in western Germany, under the control of the British? On numerous occasions, Slava had expressed her dread that Stalin's goons would find them and drag them back. He did not believe that could happen, but now, seemingly, her fear was coming to fruition. "Let me wash up. Were you able to find anything for dinner tonight?"

"Dinner! Dinner! You've scaring me to death and you ask about dinner?! Tell me what's wrong and don't try to stall."

Still holding Victor in his arms, Vladimir flopped on the sofa. Slava immediately sat down next to him. "Well?" He began slowly, repeating the events of the day from his first encounter with the British to the meeting in late afternoon. First he emphasized that the British told him he would be retained. "That is wonderful, but then what has upset you? Tell me!"

As her husband stalled with an answer, Slava became more irritated, exhaling heavily through her nose. Not knowing how to break the bad news gently, Vladimir haltingly told her about the Yalta agreement that allowed Soviet soldiers to go anywhere in Germany, including Hamm and the camp, and retrieve their citizens. He purposely left out Jenkins's words, "By force, if necessary." Instead he tried to put more weight into the statement that Stalin promised no retribution, nor punishment, for those going back.

Slava sat dejectedly, carefully listening with bated breath to Vladimir. She felt almost a physical pain in her stomach as it knotted. "Oh God, no! It can't be happening. It just can't be! Oh God! And this promise of no punishment is a lot of bunk! When did Stalin ever keep any promises? I can't believe that the Americans or British fell for that!" Her voice became shrill. "They want the Soviets to remove us from their sight. Really, what do they care what happens to us? They must be overwhelmed with all the refugees here, and they need to get rid of us as quickly as possible. And who in their right mind, having lived under Stalin's dictatorship and having known Stalin's brutal antics and tricks, would believe this shit." She quickly clapped her fingers to her mouth. Slava rarely used such words, but what she heard from Vladimir shook her badly and left her so upset that she trembled.

Vladimir sat quietly on the sofa, listening to her, his elbows on his knees and head cupped by his hands. Victor seemed to sense the anxiety around him and kept quiet, sitting snugly at his father's side.

Her ire now expended, Slava fell silent, her eyes misty. After a few moments of dead silence in the room, she said wearily, "All right, somehow, we'll have to manage. If that's the way it will be, we'll just have to hide from them when they come until we figure out a way out of this."

"That's the spirit," Vladimir said, pleased to hear his wife's flare of optimism. "We'll find a way. And, it may very well be that no Soviet soldiers would come this far west into Germany or follow through with their scheme. Let's not worry about it until we actually see the Red Army."

The next day, more British officers and soldiers arrived on the scene setting themselves up as the new administrators of the camp. Within a few days of their meticulous management, inventories of food stocks were relocated to a warehouse on the camp grounds. Military trucks brought in shipments of captured German food stock and products confiscated from uncooperative local farmers. The supplies included flour, rice, butter, macaroni, spaghetti, prunes, cocoa, sugar, meat, soup stock, fresh vegetables, dried vegetables, and ersatz coffee.

Each individual that had been assigned to the camp at Hamm and those assigned the housing outside the camp was required to appear at the administration building of the refugee camp. There, their names, ages, and places of residence were confirmed and recorded. Then they issued rations cards to be used only at the camp warehouse, at no charge for the food. Notices posted on the wall in English, Polish, Ukrainian, Byelorussian, Russian, and German languages indicated that two thousand daily calories were allowed each displaced person through the rations and that the available food may vary from day to day.

A patient who worked in the administration told Vladimir that the responsibility to provide most of the food needed for the refugees fell on the conquered Germans. If they failed to deliver the products requested, then the British military could take what was needed from whatever source was available, such as warehouses, stores, and farms. The man also confided to Vladimir that he overheard two officers talking, and that the goal was to provide the amount of only 1,100 calories for each German. "In a way, that's so sad," Slava said after Vladimir told her of the conversation. "That's barely enough to subsist on. So many were against the war and didn't realize what Hitler was doing, yet they're swept with the same broom."

"It's a form of punishment," Vladimir said. "They've caused so many deaths, so much misery, and such destruction and chaos. Just look all around us, Germany is in shambles. I can imagine what Poland or Belarus looks like, or Russia for that matter. Europe will take years to rebuild."

"I know, I know. But I can't help how I now feel sorry for the local people as I get to know them here and there."

"I feel for them also, though I'm damned if I know why. I really should have bitter feelings after the torturous treatment I received." Vladimir's jaw clenched. His words triggered a flashback. He shivered when he thought of the arduous march lasting days and days without food or water to a war prisoner camp. Then the deadly train trip, packed in with others like in a can of sardines, while Nazi soldiers entertained themselves by shooting at the cattle cars as they passed by. He shuddered inwardly as his mind recalled how his fellow soldiers slumping onto him as they died from the stray bullets penetrating their wooden car.

"Volodya, are you all right? You're in one of those deep thoughts again. Were you thinking about the past again?"

"I guess I was. I try not to; it eats at me when I do. But getting back to German deprivations, can you imagine, now, how much more bitter the resentment will be when they hear that refugees are receiving almost twice as much food? Or that the farmers' efforts go to feed us? It can only lead to violence."

"Well, let me tell you what I heard from a German woman at a little clothing store."

"The store is still in business?"

"Yes, they try to go on with their lives. Unfortunately, there is very little inventory to choose from. The clerk thinks I'm German and tells me things. She said that with the never-ceasing flood of refugees from the east, the Germans are incensed by the military administrators requisitioning private homes, apartments, hotels, school buildings, and even factory buildings to house the refugees. It is the German families that are now displaced, leaving them homeless along with those dispossessed from destroyed homes due to the bombing raids. She lamented, 'They're taking away our food and now they're taking away our homes.'"

Vladimir and Slava prayed daily that they would not see any Soviets in Hamm. Slava lay awake at nights worrying. Three weeks had gone by and nothing more was heard about the repatriation. Vladimir was beginning to feel a little more secure, hoping that perhaps it was just a scare tactic and that they would be free from the Soviets at last. Slava's glowing smile and twinkling eyes began to rebound just listening to Vladimir's optimism.

Then one day, as Slava and Victor were playing in the backyard, she heard a plane circling overhead. When she looked up she noticed papers falling from it. One of the leaflets landed a few feet from her. Picking it up, her breath caught in her throat as she began reading it. A vise squeezed her temples, bringing on a sudden headache. *Oh God! Oh, Virgin Mary, mother of God! They're here! Oh God!* Crumbling the leaflet in her fist, she grabbed her son and rushed into the house, locking the door behind her and pulling the drapes closed, as if the Soviets were already in her backyard. Her heart raced as she plopped down on the sofa. Smoothing out the leaflet, she studied it again and then laid it on the coffee table. Then she waited for Vladimir.

Vladimir returned from the hospital earlier than normal. His cheeks were flushed, his usual smile absent. "You've seen the leaflet, haven't you?"

"No, but Bogdan told me about it. How did you come to see it?"

"It fell in our backyard from a plane. Can you believe it? Here it is" Slava said, handing him the flyer.

Vladimir read it. It urged all Soviet citizens to voluntarily return to their motherland as their country needed them to rebuild after the long and bitter war. It was their patriotic duty to do so. The leaflets assured them that no harm would come to those who return.

"Well, what do you think?" Slava asked, her voice trying to be calm, even though deep inside she churned.

"I don't know what to think. But I do see something encouraging in this leaflet."

"What could be encouraging? I don't see anything encouraging."

"They're asking for volunteers. Maybe they don't plan to force everyone back."

Slava shook her head. She didn't say anything, but her gut told her otherwise.

Additional leaflets became a daily occurrence over the next several days. Radio broadcasts and crudely printed Russian language newspapers bolstered the message for the return. The words were designed to tug at the citizens' emotions emphasizing their loyalty and love for the country. The intent was to cause extreme guilt for not returning to help their nation rebuild after the horrific devastation of the Great Patriotic War.

After permission was granted by the British administrator, the Red Army personnel set up a special collection site at one edge of the camp. From that point, those returning were loaded onto large trucks and eventually driven to assembly sites in the Soviet zone of East Germany.

This incessant Soviet propaganda campaign based on deceit and lies was clever and highly effective. In those few weeks after the war the Soviets boasted over the radio waves that four million refugees had voluntarily decided to return. The Moskalkovs could not but feel the guilt. There was also the overwhelming desire to step yet again onto their native soil. *That's where we grew up. That's our home, and that's where our family is.* They had to remind themselves repeatedly that it was impossible for them to return.

They knew the system and knew what fate awaited them if they found themselves in Soviet hands. They had to avoid the Soviet repatriation at all cost.

Chapter 44

As LONG as there was a stream of refugees volunteering to return to the Soviet Union, the presence of Red Army personnel remained minimal in the camp and the rest of the city, being confined to the collection areas. The Moskalkovs avoided those areas. They also tried to avoid the trucks which trekked back and forth from collection sites to the train station or beyond.

Soon, rumors of mass executions of those that fell into Soviet custody started seeping into the camp, reached the ears of the remaining refugees. They also heard reports that those Soviet citizens, who hade dodged a firing squad's bullets were sent to labor camps located in the harsh climate of Siberia, to build up that region of the Soviet Union. Stalin thought that to be a fitting punishment for those that surrendered to the Germans or worked on their behalf.

And then, a few weeks later, a small convoy of Soviet trucks rolled into camp. A raspy voice over the rarely-used loudspeaker announced in Russian that, "All Soviet citizens must gather their belongings and meet at the designated collection area in one hour to be transported to the Soviet Union. If they fail to do so, troops will be sent to escort them to the trucks." A British official also made the same broadcast in English.

Startled by the announcement, Vladimir's mind went numb. Hunched over at his desk in his small office, reviewing a medical text, he was unable to move for a moment. The words hit him as if a ton of bricks fell onto his head. His blood surged in his vessels. *They must have run out of volunteers. Now they're after everyone else. Oh God! Dear Jesus, save and protect us.*

Struggling to decide his next move, Vladimir's knees felt like rubber as he rose to glance out of the window. With horror, he saw Red Army soldiers enter several of the barracks. Glued to the window, he remained stiff, focusing on the activity by the barracks. Several people filed out, tugging their bundles and belongings, proceeding to a location outside Vladimir's view. Next, he witnessed families dragged out by the soldiers. He was shocked to the core of his being when he saw British soldiers assisting the Soviets, ordering people out at the point of a gun.

Vladimir sat heavily down on his chair, elbows on the desk. His hands cupped his splitting head. For fear of being stopped, he did not leave his office for hours, relieved that no one came for him. When, sometime later, he looked out the window again, trucks loaded with people were leaving the camp. He walked rapidly into the hallway, anxious to join his family. As he rounded the corner to the stairs, Bogdan Panasenko stopped him. "I need to talk to you. Come to my office. It's very important."

After both sat down in Bogdan's office behind a closed door, Bogdan began to speak in hushed tones. "Did you see what happened just now?"

"Yes," Vladimir answered. "It doesn't look good for us."

"Not at all. I saw parents and children forced onto the trucks, people pleading to stay. I knew this was coming. A Ukrainian friend from another camp told me a few days ago that there was a sweep there as well. You realize, don't you, that they'll come back to sweep the hospital. Also, the bastards are certain to search from house to house in town for whoever they think are Soviet citizens. They might be doing that right now."

Vladimir suddenly grew paler. *They're in town also! Oh my God! Slava and Victor!* "So what can we do? Tell me quickly. I need to get to my family."

"All right, I'll make this brief. I like you, and I want to help. Do you have any connection to the Baltics, Poland, or western Ukraine?"

Vladimir thought for a moment. "Actually, my wife's family is Polish and partly Latvian. And we came to Germany from Slonim. Why? What are you thinking?"

"You heard what they said about the Yalta Agreement. And about that arbitrary, magical line drawn on the map that determines who goes back and who doesn't."

"Of course, how can I forget? I noticed that Slonim is on the western side of that line."

"But did you live in Slonim before August 23, 1939?"

"No, I missed it by two years. That is certainly a problem."

"Well, it may not be that big of a problem. You seem to have connections you can use, especially if your wife and you speak Polish." On pins and needles to see to his family, Vladimir suddenly became more interested in what Bogdan had to say. He felt a surge of hope. "You see," Bogdan continued. "There are people out there that can create any documents that you need—birth certificates, marriage certificates, and so on." Instantly, Vladimir understood what Bogdan was suggesting and instantly found the notion distasteful. He knew Slava would hate the idea as well. "You're looking at me suspiciously. I know what you're thinking—that that is not right. Well it is right! I don't know about you, but I know I'll be shot if they get their hands on me. You are probably in the same boat. We survived thus far and it's up to ourselves to save our skins. We need to have those documents to save ourselves and our families. We have no other choice. I understand hundreds are already doing it."

"I certainly need to think about this. What you're saying is that someone will prepare papers that give evidence that I and Slava lived on the western side of the line in 1939. Who does that, and don't the British know of the scheme?"

"I found out about it from my friend that I told you about. Also, believe it or not, an Orthodox priest strongly suggested that I go that route. The church is actually helping people avoid repatriation. The British may know, and I guess it'll depend on who you get, but I think that they are starting to find out about the brutality of the Soviets and are trying to look the other way."

"You say the Orthodox Church is helping refugees?"

"Yes, and so is the Catholic Church. They are helpful in relocating refugees out of Germany and out of the hands of the Soviets. I can get you in touch with Orthodox Bishop Sava in England. He can try to arrange for you to immigrate, possibly to England."

Vladimir thanked Bogdan and left the hospital. On the way home, he kept looking around, fearing that a Soviet soldier may be lurking in the shadows. His mind mulled over the horrible events of the day and the startling conversation with Bogdan. *Is he right? Is that the only way out? Slava will hate it. Oh God! I need to tell her. It better not be too late.*

While Vladimir hid in his office, watching the forceful roundup of refugees in the camp from a window, Slava had decided to take Victor for a walk around the neighborhood. She had no idea of the danger lurking around her. She dressed up in her favorite elegant beige suit, white frilly blouse, and a wide-brimmed brown hat. She wore comfortable fine brown leather shoes with two-inch heels. She outfitted Victor in the typical German style for boys—short pants with suspenders over a white shirt. After she locked her door and descended the steps, she happened to glance at the neighbor's porch, and to her dismay, her eye caught two Soviet soldiers talking to the older German lady. Her previous communication with the woman was limited to an occasional friendly wave.

Overhearing parts of the conversation, Slava instantly became aware that the soldiers were canvassing the area in proximity to the camp searching for former Soviet citizens. All the air whooshed out from her lungs when she saw the woman point her out as she earnestly talked to the Russians. Stepping on the sidewalk, Slava decided to continue walking as casually as she could manage on her shaky legs, telling herself not to panic or show any fear. She began speaking with Victor in German even though her heart beat as fast as a hummingbird and her knees threatened to buckle as she fought down a rising feeling of terror.

The soldiers followed her for some distance, walking just a few feet away. She felt sweat pour down every pore from sheer fright. Even though Slava felt light-headed, her heart thudding in her chest, she kept speaking in a louder than normal voice to her son in German hoping that Victor would not answer her in either Polish or Russian. At the very moment when she was certain she would be stopped and questioned, to her tremendous relief, she heard one of the soldiers following them tell the other, "Let's go, she is obviously not one of us. Look how elegantly she's dressed. I think she is speaking in German to her kid."

They turned around and walked back to the Moskalkov house perhaps to examine the nameplate typically located on the wall next to the door. Vladimir and Slava were always impressed with German record keeping. Every dwelling bore a nameplate of the resident inside. However, at that moment, Slava praised Vladimir for having had the foresight to remove the nameplate from the wall when he had first heard of repatriation. She now realized that had the soldiers seen the name of "Moskalkov" on the wall, they would have turned back to stop and question her. From a distance she inconspicuously watched as the soldiers moved onto another block. She could now safely return home.

Once inside her house, Slava closed the windows and shades and sagged down on the sofa, her body feeling as though it had been run over by a train, her heart still racing. Victor went into his room and played with his favorite toy, a small green car, while Slava reclined, her arm over her eyes, waiting for Vladimir to return. She sat up suddenly as it occurred to her that Vladimir might be in danger at the camp's hospital. She began to pray to Saint Anthony for her husband's safety and for some miracle that will save them from the Soviets.

As Vladimir came through the door, Slava rushed up to him, almost stumbling over Victor as he ran up to hug his father. She immediately blurted out that she had been followed by Soviet soldiers and had she not been dressed as a well-to-do German, they would have taken her and Victor. "What are we going to do?! I was just lucky that time. If the Soviets don't find us, then the Brits will turn us in!"

"Slavochka, my dear, simmer down. We may have a solution."

Looking puzzled, Slava stared incredulously at Vladimir. "What in the world are you talking about? How can there be a solution?"

"Let's sit down,"

As the parents sat, Victor, as usual, squeezed himself next to his father. Vladimir placed his arm around his son's shoulder, gently squeezing him closer. Huddled together, Vladimir and Slava quietly discussed the frightening events of the day and the solution as suggested by Bogdan.

"You know I don't like it," Slava said. "And I know you don't either. We're taking a chance and it isn't right. Both of us have always played by the rules, always tried to do the right thing." She sat silently for a moment, mulling things over. Vladimir waited patiently for a further comment. "But maybe it is the right thing after all, and Saint Anthony sent us the miracle I prayed for."

"I don't think we have a choice this time. I'll talk to Bogdan and get more information. In the meantime, we need to hide from our countrymen and pray that the British don't turn us in or forcibly remove us."

Chapter 45

IF PREVIOUSLY Vladimir had any reservations about obtaining new documents, the incident with Slava and the two Soviet soldiers convinced him to do whatever he could to escape capture. As it stood, he needed to contact the Polish organization that helped former Soviet citizens avoid repatriation.

Obtaining the permission to be absent from work for a few hours, the Moskalkovs cautiously made their way several blocks across town to an old, heavily damaged, office building near the railroad station. A well-dressed, slender man with short gray hair covering his narrow gaunt face occupied the tiny, poorly furnished office on the third floor. He stood up and warmly greeted the family as they entered the office. Polish posters hung on the cracked plaster walls, advising of help available for the relocation and other services for Poles. Speaking Polish in a friendly, calm voice, he asked them if he could be of any help. Vladimir, reluctantly, admitted that they needed documents. The man asked them some background questions, looking for a Polish connection.

"Let me direct you to the man who can help you. As you can imagine, we are swamped helping hundreds with the same request, but the man I'm sending you to is excellent and can probably get what you need rather quickly." He sat down, wrote out an address on a small piece of yellowish paper, and handed it to Vladimir. "I can tell that you and your wife are apprehensive about getting the documents. Don't be so nervous and worried. Believe me, I know what the Soviets do to people who took refuge in Germany. You know you have no other choice if you want to avoid a labor camp, or worse. Plus, your wife is Polish and most Byelorussians were probably originally Polish as well." This was the affirmation that both Vladimir and Slava needed to hear. They were making the right decision. Slava nodded in agreement.

"So, the man you need to see is not far from here. His apartment is along the same street. Turn to the right once you exit this building, go three blocks, and you'll see only two buildings still standing in that block. He is in the red brick one, with boards covering the top floor. Go to the fourth floor, the first door on the right. Tell him Stefan sent you. All right?"

After thanking the man, the family left the office and proceeded toward the apartment building. Once on the fourth floor, Vladimir knocked on the door as directed. Not hearing an answer, he knocked again. A few seconds later the door barely opened exposing half of a bearded face with a glaring eye. "Yes, what do you want?" The man asked in heavily accented German.

"Stefan sent us," Vladimir answered in Polish. The door opened wider and they were invited to step inside. A pungent odor of ink and chemicals permeated the small room. A small old pine table with three mismatched chairs stood under the only window in the room. The only other piece of furniture was a frayed sofa. Without saying another word, the short, unkempt man shoved a dish and a cup aside on the table, swept away a stack of old newspapers from a chair, and gestured to them to sit at the table.

He took out a pad of paper, his eyes all the while shrewdly studying Vladimir and Slava, making them both uncomfortable. Then he glanced at their son, who in turn, studied the man with the matted hair. "I know what to write in the documents to make sure that they will help you. Just give me some information and I'll take care of the rest."

After ten minutes of questions and suggestions, their answers were scribbled down. Slava looked askance at his notes on the paper and could not understand how he could possibly decipher what he wrote. "All right, that's all I need. Come back tomorrow night. The documents will be ready. I need half my fee of twenty-five marks now and you can pay me the balance tomorrow." Vladimir expected that the fee would be higher. Pleasantly surprised, he counted out the money.

As they were walking back to their house, Vladimir saw a Soviet truck, packed with women and children, come around the corner. He immediately scooped Victor up. Slava saw the vehicle as well and all three quickly darted into an unlocked foyer of an adjacent apartment building. Through the door's small beveled window, they saw the truck pass by. "I didn't want to take any chances," Vladimir said.

They waited for the truck to be out of view before cautiously emerging back on the street to continue their walk home. As luck would have it, a few minutes later, a Willy's Jeep with three Red Army soldiers in it came into view. Ruins dotted the block that the Moskalkovs now found themselves in. If they tried to hide in the rubble, behind a pile of concrete and iron, they would be quickly spotted, plus it would look suspicious. "What shall we do?" Slava whispered nervously.

"Hopefully, they'll consider us Germans and leave us alone."

To their enormous relief, the Jeep drove past them. Vladimir kept the vehicle in sight out of the corner of his eye. Suddenly, it made a U-turn and approached them. Riddled with tension, the couple tried to present a casual and unconcerned demeanor, as they continued their promenade. Suddenly, just a few meters behind them, the brakes squealed. Slava jumped. The vehicle stopped, and two soldiers hopped out. *Oh God!* Slava's heart thudded. Vladimir clenched his jaw, expecting the worst. Both assumed that the Reds were going to approach them any minute. Instead, the soldiers picked out a person who happened to be walking just a few steps behind them. The Moskalkovs had no idea where the man came from, probably from one of the apartments they had just passed. Realizing how close they themselves came to capture, Vladimir and Slava kept a steady pace down the street, away from the soldiers. His breathing still labored, Vladimir took a quick glance back, just in time to see the hapless victim shoved into the vehicle and taken away.

The next evening, Vladimir ventured out alone to pick up the documents. The man, appearing satisfied with his work, handed him the papers and instructed Vladimir to examine them carefully.

Vladimir studied the first document, a translation, dated August 7, 1939, of his birth certificate indicating the village in Belarus where he was born in 1915. The second document, dated July 27, 1939 was also a translation of Slava's birth certificate indicating her place of birth. The third was a marriage certificate, dated June 15, 1939 indicating that they were married in Slonim on March 2, 1938, rather than 1940, the actual year of their marriage. All three documents were on official-looking paper bearing an official stamped Polish red seal displaying an outstretched winged eagle topped with a crown.

"This will be enough?" Vladimir asked, somehow expecting more paperwork.

"For sure. It has worked for many. It isn't really the content, but it's the date on the documents that give evidence that you resided in Slonim prior to August 23, 1939.

Believe me, it's enough for the British. The Soviets, though, is another matter. There had been instances where they didn't care what the documents said. If they suspect you are one of their own, they'll take you anyway and nobody can do anything about it. So try to avoid them."

Vladimir paid him and hurried home, again extremely vigilant. Once there, both he and Slava studied the papers carefully. Vladimir decided not to worry Slava with the man's comment that the Soviets did not always pay attention to the documents.

When Vladimir arrived for work the next morning, all patients and foreign staff were informed by the British authorities that all remaining refugees were required to appear within the next two days with their documents proving their residence prior to August 23, 1939. They were told again that those who resided east of the agreed line would be turned over to the Soviet authorities. *Oh God! We got the papers just in time. They better work, or we're dead. Stalin must really be putting pressure on the Brits for them to do this.*

The next day, Vladimir, Slava, and Victor found themselves face to face with a British officer who spoke fluent Russian. He asked them where they were born, then where they resided in 1939. Vladimir answered that they were in Poland, on this side of the line. They were asked for any official papers that may prove that. His heart thudding, he pulled the translated documents out of his breast pocket and presented them to the officer. To further bolster their case that they in fact had lived in Slonim and their longevity there, Vladimir produced Victor's German birth certificate indicating his birth in Slonim in occupied Poland in 1944. The officer looked over the documents and then carefully studied the Moskalkovs. With a half-smile on his face, he wrote something on a half sheet of paper, then stamped it. "All right," the officer said. "It appears that you were in Poland and resided on the right side of the border. You'll be sent to a non-Jewish Polish refugee camp in Werl, Germany. Be packed and at the rail station tomorrow by 1000." The officer winked as he handed Vladimir the papers. "Be safe."

Vladimir and Slava felt as though a boulder had been lifted off their shoulders. Tears of joy flowed profusely down Slava's cheek. Vladimir took Slava's hand, pulled her to him, kissed her and held her in his arms for a long minute. "We'll make it yet," Vladimir said. "We just have to avoid the Red Army until we get to the new camp."

Chapter 46

ANOTHER TRAIN took the Moskalkovs to Werl. From there, they were sent to several other locations—Hagen-Kabel, then to Mülheim/Ruhr, to Lintorf–Düsseldorf, to Reckenfeld and then to Münster. All were Displaced Persons (DP) camps located in Westphalia and in the British Zone of occupation. Working as a physician in each camp, Vladimir's salary grew from 320 marks per month in Werl in 1945 to 646 marks in Munster in 1949. They were moved around from camp to camp depending on the need of a physician or the consolidation of the camps as refugees emigrated from Germany to nations accepting them. In later camps, such as Lintorf and Münster, Vladimir earned additional funds by treating patients outside the camps.

Although Werl and other Polish refugee sites were located in the British zone, the Polish Armed Forces administered the DP camp, including medical services. Vladimir learned that the Polish force originally consisted of a significant number of Poles who escaped Poland after its occupation by the Germans to England and France. They formed their own fighting units, headquartered in England, and fought alongside the British army and the French government-in-exile to defeat the Nazis.

Under British authority, crimes and disputes committed by the refugees fell within the jurisdiction of Polish administrators. The British, however, were in charge of food supply for both the refugees and the local German population, monitoring it through rations. They also provided housing for refugees and oversaw local municipal operations. As the Moskalkovs had surmised, the occupiers' mission was, indeed, overwhelming with the massive refugee influx. To relieve the army of this horrendous charge, in 1946 the International Refugee Organization (IRO) was established to specifically address the task. It was implemented in 1948. At that time, the IRO took over the responsibility of the maintenance and care of the camps. It provided information and help for resettlement, vocational training, and tracing service for lost relatives.

At times, it became problematic for the IRO to keep order in the local population. Some of the Germans, particularly youth bands, held a bitter grudge for Germany's loss and the subsequent Allied occupation. British and Polish soldiers and foreign refugees were vulnerable to harassment and physical confrontations by gangs of youths. Vladimir and Slava avoided trouble by continuing to blend in with the locals by their demeanor, wardrobe, and Slava's fluent German.

In Hagen-Kabel, they purchased their first car, an old Mercedes Benz, and Vladimir obtained a drivers' license issued by the Polish Armed Forces and another one from the local German administration. Unfortunately, the dread of repatriation lingered, even the many years after the war. The Soviets, although now on rarer occasions, were still known to canvas a camp or snatch someone off a street. So when driving around in their new car, they had to be vigilant of Red Army soldiers. A sinking feeling would overcome them when they heard of a random snatching of some refugees by the Reds.

In all the assigned camp towns, the Moskalkovs' residences were outside the camp itself, in well-furnished houses, and although their rations were obtained through the camp, some of their food was also purchased or bartered at the thriving black market. Slava enjoyed her time in Germany. Even though they were surrounded by devastation remaining after the war, the industrious German population began to hastily rebuild. In just a few years, the infrastructure was restored, the currency stabilized with an influx of cash with the help of America's Marshall Plan and a variety of inventory once again filled the stores.

The Moskalkovs resided from September 1947 to January 1949 in Lintorf, their longest stay of any previous camp town. This town was Slava's favorite because its proximity to Düsseldorf, a large cultural city. The variety of goods in the shops fascinated her, particularly the beautiful and elegant lingerie. She even attended a lingerie fashion show.

Life for the family became normal and routine. Vladimir attended several seminars and lectures in continuing education at the University of Gottingen, Hamburg Institute, and other universities. Slava worked when needed as a nurse or a dental technician, bringing in extra cash.

With their somewhat stable environment, increasing thoughts of their extended family became more prominent in the couple's minds. Vladimir realized that if his mother and sisters survived the war, they would be under Soviet control in Belarus. Any communication would be dangerous not only for them but also for his family. Slava wondered if her parents had escaped Vitebsk and had gone to relatives in Latvia. "Volodya, do you think my parents may be in Germany? They are Polish and might be in one of the camps around here."

"It's possible. There must be a list of refugees in Germany. I heard that the new people now in charge can help find lost relatives. I'll go tomorrow and see if they can help."

During his lunch break at the hospital, Vladimir trotted to the administration building, found a door with the "International Refugee Organization" printed on the frosted glass and walked into the room. A counter separated him from several women working at desks. A dark-haired, petite woman, in her early twenties met him at the counter and asked in Polish if she could help him. When Vladimir asked if there was a general list of refugees in camps, she informed him that there is such a list, but that they only had a list of Polish refugees. She gave him some binders containing lists of names handwritten in ink and told him to sit down at a table by the door and look through them. After an hour's search, he gave up as he needed to return to work.

The next day, at noon, he came back to continue his search. He was beginning to deem his efforts futile, when suddenly, after turning a page, his eyes widened when he ran across entries, "Szpakowski, Wladislav" and "Szpakowska, Suzanna." He smiled and whistled to himself, *well, what do you know? I can't believe this. Slava will be so ecstatic.* They were registered at a camp about one hundred kilometers away. He could hardly wait to finish up his day at work and tell Slava the good news.

On his next day off, Vladimir drove to the camp alone. Their car was not big enough to seat Slava and Victor and bring back the parents and their belongings. When Vladimir arrived at the camp, he was informed that the camp is closing and that his in-laws had already been transferred to yet another camp about thirty kilometers away.

At that camp, with rows and rows of barracks, Vladimir received instructions on how to find the particular structure where Slava's parents now resided. He drove his car up to it and was able to park a few feet from the door. As he walked in, he immediately noticed a strong pungent odor of food cooking. Wooden walls divided the long narrow building thus providing some privacy for each family. He asked a short, thin, bald man standing by one of the windows if he knew of the Szpakowkis. "That must be the old couple that moved in a week ago. They're in the last unit down this hall," he answered, pointing as he spoke.

Could it really be them? His heart beat rapidly as he approached their compartment. He knocked on the door. "Just a minute," a man's voice answered. Vladimir smiled as he immediately recognized it. He heard the floor boards creak as the man on the other side of the door slowly approached. The door opened and he saw his father's-in-law stunned look of recognition. The old man rubbed his eyes and just stood speechless for a moment. He then gulped hard and tears welled up in his sunken brown eyes. Tears gathered in Vladimir's eyes as well. They embraced heartily, both kissing the cheek of the other.

In the meantime, Suzanna recognized Vladimir even though the light from the window was at his back. "Oh my God!" Suzanna screamed upon seeing Vladimir. "Oh my God! Is it really you? You're alive. Our prayers have been answered. Where is Slava? Is she here? Is she alive?" Vladimir answered her that their daughter is fine and waiting for them.

Suzanna took Vladimir by his hand, pulling him towards her and hugging him so fiercely that it almost knocked the air out of him. Vladimir stood back and studied the couple. The years had taken a toll on them. They now both looked sickly and so much older than he remembered. Wladislav looked thin and gaunt. Suzanna, always plump as he had remembered her, lost much weight. She appeared pale with huge bags under her eyes, which added to the numerous creases in her face, her hair now gray pulled back tightly into a bun.

Vladimir sat down on a lone wooden chair while the parents sat on their cots in the tiny room, large enough for the two cots and a small table. A hot plate, its electrical cord plugged in to a light in the ceiling, a tea pot, a few cans of food and a couple of dishes and cups took up most of the surface area of the table. Each was anxious to hear each other's accounts. They explained to Vladimir that they were able to get permission to go to relatives in Latvia from the German occupiers. "Because we were old, the Germans didn't need us, thank God," Suzanna said. "As the Soviet troops were moving into Latvia, we could have stayed, but for some reason we thought that Slava and you might have made it into Germany. That is, if you were still alive. By the grace of God, we were able to get a place in an evacuation train. That trip almost did us in. We almost starved. Since we spoke Polish between ourselves, they stuck us in a Polish camp. We kept hoping that somehow, by some miracle, you'll find us. And here you are. Praise be to the Lord." Suzanna broke out into a wail. "We thought we'd never see you again."

Vladimir rose from the chair and getting down on his haunches in front of his mother-in-law, he embraced her. "Everything will be all right. You'll soon see Slava and Victor."

"Victor?" Suzanna grinned through her tears. "I have another grandson?"

"Yes, you do. You'll see him soon."

"Oh, I can't wait to go see them," Wladislav said, he was also grinning widely as tears streaked down his cheeks. "Tell us how you ended up in Germany." After Vladimir quickly filled them in, he told them that they would talk further in the car.

"You have a car?" Suzanna asked, looking shocked. "Then when can we leave? I don't want to stay here another minute."

"As soon as I arrange for you to come with me. It shouldn't take long. In the meantime, get your things together and we'll go."

Chapter 47

RUSHING OUT of the house, Slava screamed from excitement as Vladimir stopped in front of the house. She could see her parents through the windows of the car. Victor remained on the porch gawking at the scene before him. His mother kept shrieking as she embraced the old people that his father brought home. All three carried on, hugging, crying, and kissing. His father was removing a suitcase and a box from the car and carrying items inside the house. At the age of four, Victor did not quite understand who the people were and why his mother carried on like that. His father and mother had been the center of his existence, and now these people acted as though they also belonged in their small family. Slava kneeled in front of him and explained that they were her mother and father and that they were his grandparents. It took a few days for Victor to understand how special they were to him.

Slava could not help but see how much her parents changed in the four years that she had not seen them. Both were not as sharp mentally. Her father was now forgetful and did not have much energy. Her mother was better mentally, but seemed to be quite often out of breath to the point that she had to sit and rest. Her appetite was good, though, and within a few months she gained weight, perhaps even too much. Slava worried about them, her father was only sixty-nine and her mother sixty-five, but they both looked and acted so much older. She realized that life had been stressful for them since she left Vitebsk to help Vladimir. Unfortunately, she did not have her mother with her for long. Just a few months after their reunion, on Easter Sunday of 1948, Suzanna passed away. Her passing was difficult on the family, particularly on Wladislaw. His health continued to deteriorate.

One day, Slava came home and asked her father how the day went. "Oh, it was uneventful. Oh yes, some Red Army soldiers came by. I think they were looking for someone. I didn't quite understand who. Some Soviet people. They came into the house and looked around."

"Oh God! You didn't speak to them did you? And if you did, you spoke in Polish, I hope."

"Well no, I wanted them to hear their own language so I said hello in Russian and asked them to come in."

"Oh my God! What did they say?"

"They looked at me and laughed. Actually, they insulted me, calling me an old fool making fun of them. What's the problem, why do you look upset?"

"They were here to drag us back to the Soviet Union. Please, papa, don't speak to any Soviet people in Russian. Speak Polish as you usually do." Slava explained to him about the forced repatriation of former Soviet citizens and how they had been able to escape so far. Wladislaw understood and said that he would not open the door again. A few months later, in June 1949, he passed away from a stroke.

While in the Kabel camp, the Moskalkovs befriended an elderly, well-educated lady who spoke several languages. She became known as "Auntie" to Victor. She tutored the boy in French and watched him at those times when Slava worked. Victor already spoke Russian, Polish, and German. The parents wanted Victor to learn French and as many languages as possible because they had no inkling where they eventually would end up. Vladimir had made inquiries as early as 1946 of the possibilities of immigrating to the United States. He was told that the United States was not accepting refugees from Germany. He was also informed that only a few countries were accepting any and was once again given the name of Bishop Sava of the Russian Orthodox Church in England as a person that might help them. Vladimir had written him and was surprised to quickly receive a reply. The bishop wished him a Happy Easter and suggested that he first come to England and find work. Then later, when he became established he would be able to bring his family out. He ended the letter by stating that, "One can live in England. May God preserve you all."

Vladimir refused to follow that advice. It was inconceivable to him to leave his family in Germany and go to England by himself. He continued to keep his ears open, hoping to find a country that will take the three of them, especially praying that the United States would open up their borders to them.

Vladimir and Slava realized that even though they lived well in post-war Germany, they would never be fully accepted by the Germans, since they came from Eastern Europe. They were called auslanders (foreigners) and were treated as such. Vladimir thought he probably could arrange to remain permanently in Germany, but there were too many ugly memories between the refugees and the locals for comfortable coexistence. With their Slavic name, he knew they would always encounter resentment if they stayed.

"We'll have to leave Germany sooner than later. It's already 1948," Vladimir stated, almost philosophically, as he and Slava rested under a Linden tree after their bicycle ride in the country. Victor was off running in the field, picking yellow and purple wild flowers. The parents laughed as they watched him run around, chasing a butterfly. They had purchased new bicycles, even one for Victor. All were shiny black with a bell on the handlebars. The bicycle became Victor's favorite toy, and he never ceased begging his parents, particularly his father, to go bike riding together.

"Yes, we need to talk about this again seriously," Slava responded. "I feel that with every passing month, Germany is trying harder to kick the refugees out. I guess I don't blame them. They want Germany for the Germans. We need to find a country that will take us. Is there any chance now after all this time that America will?"

"I checked with the relocation office again yesterday. The United States is not accepting any immigrants. The girl at the IRO was pessimistic about that. The other countries that have been accepting now filled their quotas except for Argentina. I picked up an application. It's in my briefcase. I'm still hoping for America. Everyone says that America is a land of freedom and opportunity. I really would like to live there, what a change that would be from the Soviet Union. But Argentina, supposedly, is accepting new people. What shall we do?"

"We don't always get what we want," Slava said. "God seems to have his own plans for us. Right now it looks as if we better start studying Spanish."

Chapter 48

ARGENTINA ACCEPTED the Moskalkov family, but both Vladimir and Slava still had their hearts set on the United States. Perhaps recklessly, they let the Argentinian immigration visa expire because they heard through the grapevine that the American Congress had voted on a bill allowing two hundred thousand immigrants from Eastern Europe to enter the country. Even though stiff opposition from a substantial minority of lawmakers existed, President Truman favored the legislation and was expected to sign it into law.

The young couple took a chance that they'll be included in that wave of immigrants to America. Vladimir made numerous visits to the International Refugee Organization (IRO) office, knowing that they aided the resettlement of the refugees through different consulates and begged for help to immigrate to the United States. Finally, after several weeks, he was handed application papers and instructions for applying. The bureaucracy involved with immigrating to Argentina paled in comparison to that of the United States. Every aspect of their lives was examined. Along with birth and marriage certificates, education, employment records, salary information, numerous letters of recommendations and references (both from a personal and a work aspect) had to be obtained and submitted. All three underwent rigorous physical examinations and were required to obtain vaccinations, including one for smallpox. The process was long and arduous, taking many anxious months.

In the meantime, while the family waited for approval to immigrate to the United States, Vladimir continued to work as a physician in Lintorf. His employment continued to progress smoothly. He had a well-furnished office, the latest in medical equipment, and even a typewriter, which he learned to use for preparation of letters and medical records. He enjoyed the interaction with patients and felt blessed that he was in that position. Then one day, a directive from the International Refugee Organization was delivered and placed on his desk. After his evening rounds, he picked up the envelope. Quickly tearing it open, thinking that perhaps it was the long awaited acceptance by the United States, he read the contents. It was not the news he hoped for. Instead, the dreadful notice informed him that a new law has been adopted and all camp physicians were required to pass an examination to show their competence in the practice of medicine before they were allowed to continue to work. The notice went on to inform that each practicing physician had to belong to a local medical society. It clearly became apparent that their income, their standard of living, their house, all would vanish if he did not pass the examination.

He had previously heard of the Belorussian Medical Society Abroad that existed in Germany. Since he graduated from a Belorussian medical school, joining it was only a matter of showing them his credentials. That would not have been a problem. It was the examination that worried him. What language would it be in? *It would probably be in Polish*. He was not as proficient with the Polish alphabet. *What subjects would be covered? Would it cover only his specialty or everything from child birth to heart surgery? What would I need to study?* The letter contained none of that information. *I'd better study it all.*

Slava took the news much better than he had expected. She had complete faith in him. "I'm not worried," she said. "You'll pass it. Don't stress over it." Vladimir always admired her for her optimism at times like this. She may complain and worry, but she seemed to roll with the punches better than anyone he could imagine.

"Slavochka, I love you so much, more each day." They kissed and immediately afterwards opened a Polish medical text that he checked out from the hospital library. Sixty days later he found himself in the examination room. The examination covered a general practice of medicine. Since he was in a Polish camp, as expected, the questions were in Polish and the answers were expected to be in that language as well. With sweaty hands, he began the test. Upon a quick review of the questions, his tension eased somewhat. He felt he knew the answers, but writing in essay form in the Polish alphabet when he was used to the Cyrillic really slowed him down. When time ran out, the proctor told everyone to put their pencils down and turn in the answers. He felt devastated that he was unable to finish the last question. *I probably flunked it. If I only had another five minutes.*

"Well, how did it go?" Slava asked impatiently as Vladimir walked through the door. The late afternoon sun rays beaming though the window focused on his face. Vladimir appeared drained, his skin lacking luster.

"Who knows? I knew the answers, but I struggled with the Polish alphabet. We'll just have to wait and see."

"I'm sure you did fine. You studied so hard—one book after another and writing in Polish over and over. I barely saw you. Did they tell you when we'll know?"

"In six weeks. In the meantime I need to set aside the thought that I may no longer have a job and keep working."

"Don't worry, darling," Slava said, kissing Vladimir and stroking his hair. "You'll be fine. I'm sure you passed the test with flying colors."

Seven weeks later, Vladimir entered his office, exhausted after performing a delicate brain abscess surgery when he spotted an envelope on his desk, similar to the one he had seen before from the IRO. Instantly realizing that it may contain his examination results, he rushed to his desk. He grabbed the letter and with trembling hands unsealed the flap. He deeply exhaled in relief when he read the heading,

"CERTIFICATE OF PROFESSIONAL STATUS." It certified that he is a qualified physician after examination of his professional qualifications by the Special Qualifications Board in the British Zone of Germany." He flopped down on his chair and laughed out loud then, as was his habit, let out a strong whistle. That evening, he did not walk; he floated home to announce to Slava the wonderful news.

Month after month passed by and still no word whether they would be allowed to immigrate to the United States. In July 1949, the family was transferred yet again, this time to Reckenfeld, Westphalia. Reckenfeld was home to a large Displaced Persons camp, built on top of a huge World War I ammunition dump. The camp had a population of over ten thousand Polish and Ukrainian residents.

The Moskalkovs were assigned a spacious, well-furnished and maintained house. As they were shown the house, the couple instantly noticed a large six-pointed Star of David with some numbers printed underneath on the front door. They exchanged looks. "I won't like living in this house," Slava whispered to Vladimir. "It obviously once belonged to a Jewish family and was confiscated by the Nazis. Those poor people will always dwell in my mind." Vladimir felt the same. They requested another home, but their request was denied.

With no choice but to live in the house, they made the best of it. On one very cold, rain-soaked evening, Vladimir descended to the cellar to stoke the boiler hopper with coal.

In the dim light he noticed a brick in the foundation that seemed to be slightly out of alignment with the others. His hand reached out to touch it. It felt loose. Grasping the brick, he pulled it out. He saw a bag hidden far in the recess of the hole. Pulling it out, he discovered valuable gold jewelry studded with diamonds and colored stones. He never beheld such a treasure before. The jewels twinkled and glistened under the hanging light bulb. He called up to Slava and showed her the surprising find. "We can't keep it," was her immediate comment. "It must have belonged to the people who owned this house."

"I know," Vladimir said. "But I thought you might want to just look at it."

"It's quite a spectacular sight, but it makes me nervous. Let's put it back. The owners may come back for it. Besides, it would be bad luck to keep it."

In full agreement and knowing that the find did not belong to them, Vladimir carefully wrapped it all back in the original linen cloth and put it away, carefully replacing the brick.

Again, months went by and still no word of acceptance by the United States. Each time Vladimir inquired, he was told that they had to wait. With September approaching, they hoped that they would be able to leave before Victor needed to start kindergarten. They wanted him to start school in the new country. He was five years old and unless they heard soon, they would need to sign him up in a school in Germany. Slava assumed that she will take their son to the Polish school at the camp. "No," Vladimir said. "I'd rather enroll him in the German neighborhood school. He speaks German as a native. And, I was thinking, in the event we won't be able to immigrate, at least he'll fit in better with the local children. He has an easygoing sunny nature and has already made friends with the neighboring German boys and girls."

Slava thought about that and agreed. The days of summer grew shorter, some of the trees began to turn and a few leaves began to fall. Still no word came whether America had accepted them. They bought Victor a brown leather flat backpack so that he could attend school just as the German boys. Victor liked school and quickly adapted to his schoolmates and teacher. Then shortly before Christmas, the Moskalkovs were transferred to Münster. Again, they were given a spacious house not far from the camp where Vladimir worked. Victor began attending the German neighborhood kindergarten in the new location. In the meantime, the family anxiously kept waiting frustratingly for word from America.

A few weeks later, Slava was handed an official-looking letter by the mailman.

Chapter 49

With trembling hands and pounding heart, Slava ripped the letter open. Quickly skimming the contents, she skipped across the room, shouting, "We are going to America! My dear Jesus, Blessed Mother, thank you, thank you, thank you!" Her heart was bursting with euphoria as tears of relief ran down her cheeks. Out of sheer elation, she broke out into a song. She could no longer hold back. Alone at home, with Vladimir at work and Victor in school, Slava felt that she had to share the good news with Vladimir right away. Shrugging into her woolen coat, which was trimmed with two full length gray fox stoles, as was the fashion for a wealthy matron, she slid into her boots and scurried to the camp hospital, the letter carefully tucked into her black leather purse.

The annoyed, elderly, gray-haired receptionist used the intercom to summon Vladimir to the front desk. Startled to hear his name called, he finished up with his patient recovering from a tonsillectomy and hurried to the reception area. Slava did not give him a chance to say a word as she flung herself into his arms, followed by numerous kisses all over his face. "What is it?" Vladimir asked dumbfounded while she bubbled with joy, her eyes sparkling and ablaze with exhilaration.

"Guess what I have in my purse," she teased him with a squeaky voice.

"Slavochka, I have no time to play games. What?"

Slava slowly fumbled with her bag, looking at him playfully. To tease him, she intentionally took her time to pull out the letter and as she started to hand it to him, at the moment he tried to take it, she quickly pulled it back, laughing.

"Slava, what's wrong with you? Stop that!" She handed him the paper and waited for his reaction. He did not disappoint. His blue eyes opened wide and a huge grin split his face. He laughed heartedly and let out a whistle. With her index finger to her mouth the receptionist shushed as she gave him a stern look. "Oh my God! This is wonderful! This is wonderful! We're going to America!"

The Moskalkov's departure date scheduled just six weeks later in February 1950 quickly approached. They were to travel by train to a processing center, then on to the port city of Bremerhaven. Vladimir gave notice of his departure to the hospital and began the numerous preparations that had to be made. He found a buyer for the old Mercedes and used the money, along with the savings they had accumulated, to purchase items that they were allowed to take to the United States.

And then their euphoric high came to a smashing halt. Unexpectedly, just a week before the family was to catch a train to depart, Victor had come down with whooping cough. Their departure was canceled. Health officials required all individuals with any infectious disease to be quarantined at the hospital. Victor would be isolated for several weeks.

The parents were distraught worrying about their sick son in a ward without them. Even missing their opportunity to sail to the United States took a back seat to the concern for his health. Vladimir wanted his son not to feel himself abandoned. He sat outside for hours, perched on a wooden bench that was built around a chestnut tree in the courtyard of the hospital. Two floors above was the window into Victor's ward. He knew that his son would look out the window at the world below. Now pale and thin, Victor saw him. He smiled happily and waved down to Vladimir acknowledging his father's presence. This became a daily ritual, with Slava sometimes joining him, until Victor's full recovery and release.

After Victor recovered, Vladimir was rehired as a physician at the displaced persons camp in Reckenfeld and allowed to continue to reside in the same house. Vladimir immediately requested passage to the United States once again.

The response was devastating. His heart sank to his knees when he heard that the ships for the following few months were filled to capacity. He was also informed that unless they enter the United States within the next six months, their application to immigrate might be voided and they would need to reapply under a new quota, if available. "Oh, and by the way," he was told, "New sponsors may have to be found."

Vladimir came home downhearted. He told Slava the disappointing news. "Oh God," Slava said, her voice trembling as tears gathered in her eyes, threatening to spill. "Does that mean we might not get another chance?"

"No, we'll go. Something will come up," Vladimir said trying to be assuring, but deep inside, he wondered if that second chance would really come their way. "I'll keep checking with the IRO to make sure they don't forget us and put us on the next available ship. Don't worry, Slavochka, everything will be all right."

"There you go again with 'everything will be all right.'"

"Well, usually it is, isn't it?"

Pausing to swipe at the tears now running down her cheeks, she said, "I must admit that we have been very fortunate thus far with all that we've been through. But maybe God doesn't want us to go to America after all. We really don't know what it is like. We may find ourselves in a much worse position. You don't even know if you'll be able to practice medicine in the new country. It is always frightening to face the unknown."

"Darling, we talked about this before. I know that it will be the best thing we'll ever do in our lives. I can hardly wait to get there. Think back at the American soldiers that we saw. They looked happy, easygoing, and certainly were generous. No, Slavochka, I have a good feeling about going to America. I feel that it is our destiny."

"I know, I know. Our destiny into the unknown. I'm just so frustrated right now and am not thinking straight. We'll get there. We'll just have to keep being patient and pray that our luck will hold out."

The family had no choice but to wait once again. While they waited, Vladimir was transferred again, this time to Lintorf. Slava, as always adapting easily as with anywhere she lived, loved the place, particularly since it was near Münster, a rather large city.

More time passed by and still no ship was available for the Moskalkovs. Vladimir made his way to the IRO office daily, reminding them that he and his family still needed transportation. On a visit in July 1950, a middle-aged Polish clerk with whom Vladimir had developed rapport over the weeks, smiled kindly as Vladimir entered the office. Her expressive round face gave him optimism. "You found a ship for us?"

"Maybe. We had talked here among ourselves and came up with a plan for you. We made arrangements to have your family transferred to the Wentorf Camp. That camp is the largest Polish displaced persons camp and the regional resettlement center for European refugees. It is by Hamburg and near the port of Bremerhaven. Once you're there, you will be in the pipeline to be reprocessed. Keep in mind that you will probably be required to update your papers and receive another physical examination and have your vaccinations checked. We feel that you'll have a good chance to be scheduled for departure on one of the twelve American naval transport ships. These vessels ferried troops during the war, but now had been converted to carry civilians. It's still a rough ride and the accommodations are poor."

"I don't care if they put us on a raft as long as we get to America. Your plan is encouraging. Thank you so much. When do we leave?"

"In two days. I've already notified the hospital. They said they'll miss you. Actually, I'll miss seeing you every day. I became used to your daily visits. You're persistent, but you've actually been very pleasant. Even courteous. I appreciate that."

"And so have you. Thank you again for all your help."

The large sign with the message, *WENTORF CAMP, REGIONAL RESETTLEMENT PROCESSING CENTER*, stood by an old oak tree next to a wrought-iron gate. The Moskalkovs were dropped off there by the bus that they took from the train station. A two-story brick building topped by an extremely steep tile roof stood on the other side of a red brick wall. They eagerly entered the camp, feeling that this may be the last one they would ever see before they sail to the United States.

As an indication that their stay would be short, Vladimir was not assigned to work, and instead of being provided a private house, they were issued a tiny apartment in a converted barrack. The Moskalkovs were told that they were there for processing and that was all. As such, they complied with the additional required bureaucracy and all three took yet another physical and mental examination. Finally, after the examinations, they heard the words they waited so long to hear, "Wait for a ship."

Two weeks dragged by and Vladimir once again began making appearances at the office requesting status. In the meantime, as they did in Reckenfeld and Münster, the family continued studying English from books they had purchased in stores.

A whole month later, Vladimir was handed an official sheet of paper which indicated that they were assigned passage on *MSTS (Military Sea Transport Service) General R.M. Blatchford* on September 20, 1950. Sprinting across the camp grounds to his apartment with the good news, Vladimir's heart pounded with excitement. As he was flying up the flight of stairs, his shoes thumping on each step, Slava heard him and opened the door. Vladimir rushed in, picked her up and spun her around. "We received passage?" Slava squealed. She understood by just the look on his face.

"Yes, we're leaving in a week. Our dream is coming true."

"Oh God, thank you. This is just wonderful."

Chapter 50

THE TRAIN ride from Wentorf to Bremenhaven was brief, but long enough for the couple to drown in apprehension now that their goal was within reach. Vladimir and Slava sat silently during the trip, each lost in their deep inner thoughts. Overall, life in Germany after the war had been good to them. America was yet another mystery. Had they made the right decision? What will life for them be like? How will they communicate? Will they be able to handle the English language? How will they live? Where will they live? Will Vladimir be able to work as a physician? Will they be accepted by the Americans? Germany was hard on foreigners, hopefully America will be better. After all, they heard that it was a nation of immigrants. As the train approached the harbor, each had an ever-tightening knot in their stomachs. Trains had played a very large role in their lives as of late. A train had always taken them to some unknown place. This time was no exception. It had brought them to a ship that will take them to yet another life.

Before they boarded the train in Wentorf, the family was issued tags with the letters, *CWS*, with a number in bold black ink underneath. A harassed attendant instructed them to wear the badge on the outer garment. "This is your pass to board the train and to board the ship," said a representative of Church World Services (CWS). "Your transportation is paid for by the Church World Services. You should repay the cost someday. Also, you should have verified that your suitcases and trunks were loaded into the freight car. Now, give me your names before you board. You must be on the list."

As instructed, once they reached the port they waited in their seats until given permission to leave. Everyone sat silently. The train stopped not far from the pier, the air here had a different, pleasant smell. "It's sea air," someone said. It was late September and already a bit chilly. They knew it would be cold, so they had dressed warmly, Vladimir in his French beret and belted, dark woolen coat; Slava in a black woolen coat. She packed a warm hat in case she needed it. The parents had purchased a sailor's coat with a double row of silver buttons and a knitted cap for Victor.

Finally, a man in a worn gray suit, wearing an identical nameplate as the man in Wentorf, entered the car and began to approach each passenger. The Moskalkovs studied him closely, anxious to hear more instructions. As he approached a passenger, he inquired of their name and made a mark on a sheet of paper. When he reached the Moskalkovs, he asked their names, perused the list and made three checks with his pencil. The passengers sat silently as he went down the aisle.

After he checked off each passenger the man made an announcement in Polish, "Your larger suitcases and trunks will be loaded onto the ship. As you were instructed, each adult may take a small suitcase with a change of clothing and personal items on board. You were all required to have a sponsor, and once in New York, that person or organization should make arrangements for you in the United States. You may leave the train now and good luck."

Vladimir and Slava were informed previously by the IRO that they were given a sponsor. An American couple by the name of Stephenson had generously agreed to sponsor them. They had no idea who the Stephensons were. All that they were told was that someone will be meeting them after they cleared immigration and customs in New York. The Moskalkovs often thought about whom this generous couple might be and where they were from. Most likely from around New York, they decided. Vladimir, always a little less trusting, wondered about the reason why anyone would sponsor them. Were they really nice people who wanted to help? But why go to the trouble to help a family they didn't know? And what did they expect in return from him or Slava? At any rate, the Moskalkovs had discussed this topic on numerous occasions. They concluded how lucky and grateful they were to have found benefactors. They didn't know what a sponsorship entailed, but they were determined not to be a burden to them.

They followed the other passengers toward the ship. Vladimir's heart pounded as the crowd, all carrying their hand baggage, trudged along skirting warehouses and other metal and brick structures. Tall smokestacks and cranes protruded in the skyline. The world around the docks didn't resemble anything he had seen before. He had never been close to an ocean or port city. He never thought, growing up in land-locked Belarus that he would ever see an ocean. He glanced at Slava, her face tense as they walked. He knew she, like him, was frightened of what lay ahead.

They passed by the last structure and there, in front of them, tied to the dock stood a massive vessel. The Moskalkovs stopped in their tracks. Victor yelled out, "Mama, Pappa, look at that ship. Are we going on that? Is that the freedom ship you told me about?" The parents nodded, standing awestruck. They had never laid eyes on a ship before. It looked huge; a gray bulk of metal with its two tall masts protruding into the gray sky, a tall, round smokestack at its rear. It looked like a factory, but they knew it had been a ship of war. Vladimir estimated that the transport was about 160 meters long and could probably carry thousands of passengers if need be. He wondered how fast such a large floating mass could travel over the water. He later found out that its average speed was 16.5 knots. Slava pointed out to her family the name of the ship printed on the hull: *General R.M. Blatchford.*

Slava gave particular attention to the five life-boats lined up on the side and shuddered, her heart already racing with the thought of traveling across the Atlantic for ten days on that thing. The prospect of sailing on a huge body of water terrified her.

They were herded toward a narrow gangplank and waited in a slow-moving line to board. In the meantime, Vladimir studied the ship and marveled how much steel it took to build it. On deck, sailors holding clipboards stopped each passenger, asked their name, inspected the number on the badge, and placed a mark on the paper. After the Moskalkovs were checked off, a courteous sailor motioned for them to proceed and pointed to a large sign taped onto the steel wall of the ship. Each read the multi-language notice informing them that men would bunk in the rear section of the ship while the women and small children would bunk in the forward sections. They could, however, visit each other's quarters during daytime hours.

Slava's worried look on her expressive face did not escape her husband. A twinge of anxiety hit her with the thought of being separated in a strange place. Vladimir took her hand and squeezed it comfortingly. "It's only for the night-time. I'll go with you to make sure you and Victor settle in, and then I'll find a place for me. Don't worry."

"I know, I know," she laughed. "Everything will be all right. You don't worry, I'm a big girl, and I've been through a lot more than just spending the nights without you."

"All right then, let's follow those women down the stairs. You see, I'm not the only man accompanying his family." The family proceeded down narrow and steep metal steps to a narrow metal hallway. There were several large rooms, all containing rows of three-tiered bunks. The first room they stuck their heads into looked already crowded, so they went on to the next and the next until they found one that seemed to have beds available. Victor was given the lower bunk. Vladimir shoved Slava's suitcase underneath. Slava took the bunk above her son's, wondering who their neighbor on top would be. Vladimir kissed his wife, held her tightly against his chest, then kissed Victor and stroked his hair. "As soon as I find a bed, I'll be back for you and we'll go explore."

Vladimir found a place in the men's section on the top bunk. His neighbor in the middle bunk was a Czech and a Pole occupied the lower bunk. They seemed friendly, but Vladimir felt they preferred to be left alone. He found just enough room for his suitcase underneath the bunk. He scanned the faces of the men, hoping that they would be honest and leave his property alone. As he looked around at the strangers in the room, he noticed the cacophony of the babble of the different languages. *Everyone is in the same boat.* He chuckled to himself at the pun. *That's funny; we are actually on the same boat. Look at us. We're all concerned about our possessions. I'll just take a chance and hope no one steals anything.*

Leaving the luggage and placing his coat on his bunk to indicate that it was taken, he rapidly walked down the crowded hall, past men still filing in, fought his way up the stairs with bodies descending, grumbling at him as they carried their belongings. He continued to make his way back to Slava and Victor. As soon as he walked into their cabin, he heard an announcement made in various languages that the ship would be departing in less than an hour. The passengers could go topside if they wanted to take a last close look at Germany.

The Moskalkovs stood by the rail viewing the port of Bremerhaven. "Good-bye, Germany," Slava said. "It's a strange feeling, Volodya, isn't it? I mean… Oh, I don't know what I mean. I just can't express how I feel."

"I know what you mean," Vladimir said, not taking his eyes off the land. "You don't have to say it. That country has turned our world upside down. We wouldn't be on this ship had it not been for the invasion of our homeland. God had kept us alive. For what purpose? Time will tell. We're guided by His hand, and He must want us in America after all. Germany took away my mother and sisters from me. You may never see your brothers and sisters again. Why? Why did this happen? It took away everything that we had known and held dear and then sucked us up and then spit us out inside its borders. We lived among the enemy, and now it's pushed us out. No, Germany, good-bye. You caused me enough grief."

"Well, I have mixed feelings," Slava said thoughtfully, also watching the port. "We can't go back to Belarus, nor can we stay here. Germany gave us the most awful years of our lives and yet, mostly under the British, it gave us good years. Even though some of the people resented us as foreigners and tried to make us feel bad, there were good people. We had a good life the last few years. Fate is such a strange thing, isn't it? Who would have thought before the war, or even after, that we would be on our way to a land that one can only dream about. Let's hope it's the right decision and good for Victor or any other children we may have. I also say, good-bye, Germany, both the evil and the good."

Chapter 51

AFTER THE horn blew for the third time, the ship began slowly edging away from its berth. At this point, most all passengers were on deck, lined up port side. Many waved to no one in particular, as if saying good-bye to Germany. The ship drew farther away, and the shore, illumined brightly by the setting sun from the west, appeared smaller with every passing minute. Soon an announcement over the blaring loudspeaker called all passengers with last names beginning with A through M to dinner. The Moskalkovs were ready. They had not eaten since they left Wentorf early that morning.

The tantalizing smell of food filled the family's senses as they walked into the huge dining hall. Nearing the serving table, their saliva flowed freely at the sight of sausages, mashed potatoes, white bread with margarine, green beans, and sliced cucumbers. There were oranges for desert, and they had a choice of water, fruit juice, or tea to drink. Milk was only available to children under three. The sailors assigned to serve were generous with portions. As they exited the food line to find a place to sit, another sailor explained to Slava that since her son was young, she could be seated with the child in the captain's dining room with the other mothers. Slava chose to be with Vladimir at the standing-height tables that were provided. The top of Victor's head barely reached the bottom of the table. Vladimir held him in his arms while Slava cut the food in bite-size pieces and tried to feed him. It was awkward and Vladimir put him down. Then Vladimir spotted a couple of wooden boxes in the corner of the room. "I bet that's for children." He went over and brought one back for Victor to stand on.

The ship had sailed past the estuary into the open ocean, and before the Moskalkovs finished their meals, a pronounced sway of the ship began. "We better not eat too much," Vladimir said. "Or all this food may start coming up." Slava laughed at first, but later she began to feel queasy. She thought it might be psychological and wished that Vladimir had not mentioned it. She pushed any thoughts of nausea out of her mind.

Finishing their meal, the family climbed up onto the deck. The slight sway continued as the ship headed deeper into the ocean. Vladimir carried his Leica camera with him, and as they explored the bow, he asked Slava and Victor to pose for several photographs. All were smiling and laughing. The refreshing sea breeze with churning spray at the bow exhilarated the family. The trip, they hoped, would be an adventure of a lifetime. Victor ran around excitedly, yelling and laughing into the wind.

As the ship picked up speed, a nasty cold wind began to blow. The slight sway turned into a pronounced pitch, up and down, up and down, as it broke through the waves. Vladimir looked down at the waves, fascinated by the energy of an ocean. Slava turned away from the scene of the endless expanse of water before her. She closed her eyes, hoping that the uncomfortable, nauseous feeling she was experiencing would go away. She took in deep breaths of the crisp sea air and tried not to think about how awful she suddenly felt.

Then, in addition to the up and down motion, the ship began to roll from side to side. Up and down, side to side, up and down, side to side, the motion continued without a break in the pattern. N through Z passengers scampered from the dining area below, lurching to the nearest railing and retching. Some did not make it that far. Odorous vomit clung to the metal steps and on the deck. Now Vladimir too began to feel a twinge of nausea. Victor, though, seemed fine, at least at first, then he suddenly vomited, almost on his father's shoe. Slava turned abruptly, ran toward the rail and heaved into the water below. She felt embarrassed and told Vladimir that both Victor and she needed to go to their cabin and lie down. "Let me see if I can find a lemon or a sour pickle for you both," Vladimir said. "That should help."

"No, no, I couldn't stand to put anything in my mouth right now, but do bring something for Victor. Come on Vitya, it will soon get dark anyway. Let's go down." But before she could take her son's small hand, she threw up again, as did Victor.

Vladimir stood in a long line for a lemon or the pickle. There were no lemons, but he was able to procure two sour pickles. He rushed down to Slava's cabin. The stairs, the hallway, and the cabin reeked with a strong acrid odor of puke. He stepped gingerly around the piles to Slava's bunk. She lay quietly with her arm flung over her eyes, Victor nestled next to her. "Slavochka, I want you to take a bite of this pickle or better yet suck the juice from it. I am sure it will help." She refused initially, but then she took a bite. Victor ate half of the pickle. In no mood to talk, Slava told Vladimir that he should go since it must be dark outside, and he should not be there.

Vladimir leaned over and kissed her sweaty forehead. He proceeded to do the same with his son. In the meantime, several women were cleaning up the mess on the floor. Vladimir was barely able to walk to his cabin because of the rocking and rolling of the vessel. He held on. *The motion and the smell is enough to make even the healthy throw up.* He made it onto to the top deck for air and held on frantically to the rail to keep from falling. The brisk sea air made him feel better, although he remained slightly nauseous. Taking a couple of bites from half a pickle that he had with him, he headed back to his quarters. The stench permeated his nostrils. A clean-up crew from the ship and some of the passengers were out, swabbing up. He joined to help them and afterward he climbed up to his bunk and fell asleep.

For ten days the ship fought its way through the stormy Atlantic. All three Moskalkovs were stricken by seasickness, especially Slava and Victor. None had an appetite, but Vladimir insisted that they eat certain foods he thought would be better for nausea so that they have the energy to go on. He feared dehydration and struggled to keep fluids down. Very few passengers escaped the illness. Pale and green, they complained of the tiredness, never-ending nausea, splitting headaches, cold sweat, restlessness, and constant yawning.

Slava appeared particularly pale and green in color. Vladimir comforted her and others by telling them that as long as they kept drinking fluids, no one would die from sea-sickness. He insisted on taking Slava and Victor up on deck for fresh air, and the three walked slowly around the ship. Occasionally, during a lull in the turbulence of the waves, Slava would spend more time on deck, dreaming of standing on solid ground with no rolling, swaying, or pitching. Even though Victor felt nauseous, looked pale, and could not keep much food down, he, nevertheless, spent much time with his father during the day exploring as much of the ship as they could. Vladimir tried to be of help to the ship's medical staff, and for him the days went by a little quicker than for Slava, who thought that the trip would never end.

The end came the evening of September 30, 1950. An announcement that in a few hours the ship would reach

New York harbor brought hundreds out to view the land of their dreams. With the reduction of speed, the pitching and rolling of the ship eased. On deck, the Moskalkovs made their way through the crowd to the bow of the ship and anxiously waited to spot their new homeland. Vladimir's stomach tightened as he thought of what lies ahead. *We should be used to tremendous changes. That is all we'd experienced since the war started in 1941.* Slava felt too sick to think about it. She just wanted off the ship. It had been a rough voyage.

Suddenly, through the receding fog, they viewed lights, many lights, such as they had never witnessed before. "That's New York City," Vladimir said. "Look how beautiful and spectacular it is. It's like the most brilliant diamond shining brightly. If that is what America looks like, it's really a dreamland." Slava nodded, and forced a smile watching Vladimir's excitement.

"It is beautiful," Slava said finally. "And the closer we get to the city, the more remarkable it looks. I've never seen such tall buildings. I already see the wealth before us and we're not even off the ship." Vladimir inched closer and circled her waist. He kissed her cheek. "America, America, our new home," Slava muttered, almost under her breath. "Dear Jesus, our Blessed Virgin Mary, please help us in this new land. Give us health and the strength to work and to study and fit in with the Americans. And above all, dear God, may we and our children have a good life."

Announcements over the loudspeaker informed the passengers that the ship will moor in the morning at Pier 4. They should return to their cabins and get some sleep. That night only Victor slept as neither Vladimir nor Slava could. They tossed and turned all night wondering what the morning would bring. During the night, Vladimir heard the ship come to a complete stop and the anchor drop. *Well, we're here.* He glanced at his watch. With the fluorescent dial he determined that the time was four o'clock in the morning. *In just a few more hours, it begins. But what begins? We'll soon find out.* He wanted to go up on deck and take a look, but then sleep finally overtook him.

After an early breakfast, the passengers, with their carry-on belongings, started filing out of the ship and were escorted onto waiting ferries. They were taken to Ellis Island. On the way there, the passengers were awestruck by the green Statue of Liberty. "That represents freedom," a passenger shouted in Russian. The Moskalkovs could not take their eyes off the statute that they read about in books.

"Vitya," Slava said. "That statute was a gift to the Americans by the French." Victor with his six-year old mind thought about that.

"But how could they have brought such a large and tall statue all the way from France?"

"They brought it in pieces, son," Vladimir said. Victor still kept staring at the work of art, still trying to imagine how it got there, and if in pieces as his father said, *how they could put it together.*

At Ellis Island, they were placed in a long line where the last names began with G through M. Once they reached the counter, an apathetic man asked their names, took their papers, and carefully studied them. He compared their faces to those on the documents, made an entry on another form, and without another word motioned for them to continue on. The entire process took more than half the day, spent mostly standing in lines. It was exhausting. After the final check by a physician, they were directed to yet another line. This one was for boarding a ferry for a return trip to the pier. The water on the Hudson River became very choppy by then and nausea hit them again.

The ferry docked and the family hurried to the exit. The solid ground felt good, although their legs continued to sway. At the pier they were met by several CWS representatives who spoke various languages. The one that spoke Polish advised the people to proceed down the pier and get into line that indicated the first letter of the last name and retrieve their luggage. Once they did, they were to search for their relatives or sponsors. The Moskalkovs followed the instructions and after some time saw their two large trunks. They pulled them out and dragged them outside the doors to a large waiting area. "How will we find our sponsor?" Slava asked nervously after seeing the waiting throng of people. "What if our sponsor doesn't show up? What will we do then?"

Chapter 52

SLAVA NEED not had worried. She could see the many people waiting on the other side of a low metal fence as the ship's passengers streamed through the gate. Most held signs with the names of individuals they were to meet printed on them. Off to the side, toward the back of the crowd, Vladimir suddenly spotted his own name scribbled on a piece of cardboard. With a huge grin, he pointed out the man to Slava, and they hurriedly approached a tall, older man wearing a gray suit, a black fedora, and a clerical collar. He charmingly returned their smiles and began to speak in English.

The Moskalkovs studied as much English as they were able, but the man spoke too rapidly for them. Except for a few recognizable words it seemed like jibber. "We're sorry," Slava attempted to say in English. "Please, could you speak slowly?"

The man understood. He laughed pleasantly. "Forgive me, I should have known better. Let's try again. My name is Reverend Burnet. I'm a minister at the Methodist Church in Asher, Oklahoma. Your sponsors, Mr. and Mrs. Boyd Stephenson, asked me to meet you. They were not able to come." Vladimir and Slava seemed to fathom every other word. They assumed that his name was Burnet, here for the Stephensons and he came from Oklahoma. They had studied the map of the United States and remembered that Oklahoma is quite far from New York, in the middle of the country. The reverend continued, "We desperately need a physician in our small town. The Stephensons instructed me to tell you that you don't have to come with me, you can go anywhere you like, but we would really appreciate it if you come back with me. Our small town is in need of your services."

With language as a problem, Vladimir knew that he needed to fully understand what the man wanted of them. He looked around in desperation and fortunately happened to espy the Polish-speaking CWS representative just finishing up a conversation with another man not too far away. "Please wait a moment," Vladimir told Burnet and ran off to get the interpreter.

After the interpreter translated the words of the reverend, the Moskalkovs were ecstatic to hear that Vladimir would work as a doctor and that they were to accompany the minister to Oklahoma. They were grateful for the opportunity. A ton of rocks lifted from their shoulders. Nodding, they enthusiastically agreed. Overwhelmed with relief and out of sheer joy, Slava embraced Burnet and kissed him on the check. He seemed genuinely pleased, chuckled, and thanked them for agreeing to go with him.

Burnet arranged for a porter to take the luggage to a taxi that took them to the railway station. On the way, the

Moskalkovs were astonished at what they saw. They could never have imagined how crowded and bustling the streets and sidewalks could be. There were thousands of motor vehicles, especially the yellow cabs that scurried about like bees around a hive. Victor could not get his fill of the various makes of cars. "Look at that one," the boy squealed out. "Look at how big and shiny that car is. Papa, can we get one? Can we?" The parents laughed at his excitement.

"Maybe someday, son. Don't only look at the cars but also at the tall buildings."

"Yes, the buildings are so tall that they stretch all the way to the sky," Slava chimed in. "I've never seen anything like this city. What an exciting place. Full of wonder. And more importantly, nothing seems to be blown to pieces."

"Don't be fooled by all of this," Burnet tried to explain, humored by the family's enthusiasm for the novelty of it all. "Our little town is a heck of a lot smaller. You can actually enjoy life there. Not like in this crazy city. Why, we don't even consider this part of America. At least not the real America." Vladimir and Slava smiled back and again understood just a little of what he said. They had no problem gathering from his demeanor and tone of voice that he didn't like New York City much and that it would be better in Oklahoma.

At the enormous railway station with its numerous tracks, Slava suddenly realized that they would once again be subjected to more sway from the train. She wanted desperately to stay on solid earth at least the rest of the day and sleep in a real bed before venturing out, but she was in no position to ask for any favors. "How long is the trip to Oklahoma?" She asked timidly, hoping it would be short, although remembering the map she knew that it wouldn't be. Burnet said something inaudible as he led the way to the right track.

For three days and two nights, the train bounced and swayed, this time on American tracks, on its way to Asher. Slava refused to eat anything while on the train. Vladimir made sure she at least drank water. She could not look at food and knew if she ate, it would all come up anyway. She felt more miserable with every passing mile. When the train stopped at stations along the way, she felt some relief by stepping outside on the platform. The respite was brief and then her torture started once again. Regardless how wretched she felt, she was curious enough to take in as much of America's countryside as her condition allowed. When she could no longer watch out of the window due to nausea and a headache, she closed her eyes, leaned against the seat-back, and listened to Vladimir and Victor describe with such enthusiasm the sights around them.

So many things were novel—the narrow-trunked trees of the forests, the beautiful canyons of the high mountains, the individual farm houses so far flung from their neighbors, the neatly contoured fields with large towers (they later learned that those were grain silos), and the brown grasslands of the prairies stretching out as far as the eye could see. Reverend Burnet tried to point out different things along the way, and Vladimir could see how extremely proud he was of his country. The closer the train inched toward Oklahoma, the more excited Reverend Burnet became.

Even the food they were served seemed to have a different taste. They grew up with heavy dark rye bread, but here the bread, an important basic item, was white and fluffy. Vladimir commentated that it didn't have any substance to it, "It's like eating cotton."

The depots, where their train made its stops, were small, constructed of either wood or bricks and there with hardly any passengers. These were so unlike the large stucco or stone stations of Poland and Germany, always crowded with people. Then there was the difference in the weather. Throughout the trip, the sun beat down on the train. It was hot and not at all the cooler climate of northern Europe with its fewer sunny days, especially in late September.

The Americans they encountered were friendly, always ready to smile, but they were dressed so differently than Europeans. Some men wore suits, ties, and hats, but the majority wore a certain type of pants that Slava later learned to be jeans. Their shirts were of all patterns and colors. The women, too, were dressed in light colorful fabrics, rendering a happy, carefree appearance. Slava compared her family's apparel. *Our heavy formal German fashions simply do not fit in with what I've seen. Especially what Victor has on. Those short pants, frilly shirt, and jacket will obviously have to go.* Both Vladimir and Slava began to realize that they, indeed, came to another world altogether.

As all three Moskalkovs relaxed into the comfortable soft seats of the railcar, Vladimir took another careful look at the coach and the passengers. The seats faced each other. The passengers were reading, talking, laughing, and walking up and down the aisle, going to other cars and to the dining car. Again, so different from the trains they rode in Germany with their third-class wooden seats and, on some, shattered windows. *Circumstances were so different then. I don't see any stressed, scared faces worrying of an imminent attack from partisans or falling bombs. But yet we're on a train once again.* He suddenly realized that ever since he left his home, he'd been on one train after another. "Slavochka, do you realize we are on a train again?"

"No, what gave you that idea?" Slava said, amused at the obvious comment.

"No, I mean we're on a train again. It all started in Vitebsk, then Baranovichi, then again at Slonim, then at various towns in Germany, and now in the United States. The train, that hunk of steaming metal, has taken us steadily on a westerly journey. Always to the unknown."

"I know. We never knew where we'd end up or what would become of us once we got there. I guess it is ironic. Fate uses the train to draws us further and further away from everything we had ever known. Only memories will remain of who and what we left behind. With time, probably even those will fade."

"Slava, you're crying. I'm sorry I brought it up."

"No, I'm not crying. I'm just cleansing my eyes," Slava said with that precious mischievous smile that he loved so much even though he noticed her pale, weary face, still greenish from the motion sickness, "I do hope though, that we get to wherever we're going soon. I don't know how much longer I can bounce around on this train." She leaned back, closed her eyes and again the same thought entered her mind. *What faces us? It will be tough. We will be foreigners in such a different place with a lot of learning to do—the language, the customs.*

"Folks, we're approaching the suburbs of Oklahoma City," Reverend Burnet gleefully blurted out as he pointed out the window. "Once we get to the station, we have to change trains and head just a short distance south to Asher. We're almost home." The Moskalkovs understood that they're coming to a destination. Burnet began gathering his belongings, and Vladimir followed his example. Once off the train, and realizing that there will be yet another train to catch, Slava sat dejectedly with the others at the depot, while Burnet looked at his watch and studied the train schedule. "Only looks like an hour's wait, by golly. We'll be there in no time."

Switching trains, the family bounced and swayed some more as the engine pulled them along. They understood

Burnet to say, "Just a short trip," but what did that mean? The largeness of America came somewhat as a surprise to them. It stretched for so many kilometers and they knew they were only halfway into the country. It may be a short trip for their escort, but would there be another day's travel? "How far?" Vladimir said, pointing in the direction of the train.

Burnet studied his watch. "Oh, we should be coming into Asher in about twenty minutes." He slapped Vladimir's leg as a friendly gesture and said, "I know you'll love it there. The people are great. Don't worry, you'll fit in fine." Vladimir smiled, understanding again just a few words, focusing mostly on twenty minutes left. He dwelled on the words, *fit in* and concluded that meant to belong. Suddenly he realized that they may not be the only ones worried on how they'll thrive. Burnet also seemed to fret about mutual acceptance with the townsfolk. That made Vladimir feel a little better knowing that they'll need to all work together to make their life easier.

"OK, here we are."

The Moskalkovs took a look at the small, wooden depot outside the windows. The word, "ASHER" was written in bold letters on a sign. There were many individuals milling around the platform for a small station such as this. A few passengers got up to leave, and Burnet seemed to stall the family until everyone left first. "OK, let's go," he said with a strange grin on his face. Gesturing for the family to go first, he followed them down the aisle and to the exit door. As Vladimir was walking out, he glanced out the window again and spied even more people now gathered on the platform.

As Slava stepped off the top metal step of the coach followed by Victor and then Vladimir, a small band began to play and the people at the back of the little depot applauded. "Welcome, welcome," shouts were heard followed by more applause and some whistles. Vladimir glanced at Slava. Her eyes overflowed with tears. Totally overwhelmed by the warm and surprising reception, he told his family, "Slava, Victor, we are indeed home. America! God bless you!"

Epilogue

UNFORTUNATELY FOR the residents of Asher and the Moskalkovs, Vladimir was unable to stay and be their doctor. An Oklahoma license to practice medicine was required. That would take many months of preparations for several examinations and a state review of qualifications. The Moskalkovs' sponsors, Mr. and Mrs. Stephenson, tried to obtain an exception for Vladimir, but to no avail. After six months of trying, a solution was made that Vladimir would be allowed to practice medicine at the Central State Hospital in Norman, Oklahoma under the auspices of a licensed physician. The Moskalkovs rented a duplex in Norman. Soon thereafter, a daughter, Mary Veronica, was born, and with a salary of $250.00 per month, they were able to get by quite well.

Vladimir, however, was never one to just sit and let things be. He began writing letters to hospitals in neighboring states, asking to work as a physician. In 1953, Dr. Naramore of the Larned State Hospital in Larned, Kansas offered Vladimir a job as Staff Physician III with a salary of $480.00 per month plus housing on the State Hospital grounds. Elated, the four Moskalkovs happily moved to Larned. Dr. Naramore arranged for Vladimir to receive from the State of Kansas a special license to practice medicine within a state hospital in Kansas. A condition of his employment was that he had to pass the Educational Council for Foreign Medical Graduates (ECFMG) examination and a Basic Sciences Examination. After intensive study, Vladimir passed the examinations.

Vladimir progressed well, took numerous seminars. He attended the Menninger Clinic in Topeka and received the award of a Fellowship in Psychiatry. While at the hospital, he was drafted as a physician and would have been sent to Korea; however, Dr. Naramore wrote a letter to the draft board stating that Vladimir is essential in the operation of the hospital and requested that he not be drafted. It worked. Vladimir did not have to go back again into a war zone so soon after what he lived through. In a few years after he moved to Kansas, Vladimir's salary increased as he went from Staff Physician III to Staff Physician I.

Again, searching for a greater advancement, Vladimir wrote to other State Hospitals and in 1958 was offered a job as a clinical director of the Wyoming State Hospital in Evanston and given a salary of one thousand dollars per month plus housing. Also provided to the family were bakery and dairy products produced on the hospital campus. In Wyoming, he took and passed the State licensure examination and obtained a Wyoming license to practice medicine.

He found a greater opportunity and more pay at the New Mexico State Hospital, in Las Vegas, NM, then on to the Colorado State Hospital in Pueblo, CO. As a physician,

Vladimir was outstanding, admired, and well respected by both his patients and colleagues.

Slava could not quell his entrepreneurial and capitalistic spirit. While in Kansas, his peasant roots yearned for a farm. He purchased a 160 acre farm in Trousdale and founded an egg producing farm in Larned. While living in Wyoming, he purchased three small rental houses and a five-story apartment building in Salt Lake City, UT. In New Mexico, he purchased commercial buildings and a strip mall. In Pueblo, he owned several pieces of commercial property. When he moved on to another state, the properties were eventually sold.

In addition to the real estate, mostly as a hobby, Vladimir and Slava ventured into small retail stores. In Las Vegas, NM, they founded and operated the House of Flowers and Gifts, House of Music, and House of Pizza. They purchased the El Nido Cocktail Lounge and opened a fine-dining restaurant and bought an existing flower shop, Gloria's Flowers. When they moved to Colorado, they transferred the House of Flowers and its FTD and Teleflora affiliations from Las Vegas to Pueblo. Slava was exceptional as a flower designer and enjoyed working in the shops. During this time, in addition to his school work, Victor managed the real estate and the retail stores. While attending a university, their daughter, Mary, took a course in flower design and often helped out at the store making beautiful arrangements. Victor received his Juris Doctor degree, and Mary received a Master's degree in Mental Health Counseling.

America was good to the Moskalkovs. It was truly the land of freedom and opportunity that they hoped for when they set their shoes on the pier in New York City. As soon as they were able, they obtained United States citizenship. At that time, they had the opportunity to shorten their family name from Moskalkov to Moss. Vladimir took on the name of Walter, making it easier for his patients to pronounce his full name. Vladimir and Slava did not make a fortune, as the retail shops mostly provided employment for others, but they lived comfortably and interestingly. Both passed away in Pueblo, Colorado—Vladimir in December 1983 and Slava in July 2005.

To this day, their children and grandchildren miss them very much.